REGGIE AND DELILAH'S year of Falling

Also by Elise Bryant
Happily Ever Afters
One True Loves

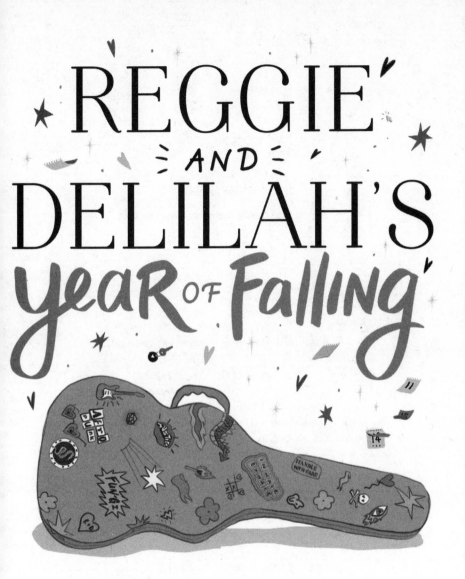

REGGIE AND DELILAH'S YEAR OF Falling

ELISE BRYANT

BALZER + BRAY

An Imprint of HarperCollins*Publishers*

For Joe—

You make writing love stories so easy

Library of Congress Control Number: 2022946657
ISBN 978-0-06-321299-2

Typography by Catherine Lee
Interior art by Michelle Rosella D'Urbano

22 23 24 25 26 LBC 5 4 3 2 1

First Edition

NEW YEAR'S EVE

DELILAH

I'm sitting in the hallway closet with two beach towels shoved into the crack under the door, trying to make myself sing.

Now. I have to do it now. I'm running out of time.

I take a deep breath, shake out the nerves, open my mouth, and—

There's a loud bang on the door.

"Delilah, why are you in the closet?" Georgia, my sister, yells from the other side. "Are you doing something weird?"

She pulls the door open, filling the small space with bright light, and I squint up at her. She has a sparkly, plastic New Year's Eve crown perched on top of her cloud of tight auburn curls, and her lips are stretched into the shining smile that got her the role of Glinda in Willmore Prep's production of *Wicked* last semester as a freshman.

I stand up, kicking the towels out of the way. "Shouldn't you wait for my answer to that question before barging in here?"

"Where's the fun in that? Though I gotta say, this is a bit of a letdown." She taps an old fleece *Frozen* blanket on the floor next to me with her foot. "Are you just, like, taking a nap?"

"No, I'm, uh—"

I'm trying to finally sing. Really, actually sing.

Not the quiet singing that sometimes sneaks out when I'm sitting in Mom's car and the song is so good it just kind of pulls it out of me before I can think about it too much. Or the halfway singing I've been doing in band practice, trying to get every one of Charlie's lyrics, scribbled in his precious Moleskine, exactly right. Even with the mic in my hand and all the guys' expectations, I feel like I've been sprinting right up to the edge of a cliff with my voice, ready to leap, but then I just . . . stop. My voice sounds like I'm gripping the earth with my toes, staring at the ocean below.

And that kind of singing isn't going to cut it in a few hours at The Mode, where we'll be playing our New Year's Eve show.

Our show, not just their show. As in . . . including me.

Instead of tagging along and trying to push the guys' merch at a table in the back, as I've done most Saturday nights for the past few months, I'm going to be up on that stage with them for the first time tonight.

Because I am officially the new lead singer of Fun Gi.

Me. The girl who can't read a single line of music. The girl who can only carry something tune-adjacent, at best. But who even knows when I still haven't made myself *actually* sing?

Georgia smirks and twirls her hand in front of her, waiting for an explanation. But there's no way I can tell my Broadway-bound sister all that. She wouldn't understand.

Before I can make up a reasonable excuse for why I'm sitting in the dark with the extra linens, though, Mom appears behind Georgia, wearing tuxedo-printed pajamas and a matching gold crown.

"You were hiding in the closet?" Her face cracks open in concern. "Oh no, honey. You know you don't have to go. You can stay home and watch the *House Hunters* marathon with us until the ball drops."

My whole body tightens and she reads it right away. "Not that I don't think you can do this. I know you can do this, and I'm proud of you for putting yourself out there, but . . . if you're hiding in the closet . . ."

"Yeah, this is weird," Georgia cuts in. "I feel like we all need to acknowledge that this is weird."

"I wasn't hiding in the closet!"

They both cross their arms and narrow their identical dark brown eyes at me.

"Okay, I was *in* the closet," I admit, crossing my arms right back. "But I wasn't hiding. I was practicing."

They both start talking at the same time.

"Oh, Lilah-girl, do you not want to sing in front of us? I'm sure your voice is so beautiful and there's no reason—"

"Is it because you think I'm going to judge you? Because I won't. I know a voice like mine only comes around once in a generation."

"Even if it's not, um, conventionally beautiful, as long as you believe in yourself, that is what will shine through!"

"And I can help you if you'd just let me already. I've got some good vocal exercises we can do together."

"There is only one you, and you have something special to bring that no one else can."

"Like, *Mommy made me mash my M&M's!*" Georgia holds up a finger as she stretches the last note of the gibberish she's started singing for some reason. That's enough to pause Mom's self-love speech.

And this is why I was singing—or *trying* to sing—in the closet. Alone.

"No. It's not that," I say before they can start back up again. "I was just in here for . . ." I lean down to pick up the Frozen blanket, folding it in front of my face as I mumble, ". . . the acoustics."

"Right." Georgia arches an eyebrow. "The acoustics."

"We can go with you." Mom reaches forward and squeezes my hand. "Be your moral support."

Because that's definitely who I need in the front row of my very first show as the lead singer of a punk band: my mom being all *You're doing amazing, sweetie!* and my superstar little sister, who will most definitely be judging me.

"Okay, okay. I know what that look means," Mom laughs, rubbing her finger along my wrinkled nose. I smooth it out with a small smile. "But know that we're rooting for you, honey."

"Yeah, you're gonna break a leg, sis," Georgia adds. "Or, like, whatever the equivalent is."

"And when you're done, we'll be here waiting for you with these fools!" Mom gestures her thumb toward the living room, where a couple's argument over crown molding is blasting loudly from the TV. "This family has a two-hundred-thousand-dollar budget and they want a separate dining room. In West Hollywood!"

That's how we've spent New Year's Eve since Mom and Dad divorced. Just the three of us watching HGTV, drinking apple cider and kissing each other's cheeks at midnight. But this year I'm doing something different.

"Now, don't forget your migraine medication. Just in case—"

"And if you get nervous, remember to picture—"

"I'm fine," I say, stepping out of the closet and shutting the door behind me. "Totally fine."

I'm not fine.

Not even close to fine.

And yet I'm still loading Beau's shiny purple toms into the back of Asher's mom's minivan and grinning as if I'm *not* completely certain tonight is going to be a disaster.

"Cheer up, buttercup," Beau says, nudging me with his elbow. He sits his cymbals in their cases on top of the amps, and then adjusts my placement of his drums, just so.

"I'm cheered," I insist. "The cheeriest."

I stretch out my plastic smile until my cheeks ache and pick up his bass drum to throw it in the back. But he rushes over and gingerly takes it from my hands.

"Your handling of my babies is telling a different story, Delilah," he says, stroking the damn thing. "Please don't take it out on the kids."

He's so particular with his drums, which is why we have to load them all up instead of sharing backline with the other bands on the lineup tonight. I don't get it and never have. The sets all look pretty identical to me.

"It's the nerves," Asher says, pushing his glasses up on his nose. The frames are so tiny that he definitely can't see out of them, but that doesn't really matter anyway. He's just wearing them for the aesthetic. "I remember my first gig. Man, I had the bubble guts all day. I was like Charlie and Grandpa Joe in that *Willy Wonka* scene, where they have to burp in that big ol' metal tube. All, *bloop, bloop, bloop*."

"Nah, that is not a thing. There's no burping scene in that movie. Why would there be a burping scene?" Beau says, shaking his head. His bleached blond hair falls into his eyes, and he pushes it away in a perfectly practiced move that makes girls melt when he's on stage. I've watched it happen from the back of the crowd countless times. "Also, *bloop*? That's what your burps sound like? *Bloop*?"

"Watch it again, bro. I swear. They had to burp to, like, save their lives," Asher says. "And, uh, I don't need to be burp-shamed."

"Burp-shamed?" Beau laughs.

"Yes, burp-shamed," Asher doubles down, his permanent sarcastic smile dancing at his lips. "I mean, I'm just trying to make Delilah feel better about our gig." He leans in, nudging me with his elbow. "But I get why you're nervous. The crowd is going to be huge."

I start to picture that crowd and my head spins, but I look down at the ground to hide any terror that might be revealing itself on my face. "You guys. I'm chill," I say, keeping my voice steady and convincing. "Stop stressing."

I wish I could say this was out of character. But I've shrugged and *yeah, whatever*-ed my way into a lot of things I never thought I would've done since I transferred to Willmore Prep and met the guys in September. Like if I keep playing the cool girl—the girl they think I am—maybe I'll actually become her.

But also, they're my friends. This is what friends do. They needed a new lead singer, and in a couple weeks, I molded myself into exactly that for them.

"Of course she's chill," Charlie says. "Delilah is a star. *Our* star."

He walks out of Asher's garage, where they store all their gear, and stands next to me. I can feel his warmth, and I have to fight the urge to lean in to him, like a plant reaching for the sun. Because that would be ridiculously awkward. We're not like that. We're just friends.

Except . . . Well, I guess I'll admit it: Charlie's probably half the reason why I agree to everything. Especially when he asks me in that rumbly low voice that I feel in my chest. Or when he wraps his arms around my shoulders and makes his bright blue eyes all big and purses his lips in the perfect pout.

But, no.

Our star, he said. Not *his*. Never his.

"Yes, the star, and you better not forget it," I say, bumping him with my shoulder. Charlie laughs and throws his arm around me, squeezing me tight. As friends do.

"Ah, the ego on this one! Already!" Beau says with a snort, laughing too. "We gotta watch you."

"I'm just saying. Bubble guts are normal," Asher continues. "There is no shame in the bubble guts."

"Asher, I don't have the bubble guts!" I yell, throwing my hands up. I totally have the bubble guts.

Charlie lets go of me to put his guitar in the van, and I feel the loss of his touch like blankets thrown off in the early morning. But I keep my face blank. Chill.

"Did you practice the lyrics some more?" Charlie says, turning back to me. His strong jaw sparkles with stubble and his wavy dark hair is tucked into a burgundy beanie. "During practice Thursday, I noticed you kept getting tripped up on the bridge of 'Parallelograms.' Remember you kept saying 'bird' instead of 'blurred.' And you've gotta make sure you stretch out 'soon' into two syllables in the second chorus."

I messed up the lyrics because they make no sense. I swear sometimes Charlie writes esoteric stuff just for the sake of being esoteric. I would never *tell* him that, though.

"Yeah, I practiced," I assure him. "I've got it down."

He nods and keeps going. "And did you watch those videos I sent you last night? Of the other girl singers? I had more but I didn't want to overload you. I really think those two are, like, the masters when it comes to stage presence."

Yes, I watched Karen O, front woman of this old band the Yeah Yeah Yeahs, screaming and spitting and spinning across the stage, owning these huge audiences with abandon. And Courtney Love, lead singer of Hole, growling in her babydoll dresses and smeared makeup, dripping confidence.

They were badass. My jaw dropped in awe as I watched both of them. But it was quickly replaced with fear. I'm not like that. I could *never* be like that.

So I went searching on YouTube for other women musicians that were more my speed, and I found even older videos—like before-my-parents-were-born *old*. Patti Smith, with her baggy clothes and howly voice that hits you right in the gut. And Poly Styrene from X-Ray Spex, a biracial Black girl like me, whose yelpy crooning commanded attention.

And of course, there's my real music role model, Taylor Swift, who's written every single one of my favorite songs. But I would never, ever mention her to the guys. They wouldn't let me live it down until I was a senior citizen.

So instead I just shrug. "Yeah, I watched. They were cool. But I think I might go for, I don't know . . . an X-Ray Spex vibe?"

He nods approvingly.

"Okay, and remember, especially during the last verse of 'Bronze Statue,' sing with me. We'll share the mic. It'll look so good."

I need this reminder even less than the other ones. Every cell in my body is still vibrating from when we sang this song together last night at practice. Our breath mingling over the mic, his eyes locked on mine. I know it's only for show, but it felt so real.

"And one more—" Charlie starts, but Asher cuts him off.

"Lay off her, bro!" Asher slaps his shoulder. "If she wasn't nervous before, this goddamn third degree is definitely going to change that."

Charlie winces, and then smiles, throwing his arm around my shoulder again. "You're right. I'm sorry. I just want everything to be perfect tonight. It's hard for me to . . . let go."

"I know. I get it."

Fun Gi is his baby. He started this band back in seventh grade with Asher, and Beau joined at the beginning of freshman year after their old drummer moved from Long Beach up to northern California. And until now, Charlie's always been the front man.

But after Fun Gi had been upstaged at yet another show by Ryan Love and the Valentines, this supercool all-girl rock band, they decided they needed to do something different to stand out. And there I was—the girl who'd started hanging around their practices for the past few months, just happy to be included. Charlie's the one that suggested I step in, only three weeks before this big New Year's Eve performance at The Mode, a venue downtown. And I went along with it. I've been going to every practice, learning every one of their songs—even though I know I'm not cut out for this at all.

And also . . . it's not like Fun Gi's lack of feminine energy is the reason they kept being upstaged by Ryan Love and the Valentines. It's because the Valentines are better. Ryan's voice is bubbly and bright. Her lyrics get stuck in your head.

And I'm not a musician—not like Charlie, Beau, and Asher all are. Or like any of these women I watched last night, or Ryan Love. I can't play guitar. I can't write lyrics. I couldn't even get a handle on the recorder in third-grade music class. So what do I know?

"Okay, one more question though," Charlie says, and Beau, Asher, and I all groan. Charlie smiles sheepishly but keeps going.

"Don't hate me," he says, holding up his hands. "But have you thought any more about those outfits?"

We went shopping last week at some vintage stores on Retro Row, searching for the perfect stage outfits. Ryan Love's well known for the sequined capes and embroidered tulle skirts she wears on stage, and I think Charlie was trying to help me figure out a stage look of my own. He picked out shiny gold leggings, crop tops with balloon sleeves, and a short romper covered in feathers.

They were so not me. Though I guess that's the point. *Me* wouldn't be doing this in the first place.

"No. No—forget it," he says, waving that away. He pulls me close. Our hips touch and he runs his hands up and down my arms. "You look great." I'm wearing what I usually do when I'm not in the Willmore Prep uniform: high-waisted jeans, a plain white T-shirt, and my checkerboard Vans. I threw a flannel over it tonight because the temperature has dipped below sixty-five and I'm freezing. But when he says it that way, touching me like this, I get pretty close to believing him.

"Really, kid, you're made for this."

Kid. I don't remember exactly how that nickname started—he said it and it felt like the way things were supposed to be. Just like how Charlie and I became friends.

One day I was sitting all alone at lunch at a brand-new private school, and some cute boy sat down next to me and said, "Oh, *you* I need to know." The next day I was in their group, drawn into their orbit. I felt special, chosen.

Am I really made for this?

I don't know. I don't *think* so.

But I've always believed in the magic of the new year. Even though it's just a day on the calendar, I love the idea that we get a chance to start over. Maybe when I step onto the stage tonight, I'll feel like I belong there. Maybe the spotlight will make me into someone I've always wanted to be.

I keep that corny shit to myself, though.

"You ready?" Charlie asks, sliding open the door to the back seat. Asher and Beau are already in the front, arguing over what we're going to listen to on the way.

No.

That's the honest answer. But I pull on my chill exterior and shrug.

"Yeah, whatever. Let's go."

REGGIE

I really fucking hate New Year's Eve.

There's always this big expectation that your life is going to change. Like, you couldn't get your ass together the rest of the year, but somehow, through some woo-woo holiday magic, you're all of a sudden going to start running marathons or figure out what exactly a 401k is or fall in love just because the clock strikes midnight? And, like, according to some arbitrary calendar created by whoever, it's time for a fresh start?

Yeah. Sure. That's all *completely* reasonable.

That's why I'm ignoring this bullshit holiday and spending tonight like I spend every Saturday night. As a cloud giant named Slarog.

Well, I'm not always a cloud giant. But he's my favorite NPC. Slarog shows up in all the Dungeons & Dragons campaigns I run.

"As you enter the grand vault," I say, keeping my voice low to build tension, "your limbs still ache with exhaustion from the climb to the Infernal Slopes, the steep mountain peak where Slarog's castle sits perched high into the clouds. The room is so immense that it's difficult to decipher where it ends, if it even does at all. A ceiling of mist overhead seems to reach the night sky. Walls of great boulders loom above your heads."

"Oh, those boulders are coming into play! I'm calling that shit right now," laughs my best friend, Yobani—or as he's known on Saturday nights, Trickery, the tiefling bard. He grabs a handful of Hot Cheetos from one of the bags scattered around the outskirts of my dining room table. "I love it."

"Boulders, though?" Greg says, raising a thick eyebrow. "I find it hard to believe that a cloud giant would keep his precious collection in such shabby quarters, as they value wealth and status."

Greg is Gruldaito Gloomcloud, a human fighter—easily the most boring option in D&D. So it's a perfect choice for Greg.

Yobani groans. "Not your campaign, Gruly."

Leela (or Walona, the half-elf sorcerer) jabs him with her elbow. "You know he hates that."

"Gruldaito," Greg corrects him sternly. "And I know. I just want to make sure that Reggie has at least consulted the Monster Manual and we're not going *entirely* home brew here. Maybe the walls should be gilded, or at least composed of something rarer, like . . . obsidian? Just an innocent suggestion." He purses his lips and shakes his head like he doesn't care, even though he *always* cares.

"Boulders," I repeat. "Massive boulders."

It's been the four of us every Saturday night for . . . well, as far back as I *want* to remember. Being an awkward, geeky kid who spends a significant amount of time thinking of the subtle differ-ences in temperaments between green dragons and blue dragons is a lot more fun when you have friends who do the same.

Leela and I met playing D&D online in sixth grade, and luckily when my parents took me to our designated meeting point at the library months later, she actually was a twelve-year-old girl who lived in Long Beach just like me. Yobani was a kid that kept mak-ing fun of our big Monster Manuals at the Mother's Beach summer day camp, and eventually we realized it was because he wanted to look through them with us instead of kayaking. And we met Greg at a game shop in Lakewood when he informed us we were buying "the dice of amateurs" and offered his expertise. It was like one of those "getting the gang together" montages in the Fast & Furious movies, except we were all in various stages of orthodontic work and way, way less cool.

Greg used to be the Dungeon Master for our group, but he was constantly trying to make us act out the fantasy novel he's been working on since, basically, birth. So we booted him from the role and I took his place. Except no one had the nerve to, like, fully kick him out.

"Okay, I will suspend my disbelief and go along with these . . . boulders," Greg sniffs.

I take a bite of one of the massive chocolate chip cookies Greg's mom always sends with him in a Tupperware. They might have something to do with why we tolerate his "innocent suggestions."

"Your eyes are drawn to the center of the room," I continue, "where Slarog's fabled treasure lies, sparkling with light, even though the grand chamber is shrouded in darkness. Large chests, more than you can count, spill over with coins and a rainbow of jewels. And in the center of it all, perched on top of a gold pedestal, is what you are seeking, adventurers: the Chalice of Rejuvenation."

"Yes!" Yobani calls out, pumping his fist. Leela gasps, and even Greg, I note with satisfaction, looks excited.

This is the payoff I was hoping for, after all the time it's taken to get here and all the work I've put into this story. Last Saturday, they'd finally retrieved the Queen's Heart from the Tomb of Odall. And now they've just got the Chalice of Rejuvenation left to steal and return to the wizard Zorciar so he'll lift the plague he cast over their village.

Zorciar is about to ghost them as soon as they give him the goods, so they're not as close to the end of this campaign as they think. But only I know that right now.

"I don't know, you guys," Leela says, shaking her head. Her long, shiny black hair falls forward, and she scoops it back around her right shoulder. "I find it hard to believe that no one has stopped us so far? I mean, we just strolled right through his garden. That was weird, right? This feels a little too easy."

I nod and press my fingers together in a steeple. "It sounds like you want to—"

"Perception check," she says, picking out a d20 from her pile of sparkly lavender dice. She rolls a twelve.

"Walona uses her darkvision to peer around the vault and spots movement on the far end of the chamber. There are wyverns patrolling! But luckily they cannot see you, adventurers, because of the invisibility spell that Walona cast before you descended the stairs."

"I knew it," Leela says, and it's taking all I've got to keep a mask of indifference on my face. Her roll was high enough for me to reveal the wyverns, but not high enough for me to reveal that Slarog, the cloud giant himself, lurks in the mist above their heads, watching and waiting.

"I'm going in," Greg says, his eyes narrowed in determination. "The longer we wait here, the more likely it is that we'll be found out. We've put too much into this to not act now."

"Gruly, you need to chill," Yobani snorts. He's rocking his chair on the two back legs, a smirk on his face. His favorite part of Saturday nights, easily, is fucking with Greg. "You're always trying to swoop in the save the day, when no one asked you to cape for us. Do you remember what happened at The Mighty Worm? Almost blew up the whole tavern with—"

"Gruldaito, still protected by Walona's invisibility spell, moves toward the chalice."

"Roll for stealth," I instruct, but Greg is already throwing his dice. Eighteen. He throws his hands up in celebration. Yobani shakes his head and takes another handful of Hot Cheetos.

"Gruldaito creeps closer to the chalice, his footsteps making no sound," I say.

"I'm gonna go for it," Greg says, all pumped up like he's about to jump into a boxing match. Leela leans forward in anticipation.

"All right." I rub my hands together. "Roll for sleight of hand."

Greg throws the d20 again, and I swear I see his soul leave his body when it lands. One.

"Critical fail!" Yobani yells, his face full of delight even though this hurts him, too. Greg puts his head in his hands. Leela reaches forward and pats his shoulder sympathetically while Yobani cackles.

"You knock the chalice to the ground, and the loud clang echoes throughout the chamber. You hear the flapping wings of wyverns as they fly closer, and the mist above your heads begins to grow thicker, darker. It encircles you—"

"Oh, shit," Leela mutters.

"I told you, Gruly!" Yobani shouts with glee.

"'Who dares to enter my chamber?'" I say. I pound the table to accentuate each syllable, all extra, and make my voice deep and loud. Man, doing the voices is my favorite part. "Slarog's words make your bones rattle, your blood run cold. His solid form appears out of the mist, towering above you, sixteen feet tall. Though he can't see you yet, he feels your presence. 'Show yourselves and prepare to die,' he commands. What do you do next, adventurers?"

I scan their faces, and Yobani and Greg are right there with me, eyes wide and mouths dropped open. But Leela is looking at her phone, and I'm a little annoyed, because I've put so much into this campaign. It's taken us months to get to this point. What could possibly be happening on her phone that's more important?

"I say we run," Greg suggests.

"Ha! Of course you do," Yobani laughs. "After you get us into this mess by trying to play the hero."

Greg gives him an epic side-eye. "In case you are not aware,"

Greg says slowly and with great enjoyment, "Walona's invisibility spell ends as soon as we attack or cast any spells of our own. I say we get out and regroup, now that we know what we're dealing with."

"Maybe he's right," Leela says, and Yobani falls back and clutches his chest like he's wounded. "Hey! Don't be like that," she continues with an easy laugh. I'm happy that her phone is face-down and she's back with us. "Gruldaito makes a good point."

"Well, I don't care what y'all say," Yobani says, picking up his d20. "We've come too far to just scurry away now. We are getting that chalice. Ol' big-head Slarog don't scare me."

I look around the table. Greg exhales loudly and shakes his head. Leela thinks about it, but then finally nods, relenting. "Fine. Let's do it."

"Okay. Roll for initiative," I say. I know it's a bad choice, but I can feel my body buzzing because this is going to be fun.

"Yeah, that's what I'm talking about!" Yobani shouts. They all throw their d20s, and I roll for Slarog and the wyverns. Leela, Yobani, and the wyverns all get low numbers, but Greg gets a seventeen and I roll a sixteen for Slarog.

"Gruldaito, you make the first move."

"Gruldaito lunges toward Slarog with his great sword," Greg says, hefting both hands up like the sword is really there. He takes a deep breath and rolls. One again. The whole table groans and Greg puts his head down.

"You miss, and the invisibility spell falls away. Slarog wrenches the sword from your grip, his cruel laughter shaking the room."

I roll for Slarog. Nineteen.

"Oh shit, oh shit . . ." Leela is practically vibrating in her chair.

"Slarog throws the boulders down—"

"Never should have dissed the boulders, Gruly," Yobani laughs.

I roll four d10s for damage, and it's bad. Real bad.

"The boulder breaks apart as it crashes into Gruldaito's armor. He falls to the ground." Greg looks crushed, and I almost feel bad. But also, that's just how it goes. And I live for these battle scenes, when all of my plans fall away to chance and I have to think on my feet. "Yobani, your turn. What do you wanna do?"

"Trickery casts the vicious mockery spell!" Yobani yells, a huge smile stretched across his face.

I raise an eyebrow. "Against Slarog?"

"Nah! Against Gruly, for getting us in this mess."

"What does that even contribute, Yo?" Leela asks, rolling her eyes.

"It's for my amusement," Yobani laughs. "Hey, probably Slarog's too!"

Greg's neck is getting red, like it always does when he's upset. "You can't attack me! We're in the same dungeon party!"

"Says who?" Yobani asks. "We're playing by Reggie's rules! Not Gruly's!"

"Well, then I'm going home!" Greg stands up and his chair falls back in the process. I can tell by his stricken face that he didn't mean to do that, but then he scrunches his face up and crosses his arms, going with it. "I'm so tired of you always messing with me just because I want us to play this game accurately—"

"More like boring-ly," Yobani interrupts. "Hey, Reggie, I changed my mind. I want to cast the sleep spell. On Gruly. And leave him behind to be Slarog's dinner while me and Walona peace out."

"Humans are not even part of the cloud giant's regular diet!" Greg shouts.

"*That's* what you're taking away from this?" Yobani throws his hands up.

"Guys! Shut up!" Leela rarely raises her voice, so when she does it gets everyone's attention.

"You're being a dick, Yobani," I say, and Leela nods in agreement. Greg gets on my nerves when we're playing too, and some shit-talking is pretty standard in our games. That's what happens when you've been playing together as long as we have. But I don't want him to feel unsafe at my table. This is the one place where I can be completely and totally myself, and I want it to be the same for my friends.

"I know, I know," Yobani says quickly. "Sorry, Greg! Trickery just . . . brings it out of me. It's the tiefling way."

"Don't blame this on Trickery, Yobani," Greg grumbles. "You're a dick even when you're not an infernal being."

Yobani smiles. "What came first? The Trickery or the dickery? The world may never know." He waggles his eyebrows. "Eh?"

I sigh. "No."

"I think, maybe . . . we should call it for tonight," Leela says, grabbing her phone again. "It's already nine."

Greg starts to nod, and even Yobani looks like he might agree.

But this is the last thing I want.

"Nine?" I say. "I thought we were going to play until midnight!" I may hate this holiday, but that doesn't mean I want to spend it alone. Ringing in the new year in Slarog's castle is the kind of festive I can get behind.

"Sorry, Reggie." Leela bites her bottom lip. "I told you I couldn't play forever tonight. Ryan has a show at The Mode. And, I mean . . . even you can admit this is a good stopping point."

Ryan Love is Leela's girlfriend and the lead singer of this sorta locally famous rock band. Her shows have been getting in the way of our Saturday-night games a lot more this year, as the band has gotten more popular around Long Beach. We even had to switch to a Sunday afternoon one week, and it threw off the whole vibe.

"You all could come?" Leela offers. She always does.

But I turn her down the way *I* always do. "Nah, that's okay. You know that's not really my scene."

I've never actually been to one of Ryan's shows to know that for a fact. But I know Ryan, with her half-shaved head and over-the-top costumes—so I'm pretty sure I'm correct in that assessment.

See, Leela is different from me. Even though we were both nerdy kids with rubber bands on our braces, searching online for people to play a role-playing game with us—she's also a chameleon. She always has been. She can talk to anyone, be at home anywhere. The only place I feel at home is here at the table, running my campaigns. Well, and also online—talking, anonymously, to other people about what goes down at their tables. I feel like I spend all week waiting in anticipation for the escape from life that our

Saturday-night games will bring, but Leela is always a reminder that people are out there living, like, all the time. And she wants to get back to that real life right now.

"Let's go, Reggie," Yobani says. The traitor. "I kind of hate Ryan's music—no offense, Leela—but it'll probably be fun anyway."

"First of all, Yo, just because you say 'no offense' doesn't mean what you say isn't offensive," Leela says, putting her dice away. "And second, I feel like you don't get a say here. All you listen to is lo-fi versions of video game themes."

Yobani shrugs. "Hey, that Zelda one is a bop."

"Well, I'm busy." Greg puts his character sheet into his shiny green folder and tucks it into his backpack.

"No one invited you, Greg."

"Greg is invited," Leela says, narrowing her eyes at Yobani.

Everyone is putting their stuff away: Yobani rolls up the bags of Hot Cheetos and cheddar and sour cream Ruffles. Leela is sweeping up all the crumbs with her hands. Greg is scooping up his main dice and his backup dice. And I'm filled with disappointment. Just like that, we're done? The wyverns didn't even come into play, and I had some cool shit planned for the wyverns!

I hear the creak of the front door opening, followed by footsteps. Lots of footsteps. And yelling. Quickly, my disappointment is replaced with dread.

"Honey, I'm home!" Eric, my older brother, calls from the front of the house. Loud laughter follows, almost like a sitcom laugh track, because Eric always surrounds himself with people that will reliably think he's the funniest guy in the room.

A Vince Staples song starts to blast on Dad's stereo system in the living room, and I groan. This isn't some quick pit stop. They're staying.

We never play at my house. Mom and Dad know about the game, but actually playing in front of them? Yeah, that's my worst nightmare. And playing *in front of my brother* . . . What's worse than a worst nightmare?

So we always play in Leela's family room, our only soundtrack the muffled sounds of the Patels' *Law & Order* marathons coming from the front of the house. But my parents decided to drive down to San Diego to drink wine and dance like they're young with their old college friends, and Eric bragged about some big party in Belmont Shore he was going to. I thought this would be the perfect opportunity to finally play on my home turf.

"Hope we're not interrupting your party, baby bro," Eric says, his voice sounding like he cast Trickery's vicious mockery spell. He explodes into the room, blowing into a loud silver noisemaker and holding up a bottle of champagne. Frankie and Tyrell, his two closest friends, trail behind him, along with three girls I don't think I've seen before.

"Bruh, what is this?!" Frankie laughs, gesturing to the table. We've cleaned up a lot of it, but my hand-drawn map is still in the center, along with my player's handbook and some character sheets.

"This," Eric says, stretching his hands out wide, "is what Reggie does for fun. They be, like, casting spells on each other. And pretending to be gnomes and unicorns and shit. For real!"

He falls forward laughing, and they all take the cue and join in.

"Hey, thanks for getting the snacks," Eric continues, grabbing Greg's Tupperware of cookies from his hands. "No Oreos? I know *those* are Reggie's all-time favorites."

He snorts and loses himself in another fit of laughter. "Ha! Cause he's an Oreo!" Tyrell clarifies, just in case anyone didn't catch that sweet, sweet burn. Thanks, Tyrell.

"I've heard of this before," one of the girls says, stepping forward. She's wearing a festive sparkly thing and has her hair in long twists. "But I thought people, uh, dressed up? And did this outside?"

I don't think she was trying to make fun of me, but that sets Eric off even more. "Yeah—where—" he gasps out in between laughs. "Are your capes? And—WANDS!"

"That's LARPing," I mumble. "This is way different."

Not that LARPing wouldn't be fun, but, like . . . I could never be out in the world like that. Look at the shit I'm taking for just this.

"LARPING!" Frankie shouts, slapping the table. "Fucking LARPing, fam!"

I stand up.

"Leela, actually, I think I'm gonna go with you after all."

It's definitely not how I want to spend my New Year's. And I am still firmly against the idea of this holiday bringing about any sort of change. That's not what's happening here. It's just that anything would be better than being stuck in this house with Eric and his asshole friends while they laugh at everything I love.

"Good," Leela says, wrapping her arms protectively around my shoulders. Yobani gathers up the rest of my D&D stuff while Leela fixes Eric with a death stare so brutal that his giggles actually slow.

"I'll take those back," Greg says, snatching his Tupperware from Eric's grip. He looks Eric up and down, throws on his backpack, and struts out of the room.

Leela, Yobani, and I follow him, and Eric, not one to give anyone else the last word, calls after us, "Hey, yo, you better not be walking out this house with those ashy ankles! People know you're related to me!"

We can still hear his friends laughing after we slam the front door.

DELILAH

"Okay, top three . . ." Asher starts, throwing his bass in its case over his shoulder, "um . . . Girl Scout cookies. Go!"

"Definitely Thin Mints," Beau says. He grabs his cymbals, rounding up this final load, and closes the trunk behind him. We start the walk from the parking lot to The Mode. Only the bands with the most cred get to park their cars in the small loading zone at the back of the venue. We had to make three trips.

Asher nods approvingly. "Samoas. Obviously."

"And Trefoils," Charlie says. Both Asher and Beau wrinkle their noses at him.

"No one likes Trefoils, bro," Asher says with certainty.

"Uh, obviously someone does or they wouldn't keep making them," Charlie says. "Okay, now, top three . . . dystopian stories. Go!"

"You *would* go from freakin' cookies to something all left field like that," Beau says, rolling his eyes. "Gonna go with . . . *Mad Max*!" He claps his hands and points to me.

I rack my brain trying to think of a good answer. Maybe *Parable of the Sower*? I've seen that on my mom's bookshelf. But Asher cuts in before I get a chance: "*The Tribe*! Oh, definitely *The Tribe*!"

"What the fuck is *The Tribe*?" Charlie asks.

"One of the great masterpieces of our time. It's on YouTube. Enlighten yourself. You're welcome."

"Nah, nah. That does not get to be in the top three," Beau scoffs. "Try again."

"You let Charlie sneak in Trefoils!"

"Trefoils are delicious," Charlie mutters. "*The Tribe* isn't even on the same level as Trefoils."

Asher hops around in front of Charlie and points one of Beau's drumsticks in his face accusingly. "Blasphemy!"

I know the guys are just trying to kill time with endless rounds of their favorite game, but I kind of wish they would be quiet. Instead of distracting me from my wobbly stomach, it's making my head feel fuzzy and crowded. I would give anything for silence right now. But I guess silence isn't happening anytime soon.

We get to the front of The Mode again, sandwiched between a hair salon with its steel shutters pulled down for the night and a twenty-four-hour donut shop, and Beau opens the heavy wooden door. The sound is overwhelming. The heavy bass of a punk song I've heard the guys play before makes my whole body shake. People are talking, yelling, filling up every inch of the place—starting at the front, where the owner, Jimmy, is swiping cards and passing out wristbands, and pressed up against all of the painted black walls of the lobby. And the first band hasn't even gone on yet. It's only going to get louder.

I feel the eyes on us immediately.

At this point, I'm kind of an expert in the eyes—the heavy, oppressive feeling of having others staring at you. Especially after this past semester. That's what happens when you're moved from a perfectly good public school to a prestigious (code word for *expensive* and *extremely white*) private school at the beginning of sophomore year because your dad is sending his new kids to kindergarten there and doesn't want to look bad or feel guilty.

When you're one of the only Black kids in a building, you feel it in your bones. The stares that linger too long, the too-wide smiles that hide all their expectations and discomfort—man, it made me want to shrink and hide. I begged Mom to let me transfer back to Bixby High, but she insisted that my sister, Georgia, and I weren't going to turn down this opportunity. And it's not like I was leaving behind some big social life. My old friends Tamir and Rachel lost patience with me constantly cancelling plans because of my migraines, even when they saw me every day at school. Like so many people, they didn't understand why I couldn't just take an Excedrin and keep it moving. So after I left, the invitations trickled down to nothing pretty quick. Out of sight, out of mind sure was easy for them.

Charlie presses his shoulder to mine, and Asher moves in close to weave around a group of guys I recognize from school with pointy silver hats and noisemakers. And it reminds me that things are different now than they were in September. This is me choosing the eyes, choosing to stand out.

Because the guys are always the center of every room they walk into. Beau is super tall and always rolls up his sleeves, even the uniform shirts, to show off his tan arms, ripped with muscles from drumming. Asher has light brown hair, deep-set sparkling eyes, and style that makes you turn your head. Tonight he has on cropped, ripped jeans over his butter-yellow Crocs and an oversized neon floral-print silk shirt. And then there's Charlie . . . Well, I've already talked about Charlie. And I'm only one entry on the long list of girls who have taken notice.

They're like teenage boys in some Netflix movie: clear skin, unlimited charm, devastating smiles, and good hair that they always seem to be running their fingers through just so. But, you know, real. And as soon as Charlie ushered me in, I moved to the center too. In a good way this time.

I see a girl with a septum piercing and pink hair sizing me up, the question so obvious on her face: Who is *she* to be with them?

But the guys make me feel like I belong. I'm protected in their cool.

"Hey, Jimmy!" Charlie calls, steering us over toward him. "Meet our new secret weapon!"

"I know Delilah," Jimmy says, handing change to a kid in a faded Sonic Youth T-shirt and then smiling at me. I've spent quite a few nights in the back of The Mode with Jimmy, selling the occasional Fun Gi sticker while the guys are on stage. He's old, somewhere between thirty or forty, but still manages to pull off silver earrings and a leather jacket without looking too try-hard. "These knuckleheads talked you into going on stage with 'em?"

I take a deep breath, trying to settle my nerves. "Looks like it," I say with a shrug.

"After tonight, people are going to be like, Ryan Love who?"

Beau says. Jimmy just chuckles and shakes his head. Probably because there's no way *that's* going to happen.

He points to the wall, where a list in his chicken-scratch handwriting is posted underneath an illustrated flyer for tonight. "Well, I can't wait to see it! And we're about to throw you into the deep end, darling. You guys are up first tonight."

"First?!" Asher yelps, jumping in to study the list for himself, as if it's going to change.

First is bad. First is who plays while people are still taking selfies and gulping down vodka out of water bottles outside.

"C'mon, Jimmy," Charlie says, leaning on the counter in between us. It's covered in faded stickers from all the bands Jimmy has hosted here over the years. "Haven't we paid our dues?"

Jimmy laughs again. "That's just the way it goes, kiddos. Feline is playing last tonight—that's who's selling all the tickets."

"But that doesn't mean we have to play first. Why isn't Ryan playing first?" Charlie asks.

Jimmy waves that question away. "You guys better get a move on. Feline just told me they want to be on stage at midnight. Got confetti cannons, or something like that. You know how they are. So if you want a full set, we need to start soon."

I gulp. "Soon as in . . ."

"Soon as in twenty minutes, darling," Jimmy says. And he must see the color drain from my face, because he quickly adds, "You'll be all right."

Twenty minutes.

I thought I had time to go over the set list one more time, maybe run through Charlie's lyrics. But twenty minutes . . . that's not even enough time for a real sound check.

As the buzz in the room starts to get even louder, my stomach dips and my head spins. And I realize this isn't just nerves. No, this is a migraine coming on. The warning signs are as familiar to me as an old friend—or really, worst enemy—because they've run my life since I was twelve. But I wasn't paying attention tonight. I was distracted and didn't catch it in time to head it off. And I brought my meds, like my mom reminded me to, but they're buried in my purse in the minivan and Charlie is tugging me back through the double doors into the main space, where things are about to get a lot louder. I'm going to have to suck it up, though. There's no time to run to the parking lot, and I can't back out now.

So twenty minutes later, I'm standing on a dark stage, holding on tight to the microphone stand like I'll fall over without it. And I might.

The sound of the crowd is so loud that I feel like I'm underwater, and the *thump-thump-thump* of my heartbeat is pounding in my head. I don't know how I'm going to remember any of the words, any of my cues, when my mind is so fuzzy and only getting worse. The lights flick on, so bright and sharp, I swear I'm going to puke.

But then Asher's velvety bass line starts, followed by Beau's steady drumbeat, and it centers me. Charlie comes in with his first chords, beaming at me like I belong there.

And I want to.

I close my eyes, open my mouth, and sing.

REGGIE

"Do you think I was too hard on Greg?" Yobani asks as we're standing in line for tickets at The Mode. With a wave to the guy in a leather jacket at the front, Leela slipped backstage to see Ryan, leaving us to fend for ourselves.

"You know you were," I say, and Yobani jumps back dramatically.

"*You take that back!*" he shouts, getting a few stares—which is saying something, considering how loud it is in here.

I laugh and roll my eyes. "Bro, you know you need to reel it in. He can be annoying sometimes, but, I mean, there's a limit. He might *actually* peace out, and then we won't have enough people to play. Or the cookies."

"Those goddamn cookies. Why must they be so delicious?" He shakes his head, looking wistful. "It just drives me crazy how he's always trying to critique you, dude. You know he's jealous, right? 'Cause, like, you just go off the dome and don't need pages and pages of notes like him."

I don't need notes because they would only get in the way and slow me down when I'm DM-ing. See, I have dyslexia, and storing everything up top is much more reliable than the way letters get all mixed up on a page. "I don't know if that's anything to be jealous of," I say, but Yobani waves that thought off.

"Nah, don't even. You're legit, Reg," he says with certainty. "Plus remember how he used to put his stupid notes behind that stupid screen? Like we were going to *cheat* at fucking *D&D*? The WORST—"

"Two?" The question interrupts Yobani's Greg rant, which is a good thing, because he could go for hours if unchecked. We've somehow made it to the front of the line, and the leather jacket guy, with leathery skin to match, is holding up a sheet of neon pink wristbands. He's intimidating, like aggressively cool, with tattoos starting at the collar of his T-shirt (featuring a band I've never heard of) and ending up by his ears. It makes me hyperaware that I don't belong in this place, where almost everyone also has tattoos and obscure shirts, plus dyed hair and a significant amount of eyeliner. It's like a tavern scene in one of our game sessions, where it's so clear that the adventurers are headed for trouble. But then I say, "Yeah, two." And the leather jacket guy smiles this big goofy smile that reveals a chipped front tooth and changes his whole face.

"That'll be twenty, then," he says. Yobani and I hand him our bills and he passes us two of the wristbands. He leans his head toward the door, where a steady drumbeat and the low sounds of a bass have started to make the walls vibrate. "Sounds like the opener, Fun Gi, is starting if you wanna catch 'em." He starts to bob his head, rapping his knuckles on the sticker-clad counter. "Actually I think I'm gonna take a peek. They got a new lineup tonight." He nods to a vampire-pale guy with two nose rings, who takes his place at the counter, and then pulls open the heavy door. The sound gets even louder for a moment—a scratchy guitar and piercing voice have joined the bass and drums. But then it quiets again when the door shuts behind him. He's not waiting for us to make up our minds. And I'm glad, because I have zero interest in watching some band with a stupid name like Fun Gi. I don't even want to see Ryan's band.

"Gotta piss!" Yobani shouts, weirdly loud in this crowded room again. "Be back in five to seven. Longer if those Hot Cheetos got something to say."

"Yo, we talked about this. You don't gotta give me all your bodily function details."

"Just being courteous!" he says over his shoulder as he heads toward a dingy-looking door with a spray-painted toilet on it. Leaving me all alone in this room I have no business being in. Like, surely the Cool Patrol are about to swoop in any minute and remove me from the premises for being so tragically uncool.

I look up from the spot I've been studying on my dirty Converse and, as if she's read my thoughts, a girl is staring right at me, her eyebrows pushed together in confusion. Well, not at *me*, I realize. At my shirt. Shit.

Leela gave me this shirt as a joke when I took over as Dungeon Master. It says "CARPE DM" in bright yellow letters with a giant d20 dice. She found it on Etsy or something. And it's, like, so cringe, but that was kind of the point? I started wearing it on game nights and then it just became part of the tradition. I was so ready to get out of my house because of Eric and his asshole friends that I didn't even think about changing. Which I DEFINITELY should have done.

I zip up my hoodie and then pull the hood on for good measure. But then I quickly pull it off, because that's bringing attention to me in another way. A way I *also* don't want to deal with right now.

I mean, it's not like I'm the only Black person here, but the crowd is "diverse" in the way that woke white kids think of diverse. Just a few of people of color sprinkled around the room, the only-the-lonelys in their friend groups. Like the cilantro in the white rice at Chipotle, you know what I'm saying? That rice is freaking delicious, but I'm not trying to live in it.

Man, I just want to go home, but that isn't safe right now either. Plus Leela would be pissed if I bounced without saying anything. So I'm stuck here. Damn. I pull out my phone. At least there's one place (other than my table) where I can always keep it one hundred.

There are a bunch of notifications on my screen, comments on my most recent essay on Medium. I threw up the post on the insidious othering of orcs yesterday morning, and it's been getting a lot of engagement. I know you're not supposed to read the comments—that's like Internet 101—but I always brave the trolls to see the comments from my regular followers. They've been around so long that I recognize their screen names and actually want to hear their feedback.

I've been writing essays critiquing the racism and colonialism in Dungeons & Dragons for a couple years now. It began as just ranting to my friends, but then Leela suggested I actually do something with those rants. So I started getting my thoughts down, using this transcribing app my resource teacher turned me on to, and Yobani stepped up to edit all my posts. It's become a real thing now—something I spend more time on than homework, that's for sure.

Which might seem weird, because I play D&D every week and overall just devote a significant amount of my brain space to this game. But, like, nothing you love is above critique. And if you love something, you want to make it better. I've gained a lot of loyal followers, especially in the past six months or so. Black people and people of color that love the game, live and breathe the game like me, but they have the same issues with D&D that I do and are happy to see it all out in the open. I've gained a lot of haters, too, though.

And *ah, yes*—I scroll through the notifications. That's who these comments are from. The trolls are out in full force. I put in an AirPod and have my text-to-speech app read them to me.

I'm so tired of these SJWs playing the race card

I can't take anyone seriously that would have all these typos. (I always have typos, even with Yobani editing, but, like, whatever. They get what I mean!)

if u don't like the game, then stop playing. wizards of the coast don't need ur money!!!!!! (I don't know . . . I give them a lot of my money.)

PLEASE tell me again how this fictional world is VICTIMIZING you! BLACKS are always trying to play the victim but THEIR NOT. (Oh, you can hear the hard-R about to jump *out* in that one.)

Comments like these are why I post my essays under an anonymous screen name, KeepinItd100. I don't need these assholes knowing any of my personal details. And I definitely don't need anyone outside of my friends being able to search up my essays on Google. What would Eric—or, god, *my parents*—think if they knew just how much time I was devoting to this nerdy game? I would never live it down.

I take out the AirPod and shove the phone into my back pocket. So much for looking to the internet to make me feel valued and respected tonight.

Someone opens the door, an explosion of sound coming from the main room. And I realize I've been hearing this back-and-forth the whole time in the background. The lobby is a whole lot emptier too. People seem to be giving this fungus band a chance.

Yobani's Hot Cheetos prophecy must have come to pass, because he's been gone for a while, so maybe I'll give this band a chance too. It beats standing around this lobby feeling sorry for myself.

I pull open the heavy door, and it's like walking into a different realm—the sound is so loud and the air is thick with sweat. All around me, bodies are moving, running the spectrum from subtly bobbing their heads to crashing together in a mosh pit that's formed in the middle. But no one's having snarky side conversations or checking their phones. No—everyone's full attention is at the front. I follow their eyes to the stage and I feel like I've forgotten how to breathe, like my brain doesn't even have space for basic bodily functions anymore. Because all I can process, all I can see, is the most beautiful girl in the world.

I know that insta-love is bullshit. It's a necessary evil in some of my D&D sessions because I'm trying to move the game along, but, like, it doesn't actually happen in real life. I *know* that.

Except, I'm pretty sure I'm in love with the girl in the middle of the stage.

She has dark, curly hair that falls on her shoulders, a wide nose, and pillowy lips. She's wearing a red and white flannel with checkerboard Vans and a sliver of her golden-brown skin peeks out over the top of her faded black jeans. And I wish I could wax poetic over the color of her eyes, but they're squeezed shut, a starbursts of lines bursting from the edges of each one.

Even though her eyes are closed, her energy is still electric. She stands on the tips of her toes, bouncing and shimmying, as if only her tight grip on the mic is what's keeping her on the ground. And her voice follows the same pattern, hopping around the harsh guitar and the fast drumbeat. It's high and loud, like a ringing bell, but just when you're getting comfortable, there's a hard edge, a near shriek, that makes you stand at attention.

The song ends with one last riff on the guitar, leaving me reeling to catch up, to fully comprehend what I'm seeing.

"This next song is going to be our last one," the most beautiful girl in the world says, speaking to the ground instead of the audience. Her voice is quiet, tentative, even with the mic. A few people in the crowd groan, clearly as disappointed as I am that this band is almost done. "It's a cover. You might know it. Um, yeah . . . Happy New Year."

The music starts back up, fast and heavy. And the girl squeezes her eyes shut again, like she's singing alone in her room.

"When the bells all ring and the horns all blow . . ."

But then all of a sudden she's wide-eyed, shock taking over her face. And then a small smile finds her lips, like she's just heard a joke that only she gets. Her voice gets louder, bolder. She swings her hair around and stares straight out at the audience, straight at me.

"What are you doing New Year's, New Year's Eve?"

And, okay, I know I said I don't believe in insta-love. And I know I said I don't believe in the woo-woo magic of New Year's Eve. But I also know for sure that I was supposed to be right here, right at this moment, seeing the girl of my dreams.

DELILAH

I am on stage.

I am on stage and I am singing.

I am on stage and I am singing and I think I may be . . . good?

For the first couple of songs, I was focused on getting the lyrics right. I held on to the microphone stand for dear life and kept my eyes shut so I couldn't be distracted by grimaces and eye rolls—or make my growing migraine even worse with the bright lights.

Then, I don't know if it was the fault of my fuzzy head or divine intervention, but when we got to "Starshine Monologue," something different happened with my voice. A little yelp, I guess, at the end of the first chorus. And I heard this *woohoo*, even over Asher's bass solo before the next verse. I decided to risk a quick look at the audience, sure someone was making fun of me somehow, maybe even pissed about having to wait through our set to get to Ryan Love or Feline. But a guy in the front with a thick mustache and neon green hat was smiling and pumping his first. The whole front row looked just as excited. We *had* a front row—when we first went on, the only person standing by the stage was a girl with a homemade Feline shirt, obviously trying to stake out her spot for their set. But now the room was getting full, people were dancing, moshing. It was definitely livelier than I've ever seen a Fun Gi show get from my usual spot at the merch table.

So I closed my eyes again and tried the yelp a few more times. I moved around more. I let my voice get looser, brighter. And at the end of the song, there was no doubt—the applause doubled. Maybe even tripled. It made me light up inside, even as my head pounded along with it. Charlie beamed at me, and Beau gave me a thumbs-up from behind his kit. They could feel the change in energy too.

Once we get to the last song—a fast, frantic cover of "What Are You Doing New Year's Eve?"—I feel like I'm really getting into my groove. Mostly because, well, I don't feel like myself. I would never be this loud, command this much attention. And I definitely wouldn't kick my leg out on that high note, like I just did right now, to cheers from the audience.

But there's something so . . . exhilarating about that? Because I'm not being myself, so I guess that means I can be anyone. And if I'm anyone, that means I can do *anything*. In this moment, I'm not Delilah, with all my hang-ups and overwhelming desire to shrink myself. I'm someone else. And I don't think I've ever felt that sort of freedom before.

At the end of my next line, I decide to open my eyes and take in the audience again, risking a full stare this time. And I'm shocked.

How did this room get even more crowded? The whole place seems to vibrate with their excitement, a blur of sparkles and ironic plastic New Year's hats and leather and denim. All of it for us. For me.

I smile to myself. I can't believe I *yeah, whatever*-ed myself into this ridiculous, exhilarating situation.

I launch into the rest of the song, the adrenaline pushing away my pounding head and the nausea, and I give it my all. I make my voice high and sweet, like a teakettle about to blow. I take the mic off the stand and jump over to Charlie, singing to him. I play around, trying sharp yelps and sugary coos, channeling the videos I watched of all those formidable front women.

And I'm singing. *Really* singing. Finally. I feel like I've leapt off the cliff at last, but I'm not falling. I'm flying. My voice is powerful, lifting me higher and higher.

When Charlie strikes his last chord, the crowd explodes. But instead of basking in it, I speed off the stage, scared that the magic will evaporate.

"We're Fun Gi!" I hear him yell into the mic. "If you liked that, then find us online because we've got more coming! Good night!"

My first thought when I reach backstage: *I can't believe I fucking did that*.

My second thought: *My migraine has officially arrived*.

The sharpness and steady pounding that was at the edges before has now taken over. The back of my head feels tight and achy and the front feels like it's being squeezed in a vise. Everything is too bright, too loud, and if I don't take one of my pills soon, I'll be completely knocked out. For the night and maybe even for days. I'm so stupid. I can't believe I just left them in the car when they're my lifeline.

The guys run off the stage. Beau screams my name, waving his hands in the air. Charlie grabs me by the waist and twirls me around. It should feel so good, but I think I'm going to puke.

"You were fucking incredible!" Asher says, shaking me by the shoulders. His cheeks are flushed red and his hair is spiky with sweat.

"Our girl is a star," Charlie says, kissing me on the cheek.

He has never done *that* before. My body goes haywire trying to process that at the same time that my brain is shutting down. Okay, meds first, analyze what the hell that means later.

"Great set, you guys." Jimmy walks up and claps Beau and Asher on the back. "Delilah! A triumph! I'm loving the Poly Styrene vibe."

"That's exactly what we were going for!" Charlie answers before I can even respond. Which is a little annoying, because I'm not even sure Charlie has listened to X-Ray Spex before. I found them all on my own.

Charlie has started a monologue on all of Fun Gi's many influences when someone touches my shoulder. I turn to see Ryan Love standing there in all her glory. She's wearing a lavender organza dress with a short, full skirt, and shiny black Doc Martens. Her half-shaved hair is dyed electric red and slicked back under a gold star crown, and her septum piercing has a dangly star to match. I swear she glows, but that also might be the effects of my increasingly blurring vision.

"Delilah, right?" Her voice is musical, like twinkling chimes. I nod, and she beams at me. "Girl, that was everything."

I'm grasping for the right words, but my brain is jumbled and I feel like I'm trying to pluck them out of a thick fog. "Thank you," I squeak out, finally.

"Well, we're about to go on," she says, gesturing to her band-mates. A girl in a sage-green jumpsuit is helping Beau pack up his precious drums so she can move her own kit in. "But we *need* to play another show together. You are so badass!"

"Yeah." Another simple word that takes way too long to find. "For sure."

She skips away and I turn back to Charlie. I tap him on the shoulder, interrupting his conversation with Jimmy.

"What's up?"

"Will you come with me to get my meds from the car?" I point to my head.

"You got a headache?" I wince. Not a headache. A migraine. They're very different things. But I don't have anything left in me to argue semantics now, so I nod, my head punishing me for even that slight movement.

"Uh . . ." He sighs, leans in closer. "It's just that . . . Jimmy and I are talking about booking another gig. And I don't want to miss Ryan Love and the Valentines' set. It's bad form." He rubs my back and hands me the van keys. "I'm sorry, but you get it, right? Maybe one of the guys can go with you?"

Beau is busy with his drums, and Asher is talking to two girls on the ripped floral couch they keep backstage.

"It's fine. No big deal." I force a smile and walk out alone.

Thirty minutes later, I'm sitting on the curb outside of the donut shop, willing my body to get its shit together.

I took a pill, but they don't work immediately. And even when it does kick in, it makes me feel less awful, but not exactly better. My limbs get all shaky and weak. And everything is on a delay, my mouth moving before the words get there, as if my wi-fi is lagging. My head feels like it's filling up with cotton balls.

Plus, the relief is so fickle. If I move my head too much or hear something too loud, the migraine will come thundering back. But I won't be able to take another pill for hours.

So even though I can hear the first guitar riffs and Ryan Love's signature scream start up, I have to stay out here, alone. I can't risk these meds not working and this migraine haunting me for days.

This is just my life. I don't get to enjoy anything all the way. I always have to worry about things being too much. I should have been keeping better track, so it didn't get this far tonight.

God, Ryan probably thought I was cold, standoffish, with my clipped answers. I hope I didn't ruin the band's connection with her. Or Jimmy. I hope he doesn't think I'm rude for not being in there right now. I don't want to mess up things just as we might be on an upward trajectory. Not that we're on an upward trajectory because of me, I guess. But . . . I don't know. Maybe.

The music gets louder and then there are footsteps. My head jerks up. I regret it immediately.

And it wasn't even anything to worry about. Just a guy walking out of The Mode. He has deep brown skin and a low fro with a taper fade. He's wearing round gold-rimmed glasses and a black hoodie. He's not threatening. Looks pretty geeky, actually. I feel my shoulders relax.

"Hey," he says, noticing me looking at him. He gives a little wave, but then looks at his hand and quickly shoves it in his pocket.

I nod back, not trusting myself to speak without puking. But then that just makes it so much worse, so I attempt a smile and then put my head between my knees and wait for the world to stop spinning.

REGGIE

I didn't intend to follow the girl outside. I promise it wasn't like that.

I mean, I *thought* about following her when she ran offstage so fast. I probably could have got backstage with Leela's help. But by the time I was done going back and forth, obsessing over what I might actually say to her, Yobani came back from his marathon shit session. And then before I knew it, Ryan Love and the Valentines were going on and it would have been weird to peace out then. So I stood off to the side, nodding my head even though this type of screamy, scratchy music isn't really my jam—at least it wasn't until I saw the most beautiful girl in the world put her spin on it.

I was there for a few songs when Yobani decided to jump in with the people thrashing and slamming into each other in the middle, leaving me behind. And Leela was in the very front, all heart-eyed as she swayed and mouthed along to all the lyrics. So I figured my friends were too busy to care about me dipping out for a second.

Not to go look for the girl. Just because it was hot. Like, really hot—so hot I had to unzip my hoodie and put my dorky shirt on full display again.

And yeah, I noticed that the girl wasn't standing with her bandmates. But I *did not* go searching for her. I needed some air. That's all.

When I did see her sitting on the curb, though, I wasn't mad about it. Except I had to go and ruin it, like, instantaneously, by waving. Waving! Like a goddamn toddler. Then she nodded and gave me a fake smile, showing me mercy instead of giving me the full-body cringe I deserved. And before I had a chance to redeem myself, she put her head between her legs, shutting down any minuscule chance I had left.

I should leave. I should walk away and pretend this never happened. We don't go to the same school—I would *definitely* recognize her if we did. No one has to know how little game I actually have.

She's sitting outside by herself, though. She's not listening or looking around her. And outside of a donut shop, no less, which is extra dangerous. Because as we all know, there are *way* too many donut shops in Long Beach for them to all be financially viable. So, like, at least fifty percent of them have to be a front for more nefarious enterprises, and I'm not trying to be interviewed as a witness on a murder podcast next month.

I can't leave her alone.

So I stand here, listening to the muffled sounds of Ryan Love and the Valentines. Ten minutes. Fifteen. I check my phone, and then remember I don't want to see any of the notifications, so I shove it back in my pocket.

Twenty minutes. The girl stirs, and I think she's going to sit up, but she just rolls her shoulders and stretches her neck.

I hear shouts and applause inside and then the sounds die down. The Valentines' set must be over. The door behind me opens, but it's not the guys in her band. (*Where are the guys in her band?*) It's two girls in Feline shirts, passing a vape pen back and forth and giggling at something on a phone. They're gone a few minutes later.

When it hits thirty-five minutes, I start questioning my whole decision-making process here. Yes, leaving her alone is not the right thing to do, but is standing above her like a creeper much better?

I take a deep breath. Okay, all right. I'll sit down. A safe, non-threatening distance away. Here I am, a regular guy, just trying to make sure you're not kidnapped by someone pretending to sell apple fritters.

"Oh, you're still here." I startle. The girl is looking right at me. Not smiling, but not horrified either. My brain rushes to memorize all the details of her face like I'm going to be tested on them later: the light dusting of freckles on her nose, a deep cupid's bow, long bottom lashes. Her eyes have dark bags under them, though, and her brown skin looks a couple shades lighter than it did when she was on stage. She still looks unbelievably gorgeous, but it's clear she's feeling sick. Why is she out here alone?

"Yeah, I'm sorry. I didn't want to just leave you here." I put my hands up. "Not in, like, a weirdo way. Because it was the right thing to do. I would have done it for anybody. You can't be too careful with, you know—" I wave my hands behind us. "The donuts."

Her dark eyebrows push together in confusion. Because of course she's confused.

"Thank you?"

"I can, uh, leave if you want me to now. Now that you're alert and . . . safe. Not that *I* kept you safe. I'm sure you're perfectly capable of that on your own." Why am I still talking? I need to stop talking.

She laughs, but it's not a mocking, *what the fuck is wrong with this guy?* laugh. I know that one well. No, it's warm and kind. She smiles at me, that same small smile from the stage—just a slight upturn of her lips. And I swear to god, my heart legit skips a beat. Like, I might need to go to the hospital.

"I appreciate it. Really." She looks around us, and I can hear the heavy bass of the next band, Feline, starting up inside. "I shouldn't have been out here like that alone. That was stupid. My mom would *kill* me . . . if I didn't get killed, that is."

I laugh, and I notice her wince. "Are you okay?"

"Yeah, I'm fine," she says quickly, as if it's a standard reply she has ready to go. "I have a migraine. Well, had a migraine. I think it's mostly gone now. I took my medicine and I was waiting for it to kick in."

"Oh god, I'm sorry. That is rough." I make my voice way quieter so I don't make her feel worse. "And you put on a show like that with a migraine? Wow. I mean, I was impressed before, but that is some superhero shit."

Her cheeks flush red, and she smiles at her knees. "Thanks. It was my first gig . . . ever."

"Ever? Like, *ever* ever?"

"Mm-hmm."

"Well . . . damn. Don't forget me when you're famous then. Because if you rocked your first show *that* hard, you about to be." That makes her smile slightly bigger, so I keep going. "Reggie. R-E-G-G-I-E. The guy that stood next to you awkwardly for thirty minutes in front of a donut shop right before your big break. I want to be name-dropped in the first documentary."

"Reggie," she repeats. "I'm Delilah."

Delilah. It's music.

"Well, I'll be bragging about this night someday, Delilah."

"I don't know about all that," she sighs. "I was just helping out my friends."

"Hey, give yourself some credit. I mean, I'm no expert here, and I'm sure your friends are great musicians or whatever. But you're talented too. What you did tonight . . . it was something special." I worry I took it too far, basically waved a flashing neon sign that said "I HAVE A MASSIVE CRUSH ON YOU" in her face. But she waves it away with another little smile.

"What does your shirt say?" she asks, changing the subject. Changing it to *the worst subject*.

I was starting to think that I might actually have a chance here. We were vibing, even. But she's cool. Like ridiculously cool. Singing-in-a-punk-band-in-front-of-a-hundred-people-as-a-favor-to-her-friends cool. Whatever ground I gained will surely be obliterated once she finds out that I make up stories about cloud giants and wyverns on *my* Saturday nights.

The way I see it, I only have two choices here: I could tell her what the shirt says and explain it away, act embarrassed. But then if I even had a minuscule chance with her, it will be completely gone. She's so cool, so *herself*—any insecurity on my part would be the end, a critical fail.

No, the only thing I can do here is own it. Fake all the confidence in the world. Most likely she'll laugh. Maybe roll her eyes and write me off. But there's a small sliver of a chance that she might . . . not.

"Oh, it's a D&D joke. Dungeons & Dragons," I say, forcing my voice to be steady and strong. "I was playing with my friends before I came here. I'm the Dungeon Master. So, you know, the person in charge." I look her in the eyes and smile.

DELILAH

"Dungeons & Dragons?" I ask. "So you were, um, playing together at a park? With costumes?" I inspect Reggie's outfit again, searching for something shiny or cloak-like that I missed before, but it looks normal.

He leans forward and laughs. It's a low hiss, like air being let out of a balloon. "Damn, why does everyone think that?" He shakes his head, slaps his knee. "Nah, that's LARPing. Live-action role-playing. But for real? Those guys are dope, like aspirational. Do you know how long those costumes take? It's some serious artistry."

He smiles and I can't help but match it. His energy is infectious. "Okay, no costumes or acting out . . . so is it like a video game?"

"No, it's not that. Though I won't front: I do love my Switch." He claps his hands together, lightly so there's no sound, and points at me. "All right, so, Dungeons & Dragons. The official spiel: It's a tabletop role-playing game where you create your own fantasy adventures. But, like, it's so much more than that. It's storytelling. It's an act of friendship. It's creativity in its purest, most uninhibited form."

"So like . . . Monopoly?" I ask. "My mom has game nights with her friends sometimes too. They really like, um, Yahtzee."

Reggie reels back and clutches his chest, all dramatic. "Oh, you're breaking my heart, Delilah." His nose wrinkles and he lets out another long, hissy laugh. It's a good laugh. "That's like comparing a paint-by-number set from Target to, like, the *Mona Lisa*."

"I don't get it . . . but I'm intrigued." Especially because he seems to like it so much. "Explain it to me. Like I'm five."

So he tells me all about the long stories he plans out just for his friends—Yobani, Leela, and Greg—to play every Saturday night. He explains the manuals and the dice and the amount of effort and time it all takes. I still don't *fully* get it. But what I do get is how excited he is talking about a long story—or I guess *campaign*—he's been running for a while involving a quest for a jewel and a fancy cup they were supposed to get tonight. I understand the way his eyes light up when he tells me about the essays he posts online, sharing his perspective of D&D. There's so much love, so much passion, there.

I'll be honest: I thought D&D players were these pale white guys that lived in their parents' basements for eternity and had closets full of tie-dye shirts with wolves on them.

But Reggie's not that. Not that there's anything wrong with that. People should do what makes them happy.

It's just, Reggie is so sure of himself, so solid. He seems to be exactly who he is, without any anxiety about how others may perceive him or judge him. And, wow . . . I want to be like that. I want to, at the very least, be *around* that.

"You're still sitting here," he says. He's squinting at me like he's trying to figure something out, and his short, curled lashes sparkle at his lids under the bright security light outside of The Mode.

I shrug. "We both seem to be pretty good at that."

"Being unnaturally quiet, going unnoticed. These are skills I had to develop as a bony seventh-grader with a voice that took its sweet time dropping and braces that made me spit."

"Oh no."

"Oh yes."

"Now that you mention it, you *do* talk very quietly, even when you aren't protecting me from donut shop employees." I nudge him with my elbow, smile. "You still waiting for your voice to drop? Trying to cover it up?"

"No, that was for—" He clears his throat, and his voice is still quiet but it drops an octave. "That was for you. For your migraine."

"Oh. Wow." My breath catches in my throat as I take that in. It's a little thing, but it feels really big. My family, my friends—they don't even remember to do this all the time. But he got it right away. "Thank you."

"It's really nothing."

"No, it is. It's something."

"Well, Delilah. I don't know you very well yet, but I'm pretty sure you deserve all the somethings."

His finger reaches out to lightly touch my wrist. It's quick. It should be insignificant. But it's like that single touch sets off all the rest of my nerve endings, every inch of my skin on high alert. I'm trying to figure out what to say, how to get him to do that again, when I realize the music inside has lulled. And then I hear the whoops and yells of the crowd, someone on the mic leading them.

"Ten, nine . . ."

The countdown already? Have I really been out here that long? I've gotta pee (another side effect of the meds), and I should probably find my friends. But more than anything, I want to keep sitting here, in this quiet easiness with Reggie. My whole body feels warm, light—such a difference from how I felt when I first sat on this curb. And it's so clear that he's the source. What would it be like to feel this way all the time?

"Six, five . . ."

And now, looking into his eyes, seconds away from midnight, I also can't help but think what people usually do when the clock strikes. I feel myself leaning in closer to him, like my body is taking the wheel from my brain. And is he? Yes, he's tilting his head in, too . . .

"There you are!" I turn around and see Charlie walking out of the venue. I stand up off the curb, and Reggie follows. "Feline finished their set and I realized you never came back in." Charlie presses his eyebrows together as he looks between Reggie and me, the question clear.

"This is Reggie. He was helping—"

Cheers of "Happy New Year!" erupt inside, and Charlie pulls me by the hips in close to him, planting a kiss on my cheek for the second time tonight. He's sweaty and hot, and I can feel the kiss all over me, even after he pulls away. My cheeks flame and the rest of my body follows. This is everything I secretly wished for, even just this morning, but now . . . I'm not sure.

"Happy New Year, kid," he whispers in my ear. His arm stays around my waist. "This is gonna be a good one for us."

He's probably not talking about *us* us, just *the band* us. But I know how it sounds, and I turn back to Reggie to try to . . . reassure him? But that's so dumb. Try to reassure him of what, exactly? We just met; we don't know each other. That definitely wasn't an almost . . . *something*. Why would he care that Charlie and I are not dating?

Sure enough, Reggie is already on the move. Probably going to find his friends. "Well, uh, bye, Delilah," he says, eyebrows furrowed, looking past me. He quickly turns and starts walking toward the parking lot.

I want to thank him again for looking out for me. I want to ask him the name of the website where he posts his essays. I want to get his number so this won't be the last time I ever get to talk to him. But he's already far away, moving fast. He probably doesn't even hear my disappointed "Bye, Reggie."

"Your headache gone?" Charlie says, but he doesn't even wait for my answer. "Jimmy wants to talk to us about playing again in two weeks, and we should probably network a little bit more before we leave. The keyboardist from Feline puts on these fucking amazing guerrilla shows I want to get in on, and he wants to meet you."

His arm drops from my waist as we walk back inside.

REGGIE

Man, I was really feeling myself for a second there. I really, truly believed that if I just put on a front, faked some confidence in who I am and what I like, that this perfect girl might actually like me. That we might have actually . . . well, whatever we almost did.

But of course she already has a boyfriend. A guitar-playing, brooding white boyfriend with sweat that doesn't even stink—and stubble. Legit, non-patchy stubble! In high school!

Of course she's with someone who doesn't have to role-play cool. He just is.

That's why I like my games more than reality. None of the normal rules of life have to apply. I'm talking status, stereotypes . . . stubble! It's all chance, so I actually *have* a chance. And it's clear to me now that I had no chance with Delilah at all.

VALENTINE'S DAY

REGGIE

"Well, that took a lot longer than I expected," Dad says as we walk into the house. He checks the time on his phone for like the hundredth time in the past hour. "Were they always that long? I don't remember them always being this long."

"It's that transition section at the end." Mom puts her hand on my shoulder to balance herself as she slips out of her heels. "They added it when he was in middle school, and it's a whole 'nother thing we need to go over. You know this, Winston."

"Yes, I'm aware." Dad puts his wallet and his keys on the entry table and takes off his shoes too. "I'm just saying, it felt especially long today. You know what I mean, Reggie, right?"

I shrug and then nod. "Yeah, it was pretty long."

We just got home from my annual IEP meeting—the third one since I've been at Tom Bradley Charter, my high school. IEP stands for "individualized educational plan," and we meet once per year to go over this thick-ass stack of papers that basically outlines everything about my disability and all that the school is supposed to be doing to help me with it—or in teacher-speak, "limit the impact of my disability in order to improve my educational results." All these people show up to the meeting. My resource teacher, Ms. Thompson, runs it; one of my gen ed teachers is always there. And the assistant principal, Mr. Colby, hosts the whole thing in his office. I think it's all required by law or something.

And my dad's right. I've had these meetings since I was officially diagnosed with dyslexia in second grade, but this one did feel *particularly* long. Probably because Ms. Thompson always talks this big game about how it's a collaborative meeting and we're creating the IEP together, or whatever, but that lady, like, *loves* to hear herself speak. So it ends up being a lot of her talking and everyone else nodding and agreeing, and today she was especially on one.

"I was hoping I could pick up another load this afternoon. A lot of people are taking off early for the holiday." Dad lets out a heavy sigh and checks his phone again, as if the time will magically change. "But it's definitely too late now."

My dad's a truck driver for a fertilizer company, and because he's an independent contractor, he gets paid by the load. So an afternoon spent listening to Ms. Thompson wax poetic over the nuances of each accommodation the school can offer me is pretty much money flying out of his pocket. My stomach gets tight, but I try to push the guilt away. He comes to my IEP meetings, all of them, because he *wants* to be there. He says they're important to him.

But still, I don't hear him complaining about the time and missed loads when it's one of Eric's away games.

I guess those are a lot more fun, though.

"Well, I'm glad I've got my valentine for the rest of the day," Mom says, wrapping her arm around Dad's waist as we walk into the kitchen. He kisses the top of her head, and she bats him away. "Now, you know I just got this done yesterday."

Mom takes off her blazer, with the name tag for the bank she manages on the lapel, and drapes it on one of the chairs at the counter. She had to take off work too, but at least she has personal time saved up. "We're really proud of you, baby." Her brown eyes crease at the sides as she beams at me and clutches her hands to her chest. "You know that, right?"

"Yeah," I say, even though I don't know exactly what for. The whole meeting was focused on me and yet I stayed pretty much silent the entire time. That's what I usually do, just smiling and nodding when it's appropriate—Ms. Thompson makes it pretty easy.

The only time I wanted to say something, came *so close* to finally opening my mouth, was when Ms. Thompson started saying something about how she wanted to make sure I didn't overuse my text-to-speech app, that I needed to eventually phase it out. I wanted to ask why I needed to phase out an accommodation if it's working for me. Because, like, I'm always going to be dyslexic. And if it works for me, then why is it a bad thing? Why is the goal to *not* need it?

But I chickened out. Kept quiet, kept it moving.

Ever since New Year's, I've been wanting to try out the new Reggie that I put on that night. The Reggie that was self-assured, confident in who he is. It didn't work out for me then, but maybe it could help in some other areas, you know? I've stopped hushing Yobani when he talks about the D&D campaign all loud at lunch. And one day I even stayed in the living room for five minutes when Eric's friends came over instead of leaving immediately.

Okay, yeah, just little things. But still! It's a weird thrill to be someone so different from myself, if even for a moment.

And I don't have it in me to do the big things—not again, not yet. The things that might make everyone around me look at me like Delilah did that night . . .

"You're working really hard," Mom continues, before I can let my brain go too far down that road. "We know it's not easy—that the way school works isn't always set up for you. But you are doing your best every day. Ms. Thompson made that very clear."

"She's right, son. We see you putting in the effort, not giving up," Dad says. He claps me on the shoulder with one of his massive hands, and his warm, earthy scent fills my nose. It reminds me of driving around in his pickup that year I was diagnosed with dyslexia. His schedule is more flexible than Mom's, so he's the one that ended up taking me to all the evaluations and second opinions before we finally had a name for my reading struggles, and a plan. And he always reminded me that it wasn't something wrong with me, but something wrong with the way I was being taught—that all these tests would help the teachers figure out how to do right by me.

"That tenacity, that . . . that *gumption*. I know you're tired of me telling you this, Reggie, but those traits would do you well in some sort of sport." He rubs a hand over his mostly gray hair and shakes his head. "It doesn't have to be competitive or even a team one, but maybe running or something. You've got a marathoner's mindset, and if you just took half the time that you give to those, uh, dragon games . . ."

And poof, just like that, all those proud, happy feelings are gone. Dad may not outright diss me like Eric, and yes, I *know* there were some compliments there. But he can never quite let me forget that what I like, how I choose to spend my time, is wrong.

"So, Reggie, when does your shift start?" Mom says, changing the subject so we don't fall into this same tired conversation right now.

I look at the clock on the microwave, happy to avoid Dad's gaze. "In about an hour. I probably better leave soon."

"Oh yeah, I'm sure it'll be busy tonight with the holiday." Her voice is overly bright and cheery. "You'll get a lot of tips?"

I really hope no one's bringing their dates to Cultured, the chain yogurt shop where I work, for Valentine's Day. But at least if they do, it will be some good entertainment to make the night pass by faster.

"It's a shame you couldn't get the night off for a Valentine's date of your own," she continues. "Is . . . Leela busy?"

Mom doesn't blatantly disapprove of my D&D passion like Dad does, but I swear it's only because my Saturday sessions ensure I get regular contact with at least one person of the opposite sex.

"Mom, Leela likes girls," I remind her, for like the billionth time. She nods. "Well, maybe she can introduce you to one of those girls. The ones she's not with, I mean. Or, you know, maybe you could meet some if you weren't so busy every week with . . ."

She trails off, seeming to catch herself before she brings back the uncomfortable conversation we just narrowly avoided.

"Well, your daddy is taking me to that new wine bar over on Willow. So don't wait up!" she says, pointing at him and shimmying her shoulders.

"Oh I am, am I?" he laughs.

"Yep, and then we're going to pick up some of those little Bundt cakes from that place in Bixby Knolls after. I already pre-ordered a dozen."

"Now, how do you know I don't got something already planned, Mae?"

She cradles his face in her cheeks and smiles up at him. "Because I told you I didn't want to do anything tonight, and after twenty years, I know you still took me at my word."

"Because *I* know whatever I did plan would be canceled for what you really wanted to do anyway." He shakes his head and kisses her, and I take that as my cue to head out early.

"We love you, baby!" Mom calls after me.

"I love you too."

Fifteen minutes later, I have on my teal work polo, and I walk out to the curb where Bessie, my 1999 Ford Escort cornflower-blue station wagon, is parked. She isn't pretty—with her dented bumper and dishwater-colored interior—but she gets the job done. And I bought her all on my own with my Cultured paychecks and tips.

I slide my key into the lock, jimmying it to just the right spot—Bessie is temperamental like that. And while I'm waiting for her to warm up, I find myself quickly pulling out my phone and navigating to the app, the profile, that I've been checking daily. Okay, hourly. I look at it so much that I swear my fingers click there all on their own. It's, like, muscle memory at this point. And I had to resist all through the IEP meeting and the time with my parents after, because I definitely couldn't deal with their prying eyes and judgey questions.

Fun Gi's Instagram page doesn't have any new posts since I last checked (likely because they all have lives . . . unlike me), so I scroll to my favorite video: Delilah's debut on New Year's Eve.

I need to get over that night. I need to get over this fixation on *her* and who I was with her. Today was a perfect reminder of who I actually am and how the people in my life will always see me.

But as I watch the video of her performing again, I know I'm not ready to get over her. Not yet.

DELILAH

"You're going to wear that?"

I look behind me in the mirror to see Georgia perched on her bed like a throne, wrinkling her nose at the dress I put on.

"What's wrong with it?"

"It's fine," she says, looking me up and down. I keep staring at her because with Georgia, I know that's only the appetizer in a five-course meal of opinions.

"It's just that, well, you don't really look like yourself. Or, you look like yourself, but, like, yourself if you were the nerd girl in a CW show who goes through a makeover to try and get a boyfriend. But the makeover is just, you know, her taking off her glasses and putting on a dress like that. Not that you are a nerd. I mean, your grades aren't good enough for that. But that's what the dress reminds me of . . . one of those dramatic makeover dresses that are, like, all about the male gaze. Where did you get it, anyway? Is that from eighth-grade graduation?"

I decide to focus on the final question. "No."

I pull down the hem of the spaghetti strap black slip dress that is *actually* from the eighth-grade farewell dance. It's suddenly feeling a lot shorter.

"Hmm." She manages to say just as much in that single noise as she did in her rambly dragging of my outfit choice. And also entire identity.

"Okay, I'm going to save you here. Please remember this tremendous act of kindness when Mom asks you what time I got in from the cast party last night." Georgia pops off her bed and goes to our shared closet, maneuvering around a pile of scarves, the teetering tower of her playbill collection, and a bowl of Lucky Charms cereal (minus the marshmallows) even though I'm pretty sure we ran out last week. We don't have a line of blue painter's tape across the floor of our room like we did in middle school, but it still feels like it's there. My side is clean, organized. The walls are empty and my schoolbooks (for the classes that, yeah, I do *just okay* in) sit in a tidy stack at the foot of the bed that is always made unless I'm lying in it. Georgia's side is an explosion, right up to the very edge of our imaginary line.

"So I'm going to assume that this sudden interest in your appearance is because of Charlie," she says, flipping between two puff-sleeved cottage core dresses that I'm definitely not going to wear. "Not that I'm trying to shame you or stop this journey of self-actualization, D! Lord knows I've been trying to get you in something other than your flannels and dirty sneakers for years."

"No, it's not," I sigh. Why didn't I wait until she was out of the room? "I was just . . . trying something new."

Her eyes narrow. "So you're not hanging out with Charlie tonight?"

I feel my cheeks heating up. "I am, but—"

"And correct me if I'm wrong, but is it *not* Valentine's Day?"

"Okay, yeah, except—"

"So, you're going to be with Charlie, the boy that makes your cheeks look like you took a red Sharpie to 'em every time his name is even spoken aloud, on a holiday explicitly created to celebrate love or at least, like, making out."

I consider protesting some more, but instead I just shrug. There's no fighting this.

"That's what I thought," she says, turning back to the closet.

Usually it's the little sister that's the follower, the one trailing after and annoying and imitating, but with us it's the opposite. I've always had to hop on Georgia's train, or get run over in the process.

"So, is this actually a date?" she asks, pulling out a dress that I'm pretty sure she wore in a summer camp production of *Hairspray*. "Or are you two still doing that friends with benefits thing."

"Oh my god, Georgia! There are no benefits." I feel myself blush again and check to make sure the door is closed. Mom would lose her mind.

"Hmm." Another one of her annoying judgey noises. She throws in a side-eye because she's dramatic as hell. "I mean, he's always so touchy with you at lunch. I figured there was more going on in these . . . band practices."

"That's just how he is. And the only thing going on in our band practices is practicing. For our shows." We've had two more since the New Year's Eve performance—another one at The Mode and one at this senior kid's house party in Belmont Shore. I was worried that the magic would wear off. That my first performance was all a fluke. Or—no longer distracted by an impending migraine—I would realize that my singing was really a cringey, screechy mess and everyone was just humoring me. But instead I'm really loving it . . . leaning in to this person that's not me, but me-adjacent, who has the freedom to scream and dance and own it on stage. At night before I go to sleep, I watch videos of Poly Styrene on my phone, replaying the ones that have quickly become favorites and searching for footage I haven't seen yet. And instead of being filled with terror like I was before that first show, I only see the possibility of what I could be.

And the audiences have been right there with me. I can see their faces sparking with interest and then excitement—it's a thrill unlike anything I've experienced before. We're up to a few thousand followers on IG, even more on TikTok, and our streams on Spotify have doubled (along with the DMs on our socials asking where the girl's—*this girl's*—voice is on those recordings). People are liking what they hear, telling their friends.

So the guys are happy. Charlie is happy. I can tell by the way he looks at me, leads me around with his hand on my lower back, like I'm someone special, important. He hasn't kissed me on the cheek again like he did that night, and that makes sense. We're just friends.

But . . . I guess I *am* hoping that maybe this is the night when all that finally changes. He asked me—and only me—what I was doing tonight at lunch today, said he'd pick me up later so we could "chill." Do "just friends" "chill" on Valentine's Day?

My face must be telegraphing all this to Georgia, because she gently grabs my wrist. I'm expecting another side-eye, but instead her eyes are soft, almost pitying. Which may be even worse.

"Be careful with him, okay? Protect your heart. I know we're, like, genetically predisposed to fall for any boy that plays the guitar. But you are a prize, sis! You don't need to be anyone's chick on the side."

Her words make my body tense. It's *not like that*. And I don't need to be talked down to.

"I'm fine," I say. I slip into my checkerboard Vans, silently but clearly building up my wall in this brewing battle of the sisters. And because I just can't stop myself, I throw a bomb over the thing. "Hey, did you ever call Dad back? He told me he tried you a few times this week but kept getting your voicemail."

Both Mom and Dad told us not to choose sides after the divorce six years ago, even though Dad left us and started his new family. I still see him and talk to him because it's easier that way; it keeps the peace. But Georgia only sees him when she's forced to on holidays and doesn't ever want to discuss that, thank you very much.

"No, I didn't." Her face gets all cheery, but I know what a good actress she is, so I'm already bracing myself when she chirps, "You know, that's who Charlie reminds me of! Dad! I've been trying to place it. They both have the same crippling fear of commitment and an inability to keep their hands to themselves."

I can feel my face on fire again.

And of course that's when the doorbell rings.

"You know, that's probably . . ." she starts, nodding toward our door and raising her eyebrows meaningfully. I know exactly who she's referring to, and it's a white flag, pausing combat.

"Yeah, and we haven't even really talked about . . ."

"I feel good about it. Do you?"

"I do, but also . . ." I exhale and shrug.

"I know. Me too." She bites her bottom lip and takes a deep breath. But just as quickly a mischievous grin takes over her face, and I know our truce is gone. "Or it could be Charlie. Do you think he'll call Mom Anita again instead of Ms. Tyler? You know she *loved* that."

I grunt and throw my oversized denim jacket on over the slip dress, sprinting out of the room. I *need* to get to the front door before Mom opens it and makes this night any more awkward.

But of course, Mom is already at the door, and when she opens it, she smiles wide.

"Hey, beautiful!"

I'm relieved it's not Charlie but the other possible candidate behind Door #1 in this bizarre version of *The Dating Game* (not that Charlie and I are dating!): Andre Dobson. Mom's first date in . . . forever.

He walks in and kisses her on the cheek, which makes my breath catch in my throat. Not that it's wrong, it's just, I don't know. Different. I didn't realize they were like that already. But even though this is their first official date, they've been friends for years. Andre is a PE teacher at the same middle school where mom works as a counselor. I shouldn't be this surprised.

"I do look good, don't I?" Mom's wearing a peach wrap dress that pops against her dark brown skin, with matching tassel earrings and bright red lipstick. The shiny curls from her twist-out bounce as she strikes a pose. Mom's voice has a lightness to it that's familiar to me, but it's strange hearing it with someone else. Usually it's just reserved for me and Georgia, in the walls of this apartment.

I feel Georgia come up next to me, and she slips her fingers through mine. Another truce.

"Mm-mmm. Yes, you do." Andre's whole face is sunlight, beaming at Mom. And then he shines it in our direction. "Hey, you two! Thank you for sharing your mom with me tonight."

We wave and mumble hello. I feel like an explorer, venturing into a brand-new world. I want to approach slowly and get my bearings.

"But now, what have you got on?!" Mom says loudly, with a sly smile. She steps back and gestures to Andre's tan pants and button-up in a slightly different shade of tan. "I can't be walking into the restaurant with a Colors of the World crayon on my arm. You need to step up your game if you want to be my valentine!"

I know she's joking, but I still tense.

Dad was obviously the cause of the divorce. They never explicitly told us he cheated, but he did move on with Sandra, his now wife, alarmingly fast. I also can't help but wonder, though, what small part Mom might have played by being just a little too bold, a little too much. By the end, everything about her—her sarcastic humor, her strong convictions—triggered Dad and led to an inevitable fight.

But I guess Dad wasn't always like that. He had to have laughed at her jokes and been charmed by Mom's big personality. They had us young, though—their wedding anniversary only five months before my birthday. Before Dad stepped into the executive position at Grandpa Cole's company that's been waiting for him since birth. Before he started thinking he needed a life, and a wife, to match. And Mom is not someone who will let herself be molded by anyone. No matter how good it started between them, it was bad as far back as I can remember.

So how do you know when it's going to shift? I don't want to see the same thing happen with Andre. For their relationship to blow up before they've even really begun.

"Nah, nah. My fourth period said the monochrome look is in!" Andre says. He juts out his hip and throws one hand behind his head, striking his own goofy pose. "You need to get hip like me, Annie!"

Georgia rubs her thumb across my hand, and I realize just how tight I was gripping her. Right. Andre isn't like Dad. But I still wish Mom would be more careful.

"Well, if you two young ladies are still all right with it," Andre says, looking at us again, "I'm going to take this beautiful woman out on a date. Now, tell me, what's her curfew for the night? Be easy on us here!"

Georgia crosses her arms. "I think ten is reasonable. Because nothing you have any business being involved in happens after ten—at least that's what she tells me."

"Yeah, you know, that reminds me," Mom says, fixing Georgia with a look. "I think I heard someone coming in at ten thirty-six last night after a certain cast party."

My phone buzzes in my pocket, just in time. It's a text from Charlie.

We're here

My stomach drops. *We? Who's we?*

"Hmm." Georgia smirks, reading over my shoulder. Even though she's caught, of course she's still in my business.

I roll my eyes at her and grab my bag, slipping past the happy couple. "I'll be back by *my* curfew."

Turns out "we" includes Asher and Beau in the back seat of Charlie's Volvo, and our fancy Valentine's Day destination is Cultured, one of those frozen yogurt shops with a sneeze guard over the get-it-yourself toppings.

I clasp my hands tightly in my lap and try to keep a plastic smile on my face to hide my disappointment. It's . . . whatever.

"Okay, top three yogurt toppings! Go!" Asher shouts over the music blasting on the stereo. It's one of Charlie's favorite songs, "Search and Destroy" by the Stooges.

"Blueberries," Beau chimes in immediately.

"Blueberries! Blueberries?!" Asher hollers like he's been personally offended. "They have M&M's, gummy bears, and those little chocolate-chip cookie dough morsels that don't even make you sick *right there,* and you're out here trying to make a healthy snack? Bro!"

Beau shrugs. "I just like the plain yogurt and blueberries."

"Help me out here, Delilah!" Asher leans forward, wrapping his arms around the back of my seat on the passenger side. He's wearing a holey green cardigan, but the expensive kind that's sold that way. "We cannot destroy the credibility of our Top Three empire by allowing this list to have only blueberries!"

"Uh . . . sometimes I like to add mochi to mine?" And I would have liked to do that with just Charlie tonight.

"Thank you! Thank you! Someone sees the light!" Asher flops back in his seat, his hands up in the air.

"How about top three members of Fun Gi?" Beau asks, with a smirk.

"Well, *obviously* we're all going to pick ourselves. So I'll start. Me!" Asher says. He counts off with fingers in his palm. "My bass solos regularly melt people's faces off. I bring some much-needed diversity into this band, so you're not just another group of white guys playing punk rock." Asher is biracial like me, but Japanese and white. "*And* I have the skills of Chuck Dukowski, Mark Hoppus, and Mike Watt—COMBINED! Boom! The end! Case closed!" He smacks his hands together.

"Um, okay. That was unnecessarily intense," Beau says. "But yeah, I'm gonna say myself too." He flexes, showing off his arms. Even though it's February, he's wearing a Nirvana shirt with the sleeves cut off. "Pretty sure half the audience comes just to see these boys."

Asher shakes his head. "Your biceps are *boys*? Have you named them, too? Do you feel no shame?"

Before I have to worry about responding, Charlie turns the radio down and clears his throat. He's sat out all the Top Three rounds until now. "I gotta say Delilah. She's brought us a refresh and, this new . . . energy that we've needed. Plus her voice is kick-ass, and"—he laughs—"she's got you beat on the diversity points, Asher!"

Okay, I kind of wish he'd left my "diversity" and its alleged "points" out of it, but I gather up the rest of the compliments like a kid at a birthday party after the piñata breaks. They don't come often and I want to remember them to savor when I'm alone later.

"Oh, please!" Asher shouts, banging on the back of Charlie's seat. "We all know you really think yourself!"

"Whatever, man," Charlie says, twisting the dial far to the right so the intense opening of "I Wanna Be Your Dog" shakes the car.

When we pull up to Cultured, in a little shopping center between a Subway and a dentist, Beau and Asher jump out of the car and bound into the store, excited for their candy and blueberries. But before we reach the door, Charlie touches a hand to my wrist, holding me back.

"Hey, I'm sorry about . . . the guys. Being here, I mean," he says, ocean-blue eyes focused on mine.

The questions spin around in my head. *Did they invite themselves? Was this really supposed to be a date? A Valentine's date? Do you like me like I like you?*

But instead I shrug and say, "It's cool."

He reaches up to my shoulder, where my denim jacket has

fallen slightly and pinches the thin strap of my black dress between his fingers. "This is nice."

His guitar-callused hands brush my bare skin. My stomach aches, and it's very likely that I'm going to spontaneously combust right here. Whatever irritation I was still harboring toward him for this night—and all the nights of things being so unclear between us—go up in smoke.

"Thanks," I say, and he grins, stepping closer. He's so close that I could count every one of his long lashes, I could reach out and touch the triangle of light freckles next to his left eye. And this definitely isn't how I expected my first kiss to go. There's nothing romantic or dreamy about standing outside of a Cultured while our friends swirl self-serve yogurt into their paper bowls. But with Charlie . . . maybe it could be?

"Excuse me. You are blocking the exit," a voice says behind me, making me jolt. I turn to see a man with a gummy-bear topped yogurt creation and an exasperated scowl.

Charlie scoots over to the side and I follow. He nods toward the door. "So should we join 'em, kid? Those boys are going to destroy that toppings bar if we don't keep them in line."

So much for ending this back-and-forth, he-likes-me-he-likes-me-not for good. But I guess I got my answer the moment I saw Asher and Beau in the back seat. I'm searching for subtle signs when he's already practically painted a billboard for me.

"Sure, yeah. Let's go."

We join Asher and Beau inside, where they've already started sprinkling toppings on their impressively high mountains of yogurt. The place is decorated for Valentine's with swirling red and pink streamers hanging from the ceiling and paper conversation hearts taped to the walls. It's another great reminder of what I expected from tonight and what I'm actually getting.

We're standing in line to pay for our yogurt (strawberry with mochi and mini chocolate chips for me), when Charlie's phone rings. He's one of those rare people who don't keep it on silent at all times.

"Oh shit!" Charlie's eyes go wide when he looks at the screen. "It's the guy, Neil, from Brass Knuckle! He's finally calling us back."

Brass Knuckle is a recording studio we've been trying to get into ever since the New Year's show, so we could re-record the old music with my vocals and also record new stuff the guys have been working on.

"I better take this outside," Charlie says, gesturing up to the speakers that are blasting "Stupid Cupid."

"I'm coming too, man," Beau says. "He's only calling you back because of that favor I called in with my buddy Joe."

Asher puts his giant cup of yogurt down, scattering rainbow sprinkles. "Well, I'm bankrolling this operation! You can't leave me out of this call!"

Charlie is already out the door, with Asher close behind him. Only Beau pauses to consider me standing there alone with four cups of yogurt. "Can you take care of this, Delilah?" he asks, scratching the back of his head and revealing a shock of dark armpit hair. "We'll be right back."

"Mm-hmm. It's fine."

"You're the best," he calls behind him as he follows the guys outside.

I'm the best, but they didn't even consider including me in this phone call. Right.

Sometimes I wish I could scream and kick in real life like the girl I've started to channel on stage. How different would things be if I was loud and wild and let out everything I'm holding in?

I definitely wouldn't be scooting their cups along the counter to the register. Taking out my own wallet to pay for them. On Valentine's Day.

"Whoa, hey!"

Wait . . . I know that voice. I look up and smile.

REGGIE

"It's um . . . okay, don't tell me! It starts with a D . . ." I snap my fingers and pretend I don't know her name, even though it's been repeating in my head like a heartbeat ever since I saw her outside standing all close to her boyfriend. *Delilah Delilah Delilah.* I can't let her know that though. "D . . . Delilah! Delilah, right?"

The corners of her lips turn down, just slightly. If you blink you'd miss it. It's as if her face is determined to remain in neutral at all times.

"Right. Hi, Reggie," she says, dropping my name easily. And I'm torn between absolute joy because SHE REMEMBERED MY NAME and absolute panic because maybe I've miscalculated and ruined everything by trying to play it cool.

"Of course I remember you. Delilah. *De-li-lah!*" I was trying to walk it back, but now I'm holding my hands out and singing her name and this is way too much. I clear my throat, try again. "Sorry, it's just been a minute."

"Yep, that's me." Her lips quirk into a small smile. "I looked for your essays online, you know. The Dungeons & Dragons ones? I couldn't find them."

And okay, now I'm pretty sure that I passed out. Fainted, knocked my head on one of the frozen yogurt dispensers, and now I'm in a hospital bed dreaming up a fantasy. Because surely, SURELY, this beautiful girl didn't take time out of her supercool life to go Google *my* essays.

"Really?" I croak out.

"Yeah, really. They sounded interesting." She shrugs. "But I guess I didn't have tons to go on. Just your name and the game . . . I should have asked you for the website."

I still can't believe this conversation is real. I fight the urge to pinch myself. "Well, I *do* write under a pseudonym, so they wouldn't have been easy to find."

"Oh yeah? Why a pseudonym?"

Because I don't want anyone in my real life finding the dozens of essays and mocking me mercilessly. Because just the thought of Eric, of my parents, reading them makes my skin start itching with imaginary hives—which, good thing I'm actually in the hospital right now because they can probably help me with that.

But I can't say all that to Delilah. It doesn't match the chill, confident Reggie she met last month. The one she SEARCHED FOR ONLINE.

"I don't know . . . I guess it's because I started that way. Then I got, like, a pretty big following and I didn't want to mess with that by changing my name. But, man, I probably *should* change it to my full name and get credit for all this knowledge I'm dropping."

I sound convincing. I believe myself.

"You should," she says. "But what's the pseudonym? So I can find you in the meantime?"

"Keepin' It d100." I say it loudly, without hesitation. Even though my natural instinct is to mumble or immediately make fun of myself.

"Ha! I get it!" She points at me, doling out another tiny smile. From anyone else, I would be searching for the insult, because there's almost always an insult, but I can feel she's genuine.

It makes me feel even bolder.

"You forgot something," I say.

"I did?"

"Yep." Before I can overthink it, I grab a thing of rainbow sprinkles and shake them over the top of her yogurt. "Here. You need something special. Because, you know . . . you're special."

Her cheeks flush and she looks down at the counter. "What if I hated sprinkles?"

"Oh, damn . . . oh my god. That was— *I'm* so stupid. Let me remake—"

Her giggles interrupt my tragic attempts to regroup, and I realize she's not backing away in horror. She's smiling. "I love sprinkles."

"Me too." And I smile back, hopefully in a completely normal way that doesn't give away how my heart is doing somersaults and cartwheels and probably a whole-ass Simone Biles routine.

"Well . . ." She scoots the other three containers of yogurt onto the scale. Because—oh my lord, clearly!—she didn't come to Cultured just to ask me about my D&D essays and make my heart try to win an Olympic gold medal. She's here with her boyfriend—her goddamn *boyfriend*—and the other guys in her band. This was all a coincidence, not her seeking me out on purpose.

And was I really trying to flirt with sprinkles?! Man, what is wrong with me?

"Yeah, yeah, sorry about that." I ring her up, tell her the price. I see her wallet out, but I can't stop myself from asking, "So um, is your boyfriend coming back in to pay for this?"

Her big brown eyes go wide and her cheeks and neck turn pink. I can tell immediately it's not the good kind of blush like before. "My boyfriend?"

I nod to the glass doors behind her, where the three guys from her band are huddled over a phone, talking so loud that we can hear the rumble of their conversation from here. "The guy that came outside . . . on New Year's?" And kissed your cheek and looked at me all smugly and made me feel like a total idiot for thinking I even had a chance.

"Charlie? Charlie's not my boyfriend," she says, but it's clear from her strangled voice and flaming cheeks that's not the whole story. "They're all just my friends . . . or, I guess, band now? We all, uh, met at Willmore. Willmore Prep?"

The fancy private school over by El Dorado Park? Well, that explains why I've never seen her before.

"Oh, all right. My bad."

"Yeah, Charlie and I . . . we're not like that at all. That's why we're here, with Asher and Beau, getting yogurt on Valentine's Day." She lets out this strange fake laugh and holds up her cup. Yup, definitely something going on there.

I gesture behind her, where two kids are filling their cups with so many marshmallows that they're spilling out onto the ground. I'm gonna have to clean that up later.

"Not your ideal date spot?"

"Definitely not."

Should I say it? I have to just say it. New Reggie would *say it*. And if she's really not with this guy . . . maybe New Reggie has a chance?

He may have taken an L with the sprinkles, but New Reggie is still winning! New Reggie is living his best life!

"Well, whatever he is to you, it's kind of shitty that he left you in here alone to buy his food. That they did, I mean—"

"Thanks," she cuts me off. Her voice is ice, and her face matches it, hard and cold. "But I'm good."

Well, shit. New Reggie just crashed and burned.

DELILAH

I know he's just being nice. I know he's not trying to make me feel bad or whatever. But his words drum up all the same crappy feelings that Georgia's talk did earlier. And I feel silly and stupid that it's so clear, even to Reggie, who I've only spent one cumulative hour with, that I'm being strung along by this guy who obviously doesn't like me like that.

I'm such a fool. And everyone knows it.

He probably just called me special before to try and soften the blow he saw coming. A pity thing.

"I'm sorry, I wasn't trying—"

"No, it's fine—"

"It's not my business, and I shouldn't have—"

Our awkward word tango is interrupted by Charlie, Asher, and Beau bouncing back into the shop, all smiles.

"We're in!" Asher whoops.

"He's gonna get us into the studio next weekend, kid," Charlie says, shaking my shoulders in excitement. "Five songs, fully mastered. We'll be able to upload them by the end of the month!"

"You okay, Delilah?" Beau asks, the only one who's realized I haven't paid for the now melting yogurt. "Did you not have enough?"

"No, I just—this is—" How do I describe who Reggie is to me? Someone who I really barely know, but it feels like he sees me more than most. "This is Reggie. I met him outside at The Mode."

"Oh yeah! You're the curb guy!" Charlie shouts, and—I know it's not just my imagination—he slides in closer to me. His hands relax on my shoulders like they belong there. I hate it. But I also love it. And then I hate myself even more for that. "Hey man, thank you for taking care of our girl, Delilah, that night. You were a real lifesaver."

"No problem," Reggie says, eyes on the screen. He repeats the total and Beau pays for us all. The guys head toward the door with their yogurt, already slipping into a heated debate over what five songs we're going to record.

"Well, it was good to see you," I say to Reggie. His brow furrows and his lips pinch together, clearly the flicker of something he wants to say. I don't know if I want to hear it or not, with how quickly he cut to the root of my Charlie drama minutes ago. But finally he just says, "Yeah, um, same. See you around."

I wave and follow the guys outside.

REGGIE

In a campaign, I could just go on another quest to win Delilah's heart, but there's no magic, no rules in play here. Seeing her again, that was a very lucky, very unlikely coincidence, and coincidences like that don't happen again. I didn't get her number. I didn't even get her last name. And she probably wouldn't have given it to me anyway after I offended her by butting in with my stupid opinion that *she didn't fucking ask for.*

But . . . am I totally delusional to think I might have been getting somewhere? Before the comment that made her bristle, before her friends showed up—we were vibing, right? I mean, she didn't just remember me—she looked for my essays! She must like something about the front I was putting on to waste her time doing *that*.

I'm still turning it over in my mind as I head home after my shift. Maybe it doesn't have to die here? I can always look up where her band's playing, and I know where she goes to school now too. It wouldn't be hard to see her again, and get yet another do-over. But would that be charming or totally stalkery? Damn, it's a fine line.

It's dark when I open the front door, but I can hear the sounds of *Super Smash Bros.* blasting from the speakers in the living room. I'm surprised to see Eric there, glowing in the blue light of the TV with a giant bag of conversation hearts at his side. I thought for sure he'd be out on a date, or at least with his boys. Unlike me, he's rarely alone, and I want to ask him about it, but there's no way that'll go well.

"Yes! Let's go!" Eric pops up and claps his hands together as celebratory music plays. I walk into the room and see Bowser holding out his claws in triumph on Dad's ginormous flat screen. Eric nods at me in greeting and then grabs the other Switch controller. "You want in?"

"Yeah," I say, plopping down on the other end of the couch. I grab a couple conversation hearts from his bag, toss them in my mouth, and then immediately regret it. I forgot these things are basically chalk and can crack a molar.

"Work good?" Eric asks, as he's picking the stage for our match.

"Mm-hmm."

As the countdown starts on the screen, I wonder what he would say about the whole Delilah situation—if he was the kind of brother that gave advice and I was the kind of brother that asked for it. But, of course, we're not those brothers.

Eric's Bowser comes at me with a shell spin. "Yo, Kirby's about to get his ass beat!"

I laugh and hit him with Kirby's inhale. "Bet!"

And instead of talking, we play.

DELILAH

"So who was that guy anyway?" Charlie asks. He reaches forward to put his hand lightly on my hip. My stomach flutters and my legs move on their own, stepping closer to him.

We drove back to his place after—again, *we* as in Charlie, Asher, Beau, and me. And after an hour of watching them play *Call of Duty* on the Xbox and pretending to be interested, I stood up and walked away from the couch, ready to end this stupid night already. That seemed to be the nudge Charlie needed to remember I exist. But why, of all things, is he asking about . . .

"Reggie. I told you. You said you remembered him?"

"Yeah I know." He looks back at the screen, clocking what's happening in the game. But just as fast, his blue eyes are back on me. His touch on my hip radiates my whole body with warmth. "It's just that, it looked like something more. Did he say something weird to you? Like, I don't know . . . try and ask you out?"

"What? No!" I'm so loud that Asher and Beau look away from

their battle. I take a steadying breath. "It's not like that."

Not that I'm 100 percent sure what it is with Reggie . . . or even what I want it to be. Who knows what Reggie even thinks of me now after I was so cold to him?

"Oh, okay. Good." But quickly, before I can let myself get excited about that *good*, his hand drops from my hip. He flashes a quick smile at me and then he's back on the couch, throwing himself down between Asher and Beau. The fluttery feeling in my stomach is gone, and now it just feels empty, hollow.

This up-and-down with him is like a roller coaster, and at least right now . . . I want to get off.

"Should we pack a bowl?" Asher asks, taking his stash out of the backpack he always carries around for just this purpose.

"Yes we should!" Charlie says, and grabs a lighter off the table. "Hey, Delilah, can you shut that door so it doesn't get out? My mom was pissed last time because her Bunco group could still smell it on the pillows the next day."

"Actually, I'm going to head home." I don't want to look like a baby. But the smell is also impossible to get out of my hair, and I don't want to deal with explaining *that* to Mom tonight.

"Oh, all right then. We're going to miss you, kid," Charlie says. He waves from the couch but then quickly turns to Asher. "Oh, bro! That's the good stuff! Why have you been holding out all night?"

I bite my lip and stand there awkwardly, waiting for the joke. Is he really not going to offer to drive me home? I'm fine taking the bus. I do it all the time after our practices. But it's late . . .

"I'll drive you, Delilah," Beau says. He stands up and swings his keys, with a Pearl Drums keychain, on a finger.

"Guess just Charlie will be my Valentine's date then!" Asher jokes, and the laugh that escapes out of my throat sounds hysterical and wrong.

Beau plays some weird folk music with a warbly singer that I don't recognize as we drive down Ximeno toward my house. I can tell he wants to say something to me. His right hand grips the wheel and then flexes, like a visual representation of his mind going back and forth.

Finally, he exhales and looks at me, and I'm sure I'm going to have a talk about my hopeless and obviously misguided crush on Charlie with Beau, too. That seems to be *the thing* tonight.

"I'm sorry," he says, with a nervous smile. Now, that's unexpected.

"For what?"

"Back at the yogurt shop . . . that wasn't cool," he continues. "You should have been involved with that call to Brass Knuckle, and we just, like, peaced out on you to take it. That wasn't right. This is just as much your band too."

I feel a little breathless as I take in his words. I didn't have any expectations to be included. I guess I still think of this as *their* band. And I'm just a guest—someone who doesn't really belong but is along for the ride. But maybe I don't have to keep feeling that way.

"Wow, um, thank you." I nod. "I appreciate that."

"And Charlie . . ." he starts as we pull up to my apartment complex.

"I don't want to talk about Charlie."

"Fair enough," he chuckles and taps out a beat on his steering wheel. "Hey, I'll wait here until you open your door."

I smile, grateful for his kindness. "Have a good night, Beau."

I don't hear Mom's loud laughter or reality TV shows when I walk inside, which means she's still out on her date with Andre. And it must be going well. For a second, I think Georgia is out too, but then I hear some soft music drifting from our half-closed door.

She's sitting on her bed in a lilac sweatsuit, with her curls pulled up in a massive, frizzy bun on the top of her head. Her laptop is balanced on her lap, but she pauses what she's watching and smiles at me.

"Was it everything you dreamed?" she asks.

"Yeah . . . no," I say, flopping onto my own bed. "Definitely not."

I realize I never asked Georgia what she was doing tonight for Valentine's Day. I guess we were fighting earlier, but that's still an asshole move. She's always seeing some boy—they practically wait in line for their chance with my shining star sister.

"No Ben?" I ask. I'm pretty sure that's the name of her most recent guy.

"No Ben." She snorts and shakes her head. "Turns out he thinks seeing the original *Hamilton* cast on Broadway is acceptable as a primary personality trait. And I'm like, 'Dude, you were eight. Move on.' Plus he got all weird when I said I wasn't gonna try out for Liesl in *Sound of Music* just because he was going for Rolf. I cannot be with anyone who doesn't know I was born to be Maria."

I smile. "No one else at Willmore even stands a chance."

Georgia's always been that way, practically came out of the womb belting "Don't Rain on My Parade" and demanding what's hers. She knows she belongs in the spotlight. She would *never* hold herself back or make herself small for a guy . . . for anyone. And here I was being completely desperate for even the smallest crumbs of attention from Charlie that I'm never going to get.

"Anyway, I think I'm done with dating," Georgia says. "I'm just going to focus on my career."

"Your career?" I shake my head. "Georgia, you're fourteen."

She rolls her eyes and waves that away, as if it's a minor detail. "Hey, Mom's not back yet. It must be going well with Andre."

I give a noncommittal grunt in response. I hope Mom is having a good time. I really, truly do. She deserves it. But still . . . it was a lot easier to handle the idea of my mom going out on a Valentine's date when I thought I was doing the same.

"Hey, what's up?" Georgia says, and I give her a look. That's all it takes—I don't have to detail all the ways that tonight went wrong or tell her she was right. She just gets it.

"I know what you need." Georgia hops off her bed and turns on our Bluetooth speaker, then scrolls to something on her phone. Seconds later, the sweet sounds of "Death by a Thousand Cuts" by Taylor Swift start to play from the speaker. Georgia starts to sway and picks up her Denman brush to use as a microphone.

It feels like sisters can only exist as polar opposites. I guess it's evolution or something, so that we each can justify our place since we're not like . . . furthering the family name? But this is the one thing that Georgia and I do have in common: our love for Taylor Swift. And our firm belief that losing yourself in one of her songs can make anything better.

Taylor was there when Georgia was cast as Milky White instead of Little Red Riding Hood in *Into the Woods*. When the orthodontist said I had to keep my braces on for an extra six months. When our parents got divorced. Georgia even used to put on this rain noise machine when we were younger—to "get the full Taylor crying-in-the-rain experience" . . . Georgia is dramatic like that. But it helped to block out the sounds of Mom and Dad fighting. Our Taylor Swift dance parties have gotten us through so much.

So even though it would be a lot easier to go to bed and wallow in my feelings, I get up and sing along to "Teardrops on My Guitar" and scream along to "Fifteen" and fling myself around in some weird interpretive dance to "cardigan." And by the time "Last Kiss" comes up on Georgia's playlist, my chest is heaving and my heart is speeding, but I feel better. I always do.

We're both lying on our beds, listening to "All Too Well" and staring at the glow-in-the-dark stickers on the ceiling in the low light of the room when Georgia turns the volume down.

"Hey, you don't interrupt a Taylor Swift bridge," I say. "Especially *this* bridge."

"Well, I'm going to now because this is important." I turn to look at her, and she's on her side, looking at me all serious.

"I just want to say that I've watched the videos online, of you guys performing, and you're really good. And, like, I shouldn't even be surprised. You've always had such a great voice—I hear you in the shower when you think no one's listening. But I want you to know . . . you're amazing, sissy." She slips into the nickname she used to have for me when she was little and still wanted to play with me all the time, insisting we put on a show with the Barbies.

I wave that away. "I don't actually know what I'm doing, not like you. I'm just messing around." Delilah's voice makes audiences break out into chills and cry and, I don't know . . . reflect on their lives. My voice is just screechy screaming.

She rolls her eyes. "Oh, shut up. It's not a competition. It's different. But I'm glad you've found this. I'm glad you're getting a chance to shine."

She doesn't mention Charlie but I can feel the subtext in her raised eyebrow and pursed lips: *Make sure you shine. In all parts of your life.*

And I know she's right. I know it's not right with Charlie. Tonight made that so clear. I need to let those hopes go, once and for all. Somehow. While I'm still in a band with him. Singing into the microphone with him and standing so close and smelling his sweat and . . . Oh god.

I'm done. I want to be done. But it's also really freaking hard to be done.

"I have someone I could set you up with, actually. Not a freshman! Don't worry. He's this junior, Damien. He's part of the production crew, he helps make a lot of the sets. And he, um, wears a lot of black like you?"

I quickly shake my head. If I even wanted to do that, it wouldn't be one of Georgia's theater kid friends. It would be someone . . .

well, someone like Reggie. Someone it's easy to be around. Someone not worried about cool, but just, I guess, himself. After how weird I was tonight, though, *that's* not happening.

"Thank you, really, for the matchmaking offer," I say. "But I think maybe . . . I'm done with dating too? I just need to fall in love with myself a little bit more right now, you know? Before I can even think about something like that."

She pops up off her bed and claps her hands. "Yes! Love this for us! We'll make a pact!"

"Whoa, whoa." I hold my palms up. "Not exactly a pact. That's a little too dramatic—"

But she's ignoring me, scrolling on her phone with intention. "Okay, you know *Reputation* is my least favorite Taylor album, but I think this moment calls for some *Reputation*."

My throat is already sore and scratchy from singing and I'm pretty sure our neighbors are going to start banging on the ceiling soon, but I snap my fingers and point at her. "Play it, Georgia."

We belt out every lyric and dance furiously until we're dripping with sweat and Mom comes home, hollering for us to cut it off.

REGGIE

"Reggie, my man, clear your schedule!" Yobani claps his hand on my shoulder mere seconds after the dismissal bell rings and I've walked out of the resource room.

I spin around and take him in, and the words and giggles rush to escape at the same time, getting stuck in my throat. "Wh— Wha—"

"How did I get a copy of *Meron's Monograph of Mischief* before its official release date on Tuesday, you ask?" he says, waving around a copy of the D&D sourcebook. "Eduardo let it slip that they had arrived and I basically had to promise him the car on every Saturday night from now until eternity. Steep price to pay, yes, but obviously worth it!"

Eduardo is Yobani's older brother, and the assistant manager at our favorite comic book and gaming store, Story Sanctorum. And also, apparently, a very cutthroat bargainer.

And, like, I'm way excited about early access to the sourcebook.

This one is supposed to be filled with new spells and characters, and I can't wait to add them to our current campaign and maybe write about them too. But first there's the issue of the rings.

"*What* are you wearing?"

Yobani has on his regular uniform of a faded black T-shirt and jeans, not too different from my own. But today there's a significant difference. Eight of his ten fingers are decked out in shiny gold rings, some so big they reach his knuckles. I hadn't seen him all day because our lunches didn't line up with the midterm schedule. But if I had, I would have advised him to take those suckers off immediately.

"You like?" he asks, holding his hands out so I can take them in. One has a large skull that legit seems to be staring at me like we've got beef. "I think I could be a person that wears rings."

I shake my head. "No, Yo . . . just no."

"But maybe also . . . yes? I think yes."

"Where did you even get all these?"

"The ring store. Obviously." He throws his head back, laughing at himself, and I shake my head, joining in. But then I realize that he's getting looks in the still crowded hallway. Being all loud, holding up a big-ass book with a half human, half demon on the cover, wearing *rings*—that's basically just asking for trouble.

I take the book from him and subtly shift so I'm facing the wall, the book out of view.

"Have you looked through it yet?"

"Of course! Ms. Robertson's Geometry test was easy as hell, so I had like an hour. And check this out . . ." He reaches over, flipping to the back. "There are these one-off adventures back here. I was thinking we could play tonight, maybe? Like as a pre-game before we get back to the regular campaign on Saturday night. I already checked with Greg and he's down, but we'd have to do it somewhere else, because Leela is going to one of Ryan's shows."

"A show?" I ask, trying to sound casual.

"Yeah, at that same place she made us go on New Year's," Yobani says, waving that away. "But we can still play, just you, me, and Greg. Maybe we can even let him DM, give him a little thrill so he'll stop being such a control-freak on Saturdays—"

"The same place from New Year's? You mean The Mode?" So much for being casual. My voice cracks when I say the name of the venue, probably hitting one of those pitches only dogs can hear.

"I think? She said they got added to something last minute . . . I don't know. I stopped listening." Yo stops, eyeing me all suspicious. "Why do you care?"

And like, I know I need to play it cool, because as soon as Yobani finds out why I'm all of a sudden so interested in a Ryan and the Valentines show, the shit-talk is going to be relentless. Nonstop.

But my heart is speeding up and my pits have started perspiring a troubling amount, and any hopes of playing it cool are flying out the window. I'm as conspicuous as Yobani's stupid rings. Because, see, another band is playing The Mode tonight. A band whose social media I scan daily. A band fronted by the most perfect girl, who I haven't given up on yet—even though doing so has been looking more and more rational as we've gotten further from Valentine's Day.

That night I went home and composed a long DM to Delilah: apologizing for my mess-up, complimenting her on her music again and slipping it in there at the end that maybe we could even meet up sometime. It was good. I ran the spell-check, grammar-check, everything. But right as I was about to send . . . I froze. Because if I sent it and she never responded, or worse, hit me with a *How did you find me?* and *Cease and desist, weirdo*—well then, that would be the end. Officially. Zero chances after that.

So I decided that maybe I could run into her again, but be ready this time. Brainstorm what to say. Get in the New Reggie zone and be my most charming self. Fun Gi's social media makes it pretty easy to figure out where she'll be each week. Except, that may be even weirder, to show up to one of her shows on my own. And how would I explain to my friends why I'm willing to cancel a Saturday-night session to see some random band when I've given Leela so much shit in the past?

No, that wouldn't fly. So I've been waiting patiently for the perfect opportunity, for Fun Gi and Ryan's paths to cross again and make it totally normal, totally not weird for me to go to a show. And it seems like it's fallen right into my lap. Tonight is the night. The universe is on my side.

"You know, maybe we should go and support Leela," I say, avoiding eye contact with Yobani.

"Support Leela supporting Ryan? Seems sort of unnecessary, bro."

"I don't know. It might be fun. That place was sorta cool." I shrug. "And where would we even play tonight? My house is out."

"We can go to Greg's place. I know his mom is kinda

helicoptery, but there's the cookies. Also"—Yobani grabs the book from me, and flips a few more pages forward—"there are almirajes in this one. Fucking unicorn. Bunnies. Unicorn bunnies! Like, how can we not play that immediately?!"

I'm about to make another case for seeing the show instead when I feel something wet and slimy swipe across my cheek.

I jump back and see Eric's friend Tyrell standing there, a wide, wicked smile on his face.

"Hold up, I'm just trying to see . . ." He licks his thumb and then reaches for my cheek with it again, but I dodge him this time. "Now come here, I'm trying to see if the black comes off, because there's no way you can be here reading about fairies and elves and actually be Black."

"Tyrell, what the fuck?" I say, weaving around another attempt.

"Chill, I'm just playing with you, baby bro," Tyrell says, cackling and clapping his hand on my shoulder. "But for real, though, you need to put that shit away. You can't be prancing around here with that!"

I'm so mad that I can't speak. My chest feels full of fire, the flames curling at the back of my throat. I know I should just brush off the joke; it's the same one Eric's always making about how I'm not really Black. Of course Tyrell, with his unoriginal ass, is repeating the same thing. But this feels like a violation. To get in my space, to put his fucking spit on me, here in front of everyone. I want to kick him in the balls. I want to smack the smirk off his stupid face.

All I manage to get out, though, is "I'm not your bro."

Yobani steps to him. "Man, what is your problem?"

"Oh shut up, Mr. They're Magically Delicious," Tyrell scoffs, his smile turning into a sneer. He points at Yobani's rings. "Is that all the gold at the end of your rainbow? Get out of here with your leprechaun ass."

Nah—I can make fun of Yo's rings, but fuck anyone else that tries. My fists clench at my sides . . . but that would be stupid. He'd win. And it would be just another chance for everyone to laugh at me. I can feel all the eyes in the hallway starting to migrate our way, waiting for a show.

"What's going on here, y'all?" I feel a hand on my shoulder and Eric appears next to me. Did he see what just happened? His eyes are narrowed, looking between Tyrell and me. Maybe he's about to set him straight, kick his ass, like I can't.

Who am I kidding, though? Even if Eric did see that shit Tyrell just pulled, my brother makes fun of me all the time. So why would he see this as going too far? Why would he stand up for me now? He's probably going to start laughing along with his buddy any second.

I don't want to stand here and be disappointed and look even stupider than I already do. I shrug Eric's hand off.

"We're gonna go," I say, nodding to Yobani. I start walking down the hallway, keeping my eyes down, but I can feel Yobani behind me. If Eric protests at all, I don't hear it.

Man, I'm so sick of feeling this way: that I'm not Black the way I'm supposed to be. That I don't like the things I'm supposed to like. That there's something wrong with me the way I am—so wrong that even my own family can't defend me.

The only time I didn't feel like that (outside of the make-believe worlds of being online or at the table) was with Delilah. Sure, that was its own kind of make-believe . . . but it's different. It's me being who I want to be, who I wish I was. I need that escape right now.

"He's such a dick," Yobani says when we're outside. "I don't see how your brother is friends with him. Man, let's Saran wrap his car. Or, no, fill his locker with glitter! I've got a funnel at home. And, like, what's wrong with leprechauns, anyway? You seen those movies? Those dudes are vicious as—"

I interrupt him. "I'm going to that show tonight."

His eyebrows press together, questions clearly brewing in his mind, but after a beat, he just nods. "Okay."

"Thank you, Yo." I gesture back at the school building. "For that."

"Of course."

"Also, I'm coming around to the rings."

He rolls his eyes and then smiles. "I knew you would."

DELILAH

I walk through life holding everything in.

Every thought that's too hard or too much. Every comment that may make someone uncomfortable or look at me differently. I push everything deep, secure the lid, and then sand down all my edges, too, until they're smooth. Presentable.

And I guess I didn't realize how much pressure that was building up, how much I needed an emergency release valve until I set foot on stage.

It's not a steady release. It's not controlled, safe. No, it's ripping the top right off.

We're at The Mode again tonight, and I'm electric. I feel like I'm plugging in when I first grab the mic, and what felt scary before, what gave me the bubble guts on New Year's, feels like relief now.

I let out syrupy-sweet screams, punctuating each line of the chorus of "Reverse." I twirl around Asher when he plays his bass solo at the end of "Parallelograms" instead of just standing there waiting for my cue like I did at our first couple shows. I let the adrenaline take over instead of holding myself back. I'm light and loose. I keep my eyes open.

And the calls from the crowd, the energy so intense I can almost reach out and grab it like something tangible—it's everything. It's the greatest reward.

I've always tried to keep myself and my life so small. I've never sought out attention. And with my migraines, it's so much easier to do nothing since I might get sick anyway and have to miss out on anything I look forward to.

But it feels good to be big, to take up all this space. To be the girl that the band, and this audience, wants me to be. That girl can do anything.

From his place on the stage, Charlie nods for me to come over to his mic, smiling around the words that he's singing, an echo of mine. I know his look, like I'm all he can see in this room, is just part of the show, but I strut over to him like I deserve it. Our voices intertwine, sharp and soft, as we stare into each other's eyes, and he winks at me when I hit the last note exactly as he told me to.

A girl in the front, with bangs that part in the middle like a curtain, looks at Charlie with want, like almost every other person in the place. He's beautiful, stepping straight out of a rocker dream. But then she looks to me, too, with wide eyes, awe. Because I'm who is capturing his attention.

It's all part of this act, of course. It's just another layer of this person I get to be here on the stage.

And when Beau starts the thundering drumbeat that opens

"Ten Seconds," I step into the center, with the guys behind me. I picture my voice weaving around the room, filling up every inch. I feel my body light up, shining. For these last few moments, I am totally free because I'm totally protected, wrapped up in this role I'm playing. And maybe it's not even a role. Maybe this is someone I actually could be.

Charlie strikes his last chords and everyone cheers. I wave and then run off, leaving the guys to bask in it and do their thing. I don't know what to say when I'm not singing, and it's highly possible that the magic will wear off and I'll turn right back into a pumpkin. Better to get out when I'm ahead.

My heart is speeding, and I close my eyes, taking big gulps of air. But shut eyes and fast legs don't mix, because I slam into another body almost instantly. I open my eyes to see Jeremy—or maybe Jared . . . definitely J-something—the guitarist of Undead Jupiter, the band that played before us. Because as Asher cheered when Jimmy showed us the lineup for tonight, "We're moving on up!" Still not closing—Jimmy called Ryan Love and the Valentines to do that when the Drivers dropped out all late. But at least it's no longer a forgone conclusion that we'll go first.

"That set was fire," he says, leaning in close. He's wearing a green three-piece suit, which may be because it's St. Patrick's Day but may also just be his general aesthetic. He's definitely been partaking in the furtive green beer drinking, as there's a lilt to his words and his breath smells like an armpit.

"Thanks." I take a step back, but he sways closer.

"Your lyrics, man . . . they really speak to me? Like when you sang 'my devotion is an inverted parallelogram,' just . . . whoa. I really felt that." He nods aggressively to emphasize his point, and I get secondhand wooziness.

I bite my lip, holding in a laugh. "Oh, I don't write the lyrics." *And I don't get them either*, I finish in my head. Probably because there's nothing to get. I know these words back and forth now, and I'm certain Charlie just throws them together for how they sound, with little care for their actual meaning.

Jeremy or Jared looks me up and down and a smug grin sits on his lips. "Yeah. Makes sense."

Makes sense? The words cut through me, and I try to decipher his intention. It makes sense that I don't write the lyrics because I'm Black? (One of the only Black people here, I'm hyperaware.) Because I'm a girl? Because I don't look smart enough? Maybe what I've taken for pretentious gibberish from Charlie is actually incredibly profound, and I really just don't get it. Of course this routine is familiar. It's all part of going through life in my body. Trying to anticipate what lens I'm being seen through, going down the checklist until—Bingo! Got your prejudice!

"They got lucky finding you to put out front, though," Jeremy or Jared continues. "Now Fun Gi like . . . stands out, you know? They got their *thing*."

"Yeah, uh. Thanks," I mumble, even though his words make me want to scream. But I can't do that now. I'm not on stage anymore.

Their thing. Is that really all I am? Just a gimmick to make the band stand out? I know I shouldn't be giving all this weight to the thoughts of this dumb drunk guy, but then again, drinking's supposed to make you honest, right? Maybe he's saying what everyone else is thinking. What everyone else *knows*.

I'm putting on a show: singing Charlie's lyrics that I don't understand, imitating other musicians. The band could do this without me, but I couldn't do this without them. I can't let myself get lost in all this and forget that.

"I need to go," I say, but Jeremy or Jared is already moving on, shuffling to greet Charlie, Asher, and Beau as they come offstage. I walk out into the lobby, keeping my eyes down so I can dodge any more reviews of our performance.

REGGIE

"All right, it's official. Something weird is going on here."

I know before I spin around that it's Delilah.

But what I *don't* know is how she figured out that I've been trying to engineer this exact moment for weeks. I thought I was slick—never accidentally liking the pictures I had to scroll way back to see, following them from my burner account and not the one with my real name. And anyway, it's not like I'm some brooding guy from a Netflix show, heavy breathing as I peer at her around a corner. I've just been, like, normal weird—not *weird* weird.

And I'm thinking all this in my head, straight spiraling, but all that's coming out is "Uh, hey, yeah . . . okay—hi—" and other indecipherable drivel, made even worse by the fact that Yobani is flicking his head back and forth between us like he's watching an intense tennis match.

"'Cause of the holidays," she says slowly, like she's throwing me a bone. But that just makes my brain start spinning even faster, because I have no idea what the hell she means.

"Ummm." Yobani's eyes are wide with curiosity and also way too much joy over my current misfortune. "I'm just gonna . . . go over there."

He walks away to nowhere in particular, and I'm grateful for his generous gift of allowing me to have my tragic downfall without an audience.

"You aren't following, are you?" Delilah says, her lips slightly upturned in that secret smile. She's wearing a baggy gray jumpsuit, and her hair is tucked under a blue bucket hat.

"Not at all. I'm, like, yards behind you. Miles."

"You . . . know who I am, though, right? You remember me?"

"Of course I remember you, Delilah!" I shout. I don't mean to shout, but I'm just so fucking relieved that this isn't going how I thought it was going. I mean, I still have no idea where it's going, but at least I'm not about to be served a restraining order.

"And I remember you, Reggie. Or should I say Keepin' It d100?" Her smile gets wider, and it feels like the first peek of sunshine in the morning. "So, it's St. Patrick's Day."

"It is." I look around at the few people wearing green. "Is this—I don't know, uh, a special day to you or something? Sorry if you told me that and I forgot. But I can see why—why you like it? Green is a good color. And, like . . . leprechauns and shit."

Before I can start spiraling again over the absolute garbage I'm spewing, Delilah falls forward in laughter, grabbing my arm to brace herself. Her touch shoots through my body, scrambling my senses and stopping my heart. But, you know, in a good way.

"Leprechauns and shit?" she repeats, laughing some more. "Oh, you're funny. I needed that."

"You're welcome?"

Her hand falls down, and it takes all of my self-control not to grab it back and hold it there forever. She tilts her head to study me, her eyes warm. "No, I'm not super into St. Patrick's Day. Though, I am like a quarter Irish or something. My dad and sister got the red hair. And the freckles."

"You have 'em too," I mumble.

"Yeah." She reaches up to touch them, almost like she forgot they were there. And I guess they are faint and I'm supposed to be a totally normal guy that's run into her casually . . . Oh no, am I being *weird* weird? Roll it back, Reggie!

"Okay, so, today is St. Patrick's Day," she says. "And last time I saw you was Valentine's Day. And the first time was New Year's . . ."

She stares at me expectantly. It takes me a couple beats, but then it finally clicks. "Holidays!" I shout, pointing at her.

"Yes, holidays."

"We keep meeting on holidays!"

"Yes, we do."

"That's like . . . that's magical!" That earns me the biggest smile from her to date, and I wish it wouldn't be *weird* weird to take out my phone and snap a picture of that smile. I want to save it to study later tonight. And damn . . . I'm really not helping my case here.

"It's definitely past just being a coincidence at this point," she says.

And I don't want her to think about that too much and realize what's really going down, so I lean in to it. "The holiday magic keeps throwing us together! It's like a movie. We're probably supposed to save the world together or something."

"Save the world?"

"Yeah, has anyone checked on Santa? The groundhog? Maybe they're being threatened and it's our job to save them, set things straight."

"I love how the groundhog is next in line after Santa . . ."

"Homeboy controls the weather! When was he supposed to come out of his hole, anyway? Maybe that's our mission! We're his only hope!"

"So to summarize," she says, smirking, "holiday magic is bringing us together so we can rescue a groundhog?"

I shrug. "Or you know, just so we can be friends."

She looks down, bites her lip. And I worry I took it too far, let that *weird* weird pop out. But her big brown eyes lock on mine. "Well, mission accomplished, I guess. We're officially friends."

My chest feels all fluttery, like a horde of butterflies got unleashed. Actually, no, this is way more significant than that. It's wyverns, flapping their meaty wings and shooting out flames.

"We did it!" I hold my hand up.

"We did." She slaps my palm, and like they have a mind of their own, my fingers go rogue and weave between hers. Her face flushes and I quickly pull my hand back.

She clears her throat. "So do you . . . come to The Mode a lot?"

Because oh yeah, this holiday magic thing is just a joke. Our joke!! But now I actually have to do some explaining.

"No, uh, well . . . you know Ryan Love and the Valentines?" Delilah nods. "Leela—who's in my D&D group. She's dating Ryan, so I came to, like, support." *Which I've never had an interest in doing before you,* I conveniently leave out.

"Ryan is so badass," she says. And even though what she's saying is objectively a compliment, there's a shift in Delilah. Her face, that was finally starting to open up, shutters.

"*You* are so badass," I say, wanting to fix whatever just happened. "That show—shit! That was so dope. You've gotten even better since the last time—"

"I don't write the lyrics," she spits out, cutting me off. Her eyes go wide, like those words popped out all on their own. "They're Charlie's words . . . I just sing them."

"Uh . . . okay," I say. And I can tell by her serious face that this is supposed to be a big admission. But, honestly, the lyrics are probably my least favorite part (well, after how close she gets to that guitarist guy when they're sharing a mic). They don't really make sense to me and I was worried I was missing something that might be really important to Delilah. So really, this is a relief.

"I think I told you that first night, I started doing this as just a favor to my friends." She pauses and bites her bottom lip. "But I'm not a musician. I don't write the music or anything. I just sing what they tell me to sing. So it's not really . . . I don't know—a big deal what I'm doing."

"No, uh-uh, you need to walk that back," I say. Her eyebrows push together in confusion, and for real, I'm kinda confused too. Because these words are coming out of my mouth before I have a chance to overanalyze them and I'm surely headed for disaster. But they keep coming! "You shouldn't downplay what you do just because you're not writing it. You are a musician; your voice is your instrument. And some people—shit! *Most* people couldn't get on that stage at all, let alone sing like that. You want to hear *me* sing? I could clear out this room in literal seconds!"

She bites her lip some more. And I have no idea what that means, so I keep going—either endearing myself to her some more or totally blowing up any chance that's left. There's no in between. "So we've established that you're already a badass musician because you're out there putting on a dope show, with the voice of an angel." She rolls her eyes, but, like, in a good way. "And if you wanted to learn how to write lyrics or, uh, play guitar, you could do that too. I mean, I don't know you like that yet, I know, but still . . . I think you could. Not because you *need* to for some cred or whatever, but for you."

Delilah nods, her face still hard to read. It's almost like all her feelings are flying through, fighting to take up space. "Maybe."

"Do you want to? Write your own music, I mean?"

"Oh, I wouldn't even know where to start." She waves her hand like she's shooing a fly.

"Hmm. I don't know. I mean, it's not really my lane, obviously. But when I'm stressing about a campaign and don't know what should happen next, I like to watch other DMs on YouTube or listen to their podcasts." It still feels bizarre to talk so openly about D&D with someone other than my friends and not have someone make a stank face or laugh, especially after what happened at school today. But I like it. "So . . . okay, who are your favorite musicians? Maybe you could find some videos of them talking about their craft. Or, like, study their lyrics."

Her cheeks go pink, and it's the cutest thing.

"Uh-oh!" I laugh. "I hit something here. What music do you listen to?"

She tugs her hat down over her eyes, and, okay, *that's* the cutest thing.

"I don't want to tell you."

"Why not?" I point to the door to the main room, where the sounds of the next band are starting to float from. "It's this kind of music, right?"

"No." She bites her lip again, seems to be considering what to say. "Don't get me wrong. I like this music. I'm starting to like it and appreciate it a lot more. But what I listen to on my own . . . it's not cool like that. I could *never* play that kind of music here."

Her eyes go all big and Bambi as she shakes her head. And I get the vibe that *here* doesn't just mean here at The Mode. *Here* means in front of her punk rock, stubble-having guy friends—or like *at all*.

It sorta feels like she's giving me a gift, admitting even this to me. And damn, that hypes me up, pumps my body full of adrenaline and my brain full of hope. I want to be the guy who she thinks she's giving it to.

"You know, I was just thinking about this because this asshole at school was hassling me today. Me and Yobani—that's my friend—we were looking at this new D&D sourcebook, and dude comes up and starts talking some mess about how I'm a nerd, how I'm not really Black because of what I like. And like . . . I just told him to fuck off. Why am I going to waste my time caring about what some dick like that thinks?" I shrug, like all this is nothing. Just another day in the life of New Reggie. "Who cares if it's cool? Who gets to determine what music is cool anyway? You gotta like what you like and live authentically."

I know I'm fronting. Or I guess, more accurately . . . straight-up lying. But her face that was so difficult to read before is clear now. She's practically telegraphing heart-eyes my way, and I swear she's leaning in closer.

She likes me. I can feel it.

And maybe this persona doesn't work in the rest of my life, but it works with Delilah. She likes *this guy*, so I'm gonna keep on being this guy with her. I'll do whatever I need to do to keep her.

DELILAH

I like Reggie. I don't mean . . . *like* like him. Though it may be that, too.

I guess I should say that I want to be like him. I want to be around him—just in case some of his confidence, his *I am who I am* attitude might rub off on me.

I want to be able to stand boldly as the person I am, to not have to wait until I'm on stage for that emergency release valve that lets everything I've been holding in out. But it's hard. How does he make it seem so easy?

"You know, maybe I can connect you with Ryan," he continues, probably totally unaware how he's blowing my mind. "She used to give lessons at that music place over in California Heights. Maybe she can teach you how to play guitar and, like, write music."

That sounds terrifying. And also . . . exhilarating. I'm already starting to list in my head all the ways I might embarrass myself with someone as talented as Ryan, all the ways I might fail. But maybe this is my first step toward being someone who does what she wants and likes what she likes. Someone like Reggie.

"Are you sure?" I ask. "Because I think I would— Yeah. Yeah, that would be awesome."

"Of course! I'm sure she would be down. We're, you know, friends." The last word comes out weird, so he clears his throat. Tries again. "We're friends."

He crosses his arms and starts to squint behind his glasses, and seconds later, when I feel Charlie's arm around me, I know why.

Charlie's touch always used to make me feel safe, but ever since Valentine's Day, it's started to feel more . . . oppressive. Controlling. And I don't want to be taken from this moment. I want to stay right where I am.

"You disappeared, kid!" Charlie says. "I was looking for you."

"You remember, Reggie?" I say, turning to Charlie. He looks unsure, and I can't tell if it's a front or for real. "He was at our first show, and we saw him at that yogurt place last month too. And get this—he's friends with Ryan Love and the Valentines."

"Hey," Reggie says, with a nod.

"Ryan and the Valentines! We love them," Charlie says. Even though just last week he called them pop punk posers, insisting that we were the real deal. It really bothered me because I like their music. It makes me feel something. But instead of contradicting Charlie, I stay quiet.

"Well, nice to meet you, man, but we gotta get going," Charlie says, tugging on my shoulder. "The guitarist from Undead Jupiter—"

I step forward, letting Charlie's hand fall. "Reggie, can I have your number?" I pull my phone out of my pocket and hold it out to him. "You know . . . because of what we talked about."

I don't want to mention the possible lessons in front of Charlie. I want them to be just for me right now. And anyway, that's not the only reason I want his number.

"Yeah, sure. Of course," he says, grinning wide. And when our fingers touch, there's a spark. I jump back.

"Whoa."

"Wow."

"It's just static," Charlie mumbles.

Reggie's nose wrinkles as he grins even bigger, pushing up his glasses. And as I watch him tap my phone's screen, I can feel my face stretching into a smile to match.

REGGIE

I don't know how long I'm standing there watching her walk away, my mouth hanging open ("catching flies," my grandma Lenore would say)—when Yobani appears next to me.

"So *that's* why you all of a sudden like punk rock," he says, jabbing me with his pointy elbow.

"That's why."

"But she just walked away with her boyfriend?"

"Not her boyfriend."

Stubble Boy was stressing, couldn't wait to get her away from me. But it doesn't even matter, because Delilah is walking away with my number. My number that SHE requested! Everything finally, finally went exactly how I wanted.

I mean, sure . . . I had to be a little dishonest to level up like this, but I can smooth all that out when she texts me. Because she's *gonna* text me!

"Reggie is! A punk rocker!" Yobani starts to sing, hopping

around like he's in the mosh pit. Except he's not. We're still in the lobby, and it's awkward. "Reggie is! A punk rocker!"

"Bro, can you not?"

He knocks into me and holds up his fist like a microphone. "Reggie is! A punk rocker! Noooooooooooow!"

I roll my eyes and nudge him away. "I don't know you." But I don't feel as embarrassed as I normally would. It's like I'm sitting on a cloud, watching this all from above, protected by the fact that DELILAH. GOT. MY NUMBER!

My phone vibrates in my pocket, and I float even higher, thinking that she texted me already, that she's as excited about this . . . this . . . *possibility* as I am.

But I'm just as quickly brought back down to earth when I see Eric's name on my screen.

heyyy so i heard what tyrell did

he said he was just playing but i told him that was some bs

you know how he can be tho

I blink at his words for a second, trying to take in what he's saying. So, he knows what happened, talked to Tyrell, but . . . all I get is "that was some bs"? No recognition of how *he* contributed to this? No apology?

I shove my phone back in my pocket and shake my head. Why would I expect anything more from my brother? They're probably laughing over the whole thing together.

I push down the sick, angry feeling brewing in the back of my throat. I'm not going to let my disappointment in my brother steal how happy I feel right now.

"So, does this mean we have to start coming to this place more often?" Yobani asks, grabbing my shoulder and clapping a hand on my chest. "Because I *will*. For you, man. But I think I may need to get some more rings. Or no, wait—a nose ring! One of those bull-looking ones! Then I'll fit in!"

"Yo, trust me. You don't need any more rings."

"Is that because you're worried I'm going to leave you behind with my coolness? Because you could get one too." He holds out his hands wide. "Yeah! I can see it now! Maybe they'll give us a deal. Two-for-one nose rings! Or, no, no, actually, what about . . ."

I tune out his increasingly complex piercing ideas as I start to plan my first text to Delilah.

Hi reggie

Hey!

Yobani what the fuck give that back right now arm rabble

Um

Arm rabble?

Oh my god I am so so sorry

I'm using voice to text and my friend took

the phone from me because he is the worst

I think arm rabble is what my screams sound like?

I have dyslexia. That's why I use voice to text

Okay cool

What was he trying to get you to say?

Hey there Delilah

A reference to some old song??

Well, good thing you got your phone back

I hate that song

And that would have been super cheesy

He just said we don't know good music and bounced 😂

Thank you for your service 🙏🏾

Happy to help!

So are you texting for Ryan's number?

Here you go

Ryan Love   RL

Thank you 😃

But also, did you know that groundhog's day already passed?

We failed him

Oh no!!!!

We've still got time to save the turkey and Santa

Or what's up next? The April Fool's . . . jester?

Bro that's some corny shit don't you want her to like you

arm arm rabble

Goddamnit

Hey yobani 👋🏽

He came back

He is the worst

Omg 💀

MON, MARCH 20 4:27 PM

The essay you posted today was so good

Thank you! That's so cool that you read it!

Of course. I really connected with it

Oh yeah?

Yeah, I know D+D is different than music, but I get that
feeling . . . of being an outsider because I'm Black
And loving something but not being sure if it loves you back
But not being able to give it up anyway
Wow ok that was a lot
Didn't mean to get so deep

No it's okay!
That makes me really happy to hear that it like
transcended tabletop games and wow even
you taking the time to message me about it
And really the deeper the better!
. . . that came out weird didn't it?

Yeah a little 😂

Hey I know you got my number to link up
with Ryan, but maybe we could hang out to?
Too*
Are there any holidays coming up
so we can keep this consistent?
If you want

No worries if not!!

Delilah?

THU, MARCH 23 7:14 PM

I'm so sorry Reggie!

I got a migraine that turned into a cluster migraine and I'm just finally starting to feel like myself again today

Oh my god! Don't apologize!

That sounds so terrible

Do you need anything? Is there something I can do??

Oh I'm fine . . . this is just my life. I'm used to it 🪦

But that doesn't mean it doesn't suck.

I'm sorry that you have to deal with those Delilah.

Thank you

I think I need to get off here for now. The screen isn't helping.

No worries!

I'm here if you need me

SAT, MARCH 25 10:41 AM

Hi! If you're not doing anything tonight, we're playing this guerrilla show in the park

As far as I've been able to tell, "guerrilla" just means we

don't have permission to play, so maybe be ready to run

Ah it's Saturday so I have D&D tonight! As much
as I want to run away from park security guards (?!)

Yeah I don't get it either . . .
I think it's a white people thing.
Have fun at D&D!

SUN, MARCH 26 12:27 PM

How was the show? Do I need to bail you out?

We didn't even get to play! The park people
turned the sprinklers on after the first band
But honestly, props to them. It was effective

Oh no!!

Do you have plans today? We could go to the
park and stare at them menacingly from the slides
Or you know just get coffee

I've got band practice ☹
But next time!

WED, MARCH 29 5:00 PM

Are you around? Rain check on the coffee?

I wish but I'm heading into work right now

Oooooo have some strawberry yogurt with mochi for me

I clean those machines and as a result I can never eat
yogurt again

Omg don't tell me anything else. Keep the illusion alive

I wouldn't want to burden anyone else with this
knowledge
Are you free Friday?

That's actually my first lesson with Ryan. I am . . . terrified.

Oh cool!
Don't stress. You'll be great!

I hope so

APRIL FOOL'S DAY

DELILAH

I get to Ryan's house fifteen minutes early, which is just as bad as showing up fifteen minutes late.

I don't have a car. Dad didn't offer one when I turned sixteen and got my license last September, even though he and Sandra get new Audis every two years. And I would never ask Mom for one—I know it's not possible in our tight budget. So I show up whenever the bus or my ride for the day decides I'm going to show up. The bus got me to Ryan's neighborhood, Cal Heights, today because I definitely wasn't about to ask the guys for a ride here and Mom's still at work. Charlie would totally drive me. He's being extra nice lately . . . actually since he interrupted me and Reggie talking at The Mode a couple weeks ago. But I don't want him to know I'm doing this. Not yet.

I'm trying to decide if I should just stand here like a dork or do a couple laps around the block when a girl pushes open a gate on the side of the house, followed closely by Ryan. The girl has light brown skin and long, shiny black hair, and she's holding Ryan's hand.

For a moment, I convince myself that this was all some strange April Fool's joke that went over my head, that Ryan didn't expect me to show up for an actual lesson. And now I'm standing here watching them on her lawn like a total loser.

But then Ryan notices me and smiles. My chest loosens.

"You made it," she says, and her girlfriend's eyes light up.

"You're Delilah!" the girl says. "Hi! I'm Leela."

"Hey, yeah. I'm here." And I think my face looks normal, like I'm holding it together. But all of sudden I'm hit with another wave of panic. Why did I think I could do this again? How could I possibly have convinced myself this was a good idea?

But Leela closes the gap between us with long, quick strides and holds her hand out. I take hers and she grips it with surprising force. "So you're Reggie's friend," she says, pumping our hands and smiling wide. "Like I'm his friend. And Ryan—Ryan is *definitely* his friend. We're all friends here!"

Ryan grabs her shoulders and delicately pulls her back. "Babe, you're being weird."

Leela side-eyes her, but then nods in agreement. "Yeah, I am," she laughs. "I'm just so excited to meet Reggie's *friend*!"

"Well, you met her," Ryan says with a playful eye roll. "Now, time for you to go. We've got work to do."

They give each other a quick peck, and then Leela heads out, giving me one more aggressively smiley look. Either the girl is actually really happy to see me or completely hates my guts. *What exactly did Reggie say about me . . . ?* But no. I push that thought out of my mind. I've got enough to worry about now.

"Thank you so much for doing this," I say, but Ryan quickly waves that away.

"Oh, of course," she says. "I'm honored you came to me. Truly. And I'm all about helping out another girl in this scene—*especially* another girl of color. There's so few of us."

I nod. "There are. And that's why I'm just so—so in awe of you. I'm such a fan."

"Awww, shucks. Same, girl!" she says with a laugh. Clearly joking, because that couldn't possibly be true. "Come on." She motions her head toward the side gate. "My space is back here."

I follow her, taking the opportunity to fully gawk at her outfit. She's wearing a floral lace dress, studded denim vest, and pastel pink Docs. Instead of red, her hair is now electric blue, and it's growing out into a cool, asymmetrical cut. So I guess her perfectly outrageous looks aren't just for the stage. It makes me like her even more.

We walk through her backyard to a detached garage. But instead of housing a couple cars or piles of old junk, like most people's, this place is decked out like a professional studio. It's maybe even nicer than the place that Asher dished out tons of money for us to record in back in February.

The walls are covered in shiny wood paneling, striped light and dark. On one side, there are six guitars mounted on the wall, in a rainbow of colors, with drums, amps, and gold mic-stand below. And on the other side, there's a lounge area with a green velvet loveseat, leather chairs, and a pink mini fridge. The whole room is cast in a rosy glow from the neon sign that says "Love" in loopy script.

"This is . . . so cool," I say, slowly spinning to take everything in.

"Right? My parents let me go all out." She beams. "They're all about my music, which I know is a huge blessing 'cause most parents aren't like that. But when I told them I was starting a band, they were like, 'Okay. How do we get you to Coachella?'"

"That's really cool," I repeat. And I *know* I'm repeating myself, but it's like my brain is robbed of all other adjectives—actually, all other words. I want to impress her, show her she didn't make a complete mistake agreeing to teach me. But that pressure is just making my mind go blank.

"My mom's only request is to use the space for her book club," she continues. "Those aunties can get pretty rowdy."

"Oh, ha-ha." Another stupid generic comment. I look around, searching for something, anything, to say so she doesn't send my cringey butt out of here right now.

"Is your last name really Love?" I ask, pointing to the neon sign on the wall.

"No," she says with a giggle, and I get another wave of mortification. Of course it's not. Maybe I should just see myself out. "My last name is Lo, but Ryan Love and the Valentines just sounds so badass. Also, Love is generic. Lo tells bookers exactly who I am. And some bookers—they don't want to give stage time to a girl named Lo."

"Really?" I squeak out.

"You'd be surprised." She stops, cocks her head to the side. "Actually, no . . . I don't think you would be. Things are easy in our liberal bubble of Long Beach. But you know as much as I do that we can cross over into the next county and enter an entirely different world . . . *especially* when it comes to their precious rock music. And I don't want to give some ignorant shit on a power trip the chance to turn me down before I blow them away."

"That's so unfair . . ." I sigh, and shake my head. "But you're right. It's reality."

"Yeah, the game's not fair, but I'm going to win regardless." She saunters over to her mini fridge and pulls out two LaCroixs, handing me one of them. I don't love them, but I'm for sure going to drink whatever this enlightened rock goddess role model gives me. She sits down on one of her leather chairs and nods for me to do the same.

"So Delilah." She leans forward on her knees, and her eyes narrow at me, assessing. I don't think she's trying to intimidate me, but my heart rate speeds up all the same. "Before we get started, I want to know your why."

My why? *My why??*

My heart races even faster, so loud she definitely hears it. What kind of question is that? I'm at a guitar lesson, not therapy.

"My why . . . ?" I ask, trying to buy myself time.

"Yeah." She smiles, like this is a totally normal, totally easy question. "Why you want to learn to play guitar, why you want to play your own music." She must see the absolute panic flashing across my face because she adds, "There's no right answer. Don't stress. I just want to make sure I'm helping you the best I can."

I search my mind for the right thing to say, because there is always a right answer. People always have a response they're looking for, no matter what they say. And I want to find Ryan's. I want to sound cool.

But my mind is still blank. And since sitting here in silence is not an option, as that would be *the most* cringe thing possible, I decide to be honest. It's all I've got.

"I guess . . . Well, I love who I am when I'm up there. On stage," I mumble, looking down. "And I—I want to feel like I deserve it. I think if I could actually play music I'd deserve it. Like the guys do."

"I get that," she says, and my head whips up in shock. Because how can *the Ryan Love* understand what I'm saying at all? But she has a smile on her face, and it's an easy one. Not stretched too wide with pity or condescension. "I've seen your show. You're good. You hold your own. But who gives a fuck what I think? The only one who can tell you that you deserve it is you."

I'm shocked by her words, how quickly she's cut right to my core. So, I just nod once, then two more times. "Okay."

Ryan stands up and walks over to her guitar wall. She presses her lips together and closes one of her eyes, studying me. I wish I could listen in on her thoughts, see what she sees. Finally, she pulls down a mint green electric guitar and places it in my hands like it's a newborn baby.

"This is a Fender Player Stratocaster. It's a limited-edition model. Maple fingerboard," she says, delicately brushing the top of it with her fingertips. "I call her Mabel. I think you and Mabel are gonna get along just fine."

When we first texted, she told me I could borrow a guitar for today, but I thought for sure it would be some dusty, dinged-up one that she didn't need anymore. But Mabel isn't that. Mabel is special.

"Wow," I breathe. "Thank you, Ryan."

"You're welcome," Ryan says. "Here, let me tune her for you."

She takes Mabel back. And as silly as it sounds, I feel the loss of it, even though we've only been acquainted for seconds.

After plugging Mabel into a small amp at our feet, Ryan takes out her phone and opens up an app. She strums on a string and the screen flashes yellow, so she twists one of those . . . twisty thingies—I need to learn what they're called if I'm going to really do this!—on the top. Then she plays again and adjusts some more until the screen turns green. I watch her, mesmerized.

"So I'm just curious," she says, moving on to the next string. "Why didn't you ask someone in your band to teach you? Charlie, he's really good."

"Yeah, he is." And normally I would stop right there, but I keep going. "It's just that . . . he can be . . . kind of judgey sometimes? I think with him I'd be scared to get it wrong. Or look stupid."

And I was totally feeling the same with Ryan only moments ago, but it feels like we've broken through that. I guess she already saw right through me, so why keep trying so hard to get it just right? I can breathe a little deeper, be a little looser. It reminds me of how I feel with Reggie.

"Well, you're gonna look stupid." She looks up and smiles. "And I probably will too. That's making music. But I get what you're saying, the judgey thing. He tried to talk shit to me about Feline one night, and I'm just not about that. And with people like that—shoot. I'm sure he's talked about my band too."

"He called you pop punk posers." I bite my lip, as if I could catch the words once they're already out, because that might have been a step too far. Was there truth serum in that bubbly water? Some sort of magic in her assessing stare?

But Ryan's head falls back in a loud cackle. "Oh, fuck that! There's always been, and will always be, some white guy with a bad haircut claiming they're the only ones who truly know what punk is. And *conveniently* it's exactly what they produce." She laughs some more, the bead hanging from her septum piercing jangling around. "Don't worry. I'm not going to say anything to him. But, man! That is FUN-NY!"

She picks the last string, getting the green go-ahead from her phone, and then strums the guitar. The sound makes my whole body feel like it's wrapped up in a blanket.

Ryan hands Mabel to me. "Okay. She's ready. What's the first song you wanna learn?"

"Uh . . . well." I freeze because the only things coming to mind are not *Ryan*-cool.

She gives me a playful look like, *really?* "I'm not Charlie, girl. Just tell me!"

"I really love Taylor Swift," I admit, bracing myself for the responses I expect, the ones I tell myself when I'm trying to do the judging before someone else gets the chance. Taylor Swift is mainstream, the pumpkin spice latte of music. Taylor Swift is for white girls.

But Ryan just shrugs. "It's pretty punk rock, calling assholes out by name, not taking sexist shit."

"So . . . Taylor Swift is punk rock?"

"Oh, fuck no!" she snorts, grinning at me. I smile too. "But what I'm saying is, you can still be punk rock even if you're influenced by Tay-Tay. Like, there's nothing more punk than owning who you are and what you like, unapologetically."

"Okay." I grip Mabel in my hands, lightly touch the strings. "Well, I like Taylor Swift. And I want to play this electric guitar and scream until my throat's sore and . . . also write lyrics that make people cry."

"Good," she nods, like that's that. "And anyway, I was just fucking with you. We'll be lucky if we get to 'Mary Had a Little Lamb' today."

REGGIE

"Bro, this is way too long," Yobani calls from his place at my desk.

"I think the length is fine," Greg counters, peering over his shoulder.

"No one asked you, Gruly."

"Reggie literally asked me. That is the only reason I'm here."

"Can we, like, not do this right now?" I roll my eyes and sit up on my bed. "I mostly just need you to look for typos. I'm feeling pretty confident on the content."

"Oh, really?" Greg says. "Because I did have some notes on this second point you made about Meron's backstory. Are you sure you're correctly interpreting the—"

Yobani cuts him off. "Of course he's interpreting Meron's backstory correctly. Here you go again acting like you know better than ev—"

"Typos, you guys. Typos."

I wrote up a new post, a review of the new D&D sourcebook,

Meron's Monograph of Mischief, and I know it's about to get the trolls all up in their feelings. So I asked Yobani and Greg to come over and look at it for me because the last thing I need is for the whole essay—which is *not* too long and *correctly* interprets Meron's backstory—to be derailed by some typos for my haters to latch on to. I know there's some. There always are, and probably even more than usual because I've been distracted by—

"Has she texted you yet?" Yobani asks. They're apparently no longer arguing about my essay and have turned their attention fully to me.

"What are you talking about?" I ask, playing dumb. But he nods at my phone, which is unlocked and gripped in my hands.

"You know exactly *who* I'm talking about," Yobani says with a smirk. "The same girl you've been checking for constantly ever since you somehow landed her number. De-li-lah!" He sings out her name like a song and mimes scrolling on his phone while he bats his eyelashes, all dramatic.

"I wasn't even looking at my texts," I mumble.

"Dude! Don't lie!" Yobani pops out of the chair.

"I have to concur," Greg says. "I mean, even if you weren't specifically looking at your texts, you were probably staring at her band's socials again. Let's not get bogged down by semantics."

Of course *this* is what brings them together.

"Okay, fine. I was checking, but there's nothing new." There hasn't been for days now.

"But why can't you just text her again?" Greg asks. "You're spending a significant amount of time thinking about her. Why not just open up the chain of communication again?

"No!" Yobani and I both shout together. Because I definitely, definitely cannot do that.

"He sent the last text!" Yobani explains. "With a thirsty red heart—"

"It was not thirsty!" I interrupt. "It was just a nice, normal heart! She was nervous. I was trying to show her I supported her."

"That is not what a red heart means. You shouldn't be allowed to send emojis if you don't understand them. Like, with great power comes great responsibility." He shakes his head all serious, like what he just said made any sense. "Anyway, regardless of the fact that Reggie tried to boo her up after only a few texts—"

"It was just a heart!"

"—*regardless*, no matter what he last sent, he can't text her again. It'll look desperate. There has to be a back-and-forth."

I sigh deeply. As much as I want to argue with Yobani, he's right. Even though I apparently need a primer course on the true meaning of emojis, I know at least this basic fact about texting. I pushed things a little too far already when she disappeared with her migraine and I sent a string of increasingly desperate messages with no response. That worked out okay, thank god, but I can't be tempting fate like that again.

"I just think this is a foolish move," Greg says. "Why play a game when you know what you want? If you like her, tell her."

And I do like her. What started out as something surface before, an infatuation with her incredibly cool persona and ridiculously gorgeous looks, has been growing steadily with just our few texts. She's been vulnerable and real and funny. She's read my writing. And when I told her about my disability, she just said okay.

Like my disability is no big deal—which it isn't. But people are always trying to make it one.

I know that I want to know more. I know I want to ask her on a date and treat her like the treasure she is and shout my feelings from the rooftops. But it's not that easy. One wrong move, and she finds out what a nerd I am and everything I've been building will be dust.

"You don't know what you're talking about, Gruly," Yobani scoffs.

"First of all, Gruldaito Gloomcloud has plus twenty-five charisma and incredible seducing prowess. It's on my character sheet," Greg says, rolling his eyes. "And second of all, I'm pretty certain that I've had more partners than you."

"Nah— You don't— What," Yobani sputters, and I crack up. Greg crosses his arms and smiles at Yobani smugly.

"That's a flex, dude," I laugh, reaching to give him a fist bump.

"Ahh, whatever. I am single by choice," Yobani says. He sits down and turns back to the screen like he's getting back to business, but I know he's just hiding his flaming cheeks.

A second later, he's screaming.

"Reggie! Reggie!!"

"Bro, chill out, you're about to have my mom in here again." She's already popped her head in twice "just checking" on us. "Greg wasn't—"

"Forget Gruly!" he shouts. "Look at this comment on your last post!"

I walk to my desk, leaning over his shoulder to read whatever's got him so agitated, and Greg crowds in too.

Which is, like, a pretty innocuous comment. I don't see why he's making such a big deal and hollering all wild. But then I see who it's from.

Darren Lumb. The host of *Role With It,* the biggest D&D actual play podcast and YouTube show. We're all obsessed with *RWI* and listen to their weekly sessions religiously—along with, like, everyone else who's serious about the game.

So whoa. This actually *is* a big deal.

"Darren Lumb commented!" Greg's voice has gone up at least two octaves. "Darren Lumb knows who you are!"

"Yobani, is this some stupid April Fool's thing?" I ask, narrowing my eyes at him. "'Cause we told you you're banned from this entire holiday after the cereal incident. Be straight with me!"

"Forget the cereal! This is real! I swear on Trickery's parents' graves!" Yobani says, shaking in his seat. I look him up and down, and reality sets in. Yobani isn't this good of an actor.

"We need to write him back. Right now!" He jabs a finger at my computer screen. "This could be fucking huge! You could be on the show!"

"No. No! Not yet." I need to think about this. I need to say exactly the right thing.

Also I have NO interest in being on Darren Lumb's show. Like, at all. I enjoy listening to it and watching it, but I don't need people seeing my face, knowing who I really am. Just the thought of that makes me feel sick to my stomach. That's why I keep this all anonymous.

Yobani grabs my keyboard like he's ready to throw down. If I don't act quick, he's probably gonna hijack my account and send it himself. And Greg, a Darren Lumb superfan, will gladly hold me down until it goes through.

Ping.

We all freeze and then slowly turn to stare at my phone on the bed. I usually keep my phone on silent like a normal, well-adjusted person. But I've had the volume full blast for the past two weeks so I wouldn't miss a text. So is that . . . ?

Ping. Ping.

Yes, it definitely is.

DELILAH

We don't even get to "Mary Had a Little Lamb."

Ryan shows me how to sit up straight and how to hold the guitar on my right leg with my hands in the correct places. She teaches me the names for the different parts of the guitar (turns out the twisty thingies are called tuning keys) and the right way to hold a pick. And I've just barely got the names of the strings down (thanks to the mnemonic device Eddie Ate Dynamite Good Bye Eddie) when all of a sudden an hour has passed.

I made a lot of mistakes. The fingers on my fretting hand are red and sore—and Ryan says they'll stay that way until I get calluses. But I feel content. I feel excited to learn more. I feel capable.

And when Ryan and I are snacking on shrimp chips and more LaCroix after the lesson is over, I realize that the best part of the day is that I have a new friend. A badass, total goals, still kind of intimidating friend—but a friend all the same.

I feel a little silly getting all excited about that. I'm not in kindergarten and this shouldn't be a major feat. But it kind of is. I was myself. I let go of trying to be cool and instead was just honest, and Ryan decided she still wanted to hang with me anyway. This has happened twice now, so maybe . . . I should start believing it's possible.

"So how long have you and Leela been together?" I ask, leaning back on her ridiculously comfy couch.

"Oh, a long time. Two and a half years now?" Ryan smiles. "I asked her out after the first meeting of Pride Club our freshman year. Would have done it sooner, but I needed it, like, ninety-nine point nine percent confirmed that she was into me, too, before I could take the risk. I was so scared!"

It's hard to imagine this Ryan sitting in front of me with blue hair and pink Docs being scared of anything, but I guess asking someone out is maybe the only time we're all sweaty, anxious messes.

"And she's okay with this, right?" I say, pointing between the two of us. Ryan arches her eyebrow and I realize how strange that sounded. I rush to explain, "Not that she shouldn't be! It was just when she left—"

"She was being really fucking conspicuous," Ryan cuts me off, laughing.

"Um . . . yeah." I laugh too.

"It's not that. I'm guessing you're straight."

I nod.

"And even if you weren't, it's not like any girl is a threat." She shakes her head, laughs some more. "It's just . . . Reggie."

The sounds of his name sets off fireworks in my chest.

"Reggie?"

Her eyebrows shoot up, and she fixes me with a satisfied smirk. "Oh, that face answered any question I was about to ask."

I reach up to touch my face, and feel a big grin I didn't even realize was there. My cheeks are warm, and I know they're turning pink. "Well, that's not fair," I say, looking down. "I can't control my face."

"Exactly."

I get the nerve to look at her again. Her lips are pressed together and she's studying me with one eye closed, like she did earlier. I swear she can see right into my brain when she does that. "So, is there something going on there? Leela thinks so."

Is there something going on? I've learned more about him by reading all of his essays online—how he thinks, what he likes. He responded to my days-long migraine cluster exactly how I *wish* people would. Acknowledging how much it sucks and offering to help, instead of brushing them off as headaches like everyone except my mom and sister does. He seems so smart, so kind, and just unapologetically himself. And also . . . he's just really, really cute.

Then again, we haven't managed to meet up, and maybe that's because he actually doesn't want to? *I* want to, but I'm scared to bring it up again. I don't want to come on too strong, be too much. I don't want to scare him away before anything really begins. And I think telling Ryan how much I like him might be the definition of coming on too strong. I have to play this cool.

"We're friends," I finally say. "I like him. I like being friends with him. He's just . . . not like anyone I've ever met. He's so confident, you know? But we haven't had luck in linking up yet."

Ryan wrinkles her nose, looking confused. But then she seems to come to some sort of decision and nods forcefully. "I'm gonna text him right now and tell him to come over."

"Don't do that!" The words fly out of me, and Ryan jumps back.

"Why not?"

"I don't know . . . I—" I sputter. "I don't want him to think . . ."

"Relax," she says. And usually I hate when people tell me that, but with her, my body seems to get the message and actually listens. "It can be just a friend thing, really chill. I'll ask Leela to come too. It won't be awkward, I promise."

Of course it's going to be awkward. I don't know how it *won't* be awkward with these three supercool people and then me—just barely starting to feel like I can exist as my actual self in the same universe as them.

But maybe . . . I can give in to the awkward, how uncomfortable I am. Look what I've already gotten out of doing just that today.

"Okay," I say. "And, uh . . . can you tell him that it's April Fool's Day?"

"Sure," she says with a laugh, and starts typing intently on her phone.

I wipe my hands and pick up Mabel, plucking the high E string and moving my fingers up the fretboard. It's slow and stilted but still so much more than I could do even an hour ago. My chest buzzes with the possibilities of what else could change.

REGGIE

Yobani dives for it, but I'm faster. My heart sinks when I see it's not from Delilah, but that sucker starts speeding into hyperspace when I read Ryan's texts.

> I'm at my place with Delilah right now. Pretty sure she's really feeling you. Get your butt over here! Let's make this happen! 🤟 😘
>
> Also she says to tell you it's April Fool's Day . . . whatever that means 😏

I read it four times to make sure I'm not getting it wrong or mixing the words up, and even then I'm struggling to trust my brain. But then Yobani starts yelling out "Oh!" and Greg starts doing this weirdo dance, and I'm totally sure that the texts say what I think they say.

"She likes me!" I yell out, holding up my arms like I just ran through a finish line. "She really likes me!"

"Not gonna lie. I thought this was a long shot," Yobani says. "I mean, yeah, there's always a chance. But I was thinking your chance was like point zero zero zero zero—"

"Hey," I say, smacking his shoulder.

"I'm just being real with you!" he laughs, smacking me back and then hopping over to the other side of the room.

I toss a pillow after him and he whips his hoodie from his waist like it's some sort of secret weapon, but before he can swat me with it, Greg steps between us. "Um, shouldn't you respond?"

"Huh, yeah . . . you're right," I say. I rub my hands over my face. "But, like, what do I even say?"

"Nothing," Yobani says. "You say nothing. You don't want her to think you're sitting around waiting for your text. That's like Dating 101."

"I thought we established you didn't have the authority to teach that course," Greg says, smirking.

"You shut your mouth, Gruly!"

"But she can see that I read it," I interrupt them. "Won't that make me look like a dick? If I just don't respond?"

"Why do you have your read receipts on?" Yobani yells, throwing his hands out. "Are you some kind of monster?!"

"I agree," Greg says. "Read receipts are definitely monster-adjacent behavior. Let's fix that for you now." He takes my phone from my hands, navigating to the settings page.

"Well, I can't go back and be less of a monster at this point." I roll my eyes. "So what do I say?"

"Tell her you're coming over." Greg shrugs and hands my phone back to me. "You want to see her. This is your chance to see her."

"You *cannot* do that," Yobani says, all intense like we're trying to diffuse a bomb instead of send a text. "You can't just run over there right when she beckons. You want her to think you have a life! Girls like it when you have a life!"

Greg shakes his head. "I'm telling you, all these games are a waste of time. People like it when you're authentic. When you say what you mean and mean what you say."

"Ugh! You sound like my father." Yobani wrinkles his nose.

"Pretty sure your parents have been married for a long time, so maybe that's not a bad thing?"

They continue to bicker, more and more concerned with dunking on each other than helping me (Gruldaito Gloomcloud's seducing prowess gets brought up again, for some reason). My head spins trying to determine the right course of action here. Yeah, I want to sprint over there and declare my undying . . . *like* for her. But I've only gotten this far with Delilah by playing games, being cool and confident instead of my authentic self-conscious, quiet, nerdy-on-the-down-low self. She likes that front, not who I really am. And maybe listening to Yobani here is the right move to keep up that front.

I type my response so the voice-to-text won't pick up the guys' argument (that has somehow come around to what went down with Slarog the cloud giant), and then interrupt them to get their eyes on it.

That sounds cool! Will head over in a little while.

"Perfect," Yobani says, miming a chef's kiss.

"It's not what I would do," Greg says. "But I guess it makes you look . . . busy?"

And I want to look busy. I want to look like I have this big, cool life—one she might want to be a part of.

I hit send. Then I stare at the clock, waiting for what can reasonably be considered "a little while" to pass.

DELILAH

Reggie isn't coming.

It was easy to convince myself otherwise when only thirty minutes had passed and Leela showed up, all secret smiles and waggling eyebrows.

But then we hit an hour. And then an hour and a half. Leela's face turns stormy as she aggressively taps out messages on her phone, and Ryan's excitement shifts to something strained.

My throat feels tight and my stomach feels sloshy when I realize exactly what has happened. Reggie is standing me up. And I need to go, *right now*, before I embarrass myself any more.

"I think I'm going to head out," I say, standing up.

"No, don't do that," Ryan says. "We can still hang out without Reggie." So, she's well aware that he's not coming too.

"Yeah, fuck Reggie!" Leela shouts, but then quickly adds, "I mean, I love Reggie. He's a really good guy. And I'm sure there's a perfectly good reason why he's not here . . . but also I kinda want to kill him right now."

I know they're trying to help, but this is just making me feel so much worse. Like I'm this delicate flower that has to be protected from what's so clearly going on here.

This all scared him. *I* scared him. I was looking for signs that he maybe liked me too, but I ended up willfully, stupidly misreading everything—just like I did with Charlie. I was searching for something that wasn't there, and this was his clear message that I should slow down, back off.

I'm mortified. And it's even worse because it's in front of an audience.

"No worries." I wave them off, trying to come across way more chill than I feel. "I'll see Reggie around."

"Are you sure?" Leela asks with her eyebrows pressed together in concern. I hate it.

"Totally sure!" I stretch my face into a big fake smile. "Thank you again for the lesson, Ryan. That was just . . . everything. And I know you said I didn't have to pay you, but I—"

She cuts me off. "It was my pleasure, Delilah. Really." She picks up a guitar case from behind her chair and gingerly places Mabel inside. "Don't forget your girl."

"I—I can't . . ." I start, but she pushes the case in my hands.

"Uh, of course you can! I'm assigning you at least thirty minutes a day of practice until our lesson next Saturday. Plus, I'm pretty sure you two are bonded now."

"You're going to keep teaching me?" We hadn't discussed anything more than today, and I guess I just assumed this would be it.

"Damn right I am!" she calls out, beaming at me. "We've got a mission: punk rock that makes you cry."

"Punk rock that makes you cry," I repeat, returning her smile, a real one this time.

As I'm walking down the street to the bus stop, holding the heavy case and a small practice amp in my hands, the disappointment and embarrassment over Reggie creeps back in, but I push it away. Before he showed me exactly where we stand, today was pure exhilaration and joy. I played guitar for the first time. I got to peel back the layers with Ryan, be myself. I got Mabel!

Yeah, Reggie boosted my confidence and connected me with Ryan and led to all that happening. But it was as a friend. I can be just friends with him. Well . . . I don't have any other choice.

And I don't need to be jumping into anything with him anyway, not right now. I don't need distractions. I need to fall in love with myself, like I told Georgia. I need to focus on becoming this girl I want to be instead of chasing some guy who doesn't want anything more than sporadic texts and random meetings.

REGGIE

I wait as long as Yobani tells me to—and then a little longer because we decide to respond to Darren Lumb's comment and it takes some time to get it just right.

But as soon as I press enter, all terrified, and send that out into the universe (Thanks, man! I'm a big fan.), I hop into Bessie and speed over to Ryan's. I can't find parking on her block, so I end up around the corner. And once I finally get Bessie locked—of course she decides to be extra difficult today—I sprint down to Ryan's house and through the side gate. I'm huffing when I get to her garage and—shit!—very sweaty. That's a sure way to scare Delilah off. So, I stand there an extra minute and fan my pits, try to construct a sweat dam with my mind, do a quick sniff check. And then I open the door.

"Hey, sorry I'm la—"

My face falls.

Because unless they've decided to play a game of hide-and-seek or whatever, Delilah is not here. It's just Ryan and Leela, and Leela looks *pissed*.

"Where's Delilah?" I ask, but then Leela narrows her eyes even more, locked on me like they're about to shoot lasers, and I know that was the wrong thing to say.

"She left, you asshole!" Leela spits out, crossing her arms. "A little while? A little while?!" Her voice gets alarmingly loud. "What could you have possibly been busy with? I know you keep Saturdays free so you can emotionally prepare for our sessions!"

And that's true, but when she says it like that—

"She was so excited to see you, and you should have seen her face when you didn't show!" She lets out a garbled yell, and Ryan's eyebrows shoot up in surprise. This is probably the most un-chill Leela has been in her entire life. "Fuck! I love you, Reggie, but I'm so mad at you! That wasn't cool."

"She was excited to see me?" I ask, quietly, and apparently that was also the wrong thing to say, because Leela throws her hands up and gives me a death stare.

"What happened?" Ryan asks, with considerably more chill, but I can tell she's not happy with me either.

"I was with Yobani and Greg and—well, Yobani told me . . . he thought . . ." I shake my head, run my hands over my face, because as I try to get the words out, I realize how completely stupid I've been. Finally I mumble, "Yobani told me to make her wait awhile so she would think I have a life."

Leela leans forward with wide eyes like she's waiting for the punch line to a joke, but when it's clear it's not coming, she yells out, "Are you kidding me?!" She pops off the couch, shaking her head. "You listened to Yobani? Yobani?! Yobani hasn't been on a date since the eighth-grade formal. And I'm still not convinced that wasn't his third cousin doing him a favor."

I exhale and fight the urge to slap myself upside the head. She's so right. What was I thinking?

"Do you think . . . can I— What can I do to fix things with her?" That's all I want. To get us back on the right track we were on before. I mean, if that's even possible at this point.

Ryan bites her lip and picks up a guitar that was on the couch, avoiding my gaze. "I don't know, man."

Leela stomps over to me and grabs my shoulders. "Stop trying to be strategic. This isn't a session, Reggie. You can't DM a relationship! Just be yourself. Usually—not right now—but *usually* I really like that person. Most people do."

Well, I know that's not going to work. Leela is seeing things through some rosy-ass glasses if she thinks most people like me just as I am. And things have only gone so well with Delilah so far because I've been playing this just right. Today . . . today was shit. But maybe I can find something in between—and real fast, before I lose Delilah for good.

SAT, APRIL 1 4:56 PM

I'm so sorry I missed you Delilah!!

I got caught up doing something and lost track of time.

I am the absolute worst

It's fine

Can I make it up to you?

Tomorrow is national peanut butter and

jelly day and I make a real good sandwich

You know because it's a holiday and

we can keep working on our mission

lol

Sorry I'm busy

TUE, APRIL 4 10:03 AM

Okay so today is national hug a newsperson

day and I'm not totally sure how legit that is

but maybe we should go find Marc Brown

You know from ABC 7?

Man my dad loves that guy. Sometimes I catch him talking

back to the screen like they're buddies or something

Marc Brown might need our help! Homeboy is a legend!

Haha

Or lol we could just hang out in a normal way

I know I messed up and I'm probably annoying you now, but I wanted to send you one more message and then I'll leave you alone for good. I promise. On that Saturday I wasn't even that busy. I was legit just sitting around with my friends. But then when Ryan texted, I didn't want to show up right away because I didn't want you to think I was just waiting around for you to call. EVEN THOUGH I WAS TOTALLY WAITING AROUND FOR YOU TO CALL!

I was playing games and it was stupid and I hope I didn't completely destroy this between us because I think you're really awesome and I really wanted to get to know you more.

Want not wanted!!

Stupid

I was talking to my voice to text app not you!!!!!

Oh man I'm going to see myself out now.

I won't bother you again Delilah

Thank you for apologizing. You should probably apologize to your app too. It's doing its best.

Hi! Yes! You're so right I need to appreciate her services

Why do you assume the app is a girl?

Ah! You're right! I don't know!! It's like the patriarchy or something and I need to let that shit go because I'm a

feminist. We should all be feminists like
that book title and yeah god is a woman!

...

Am I making you regret responding yet?

Not yet
So when you use all these exclamation marks, are you
saying exclamation mark?

I am. That's a great visual isn't it

For real though thank you for responding. The offer
still stands to leave you alone if you want me to

I was really . . . sad. But I think I'm over it. Or at least I get
what happened
Friends don't need to play games

I'm so sorry I made you feel that way!
And I do want to see you again if you're down
Are you free this weekend?

Yeah maybe Saturday morning?
I can bring my sister if you want to do a group hang
I need to get to know the famous Yobani

Okay yeah a group hang

That's totally cool

And I'll shut up about this if it's totally

stale now but it's actually a holiday

Oh yeah?

Yeah! Free comic book day

Sounds good!

FREE COMIC BOOK DAY

REGGIE

When I open the front door, Yobani is standing there in a black short-sleeved turtleneck.

"I think I could be a turtleneck person," he says with complete sincerity before I have a chance to roast him. "It goes with the rings."

He holds up his hands that have been shamelessly decked out with rings for months now. And I have to admit . . . I've come around to them. Luckily he changed his mind about the nose ring, though.

"I think you need a pendant next," I say. "Maybe a statement piece? A tiefling bust in honor of Trickery?"

"I'm gonna talk to my jewelry guy," he says, nodding his head vigorously. If he knows I'm messing with him, he's not letting on.

"Come on." I wave him in. "Greg's not here yet."

"Well, he better get here soon. I'm not trying to be last in line and miss out on all the gold comics."

"Bro, chill. We'll be fine."

Yobani follows me into the kitchen, where I grab a ginger ale from the fridge. My grandma Lenore swears ginger ale is the cure to any and all ailments—colds, nausea, probably even heart attacks. I don't know about all that, but I do think it'll do something about my stomach. Like, seriously, it's felt like I'm riding Supreme Scream at Knott's Berry Farm for hours now, all because I'm so fucking terrified about seeing Delilah again. She's giving me another chance, and it's for sure my last one. What if I totally screw it up? What if she—

"Actually," Yobani says, cutting through my worst-case-scenario brain loop. "I'm glad Greg's not here yet, because we gotta talk some more about this Darren Lumb offer. I know Gruly's all kumbaya-I-accept-your-feelings, but I'm going to keep telling it to you straight. You're making a terrible mistake!"

And oh yeah. That's making my stomach extra wavy too.

What started as a six-word response to Darren's comment turned into a long-ass email from him offering to have me on *Role With It* as a onetime guest or as a regular player at their virtual table, whatever I wanted. And I know I should be really fucking excited. I should have sent him a big, all-caps YES immediately because this is a huge opportunity in the world of D&D and table-top games. Darren's show is a legend and this would really get my name out there.

But the problem is . . . I don't want my name out there. Having my name out there is actually my worst nightmare.

"It's just not what I want. The recognition, I mean," I say now to Yobani, repeating what I already told him the fifty-leven times we've already gone over this. "It's enough that so many people read and respond to my pieces. I don't need them to, like, know who I am."

"Um, said no one ever." Yobani rolls his eyes and grabs his own ginger ale from the fridge.

"Says me," I say. As if that's really it.

But it's not just that I don't need the recognition—which for the record, I *really* don't. It's also that it's scary as hell to be a Black person online. I don't want my trolls to know my real name, where I live. I don't need them to be able to harass me more effectively. I've got plenty of people in my real life that do that already. And oh man, what if those people—Eric, Tyrell!—got wind of exactly how deep I am in this nerdy shit. Right now they think I just play once a week and read some books with dragons on the cover. They'd never let it go if I was doing YouTube videos and podcasts with my real face and name online. Like for real, at my funeral someday, Eric would still be talking about, "Here lies Reggie, the dorkiest Oreo that ever lived."

I can't.

"Anyway, I can't even think about this right now," I say, internally crossing my fingers that he'll let this go. "We're about to see Delilah and I feel like I'm about to throw up, poop my pants, and let out the loudest burp of my entire existence—all at the same time."

"Well, first, I want to see that," Yobani says. "And second . . . yeah, I can see why you're nervous. Hopefully you don't screw it up. I'm really surprised she's letting you go to bat again."

"Hey! It's your fault that I'm here in the first place."

"You listened to me." He shrugs. "Also you send corny-ass texts."

"What's this you're saying about my son being corny?" my dad asks, strutting into the kitchen.

"It's nothing," I say, at the same time Yobani shouts, "He needs help!"

Dad chuckles as he grabs a beer from the fridge and shakes his head. His laugh is just like mine—a hiss that always starts at the roof of his mouth and ends in his nose. It's pretty much the only thing we have in common.

Highlighting just that, he nods his head toward the living room and asks, "You guys want to join Eric and me for the game? It's Dodgers versus Angels."

It takes me a couple extra seconds to process those team names, his red hat and jersey. Baseball. He's talking about a baseball game.

"Can't. Sorry," I say, even though I'm not at all. "We're meeting some friends over at Story Sanctorum."

He squints like he always does when my interests are brought up, as if he thinks that looking at me differently will change me into the son he was expecting—the kind that runs marathons, watches baseball. "Why don't you invite them over here?" he presses. "The Story, uh—whatever you just said will still be there tomorrow. The Freeway Series only happens once a year!"

Why don't you just be normal for today? That's what I hear, what I know he's really trying to say. God, I'd be getting the squinty-eyed stare of the century if he saw me on *Role With It*.

"Thanks for the invite, Mr. Hubbard," Yobani says. "But it's Free Comic Book Day. Basically the most important day of the year after Christmas. And my birthday."

"All right, all right," Dad says, waving his hand, like *your loss*. He starts to head out, but then stops, eyeing Yobani. "Boy, what you got on?"

Yobani waggles his eyebrows, all confident. I don't know where he gets it from. "It's a new look I'm trying out. I'm going to add a pendant next." He traces on his chest where that totally-a-joke, not-at-all-serious pendant I suggested is going to go.

Dad presses his lips together, taking it all in. Finally he laughs and shakes his head. "Well, go on then." He grabs a bag of Doritos on his way out.

Yobani starts shimmying his hips and snapping his fingers, singing, "Mr. Hubbard approved!" in a disturbingly high-pitched voice.

"That's not what that was!" I call over my shoulder as I head toward the door, Yobani following behind.

DELILAH

"Wow, that was actually pretty good."

I'm not even plugged into the amp, so I should have heard Georgia walk in. But her voice makes me jump and drop my pick.

"Thanks," I mumble, embarrassed that I've been caught. Not that I'm doing anything wrong, but I'm just not at the point where I want to be playing for anyone.

"What song was that?" she asks, bouncing down on her bed. "It sounds familiar."

In the past month, I've mastered not only "Mary Had a Little Lamb," but the whole nursery rhyme canon, and I've even got "Oh Bondage Up Yours!" (or at least the opening chords) down pretty well. But that was . . . something else. I was just playing around, seeing what sounded good.

"Oh, it's nothing." I carry Mabel over to my bed, where the case is sitting. Before I snap it closed, I brush my fingers against the little pictures of my two patron saints of music, Poly Styrene and

Taylor Swift, that I've pinned into the golden lining. I put them there so that maybe Mabel could absorb their energy. But honestly, it's me that needs their vibes, today especially.

"Don't put that away for me! I like hearing you play. I wish you would let me go to a show already," Georgia says. Her face shifts into a smirk and she falls back on her comforter. "Hey, let's cancel our plans and we can stay like this all day. Do you know 'The Hills Are Alive'? Maybe I can talk Mrs. Horowitz into a punk rock Maria!"

I fix her with a look. "You're seriously trying to bail on me? We're supposed to be there in less than an hour."

"Chill, I was just playing." She raises her eyebrows. "Unless . . . ?"

"No. No unless. You said you would go with me, and I can't—*didn't* ask anyone else." I swallow the tight feeling in my throat. "It's important."

When Reggie apologized to me—that real, honest apology—I knew I wanted to see him again. I guess I wanted to see him again even *before* he apologized the second time, but I couldn't show him that. Not without looking stupid. And desperate. So I kept my distance, threw myself into the band and my still secret guitar lessons, until he made it clear through his texts that he really was the good guy I thought he was. That he'd made a mistake but was willing to take responsibility for it.

I didn't want him to think I was expecting anything . . . romantic, though. Not when his friend-zoning of me was so clear. I suggested a friend hang to show him that I was totally cool with that. Because that's me: an independent girl who can be friends with boys without seeking out their approval in order to determine self-worth and/or immediately trying to date them. Totally me.

Except the problem is, I don't really have any friends I could bring to a friend hang, other than people that would make it incredibly awkward (the band) or people that are already Reggie's friends (Ryan). So I had to ask, or really beg and bribe, Georgia.

"Who is this guy, anyway? Like, is he really worth taking on the full Dad and Sandra show all by yourself? I would almost feel guilty . . . if I wasn't fucking elated."

I told Georgia I would cover for her with Dad and Mom, vouch for emergency theater rehearsals that just coincidentally happen to be when we're expected over there, so she doesn't have to see him. I hate going too, but I'm better at getting through it without an inevitable blowup.

"Not for the foreseeable future," I clarify. "You get three excuses. Use them wisely. And Reggie . . . he's a friend."

"Is he in a band?" Georgia asks, narrowing his eyes.

"Do you think we'd be going to a comic book store if he was in a band?"

"I don't know. People contain multitudes." She shrugs. "Not gonna lie, though, D. That's a relief! You don't need to be dating one of these band dudes. They're bad news. Like, really, scroll through the IGs of any musician's wife! They all have sad eyes! God, I'm so, SO glad you're not mooning over Charlie anymore."

I want to address so many things she just said that I don't even know where to begin.

"Sad eyes?" I ask, finally.

"Yep." She nods like that's a perfectly reasonable generalization. "Anyway, from what I just heard when I walked in here, you might not even need that douche in your band anymore. You can break out on your own! Your new boyfriend better get ready to groupie the shit out of you and treat you like the rock goddess you are."

"Are you kidding me? On my own?" The very thought makes my heart race in panic. "I don't know what I'm doing. I'm not—I *couldn't*. I wouldn't even be here without them."

"You could be anywhere you want to be," Georgia says. And I believe that *she* believes that. But she doesn't understand how this all works, how little I actually know how to do. Just because I can play a few chords now and hold a guitar right doesn't mean I can start a whole band of my own or make my own music. That takes someone really special . . . and I don't know if I'll ever have that.

"And hey, you're not even going to address the second thing I—"

"No comment." I cut her off. "Actually, yes. Yes comment! Like I said, Reggie and I are just friends."

"Because we're both done with dating, *remember*?"

"Of course I remember, Georgia." And even if I didn't, I'm almost certain Reggie's not interested in dating me anyway.

She crosses her arms and looks me up and down. "Hmm."

"Just friends," I repeat. "So can *you* please remember that when we see them?"

"Yeah, sure. Whatever," she says, very unconvincingly. And I question whether I've made a horrible string of decisions that I'm going to regret very shortly.

But when we're walking up the sidewalk to Story Sanctorum, purple jacaranda flowers falling from the trees like SoCal snow, I know with certainty that's not true. I see Reggie talking with his friends, his nose wrinkling as he laughs at a joke. I feel his warm rumbly laugh in my chest, and my stomach goes all fluttery in anticipation of what we'll talk about. I know that bribing Georgia and dealing with her wild-card behavior is worth it to be here right now, feeling like this.

"Friends, huh?" she whispers to me. I can hear the satisfied smirk she's giving me in her voice.

She pokes my cheek, and I realize just how big I'm smiling.

REGGIE

"There goes your girl, Reg," Yobani says, nodding from our place in line.

"Well, technically she's not Reggie's girl because—"

Yobani and I both cut Greg off. "Shut up, Gruly."

"And, Yo, you too," I add, bumping his shoulder with mine.

Of course I've already seen Delilah. My eyes zeroed in on her as soon as she stepped off the bus and started walking toward Story Sanctorum from the stop. But I've been trying to play it cool, acting like I'm absorbed in a conversation and Yobani's jokes about the new Star Wars movie were actually funny. And now she's close, so close that she could possibly hear my friends' cringey comments about her, resulting in my eternal embarrassment. And also close enough that I can see her smiling.

It's not the slight upturn of her lips that I'm used to seeing. I mean, don't get me wrong, I'd be happy to get one of those, because she dishes them out so sparingly, like a teacher trying to make a large cheese pizza last for a class party. But no—this smile is a whole pie with pepperoni and sausage, plus a two-liter of Sprite and a family-size bag of Cool Ranch Doritos, all for me. It lights up her whole face and seems to make the sun shine just a little bit brighter.

I'm determined to get it right this time. I'm determined to be exactly who I need to be, so I can get this smile all the time.

"Hey!" I call when she's right there and I won't look like a total stalker for acknowledging her.

"Hi," Delilah says. The smile has turned down a few notches, but its effects are still lingering in my brain and body.

"Um, okay, well, I'm Georgia." The girl next to her steps forward and waves dramatically, and I realize we've just been standing there batting our eyes at each other, like two kindergartners that haven't yet learned what to do next. "I'm this one's sister, along for the ride today. Happy Free Comic Book Day to all who celebrate!"

This girl's got wild auburn curls and a face full of freckles, but they have the same wide noses and long lashes framing their dark brown eyes. Georgia narrows her at me, looking me up and down.

"Are you Reggie?" she asks, and Delilah knocks into her. She mumbles, "Sorry," trying to play it off as an accident even though it definitely wasn't. So that means she's been talking to her sister about me.

"Yeah, I'm Reggie," I say, going in for a handshake. "Nice to meet you, Georgia."

"Yes, it's so nice to meet Delilah's *friends*," she says, earning lethal side-eye from Delilah this time. Okay, so that means she's been talking to her sister about me *being her friend*. Great.

Everyone goes around and introduces themselves, but I can't even focus, because Delilah really was friend-zoning me in those texts. I tried to convince myself that I was just overanalyzing and assuming the worst, but this goes to show that there is no such thing as overanalyzing and the worst is PROBABLY WHAT IS HAPPENING.

". . . like, really into comics?" I catch the end of Georgia's question, and I realize I need to stop the spiral and pay attention. This isn't over. I can still fix this.

"Yes," Greg replies. "But I'd say we're more equal-opportunity nerds. Comics are just one of our many passions."

"They also play D&D. Reggie is the DM," Delilah adds. Georgia raises an eyebrow like her sister just said we twerk on the moon.

"Is that like BDSM?" she asks.

"No! Oh my god, no." I've never been more grateful that my cheeks don't show a blush, because I can feel my face flaming.

"Hey, speak for yourself," Yobani says, smirking.

"He is *kidding*! Yobani, tell her you're kidding." But instead of listening to directions, he shrugs.

Greg and Delilah are both cracking up, and Georgia's eyes are lit up with confusion but also delight. "So this is a sex thing or . . . ?"

"Not! It's not!" And I need to be quieter, because the two guys in front of us holding hands and wearing matching Green Lantern shirts are turning around to stare. "D&D stands for Dungeons & Dragons. And the DM is the Dungeon Master . . . though saying that out loud, I can see how that could totally still be a sex thing."

Seriously, my cheeks are about to spontaneously combust.

"It's actually really cool, G," Delilah says. "I thought it was, I don't know . . . guys dressing up and pretending to be wizards in the park? But it's really creative. It's more like storytelling. Reggie comes up with these epic, uh, adventures for them to play every week."

She described it perfectly. She sounds impressed, which is very much not friend-like . . . right?

"You should come play with us," Greg says, nodding to the two of them. "Reggie doesn't always follow the rules." Yobani rolls his eyes so aggressively that I'm surprised they don't pop out of his head. "But yeah, he makes it really fun. We're playing tonight if you want to drop by."

I'm grateful for the rare compliment from Greg, but oh no. I definitely don't want that. Delilah does not need to pay attention to the man behind the curtain. Plus, we're playing at my house tonight because Leela's parents are having a party. I'm on the right track with Delilah now, but it will be hard to keep it going if Eric pulls up with his friends again and totally roasts me.

"He could do more than just play with us too," Yobani adds, raising his eyebrows at me meaningfully. "If he would take the risk."

Dude, why are my friends so determined to, like, tragically blow up my spot today?

Delilah looks at me, her lips twisted and brow furrowed in a question, but then the line starts moving. Praise be to Dwayne

McDuffie and Stan Lee and all the comic gods.

As we get closer to the front, Greg turns to Yobani. "Remember the game plan." Yobani nods and they look so intense that I'm surprised they don't bump chests and start chanting. This may be the one time per year when they put all their petty shit aside in the interest of one common goal: free comics.

Georgia smiles at them, curiously. "Oh, so is this like a limited-quantity thing? Just say the word and I'll take out the competition."

"Please. Join us," Yobani says, waving her into their huddle. They start talking strategy, whispering so no one else can steal their plan, leaving me and Delilah to trail behind.

"So, I'm really happy you could make it," I start. "And I'm just so sorry again."

She holds her hand up. "You don't have to apologize any more. We're good. And I'm happy I'm here too."

She smiles again—the full-face, real one—and I feel like I've jumped into a sparkling pool in the late afternoon, after it's been warmed all day by the sunshine.

When we get to the front, Eduardo, Yobani's brother, is standing at the door like a bouncer. "Welcome to Free Comic Book Day!" he says, and someone behind us legit cheers. "The featured comics are laid out in the middle of the shop." He gestures to several folding tables covered in stacks. "The limit's one of each, and please only take what you're going to read so there's enough for everyone."

Yobani snorts out a laugh, and Greg shakes his head. I know for sure they're planning on grabbing one of everything, even if they'd never be interested in it otherwise—and have probably enlisted Georgia to do the same, judging by how she's rubbing her hands together and eyeing the tables.

Delilah and I both go to walk through the door at the same time, pressing in close. Her hair brushes my cheek, and before I even process what I'm doing and talk myself out of being such a creeper, I breathe in deep. Her hair smells like flowers—what kind, I have no idea, but I want to pick up a whole bouquet of them so I can smell 'em all the time.

"I'm sorry," I mumble. Hopefully she thinks that's for bumping into her and not for trying to suck up all her scent with my flared nostrils.

"It's fine."

Normally I'm all laser focused, making sure I carefully consider each comic and get the ones I want, but standing at the tables with Delilah, I can barely pay attention to the special edition *Avengers* or the new horror series from Dark Horse. All I want to do is grab her hand and take her to a quiet corner of the store to confess my feelings and plant a kiss on her perfect lips. But of course I can't do that without her rightfully alerting the authorities, so instead I gesture over to one of the shelves. "Do you want me to show you around?"

"Yeah, let's do it."

I lead her over to one of my favorite sections, full of individual issues and trades from Milestone Comics, an old imprint started by a bunch of Black creators in the nineties. Everyone is feasting over the free issues, so it's just the two of us.

"Oh my god." She covers her mouth, holding in giggles. "Did

you see that guy in the green shirt take two copies of that one thing? I thought Yobani was going to shoot lasers out of his eyes."

"No! What? I totally missed that." *Because all I can pay attention to is you.*

"Yeah, I'm actually a little worried for him."

"That is a valid concern. Yo never forgets and always gets his revenge. Like, there was this one teacher at our middle school that always used to say his name wrong. The guy loved Marvel movies, had a Captain America poster in his class and everything. So Yobani created all these anonymous email accounts and sent him the spoilers to every Marvel movie on release day mornings. I'm pretty sure he still keeps it up."

"That is so . . . committed?"

"It's something," I say, laughing and shaking my head. "He's a good friend to have on your side, that's for sure."

"I bet." She turns to look at the covers, leaning in to study an early copy of *Static Shock,* wrapped in plastic. "Do you read these?"

"Yeah, they're actually what got me started on comics real young." I pick up a trade off the shelf. "Well, you know, I always struggled with reading. It took a bit for me to get diagnosed, actually—my parents kept thinking I would pick it up if I just tried hard enough, read more. But I wasn't interested . . . it's hard to want to sit there and read when the words just don't look right, you know what I'm saying?"

She nods. "That must have been so frustrating."

"Oh yeah. So, my dad picked up a stack of these old comics from a garage sale. Comics aren't his thing—like, *at all*—but he was just trying to find anything to help me. And I mean, they sucked me right in, because of the pictures. I even tried to decipher all the words because I had to know what was happening. I read every issue he had bought, and then he went online, trying to find more. I have all these trades at home." I run my fingers along the spines of the huge volumes. "Of course, it didn't, like, get rid of my dyslexia. That's never going to happen. But it was the first time stories felt accessible to me, instead of just something that I would never figure out. Does that make sense?"

I hadn't thought about how these comics connected me and my dad in a while. I wonder if he even remembers that, of all people, *he* handed me my nerdy gateway drug. It seems so far away . . . especially now that our most common interactions are him trying to get me to do anything else.

"That makes total sense," Delilah says. "And now you create stories of your own."

I look down, trying to temper the huge smile taking up my cheeks. "Well, I don't know about that."

"You do!" She pushes my shoulder. It could be a total, playful friend move, but also it could be something else. "And, hey, what was Yobani saying earlier, when we were outside? About taking a risk?"

My stomach dips in dread. This is the last thing I want to talk about, and I internally wish a million paper cuts on Yobani today for bringing it up in front of her.

"It's no big deal," I say, not looking her in the eye. "There's this show, *Role With It*. It's kind of popular in the tabletop scene, like a podcast and YouTube thing. And the host reads my essays, I guess, and invited me on to play."

"What!" Delilah shouts. She does this little happy bounce with her eyes all lit up. It's the cutest thing ever. "That's so cool! When can I listen?"

"Well, I don't think I'm going to actually do it . . ."

Her eyebrows pinch together. "Why not?"

"I don't know, it's just like . . . it's hard enough being an *anonymous* Black person in this space, right? Half the people don't want me here—more than half. Once they know my real name, what I look like, it's going to take their trolling to a whole 'nother level. They're going to come for me so much harder! And the people that do like what I have to say, they expect me to be perfect, to speak for all Black people that like D&D. So what's going to happen if I mess up and don't speak for us all perfectly? It's just . . . a lot."

I'm being honest. More honest than I've been with anyone, even my friends. But as I'm talking, I see the side of her mouth start to tilt downward, that subtle slip into a frown. This isn't what she wants or what she's come to expect from me. I let myself slip.

DELILAH

What Reggie is saying, I totally get it. Because that's how I feel right now when I start thinking about making my own songs or even calling myself a musician. It's so scary to navigate it all, which is why it's felt safer to defer to and hang behind the guys. I always have my excuse that this is just for fun, a long and drawn-out favor I'm doing for my friends. I don't have to actually put my full self on display.

But Reggie isn't like me. He does what he wants, likes what he likes. And I guess it gave me hope, you know? Like maybe I deserved to do that too. If *he's* scared, though . . .

"That was my first instinct," he says, flashing me a big grin. "But I mean, I had to push past the fear, right? I can't let what other people might think stop me from doing something that I'd really enjoy, so I told Darren—that's the guy who runs the whole thing—that I'm in. It's probably going to take a while to get going with all of it, but it's happening. I just, like, haven't had a chance to tell Yobani yet."

"Oh wow. Okay!" I laugh, relieved. He's exactly who I thought he was.

So I decide to take a risk of my own.

"You know, you really are incredible."

His eyes go wide, almost like he's seen something scary, but then he smiles and pushes up his glasses at the bridge, the embodiment of "Aww, shucks." It's the cutest thing ever.

"Well, thank you, Delilah," he says. "I think you're pretty incredible, too."

I think I'm making an "Aww, shucks" face of my own now.

"So what should I read here?" I ask, and reach up to grab a book with a Black guy in red latex and a green cape. Reggie's reaching up at the same time, and my callused fingers brush against the smooth brown skin on the back of his hand. It makes my whole body feel electric, like I just stuck my finger in a socket. But in a good way. And I find myself lingering longer than I need to. I think how it might feel to flip his soft hand over and rub my fingers across his palm. But then I pull back, remembering myself, remembering we're just friends. He's made that so clear.

Except he's not looking at me the way a friend would.

Also, I'm pretty sure he was smelling my hair when we walked into the store earlier.

My phone beeps, interrupting . . . whatever this moment is. And then it beeps twice more, one after the other. I look at the screen and see Charlie's name, and I don't want to answer it. I want to stand here and breathe in the smell of comic books and Reggie's laundry-detergent-and-cocoa-butter scent (because okay, I was smelling him too). I want to brush my fingers against his again and try to figure out if he's doing it on purpose. But then Charlie texts again. And again.

Delilah omg you gotta get over here!!!!!!!

We are blowing up

A tiktok of you performing is EVERYWHERE

Like everywhere

THIS IS NOT A DRILL

"Everything okay?" Reggie asks. His face looks concerned. I wonder if he saw Charlie's name on my screen. We're standing so close that it would be hard for him not to.

"Yeah, I think. Um, let me see." I swipe over to the band's TikTok account on my phone. I keep it logged in but the notifications off because I find even the few we get a day too overwhelming. And . . . whoa. What's coming in now is a lot more than a few. It's a few multiplied by a few thousand.

"I— What," I sputter out. "I don't know what's going on."

Reggie raises his eyebrows, leaning in closer to look at my screen. "Well, that looks like a video of you and . . . Oh my god."

We both watch the like count and comments change, speeding like the numbers on a slot machine. I'm still trying to catch up and process what exactly is happening.

It's a video of me from a set that we played at The Mode a week ago. I'm wearing ripped Levis and my checkerboard Vans, and I threw off the flannel I was wearing over my white tank top at the last second because it was so stuffy in there. I'm singing the chorus of "Starshine Monologue," throwing my hands up with every yelp. At the end of the video, I kick my leg backward and swing my head to the left. The caption: THIS BLACK GIRL ROCKS.

I rarely watch videos of our shows because it's hard to reconcile that girl on stage with who I feel like I am inside the rest of the time. It's just hard for me to compute because something isn't quite right, like the feeling you get when you watch a really legit Pixar movie or robots that are almost human. That's me, but also not me?

I know I was at that show. I know I sang so hard that my throat hurt the entire next day and I bounced and spun all over the stage and scraped my ankle on Beau's bass drum. But to see it on video? That girl looks—*I* look—really, really cool. And from these numbers, it seems like other people, *a lot* of other people, think so too.

That caption, though . . . I'm not sure how I feel about it. If I were a white girl, would they feel the need to point that out? If I were white, would my performance even be remarkable enough for people to care?

But no. I can't even start to process all of that now.

"I knew this would happen," Reggie says. "Girl, you famous!"

Another text pops up on my screen.

Get over here you gorgeous girl! We gotta celebrate!!!!

I swipe it away, but I know Reggie read it or a least got the gist. I can tell from the slump of his shoulders and the step back he just took.

And I know Charlie's just being Charlie. The flirting doesn't mean anything to him, for sure, and not to me anymore either. But how do I explain that to Reggie without coming across as a total presumptuous egomaniac? He didn't say he likes me like that. He just lightly touched my hand, maybe on accident.

"Looks like you need to see your band and figure out what's up," he says. He sounds . . . colder. Again, though, that could all be in my head. Until this little mini-moment in between the comic book shelves, I was pretty certain I was being friend-zoned.

"I guess so." I see more texts popping up on my phone from Charlie, Alex, and Beau, too. I stick it in my back pocket. "But that was really fun."

"Yeah?" He beams, his nose wrinkling.

"Yeah." I nod over to Georgia, whose arms are full of comics I'm pretty sure she has no interest in reading. Greg is saying something to her about the book on the top of the stack, and Yobani is eyeing the double comic guy menacingly. "Looks like everyone clicked."

"They did, didn't they? We should hang out again soon."

I want to know who that "we" includes. "We" as in me and him? Or "we" as in all of us? But there's no time right now to shake his shoulders and demand clarification.

"Yeah, for sure," I say, with a smile. And then I go off to find Georgia so I can meet up with the guys and find out what is going on.

REGGIE

I get in line to buy a trade of *Icon* that I know I'm missing, and my mind starts racking up all the Delilah wins from this afternoon.

1. She told her sister about me.

2. She listened to me talk about comic books without her eyes glazing over—and about my dyslexia without acting all weird and sympathetic like it's some fatal disease.

3. She called me incredible. And, like, it doesn't even matter what little untruth I told her before that because . . .

4. When our fingers touched there was a spark! Again! Like, a sign from the universe or our holiday love guides or whatever, who *obviously* want us to be together and *obviously* realize that Free Comic Book Day is the holiest of holidays.

5. Also I'm pretty sure I caught her taking a big whiff of me. Because I smell good or because something stank and she was trying to find the source? TBD. But still!

Sure, she got a text from that stubble dude from her band,

calling her "gorgeous." But I mean, she said she's not dating him so many times now, and I believe her.

I think—I *hope*—this all means that Delilah might like me, too. Or that she's at least on her way there! Just the thought of that makes my whole body feel like it's full of helium and I'm about to float up to the sky like a freed birthday balloon.

"So, it seems like congratulations are in order." Yobani slides in next to me. Greg's right behind him. "Yeah, I'm really glad you changed your mind, Reg. It's too big of an opportunity to let pass you by."

"Are you— Wait . . . I'm confused. Is this about Delilah? Because I still think it's a little too early for congrats."

"No!" Yobani slaps my arm like I'm messing with him.

"I mean, that is great if you've made progress with her, though. We know that's important to—"

"What's *important* is that Reggie finally came to his senses and told motherfucking Darren Lumb that he is going to be on *Role With It!*"

The guy in front of us with a bushy beard and a "Magneto Was Right" shirt turns around and smiles. "Oh, I love that show."

"Of course you do! And my buddy Reggie here is about to rock it—"

"Arghhh!" My brain's rushing to catch up with what's happening. All I know is Yobani needs to not finish that sentence out loud to some random guy in *RWI*'s very devoted fanbase. Thankfully my strangled scream seems to freak out the bearded eavesdropper enough to make him put his palms up and turn around.

Yobani whips around to look at me. "Dude, what the—"

"I'm not doing the show," I whisper.

"What was that?" Greg asks, leaning in.

"I'm not doing the show," I repeat, probably even quieter.

"WHAT DO YOU MEAN YOU'RE NOT DOING THE SHOW?!" Yobani shouts, not getting the very clear message about volume. The *RWI* fanboy is definitely listening in, so I get out of line and the guys follow me over to the corner where all the Archie Comics are displayed.

"How did you—I mean . . . *why* do you even think that?" I ask. "Like, I don't get it. I told you it was out of the question."

"Because I heard you bragging about it to your girl!" Yobani says, all exasperated.

"You were spying on us?"

"No, I wasn't spying on you." Yobani rolls his eyes. "I was going to find Eddie to tell him about that dude taking extra copies so I could get him, like, banned from Free Comic Book Day forever. And I just happened to be on the other side of the shelf when you were monologuing about pushing past your fear or some shit."

"You were trying to snitch?" I ask, hoping a distraction will do the trick.

But Yobani waves that off. "The snitching rules don't apply when it comes to Free Comic Book Day. You know that, bro."

"It's true," Greg chimes in.

"So, anyway, I heard what you told Delilah, and I was so glad that you came around. But now I'm real confused as to why you're saying all this isn't happening. Why did you tell her you were taking Darren's offer if you're . . . not?"

Yobani and Greg both cross their arms and stare me down. I'm caught.

"I just wanted her . . ."

How do I explain this without sounding like a total loser?

"I wanted her to think I was . . . I don't know, cool. And, like, secure in who I am. I didn't want her to know how scared I am of being, like, out there with my interests and my opinions. Because I am scared, you know? If I'm on *Role With It*, everyone is going to know who I am. My trolls . . . my brother and his friends, you know what I'm saying?"

Yobani nods and twists his lips to the side. I know he gets it, even if he would probably take the jump anyway.

"But what about getting past this fear? Like you told her?" Greg asks.

"I want to do that . . . but I don't think I actually can."

We're all quiet for a bit—me because I'm embarrassed, and them . . . I'm not sure what they're thinking about me.

Finally, Yobani breaks the silence. "Sounds like a game to me," he says with a smirk.

"Yeah, whatever," I laugh, grateful he's making fun of me. I'd rather have that normalcy than us being all in our feelings. "It's not like that. I'm done with the games."

And I mean, what I'm doing with Delilah is sort of a game. But not in the same way keeping my interest vague or standing her up was.

I'm just trying to be the person I wish I was with her, my ideal self. The Reggie who doesn't give a fuck and is authentic all the time, no matter the audience. And I don't know—maybe if I keep doing this for her, keep pretending I'm this person, I'll actually transform into him.

JUST A NORMAL FRIDAY IN MAY
DELILAH

I've been coming to The Mode with the guys since I met them last fall. I've seen everything from big punk acts just past their prime passing through, to experimental folk duos with fiddles and nails-on-a-chalkboard voices. It didn't even really seem to matter what the music was, if the guys liked it or not. Being a part of the crowd, a part of this group collectively experiencing something, was the point. Tonight's crowd is, by far, the biggest one I've ever seen.

And they're all here to see Fun Gi.

I didn't let myself assume at first or get my hopes up. It was completely possible that they were here to watch Undead Jupiter or the Orange Bananas, the two bands that opened for us. But the crowd only swelled after each of their sets, and now that we're about to go on, the audience is so big that Jimmy is surely looking the other way on a fire code or two.

"Let's do this!" Charlie shouts, a giddy smile on his face. He steps out on the stage with his head held high, like it's always been like this—or at least, he's always expected it to be. Cheers erupt from the crowd, and Asher bounds out after him. Beau gives my arm a reassuring squeeze and follows. They're all excitement, no nerves. But I guess they've stayed that way through all of this: accepting the attention, blossoming in the sunshine of it—instead of feeling like an ant under a magnifying glass, like I do.

It's all because of the video. After I left the comic book store, I went over to Charlie's and the four of us completed a social media investigation, all the while swiping away the constant notifications. It started with a post on TikTok from someone that was in the audience, and then there were the stitches and duets, followed by reposts on Instagram. It even popped up on Twitter and Facebook, the old people watering holes, so my mom caught wind of it too. Andre let it slip that she even showed it to the other teachers at their faculty meeting, telling everyone who would listen that her Lilah-girl was famous.

I already had my personal accounts that I use to look at memes locked down, thankfully, so no one found me. But the band's socials blew up. Spotify streams, TikTok followers, Instagram likes . . . all the numbers are higher than I even know how to process. It's slowed down from the chaos of that first day, but we're starting to see those numbers translate to real life. Like this crowd.

Oh my god, this crowd. Just looking at all these people from backstage is making my heartbeat speed up double time and my head spin. But it's not a migraine this time. Only anxiety and imposter syndrome, which are honestly almost as bad.

I glance back at the band, and Charlie is looking at me funny and jerking his head to the side. I need to get my butt in gear already.

I walk up on stage, slow and steady, and the sound of the audience is overwhelming—definitely two times what they gave the guys. And the loudest voices of all are coming from the very front, where Georgia, Leela, and Ryan are standing. Georgia is howling and twirling her hands in the air. She promised she wouldn't be conspicuous when I finally told her she could come to a show, but we both knew she had no intentions of keeping that promise. And now I'm grateful for her presence, even as she begins to chant "DE-LI-LAH!" like she's at some sports thing. I laugh, and calm spreads through my body. I've got this. These people are here because they already like us. And that's probably the very best crowd to play for.

I step up to the mic, pull the stand close. "Hi, we're Fun Gi." They scream, and I smile wide. "We're gonna start with a song you might know. It's called 'Parallelograms.'"

Beau plays the steady beat on the bass drum that starts the song, and I take down the mic so I can dance along. But a loud voice in the audience makes me stop short.

"OH, THIS IS THE BAND WITH THE BLACK ONE!"

I zero in on a white guy in a Vampire Weekend shirt in the front. His friends next to him shush and shove him, but then they explode into laughter.

"WHAT?!" the guy shouts. His eyes are red and droopy—the kind of droopy that makes it clear he has no idea how loud he's being. Somehow in his haze, he sees me looking at him, and he just shrugs.

That's when I notice the music's stopped. I turn to see that everyone in the band is staring at me—Beau with concern and Asher and Charlie with thinly masked irritation. I missed my cue. And I must have been so late, so lost, that they couldn't even keep going and play it off.

My whole body feels like it's on fire, and from the way Charlie is glaring at me now, as I continue to draw this out even longer, I wouldn't be surprised if there actually were flames appearing at my feet.

I look back to the crowd and this time all I see Georgia. Her hands are clutched together, and she's mouthing something. The third time she says it, it clicks: "You got this, sissy."

And somehow, that's enough. I believe it.

I laugh into the mic. It sounds fake to me, but they won't be able to tell. "Sorry about that! Just got distracted by all your beautiful faces."

People—lots of people, more than just my sister and friends!—laugh, too. And from somewhere in the back, a husky voice calls out, "WE LOVE YOU, FUN GI!" They're right there with me.

Beau starts "Parallelograms" again and I'm ready this time. I hit every note, twirl and scream and howl and kick, and give this crowd the show they came for. And when it's over, I'm dripping sweat and breathing heavy and my legs feel like Jell-O, but I know with certainty that was the best set I've ever had.

I look into the crowd to see what that guy thinks now, but he's already gone. I do see my sister though, and she's bowing down to me, even being so dramatic as to try to get down to the floor. But

Ryan and Leela giggle and keep her up because they know just how disgusting those floors are. I blow them a kiss and follow the guys backstage.

Charlie starts in immediately.

"What happened, Delilah? Did you get, like . . . stage fright?"

"It was fine," Beau says, wiping his face with the hem of his ripped Minutemen shirt. "She recovered."

"Some guy in the front said something. About me being Black." My heart rate was starting to slow down after the adrenaline rush of that performance, but this is ticking it right back up.

"Like something racist?" Charlie's eyebrows press together and he steps closer to me. "That's fucked up."

"No. I don't know." I try to replay the moment in my mind, searching for something explicit and straightforward as to why it bothered me so much. Because it's not like he called me the N-word—though that's popped up in the comments online too, there for just a fleeting a moment before they're reported and erased. But it's not like that, not exactly. It's the feeling I got.

"He said something like 'This is the band with the Black one.'"

"Oh, I'm sorry, Delilah," Beau says, but Charlie just twists his lips.

Next to me, Asher sighs. "I don't know. He probably didn't even mean it like *that*. And anyway, even if he maybe did, that's his problem and you don't have to, like, let it be yours or whatever. People have said racist shit to me before, and I just ignored them. Because, like, why should I care what they think?" Then he shrugs, as if it's that easy.

Next to him, Charlie starts nodding emphatically. "Yeah. Yeah, that's right."

I want to argue that it's different. I want to argue that I'm entitled to feel however I want to. I want to remind them that I pulled it together and put on the best fucking show I ever have.

But all I do is shake my head and turn toward the door.

"Okay. I'm going to find my friends," I call behind me as I go.

"First you were like, ah! And then you were like, oh!" Georgia is up out of her seat again, reenacting my performance from earlier tonight. "And then you were like, ahh ahh ahh!" She kicks her leg up impressively high, definitely higher than I did on stage, and the bearded guy in a beanie at the table across from us looks away from his potato tacos in awe.

"It was just—ugghhhhh!" She lets out a groan that turns more heads our way. "So good! My sis is a star!"

My cheeks would usually burn red with the attention she's grabbing, but I feel all warm inside in a good way. My sister could belt out "On My Own" to an audience of hundreds at a moment's notice and still bring the house down, and here she is fangirling over me. It almost makes me forget my uneasiness about what happened before the show . . . and after.

"That really was one of the best sets I've ever seen at The Mode. Probably top ten sets ever," Ryan says. I search her eyes for a catch, a joke, but there isn't one. She really believes that. My chest swells with pride.

Leela holds up her glass bottle Coke. "Cheers to that!"

"Even after that total douchebag pulled that shit at the beginning, you still totally rocked it. You're a legend."

So Ryan noticed it too. It wasn't unremarkable to her. Or something I shouldn't make "my problem."

"That . . . that did suck, right?" I start tentatively. "I wasn't being too sensitive?"

"Not at all!" Georgia says. She slaps the table, making her carnitas tacos pop up off the checkered paper.

"Drunk ass . . ." Leela rolls her eyes and takes a big swig of Coke. "I'm glad Ryan got him kicked out."

"You did what?!" I shout, earning almost as many stares as Georgia's high kick.

Ryan smirks. "I didn't, like, single-handedly get him banned. Jimmy saw what happened, too, and escorted him out. He was really trying hard to defend himself, talking about *that wasn't his intention.*" She shakes her head. "But it doesn't matter his intention. It made you upset, and *that's* all that matters."

"I know what he said wasn't that big of a deal, I guess. In the scheme of things—"

"Nuh-uh," Leela cuts me off and wags her finger around. "We're not gonna belittle this or make excuses for him. He was being a dick."

"Yeah, 'the band with the Black one'! What was that shit?!" Georgia joins in. "He didn't announce how every other band before you was all white guys. Even though—let's talk about that!" Her body practically vibrates in anger. "How about the band with the badass lead singer that's all like, this!" She does a dramatic hair toss that I for sure did not do tonight, but I appreciate the heart behind it.

"So . . . I was right to be upset?"

"Fuck yeah!" "Of course!" "Damn right!" They all let out a chorus of affirmations, and it heals all the doubt that Asher and Charlie planted in my head. What happened felt shitty because it *was* shitty. And it feels so good to be around people who don't make me question my perceptions or ignore my gut.

"I really love you guys," I say, leaning my head on Georgia's shoulder.

"Oh, we love you too!" Ryan reaches across the table to squeeze my hand, and Georgia pulls me in close.

"Speaking of love," Leela says, a mischievous glint in her eyes, "Reggie is texting me right now. Because he loooooooooves you."

"No, he doesn't." I laugh nervously, trying to play it cool. But I have to fight every urge to reach across the table and grab her phone so I can see the texts for myself.

"Um . . . what did he say?"

Georgia throws her head back and cackles, flinging some green salsa off her chip.

"He's asking how your show went." Leela smiles. "And telling me for like the hundredth time how sorry he is he had to miss it."

He's probably texted me the same at least a hundred more times. He really wanted to be here—and I wanted him to be too, especially after all the unanswered questions I was left with on Free Comic Book Day. He was out of town this weekend, visiting family in Florida, though.

But I think *how much* he's texted me apologies for missing just one show—and the fact that he's texting his friend about it, too—gives me some of the answers to my questions. You don't do that for someone you want to be just friends with.

Leela puts her phone down on the table and claps her hands. "Okay, so can we get into it then? Do you looooove him too? When is this finally going to happen already?"

Ryan lets out an exasperated sigh. "Lee, chill. We are legit *failing* the Bechdel test right now."

"I don't even care. I love Reggie and I love Delilah and I love the two of them together. So I need answers or I'm probably going to explode. Do you want that on your hands?"

"Oh no! Definitely not!" Ryan says with a sarcastic smirk. Leela's eyes narrow at her in mock outrage, and then Ryan goes all heart-eyes back and kisses her on the cheek.

Ryan looks back at me. "Please, Delilah, save my girlfriend's life."

I'm not sure how much I want to give away. I like Reggie. As much as I've protested to everyone else, I can't deny that to myself. But do I want to tell one of his closest friends that? When she inevitably relays the message, will that freak him out?

"We're friends . . ." I start. "And I don't know, I—" I pause, trying to pick the exact right words, so it's clear how I feel. But so there's also plausible deniability, too. I don't want to come on too strong.

Before I can keep going, though, Georgia chimes in. "Well, me and Delilah have a no-dating pact."

"A pact?" Leela leans in. "Oooh, tell me more! And I promise to keep this all between us."

"I'm pretty sure I refused to call it a pact," I say, rolling my eyes at Georgia, and she rolls them right back. "Plus, didn't Ben drop you off the other day?"

"That wasn't Ben. That was Rodney."

"Who's *Rodney*?"

She waves that away, and her playful grin turns more serious. "For real though, D—I just want to say how proud of you I am for putting yourself first lately instead of getting distracted by a boy right now. I'll be honest, I didn't believe you when you said you were going to focus on falling in love with yourself after Charlie. I thought for sure you were going to jump into a thing with Reggie, but you didn't. And, like, look at you now!! It's so badass."

Any hints I was considering sending Leela's way totally evaporate. Because what can I even say after that? I feel like I've won a prize, hearing that my little sister sees me this way. But I also feel sick because I don't deserve it, not really. If it were up to me, I probably would have jumped into this thing with Reggie already. In the meantime, I've been using up a ridiculous amount of my brain space analyzing his feelings to figure out if it's a sure thing.

And do I really love myself like she thinks I do if I can't even trust my own feelings without checking with my friends? When the smallest comment from an audience member can send me spinning?

"I want to be like you," she continues. "All rah-rah, I am woman, hear me roar!" Leela and Ryan giggle. "And I mean, I really could use some pointers. Because okay, I *did* start seeing Ben again. I mean, he kisses the ground I walk on, as he should. But I think it's really starting to distract me from *The Sound of Music*. And with opening night so close . . ."

Georgia goes on talking about her Ben predicament (we're definitely scoring an F minus on the Bechdel test), but I zone out, trying to decipher all these conflicting feelings racing through my mind. I want to be with Reggie. I do. But is that going to keep me from being who I want to be—who my sister thinks I already am? If it came down to it and I had to choose: Who would win?

I don't like that this question isn't an easy one.

REGGIE

"And as issues like this continue to persist unchecked, it's no wonder that more and more BIPOC players turn to indie RPG offerings where they don't have to wonder if they're wanted—"

A knock at the door interrupts my train of thought, and I know right away it's my dad. My mom always sticks her head in uninvited when she's checking on me (which is way too often), and Eric has no interest in entering my room.

I pull an AirPod out of my ear. "Uh, yeah?"

Dad opens the door halfway and takes a tentative step in. "Just wanted to let you know that we're probably going to head out soon." His face cracks into a smile, and he gestures toward the front of the house. "Well, soon as in: your mom is doing her last check of everything packed in the car. But you know that means there's probably going to be at least one more recheck."

"So like, ten minutes?"

"Yeah, give or take a few more 'just in case' additions." He shakes his head. "I was trying to move things along, but she wasn't having any of that."

As if on cue, my mom's high voice carries in from the other room. "Winston, have you seen the extra cooler? I want to bring some more water bottles and ice just in case."

Dad holds his finger up and smirks, like *See?* and we both crack up, our identical laughs blending together.

"Well, I better get to it. Even though we're about to have enough water to send everyone at the barbecue home with a lifetime supply." He backs up toward the door. "Didn't mean to interrupt. Sounded like you were, uh, talking to somebody . . ."

I definitely can't tell him that the only "somebodies" I'm talking to are the D&D fans on the internet who might eventually read this essay I was in the middle of writing. I'm not trying to deal with the squinty-eyed stare that would earn.

"I was just getting some thoughts down," I say, hoping he won't ask any follow-up questions. I hold up my phone quickly, flashing him the screen. "You know that transcribing app that I use? It's faster for me, so I don't forget what I want to say."

He nods, crossing his arms over the grass-green polo he's wearing. "Oh yeah, that's what Ms. Thompson brought up back at your IEP meeting. I guess I've just never realized that you use it outside of school, too. That and the other one. The text-to . . . to—"

"Text-to-speech," I finish for him.

He snaps and then points at me. "Yeah, that's right. Text-to-speech. She was saying you should try not using them? To practice, right? You, uh . . . think you want to try that?"

Whatever face I make must give away how I feel about that suggestion. "*After* the summer, I mean," he corrects. "When your senior year starts."

I sigh. Do I want to get into all this right now? I know I'm not about to phase out anything—knew it as soon as Ms. Thompson introduced that idea like it was the next natural step. And I successfully brushed off her hints to go without my apps in the resource room for the rest of the semester, totally taking advantage of the fact that she's got a lot of other students to help. But I've never actually told her, or anyone, the reason why.

"Why should I give them up if they make things easier for me?" The question is out before I've fully decided if this is the right time for this conversation—or if my dad is the right person. My pits immediately start sweating, as if they've already recognized before my brain that I've made a terrible mistake.

Dad doesn't frown or squint his eyes at me, though. He leans in and claps a hand on my shoulder, which nearly knocks me over in surprise. And his words are even more surprising. "I get that. You know better than anyone what's best for you, son."

I fight the urge to pinch myself and make sure this isn't some lucid-dreaming shit. Did he really just say that? I can't remember the last time my dad didn't approach me with concern, or at the very least confusion.

If this is a dream, though, it's a good one. "Thank you." He nods once and then squeezes my shoulder.

"Winston, did you hear me?" Mom says, barging into my room and interrupting whatever father-son bonding moment was just going down. "Can you carry a couple more cases of water for me to the trunk? I'm only waiting on that, and then I'm ready to go."

"Yep." He laughs and kisses her on the cheek. "You wanna help me with that, Reggie?"

"Sure." I take out my other AirPod and go to put the case in my pocket, which makes Mom look me up and down with a raised eyebrow.

"You don't need those where we're going," she says, already shaking her head. "You can talk to your family, Reginald. You only see some of them once a year!"

And that's exactly why I *do* need my AirPods. Because the cousin I usually chill with, the only one I *like* talking to, Lenore, bailed to travel with her boyfriend this summer.

"It's just a podcast. For the car," I say.

"Mm-hmm." Mom looks me up and down. We both know I'm definitely planning to use my AirPods to dodge all the aunties and uncles I don't want to make awkward small talk with, too. "Now get a move on, you two! We're going to be late."

She swishes away, passing Eric, who takes her place in my doorway.

"You talking 'bout that dorky dragons podcast? The one about rolling?" He throws his head back, cackling.

So apparently everyone but me got the memo that my room is the new family meeting spot. And what is he talking about . . .

"You left out your laptop," he explains. "I was trying to find the senior highlights video Coach Diaz posted on YouTube, and this video of all these white guys pretending to be elves and talking all funny started playing. I didn't realize you spent, like, hours watching people sit around and play this game, too. I mean, bro!" He snorts out another laugh, making it clear what he thinks about that.

And Dad seems to be on the same page as him. The squinty-eyed look has arrived, and it's paired with a wrinkled nose, like he smells something funky. My whole body burns, and I can't tell if it's shame or anger. Probably both.

"That's enough, Eric," Dad says, his voice stern, and Eric's laughter immediately stops, like someone hit the mute button. Dad turns to me and nods to the AirPods that are still in my hand. "But you should listen to your mom, Reggie. Talk to the family."

So I guess I only know what's best for me sometimes. When I'm at school and it's not going to embarrass him in front of a crowd or reflect on him as a parent. I don't know why I'm even upset, because this isn't new.

"Now come on and help me with this water, boys." He walks out of my room, and Eric and I silently follow.

DELILAH

"Now, I thought I told you to put that phone away," my mom calls from the kitchen, fixing me with a stare that makes it clear she doesn't just *think*, she *knows*.

And I guess she has. Quite a few times. In just the past hour.

But it's hard not to be glued to my phone when there's so much happening on it, all the time.

Fun Gi is still riding the wave of that video, which is basically an eternity in social media. I thought maybe it was a fluke. That the big show at The Mode was our one shining moment before everyone moved on to some other band. And they have, for sure. But a lot of people—a lot of people with *opinions*, good and bad— have stuck around.

omg my new favorite band

delilah ur so pretty

I'm so here for this Black Girl Magic!

Did she actually confirm she was black tho??? I'm just saying . . . ☹

"Maybe she can't hear me," Mom continues, turning to Andre. "Can you hear me? AM I TALKING LOUD ENOUGH?"

Andre rolls his eyes and covers his ears. "We can all hear you plenty. I'm sure she's just finishing something up."

I'm not finishing anything, because there's no way to see it all. I could scroll forever, seeing people's opinions of my voice, my face, my Blackness . . .

I gotta stop. I put my phone facedown on the dining table and walk toward the counter.

"What's all this?" I ask, pointing to the food laid out. "I thought we were leaving soon."

"Well, someone just told me that it's a potluck," Mom says, side-eyeing Andre.

"And I just told *someone* that I could pick up something at the store on the way. That's what I always do," he fires back with a smile.

"And *someone* is trying to have me look like a fool when I meet half his family for the first time." Mom bumps his hip with hers. "So we're making my mac and cheese. We're gonna be a little late, but y'all already know everyone else will too, so we're good."

"Ha! Can't argue with that!" Andre smiles and points at her, nodding his head.

We're heading to a big barbecue to celebrate Juneteenth at a park in north Long Beach. I've never really *celebrated* Juneteenth before. For a long time it was just a footnote in a textbook, and then it was a reason for companies to send another marketing email. But apparently Andre's family has been going to this barbecue for years, and he really wanted to bring us this time. Georgia had an out with voice lessons, but I wasn't so lucky. Not that I don't love Andre. I do. It's just . . . playing happy family with a family that isn't mine is not my idea of fun.

And also sometimes I get this nervous feeling in big groups of Black people. Not like the anxiety I feel in big groups of white people, where it's immediately apparent I'm not one of them. Because regardless of my dad, I'm not *white*. White people have always made that incredibly clear. My Blackness is the first thing they see. Even now, with that video and the new followers it brought, my Blackness seems to be called out in every other repost.

And I see myself as Black, too. That's the box I've always checked on forms—and as a biracial person, it feels like you have to make that choice.

But still . . . I always worry that Black people can take one look at me and immediately tell I don't *really* belong. I'm always bracing myself for that rejection.

This means a lot to Mom, though. I could tell by the gentle way she asked, and how she bit her lip and looked all disappointed when Georgia declined. So I agreed.

"Will you get that pan out for me? The big one?" Mom is back at the stove, whisking something fast. "This sauce is almost done."

"I'm on it," Andre says, pulling a cabinet door open. They work so well together.

And okay, if they're distracted, maybe I can just glance at my screen, really quickly . . .

When I pulled the big twist with Zorciar in the game last

night I swear Yo was about to flip the table

Because that's the other thing keeping me on my phone all the time: texts from Reggie. We've only seen each other a couple more times—with his friends at the yogurt shop after he got off work, at another Fun Gi and Ryan Love show. And we're definitely *not* together. Georgia's comments have made me even more hesitant to explore how I really feel about him. But his texts are steady, a constant conversation that we both pick up when we can. I don't always know when they're coming, so it's like when you find an unexpected twenty in your wallet and the whole day turns around, feels brighter.

It had major Real Housewives of New Jersey vibes

I swear he had the same blank, raging look in his eyes as

Teresa season 1

Ok but how do you have such in depth Bravo knowledge? I send back.

Andy Cohen is right after Jesus on my mom's list of

favorite people. My dad is third.

Actually he may come after NeNe Leakes

I laugh, grabbing Mom's attention away from her meticulous layering of noodles and sauce into the pan.

"That was what? Five minutes?" she says. "Don't your eyes hurt?"

Andre comes in to my defense. "She's got fans now, Annie. Let the girl do her thang!"

"Fans got you smiling like that?" Mom narrows her eyes.

Where do you fall then? I type superfast, trying to keep my

expression neutral. I put my phone facedown. "Yep. It's the fans."

But they've already moved on. "Bread crumbs? What are you talking about, bread crumbs?"

"Bread crumbs," Andre repeats. "To put on top of the mac and cheese before it bakes."

Mom puts her hands on her hips and looks him up and down like he just suggested cooking up some garbage in the stove and serving that. And I guess he basically did.

"Are you messing with me?" Mom starts out quiet, but her voice creeps up louder with each word. "Because I know you, someone I like very much, have more sense than to suggest I sully the perfect, melty top of my mac and cheese with some dusty gravel! Bread crumbs! Really!"

In the past few months, Andre has become a regular fixture in our house. And their banter has become part of its normal soundtrack—like the dishwasher running or Georgia singing scales. But still, I feel my whole body tense. I know Mom isn't mad. This is just her way of communicating when she's passionate about something. And this is a perfectly reasonable something. Bread crumbs on top of mac and cheese is a crime.

But with Dad, this would be the beginning of an all-night blowup. Because even if she was joking, he would take offense and storm out, muttering, "Do whatever you want then, Annie." And then Mom would go after him, demanding a conversation, some sort of resolution. And then that would devolve into a screaming match, excavating every single grievance and slight and misstep since they met their junior year of college. And then Mom would eventually get quieter and passive to smooth things over and Dad would accept her apology like she actually did something wrong, so we could all eventually go to sleep. All of this because Mom raised her voice or had an opinion.

"Does that mean no bread crumbs then?" Andre says with an easy laugh. "I'm still not one hundred on how you feel about them."

Mom sucks her teeth and shakes her head, like she's annoyed. But as she begins to sprinkle cheese over the top of the baking dish, a small smile appears on her lips. Andre smiles too as he helps her.

"Thank you for doing all this for my family."

"You're welcome, Dre."

I feel my shoulders drop down as I breathe out. It's okay. I keep forgetting it's okay with Andre. He's not Dad. He doesn't get passive-aggressive or outright aggressive when Mom is just . . . herself. He likes her loud, big opinions—encourages them. With him, she never has to tone herself down or make herself small.

Did she luck out? Or is it possible for anyone to find this? I don't know.

I sneak a glance at my phone, and there's another text from Reggie. Sometimes I think I'm down there at the bottom of her list with Ramona and Vicki

I send back, Well you're definitely higher than Ramona and Vicki on my list 🫂

That's the nicest thing anyone's ever said to me.

After thirty-five minutes of bake time and a spirited debate over just how brown the cheese crust on the top should be (correct answer: dark golden), we're on our way to the park only an hour and a half late.

"So, the Parkers, they're the ones that started this tradition,"

Andre tells us as he's driving. "I think they moved to Long Beach in 'seventy-four? 'Seventy-five? Something like that. And they came from Houston, where celebrating Juneteenth was just, you know, *the thing*."

"Because Texas is where it actually happened, right?" I ask from the back seat. "There was the Emancipation Proclamation . . . but then it took a couple extra years for all the enslaved people to actually be freed?"

"Yep, that's exactly it! On June nineteenth!" Andre says, tapping his steering wheel. "I've seen how it's sorta come into fashion lately, and you know what, I'm not even going to knock that, because the recognition is good. But I've been celebrating with my family for as long as I can remember. We may not get the city setting off fireworks for us, but this is our independence day."

"Thank you for inviting us, Dre."

"Yeah, thank you, Andre."

In the rearview mirror I can see Mom smiling at him all hearteyed, and it makes me smile too.

Still, the anxiety that's been hanging around since I made the terrible choice of checking our social media earlier, a low pulsing beat, crescendos as we pull into the very full parking lot. Andre's welcoming us, yeah, but is everyone else going to feel the same? Or is this going to be the worst-case scenario that I'm already conjuring up in my mind?

And I have a lot of inspiration to draw from, because I've had people telling me I'm not really Black my whole life: Kathy Williams calling me an Oreo in third grade, my cousins from North

Carolina saying I don't "talk Black" . . . and comments online now calling out my light skin and looser curls and non-Black bandmates like they're about to start an investigation. Every one of those opinions is written on my brain in permanent marker, darker and bolder than the rest.

I'm barely paying attention as I walk a few paces behind Mom and Andre, my thoughts consumed with this identity tornado in my brain and bubble guts that may require me to make a run for the gross park restroom. And I guess I shouldn't even be surprised when I bump right into Reggie, a bright, nose-wrinkling smile on his face.

REGGIE

I'd been trying to get her attention, all the while thanking God, the universe, this magical holiday fairy—whoever is responsible for arranging that Delilah would show up right here, right now, at this barbecue. And I'd also been trying to slow down my heart rate, which started speeding double time as soon as I saw her in jean shorts and a white tank top, her golden-brown skin welcoming the sun.

But even though I'm pretty sure she's looking right at me, she keeps right on walking. And when I try to dodge her at the last second, we collide, our heads knocking together all loud like two coconuts.

"Ah!"

"Are you okay?"

She blinks at me, and for a second I'm terrified that she was trying to ignore me and I didn't get the message. Like, maybe our texts are the only place she wants to keep whatever this is going.

But no. That doesn't make sense. And then her whole face lights up, knocking over all those worries like a tidal wave.

"It's Juneteenth," she says.

"It's Juneteenth," I repeat.

"Uh, Lilah-girl, who is this?" the lady standing next to Delilah asks. Because, oh yeah, we just slammed into each other and then started full-on cheesing, which is pretty conspicuous. The lady has deep-brown skin, a slicked-back bun, and the same nose as Delilah. So, this must be her mom, and then the guy next to her is her boyfriend.

"This is my friend, Reggie, Mom," Delilah says, pointing her thumb in my direction. Friend. That fucking word again. But the way she said it . . . maybe I'm just looking for signs, but it sounded all fluttery. Very un-friendlike.

Okay yeah, I'm probably just looking for signs.

"Oh, good! You got a friend here, D," the guy I'm assuming is her mom's boyfriend says. "Who's your family?"

"The Hubbards, sir. And also the Bennetts."

He smiles, warm and easy. "Good people. I'm Andre Dobson. Nice to meet you."

He reaches out to shake my hand. Her mom is clearly still skeptical, though, assessing me with narrowed eyes and pursed lips. "How are you friends? Do you go to Willmore? Or Bixby High? I've never heard your name before."

Ouch.

"No, ma'am. I go to Tom Bradley Charter—"

"We met at one of my shows, Mom," Delilah cuts in, but that

seems to make her more suspicious.

"You're in a band? Oh no."

"Not in a band, ma'am," I say. "Just a fan of the bands. Especially Delilah's."

She lets out a dramatic sigh. "Thank god. Don't get me wrong, I'm all about this outlet for Delilah. She's gotta get those feelings out *somehow*, right? But I've told her she doesn't need to be messing around with those kinda guys."

Delilah's cheeks go from brown to scarlet in a millisecond. "Mom! We're not messing—"

"Oh, I'm being embarrassing. I'm sorry." She squeezes Delilah's arm. "Now let me go before I say anything else wrong. It was nice to meet you, Reggie, and you can call me Ms. Tyler. This ma'am stuff makes me feel old."

"You are old, ma'am!" Andre says with a playful grin, and Ms. Tyler laughs and bumps him with her hip. "Now you better be quiet! I can't take you down in front of your family."

"Yep, I know! And I'm 'bout to take full advantage of that!" He throws his head back with a single "Ha!"

"Come find us when you need us," Ms. Tyler says, giving Delilah a quick peck on the forehead. And then they make their way over to the picnic benches, laughing and slapping each other's shoulders the whole way.

"They are really cool," I say.

"Yeah, they are." Delilah is looking after them, twisting her lips to the side, and it's clear there's something else there. But I don't want to pry and make her feel uncomfortable. No . . . I need to change the vibe, stat.

I pull out my phone and pretend to be dialing, complete with old-school beeping sound effects.

"What are you doing?" she asks, looking at me now.

"Just calling TMZ." I put the phone up to my ear. "Hello? TMZ? I'd like to report a celebrity sighting."

"Oh my god, stop," she says, but the clouds on her face have cleared and the sides of her lips are slowly turning up.

"Yeah, I just saw Delilah. You know, Delilah Cole, lead singer of Fun Gi? The girl that's been the subject of about a million adoring TikToks and has taken the music world by storm."

"It's not even big like that—"

"We're at Scherer Park, off Long Beach Boulevard. That's S-C-H—"

She giggles, trying to grab my phone away from me, and when her rough fingers brush my arm, I swear an electric pulse goes through my whole body and nearly stops my heart. I want to stop fighting and pull her in close and bury my face in her flowery-smelling curls.

And those vibes must be, like, wafting off me, because all of a sudden she stops and pulls away. I might as well have hired one of those little airplanes to carry an "I LIKE YOU DELILAH" sign across the sky. Goddamn it.

"You know it's not like that," she repeats quietly. She tucks her hair behind her ears self-consciously, glancing at the ground.

"Okay, all right. I'm just playing." I clear my throat and will my speeding heart to slow down again so it doesn't give away anymore just how much a touch to my arm destroyed me. "But it must feel pretty great, right? Everyone is *loving* you."

"The band," she corrects me.

"Yeah, the band. But mostly you. That's why people care. It's not like Fun Gi was blowing up on their own before you."

She sighs heavily and then twists her lips to the side. Which is . . . not the reaction I was expecting.

"Hey. What's going on?"

"It's . . . it's nothing." She blinks a few times and brushes a finger under her right eye all quick.

I glance over at the barbecue, where Al Green is blasting from someone's Bluetooth speakers and everyone is already talking loudly and filling up plates from the five tables full of aluminum trays. I don't know what's going on with Delilah, but I know that's not what she needs.

"Do you—uh, do you want to go talk?" I nod over at a bench a few yards away.

"Oh, no . . . it's fine," she murmurs, trying to do another covert wiping of her eyes. "I don't want to take you away from your family."

My family—as in my parents, who are probably grateful I'm not embarrassing them in front of everyone? Or my brother and cousin Jerry, who are definitely waiting around to roast me? "I'd much rather talk to you."

She nods. "Okay."

We don't speak as we walk across the grass. It's covered in a carpet of slimy purple jacaranda flowers, so the only sounds are our squishy steps and Delilah's sniffles. And I'm racking my brain trying to figure out what I did or said to make her so upset. I mean,

I was just complimenting her band and all the hype they've been getting lately. That seems like pretty safe territory.

"Did something happen? Did I say something wrong?" I ask as soon as we sit down.

"No. No, no." She sighs again and studies the ground. "I'm just . . . in my feelings today, I guess. I'm sorry."

"You don't have to apologize for your feelings."

She looks up at me and squints, like she's trying to solve a complicated math problem written on my forehead, but then that shifts into a small grin.

"That's a nice thing to say."

I shrug. "Well, it's true. So, did something happen?"

"No. Actually . . . I guess, *yes*. A whole lot of things. Too much."

"Yes, that all makes perfect sense. Thank you for elaborating," I say, nodding and stroking my chin. She hits my shoulder and laughs, and I want to take her hand and hold it there.

"It's just . . . all of this, for the past month with that video. It's been really good, *so good*, for the band. People are paying attention to us that never did before and we're getting a lot of new opportunities from it. Like, we got offered a gig at The Echo."

"Whoa! The Echo!" I have no idea what The Echo is, but I can tell from her tone it's a big deal.

"Yeah, so it's all really exciting. And I'm grateful. But it's like what you were saying . . . Fun Gi didn't get this attention before, and the music is the same."

"But, I mean . . . it's not the same? Because there's *you*. You are the difference. People are responding to *you*."

She waves that away quickly, like I just tried to claim unicorns and mermaids are real. "Is it me, though? Or is it . . ." She pauses and bites her lip, takes another deep breath. "You've watched the first video right?"

"Of course! You're, like, perfection in it." *Roll it back there, Reggie. You're trying not to scare her away.*

Her cheeks turn pink, but she shakes her head fast like she's trying to physically knock a thought out of there. "Thank you. But—what I mean is, you saw the caption, then? You saw all the comments, what they all bring up?"

I try to call them up in my mind. Were people talking shit about her? Being racist? That makes my chest get tight in anger, but, like . . . it wouldn't surprise me. It's pretty much par for the course as a Black person on the internet—that's why I've been so careful. But no. Everything I've seen, at least, has been pretty positive.

"They all talk about me being Black," she says, answering her own question. "Well, not all of them, but a lot of them. And this guy at The Mode . . . I don't know if Leela already told you about that. So I keep thinking, did the video get so big, were people into it . . . because of that? Do they see my . . . I don't know. My talent for this? Or am I just . . . a novelty to them?"

"A token?" I chime in, and she starts nodding vigorously.

"Yes, exactly yes." And it's as if that small amount of recognition, of validation, was all she needed and now the floodgates have opened. She starts talking super fast, like her mouth is rushing to keep up with all the thoughts spilling out. "And don't get me wrong. I love being Black. I'm *proud* of being Black. But my whole life, I've had people telling me I'm not really Black, so much that I doubt it all the time. And that's happening now, of course. But then for other people, that's all they see. It's my primary identifying trait. And sometimes in the past, that's been a bad thing. To other people, I mean. But now, all of a sudden, it's a good thing? Especially with all these new people following us and sharing the video. So I guess I feel, I don't know, whiplash or something? It's just . . . really freaking strange."

"That's a lot."

"It is," she huffs. "Too much! And oh god, I'm sorry for unloading on you like—"

"No, I mean. That's a lot for you to be dealing with all on your own. So, like, thank you for trusting me enough to share it." I scoot my hand between us, so our pinkies touch. And then I keep talking before I can start spiraling over its significance or turn it into something totally awkward. "Okay, so number one, who's been telling you you're not Black?"

She shrugs and looks down, though her pinkie stays firmly in place. "Oh, lots of people. Some outright and some just in their behavior toward me . . . if that makes sense. Because I'm biracial, when they find that out. But also because I don't dress the way I'm supposed to dress or like the things I'm supposed to like."

"I know exactly what you mean."

"You do?"

"Yeah. I mean, I'm not biracial." My hand pops up to gesture over at picnic tables, where my family is, and I immediately regret moving my pinkie from hers, cursing whatever gene I got that made me a hand-talker. "But the not being Black enough . . . I feel that. I've had people be real dicks about it, call me an Oreo—"

"Mm-hmm. Yes!"

"But there's also the little things that let you know how people really feel. Like there was this one time freshman year, Mr. Lewis— he's the Ethnic Studies teacher at my school, and he's Black. So he was trying to get students to join BSU, walking around, passing out flyers. And he just . . . strolled on by me. He definitely saw me. We, like, definitely made eye contact. But he didn't even ask me to join."

"No!" Delilah says, eyes wide.

"Yep," I say. "And it's not even like there are a ton of Black kids at my school. It's a pretty small charter. Anyway . . . yeah. I feel it. There's this incredible pressure to be a certain way or have these, like, very specific interests to be considered Black."

"And who even decides?" She throws her hands up.

"Oh, you haven't heard of the Official Council of Blackness Arbiters? Better known as OC, uh . . . OCBA?"

"Ha! Stop!" She throws her head back, curls bouncing, and then slaps my shoulder. She keeps doing that, and my mind is jumping at, like, record-breaking levels to conclusions, while my body rushes to memorize the exact sensation.

"But for real," I continue. "I try not to let it get to me, because they don't get to decide. I'm Black. Period. So anything I like, anything I do, is something that Black people do. If people have a problem with that, well, that's their baggage. And it's okay that it makes me upset, to feel those feelings, but I don't have to let it affect me forever. I don't have to change anything for them."

As the words are coming out of my mouth, I know I'm not being one hundred. Because yeah, this is how I want to feel, how I *would* feel in an ideal world, but it's not how I'm actually living. Eric and Tyrell and random people online . . . their problems with me *definitely* affect me. Their opinions are like seeds planted in my mind that grow into something ugly and invasive and permanent, stealing all the space and light.

But I just keep talking though, chasing the approval—and something else, something stronger—that's written all over her face.

"We're not a monolith, you know? And no one's standing at the official Black gates checking percentages or, like, your knowledge of sweet potato pie and . . . Bill Withers songs. Well, except on Twitter, but that's the bad place."

"Bill Withers songs!" she repeats, laughing. "Oh my god, that's totally what my mom plays when she's cleaning the house on Saturday morning."

"My mom too! See, take that, haters! We're Black!"

That sends her into another fit of giggles. And you know, maybe it doesn't matter if I'm misrepresenting myself a little bit, smudging the facts, because it's helping her. She looks lighter, looser, than she did just a few minutes ago, as if she threw off a big ol' backpack of bricks. It's so clear that this is—no, that *I am*—making her feel better.

And I feel better too. I don't think I've ever broached these topics with anyone, not face-to-face like this. I don't think I could with anyone but Delilah.

"God, you're just so easy to talk to," she says, shifting in her seat. Her leg moves closer to mine, our knees kissing, and my body tenses, scared to move even a little and break the spell. "It's very different with the guys," she continues. "I can't talk through any of this with them. And it's been sort of . . . weird."

"Why?" I ask, immediately ready to take up a sword and fight. "Did they do something to you?"

"No, no . . . well, not really." She sounds like she's trying to convince herself. "I'm probably being too sensitive. And Beau—he's the drummer—I know he tries to go in and delete asshole comments and messages on our Instagram before I can read them. I saw him doing it at rehearsal once. So, they look out for me."

"But?" It's clear from the way she's biting her lip—I am now a scholar in interpreting Delilah's lips—that there's a but.

"But . . . it sorta feels like my Blackness is all they see right now. Like how it's helping the band?" I raise my eyebrows and she waves her hand, like she's wiping away what she just said. "Nothing big, just little things. Like this morning, Charlie—you've met Charlie—he texted me asking if we should make a post about Juneteenth on our band account. Not in the group chat, only to me. And it just felt . . . weird? I don't know. It's not anything explicit that they're saying or doing."

"Sounds pretty explicit to me."

She shrugs. "I don't know," she repeats. "But all of this . . . it's just made me feel like maybe my race was something they've been very aware of all along, even though we've never *really* talked about it. And that makes me even more hesitant to talk about it . . . Does that make sense? I don't think I'm making sense!" She covers her face with her hands, and I lightly touch her shoulder, pulling away just as fast because I don't want to freak her out.

"You are! I get it."

She peeks at me in between her fingers. "Thank you, Reggie." And before I could have written off our knees touching as an accident, but she shifts closer again and this time it's definitely intentional how our thighs are pressing together. She brings her hands down to her lap and her lips curve into a small smile, brown eyes bright. And I want to reach up and count every tiny freckle on her nose, I want to lean in and press my eyelashes to hers. But . . . does she want that too?

"It's probably because I admire you so much," she says, looking at me like I'm someone special. "How you put yourself out there, I guess—even when it's hard and this whole identity mind-fuck. You're never ashamed of who you are."

My heart drops straight down to my stomach because, oh yeah, she's looking at me like that because of the act I'm putting on. She's sitting all close to me because she thinks I'm someone I'm not . . . not really. Would she still be touching my knee, hitting my shoulder, if she knew I was just as scared as she is—probably even *more* scared—of people judging me and my identity.

"How's the stuff going with that podcast, anyway? Sorry I haven't asked!"

"Oh, no big deal, no worries," I mumble. "And it's going good. Real good! We're working out the details."

And if the veracity of what I said before was a little murky, well, this is an outright lie. No details are being worked out. I didn't even respond to Darren's last email at all. Just completely ghosted him.

But . . . she said she admires me. So maybe it's okay to be a little morally gray if it means I'm helping her and encouraging her. This could, like, push her to be a huge rock star or something and reach her full potential. It already kinda is! I'm basically doing a good deed. And maybe she'll write some huge, influential album or whatever that inspires generations to come, so this is practically a community service.

I mean, sure, it's helping me too, getting me closer to the girl of my dreams. But I'm not *hurting* anyone. I'm helping . . . both of us.

I see movement out of the corner of my eye, and when I turn my head, I realize it's Eric walking up with my cousins Jerry and Wally. My heart starts beating fast. I've got to get Delilah far away from them, and fast. I mean, I don't think they would try to embarrass me in front of her on purpose . . . at least I hope not. But family sometimes can't help but take you down a few notches—and with Eric? Add a few notches more. I can't take a chance here, not with how good things are going right now.

I pop up off the bench and reach out for Delilah's hand. At first her eyes go wide in surprise, but then, thankfully, her face softens into a grin and she places her fingers on mine.

"Hey, uh, do you want to go walk over by the pond?" I ask, nodding my head in that direction.

"Yeah. I do."

DELILAH

Reggie and I are holding hands.

We are holding hands as we walk toward a pond that smells like duck poop, the toxic scent wafting toward us before we've even reached it. It's the least romantic smell in existence. And yet, he hasn't let go.

We are holding hands after the most perfect conversation ever. It was exactly what I needed. It made me feel seen, and also pushed me to let go of all these other opinions taking up space in my brain. To stand in who I am without apology. Like my mom, like Reggie.

But.

What about what Georgia said? Am I jumping into something with a guy just for the validation? If I tell Reggie how I feel and really pursue this . . . am I going to be putting myself, and all the growth I've been making, on the back burner?

I don't know.

In the scheme of things, though, holding hands is barely a blip on the bases scale. It's not a dramatic declaration of my feelings. It really means nothing, right?

With Reggie, though, it kind of feels like everything.

And I think he feels it too. His head has tilted to the side, and he's smiling at me, moving in closer. The bright sun on his face seems to make his face glow, and I wonder what would happen if I reached out and touched his cheek, pulled him even closer. I wonder if his lips feel as soft as they look.

But.

Again.

Am I letting Georgia down? Am I letting *myself* down?

His lips part, and he's so close now that I can feel his breath mingling with my own. And all I want to do is close the space between us and finally kiss him like I've dreamed about.

Right as it's about to happen, though, I feel another sharp pang in my chest, and the indecision, the anxiety, wins.

I turn my head.

REGGIE

She swerved.

She fucking swerved.

I thought for sure it was finally happening. That this would be the end of all the back-and-forth, perpetual panic attack, and I could finally be certain—no gray area or reasonable doubt—that she actually, truly liked me too.

But no, she swerved.

And now I have to stand here and somehow hide the fact that I want to be launched into space on a one-way ticket, torched by an angry wyvern's flames, and crash into an iceberg so I can plummet to the bottom of the sea with the *Titanic*. All at the same time.

I drop her hand.

"No, um, it's not like. I just—" she starts, but I wave that away. I don't need to hear her excuses or feel her pity anymore. It was loud and clear, flashing neon on a marquee, with that move. And, like, I can't even be mad about it. I was probably reading the signs wrong, starting something that she obviously didn't actually want. If anything, she deserves to be mad at *me*.

"It's fine. No big deal. I get it."

Her eyebrows furrow, and she blinks at me, like if she does it enough times something else will click into focus.

"No, that's not what that—I mean, I'm sorry, it's—"

"Oh, please don't say sorry! I shouldn't have—*I'm sorry!*"

"No, no, no. *You* don't have to be."

"It's fine," I repeat, stepping back from her. "I'm fine. We're fine."

I'm praying that Eric and my cousin aren't currently witnessing the most mortifying, totally-not-fine thing that's ever happened to me. But with my luck, they're probably live-streaming this all with commentary.

She lets out a big exhale and looks me in the eye, her brown eyes wide and searching. "Can we just start over?"

Start over from something that will be seared behind my eyelids until I take my last dying breath? How in the world am I supposed to do that?

But I nod.

"Good." She smiles at me, looking relieved. She reaches out, and for a single, wildly hopeful second, I think she might grab my hand again. But she taps my wrist and then quickly pulls away. "Thank you. Really. For understanding."

Except, I don't know that I *am* understanding. Like, at all. The only thing I know for sure right now is that she definitely didn't want to kiss me. And I'm definitely not going to push anything that she doesn't want.

"I need . . . some more time."

I stretch my face into the biggest grin I can manage. Inside, though, my brain is pinballing from one possibility to the next. Does she need time as in she's trying to let me down easy, already plotting how she's going to ghost me after today? Or could this mean I haven't been completely delusional and she really is on the same page as me? She just needs a few more beats to get there.

"Is that okay, Reggie?"

I tell her the only thing I can, because I want whatever I can have with her.

"Of course."

Okay but why am I still dreaming of that ambrosia salad

I told you it was bomb
Ambrosia salad is usually like a bottom tier
potluck food but my auntie makes miracles

Right?? Who knew ambrosia salad could be not disgusting??
I should have found her to thank her for her service
instead of just letting you bring me more plates

I didn't mind
But I'll pass on the message

So when are we going to see each other next?

Yeah whens the next holiday?
Our record is pretty legit at this point
Oh whens International Ambrosia Salad Day??
I'm sure the universe will bring us together then lol

When's the next time we'll see each other on purpose
Not by chance, I mean
Are you free Thursday?

Well Thursday is National Chocolate Eclair Day

So my only plans were to eat a dozen chocolate
eclairs in one sitting like I do every year in celebration

Can I join you?
I can get my own dozen

Yes I'd love company
Might make it less of a chore
But wait, what is our mission? What mythical holiday
creature are we supposed to save? Who invented eclairs??

I don't care about Santa or the groundhog anymore. I just
want to see you.

Did she really just say that
Ignore that!!!!
Just a glitch in my app
I want to see you too

THU, JUNE 22 10:24 AM

Do you see that guy over there

. . . . Reggie I'm sitting right next to you

I know but we have to keep this on the down low

Thats why I'm typing

Dont look at him!!!

Does this have something to do with
what you said on New Years?
You told me you can't be too careful with donuts

You remember that?

I remember everything you say
Ok I just need to record this here too for posterity. Your
theory is that all the donut shops in Long Beach are clearly
fronts for criminal enterprises. Possibly the mob. Bc there
are just too many of them and they have too good of real
estate for them to be financially viable???

Exactly.

It all makes sense if you just pay attention

Reggie that is the most bonkers thing I've ever heard

Why is that man the only customer here at 10 on a weekday?

On a donut related holiday no less!

Probably here for a handoff

What are you doing!!!!

OMG SIT DOWN

He said he works remotely and really likes their apple fritters

You have frosting on your face

FRI, JUNE 23 6:24 PM

Are you safe or have you been taken by the
donut mob for asking too many questions?
Delilah?
Oh no I was joking but for real I'm
about to do a drive by wellness check

LOL!
I am safe
Just playing around on my guitar

Phew!
Tell Mabel I said whats up
So whens our next holiday hang?
4th of July?

I have to go to my dad's house that day 🫱
Anyway I want to see you sooner
Tomorrows National Catfish Day
And my show at The Echo
Do you want to come?

I'd love to

NATIONAL CATFISH DAY

REGGIE

"Do you think the day is referring to the actual fish, or the people that take pictures off Google Images and somehow convince their internet girlfriends they don't know how to use Zoom?"

That's the first thing Delilah says when she runs off the stage and directly up to me after her set at The Echo. And, like, I don't even know how to process her question, because her curls are wild and her brown skin is shiny with sweat that, magically, doesn't stink. And she just screamed and spun and demanded the attention of the whole room like a high priestess of punk, and out of everyone she could talk to, which is literally anyone because I'm definitely not the only person who's flashing her heart-eyes, she chose me. Me!

I still don't fully understand what she wants, what we are. But I'll take whatever this is gratefully.

"Well, what do you think?" she asks. "Because that's really going to determine the rest of the night."

I didn't expect us to hang out after her show. She has her band of cool guys. What does she need me for? And from the way the stubbly one is eyeing me right now, it's clear he thinks the same.

"I kinda don't even want to find out?" I say, finally. "Let's celebrate both."

"And how do we do that?"

"Fried catfish and MTV marathon?"

She bounces on her tiptoes, like she's still jittery with the leftover adrenaline. "Do you have a fried catfish hookup? And also cable? I don't have cable."

"I'm pretty sure there are old episodes on Hulu. But okay, for real now, Delilah." I step forward and I almost touch her arm, but I stop myself. "You were really fucking good."

"Thank you. It's whatever," she says, waving her hand. "Back to business. Have you ever tried fried catfish?"

But I ignore her attempt to change the subject. "It's not just whatever. And I'm not the only one that thinks so."

I subtly nod my head at two Black girls with raccoon eyeliner and strategically ripped clothing. They're wearing bright orange underage bracelets and look a couple years younger than us, like maybe their hip parents dropped them off. Even though most people have gone to get drinks or vape before the next set, they've been standing nearby ever since Delilah hopped offstage, whispering and sneaking looks. It's clear they're not interested in talking to the guys of Fun Gi—just Delilah.

"Go talk to your fans," I lean in and whisper in her ear. "We'll coordinate catfish celebrations after."

Her eyes go all big, and a tiny grin creeps across her face, telegraphing, *Is this real?*

It's real, I send back with an enthusiastic nod.

And after a couple false starts, she finally makes her way over in a daze.

DELILAH

They start giggling when I walk over, and it's contagious. I find myself giggling too.

"Hi."

"Hi."

"Hi."

And then there's a long pause, as they both stare at me expectantly. I'm clearly supposed to be in the lead here, which feels very . . . new.

"Um, thank you so much for coming!" I say, pointing toward the stage. As if they need the reminder why they're here.

That seems to be all the permission they need.

"You are the best!" the taller girl squeals, revealing bright purple rubber bands on her braces.

"The best!" her friend echoes. She has a dramatic, stick-straight bang over her right eye, which is a sharp contrast to her bright smile.

"Oh, wow! That's so kind. Thank you." I've gotten compliments before online and at shows, but this feels different. Overwhelming. The back of my throat is getting tight and scratchy, like I might cry. Which doesn't even make sense, because this is a good thing, a happy thing.

"We came all the way from Mission Viejo to see you!"

"Wow, was traffic—" I start.

"We are obsessed. With. You!"

"Obsessed!"

"Ever since we saw you on TikTok!" The taller girl barely takes a breath, like she thinks I'm going to run away if she doesn't get it all out now. "It's just, like, so hard to find this kind of music played by girls that look like us. Well, I don't have to tell *you* that. You know what I mean. So when we saw you, we freaked out!"

"Oh my god, wow. Thank you. What are your names?"

"My name is Jamilah, and this is my best friend, Nola." Nola flashes another huge smile and waves, and Jamilah's voice gets quieter, suddenly shy again. "And we . . . well. We want to start our own band. Just like you. And, like, you—you—" She takes a deep breath. "You make us feel like it's possible!"

Okay, I'm definitely crying now. I sneak my fingers under both eyes fast, hoping they don't notice. But even if they do—how else am I supposed to respond to this?

Since I joined Fun Gi, I've been focused on myself, trying to convince myself that I belong. And since we've started to get bigger, I've been so worried about how others are perceiving my Blackness or using it for their own gain. I didn't even consider what me being in this space could mean to others. Like what finding that first video of Poly Styrene meant to me—proof that I deserved to be here because it was so clear she deserved to be there, too.

"This just means everything to me," I say, clasping my hands in front of me. I wish I could say something wiser, something more profound. But this is all I've got in me right now.

It seems to be enough because they look at each other and squeal, eyes wide.

"Okay, we'll, like, leave you and your boyfriend alone now," Jamilah says, and she's talking so quickly I can't even correct her. "Thank you for, like, making our whole life!"

"Our! Whole! Life!"

They bound toward the door, a storm of energy, and I can hear snippets of their giddy conversation. "So cool!" "The coolest!"

I know whatever I just gave to them, they gave me back tenfold. Because that was easily the coolest thing that's ever happened to me. I have listeners—*fans*—who see me exactly as I want to be seen. I didn't realize what a missing piece that was.

I think about the song I've been working on when no one else is home to hear me playing around on Mabel or singing the words I've been writing down in my notebook. I think Jamilah and Nola might like it. I think they might get what I'm trying to do, maybe feel seen in the lyrics.

But they'll never hear the song if I keep only playing it for myself.

FOURTH OF JULY

DELILAH

I'm eating lunch with my dad and his new family in complete silence.

Well, not complete silence. There's the sound of the big oak clock in the foyer ticking and everyone chewing and forks clinking and even the faint music and laughter of their neighbor's Fourth of July party next door. But compared to meals at my house, we might as well be in one of those sensory deprivation tanks that rich ladies pay to float in.

We're sitting inside in Dad and Sandra's HGTV-set dining room because nearby fires in Orange County have tinted the skies orange and made them heavy with smoke. But I feel like Dad and Sandra probably prefer this perfect, controlled setting anyway. And it's not like anything was actually cooked outside on their expensive behemoth of a grill. It was ordered far in advance and picked up from Whole Foods this morning.

"Did you see the Yeomans painted their front door purple?"

Dad says. He's wearing a flag-printed polo. They all are, paired with matching khaki shorts. It would be a little terrifying, a little pod-person, if I wasn't used to it. This is their usual routine for every holiday. Sandra very kindly called and offered me one two weeks ago when she was buying them at Nordstrom. I declined.

"Purple?" Sandra repeats, raising her eyebrows and giving a knowing smile. "Oh, the HOA isn't going to like that."

"No, they're not," Dad chuckles.

That's been the general vibe of the conversation when it does happen—stilted and superficial. Never going deeper than necessary.

"I like purple," Atticus, one of Dad and Sandra's six-year-old twins declares, after a big bite of potato salad. Annabella, his sister—my half-sister—nods heartily in agreement.

"Purple is a nice color, sweetie. But maybe not for the front door," Sandra says.

"And remember, Atticus, don't talk with food in your mouth," Dad adds. His tone is playful, but there's an edge of chastisement there too.

When we were growing up, Georgia wouldn't just talk with food in her mouth at meals, she would stand on her chair and belt out "And I Am Telling You I'm Not Going," hands up in the air as she hit the high notes like Effie. And I would come in as her backup Dreamgirl, dodging whatever crumbs came flying out of her mouth.

But . . . I guess that always ended with Dad saying, "That's enough"—first with exasperation, then with anger. Maybe Atticus and Annabella have experienced a few *That's enough*s of their own to get the message at this point, without someone like my mom there to temper those stern reminders with lightness. Or maybe they didn't even need them. They were just born this way.

"Sorry, Daddy," Atticus says, taking his napkin out of his lap and wiping his mouth with it. "I forgot."

"It's okay," Dad says with a wink.

I wish I knew my half-siblings more to better decipher how Atticus and Annabella are really feeling. If this meal feels as stifling to them as it does to me, or if it's totally normal. But that would require sitting through more awkward, nearly silent meals, and I'm fine with the small number per year Dad requests now. Georgia finds these required get-togethers excruciating, and that's why I'm covering for her now—I still owe her for Free Comic Book Day. Mom just asks that we try.

But I don't know . . . Atticus and Annabella don't seem unhappy at all. Maybe all the things that made my childhood so tense—Dad's rigidness, his need for structure and quiet—make them feel secure and safe. I only see them on Dad's chosen holidays, birthdays, and the odd weekend, but they seem content.

"So, your mother tells me you're in a band?" Dad asks after another lull. I'd started to count each steady tick of the clock.

"Yeah, since late last year. We're called Fun Gi, and I sing— well, really scream. I'm learning to play guitar, too."

"Mushrooms are a type of fungi," Annabella says, sitting up tall in her chair.

"That's right, sweetie," Sandra coos.

"We write it as two words, though. Fun. Gi. So, like, um, 'Hey, I'm a fun guy,' or something like that . . ."

I trail off because I actually think our name is kind of stupid, and I can see through Dad and Sandra's strained, encouraging smiles that they feel the same.

"I think it's wonderful that you've found such a . . . unique outlet, Delilah," Dad says with a small smile. "Have you been putting a lot of effort into this endeavor then? It sounds like a pretty significant time commitment."

"Yeah. Yeah, I have. Actually . . . I have practice today—after this, of course. Asher—that's the bassist—he said we should take a break. For the holiday, you know. But Charlie—he's the guitarist and he writes all the lyrics, too. He said we should keep up our normal rehearsal schedule because we have a lot of really big gigs coming up." I'm talking way more than I normally do, but I feel this intense need to fill the silence, to keep this actual conversation volley up in the air.

"That's nice," Sandra says with a big smile.

"Very nice," Dad echoes.

"Thanks, yeah . . . I'm having fun."

And the ball drops.

So, I eat my food—counting the ticks of the clock during the long, drawn-out silences and smiling and nodding when something is said. Partway through dessert, Sandra drops the bomb that the Birneys' Ring camera caught the Yeomans' Shiba Inu pooping on their lawn, and I find myself gasping loudly, desperate for something even mildly interesting to latch on to. That's what only a few hours here has done to me.

I study Sandra as we watch *The Music Man* on their white sectional couch after lunch. Like the twins, she looks content. Not just content, actually, but overjoyed with her mostly silent meals and TV-perfect house. I don't think she's being controlled or repressed. This is clearly the life that she wants.

It's not like with Mom, who always looked like she was itching out of her skin when she was around Dad. Sometimes I swear she would pick fights just to get any expression of feeling out of him, to force him to veer out of neutral. God, they were so ridiculously incompatible, I don't even know how they made it so long. But they were so young, still figuring themselves out. And then I came along and they made the decision they thought was best for everyone at the time. Because of the way it all went down, it's hard not to think of us as a stop on the way to the life that was *actually* planned for Dad—that he maybe always saw for himself, too.

And Georgia took after Mom, for sure. When we were young, she never made herself quieter, smaller when he told her to. She belted out show tunes on the front porch, put on performances in grocery store aisles, dressed herself in sequins and rainbows and red cowboy boots to go to church with our straitlaced grandparents. And when we got a little older, near the end, she picked fights of her own.

But I could always get along, keep the peace.

I guess that's why I'm here right now, pretending to enjoy this old-ass musical while Mom's hanging at Andre's auntie's pool and Georgia's at her friend's beach bonfire—or intense holiday rehearsal for the community theater production of *The Little*

Mermaid, if Mom or Dad asks.

"I'm proud of you, Delilah," Dad says when we pull up to Asher's house later. I know how this should make me feel, hearing this from my dad. I know I should get teary-eyed or feel all warm inside, with his spotlight turned on me in this moment. But all I can think is: How can he be proud of me when he doesn't even know the real me? Not like my mom and Georgia. Ryan now, too. And Reggie . . . the people I trust to look behind the curtain I keep up for everyone else.

But I smile and say, "Thanks," like I'm supposed to. And he pats my arm and grins because that's enough.

I don't want that life.

The words ring in my head—big, booming—as I close the door to Dad's Audi and he drives down the street with a honk.

I can't have that life.

What Dad and Sandra and the twins have. It's too quiet, too passive. Too boring.

But am I actually reaching for anything else? I'm still playing other people's music and hiding my own because it's easier. I'm still in this strange limbo with Reggie because I'm scared of what my sister might think—or really just scared that I can't trust my own gut about what I really want. Why do I keep making myself small, thinking this is the way it always has to be?

It's not enough to just think about the girl I want to be any-more. It means nothing if I keep walking down the same path I always have, shrugging and spouting out "Yeah, whatever" and staying in neutral.

It's time for me to actually do something about it. And I'm

going to start right here, right now, by finally sharing my music with the band.

I try to give myself mental pep talks all through practice.

You got this. This is going to go better than you think. What's the worst that can happen?

But of course, my brain is pretty skilled at providing the worst-case scenario: derisive laughter, placating smiles to hide their embarrassment for me, immediate ejection from the band . . . I could go on. I'm a realist. Charlie is picky and elitist when it comes to music. He's not about to praise what I've been working on and suggest we change the name to Delilah and the Fungus or something. No, the most that I can hope for is that they'll all be open to it, accepting. And regardless of all that can go wrong, I know I can't chicken out—I have to take the leap right now. If I keep being quiet and going with their flow, nothing is ever going to change.

So after we finish a third run-through of "Infinity Kit," I take a deep breath, trying to loosen the tightness in my throat and chest.

"Bro, that last part you added on the toms is so sick."

"Yeah, but something is still off. I need to tweak it some more."

I will my voice to be steady, strong. "Hey, can I show you something?"

The guys are always doing this at practice. It starts with this simple request, and then Asher will play a riff he's been tinkering with, or Charlie will read some lyrics out of his notebook. And then Beau will come in with a beat that ties everything together. They'll adjust and refine, sometimes giving each other suggestions or critiques, but sometimes completely wordlessly, like their brains are just melding together. It really is magic to watch. It's how the music gets made.

But when I go to pick up a guitar to show them something like I've witnessed them all do countless times before, Charlie snorts out a laugh.

My whole body goes rigid.

"Ha-ha, very funny, kid," he says. But something on my face must make him reconsider his original assessment.

"What's going on?" he asks, eyebrows pinched together. "You don't play guitar."

Just like that. *You don't play guitar.* Like he knows me better than me. Like I'm stupid enough to need that reminder.

I feel all the resolve I had outside, all my hopes to finally start being the girl I want to be, drain out of my body.

"Um, I do actually," I finally squeak out. My voice sounds silly and weak and I hate it.

I want to run out of Asher's garage and pretend this never happened. I want to go back to just listening and watching and doing what I'm told. That's not scary. It doesn't make my heart beat dangerously fast like this or my stomach feel like I'm on a roller coaster from hell. But I know if I leave, if I give up now, I'll never try again.

I take another deep, steadying breath, pull a pick out of my back pocket, and start playing the song I've been working on.

I haven't really mastered playing and singing at the same time yet. It kind of feels like that patting-your-head, rubbing-your-stomach trick to me—one day it'll all click, but that day hasn't come yet. So instead, I strum the first verse, humming the melody the best I can. And when I get to the chorus, I pause and sing a couple phrases, because the lyrics and the chords kind of dance around each other in a way I'm not sure how to make happen in real life yet. It sounds really good in my head, though. The arrangement mirrors what the song is about: that same dance I've been doing trying to figure out who I want to be, around all the voices who think they already know.

I try to stumble my way through the second verse, but my hands are clammy and my finger keeps slipping on the B string.

"So, um, yeah . . . something like that," I mumble, resting the guitar in my lap. "You get the idea."

"Delilah!!" Beau yells, jumping up from his throne behind the drums and beaming at me. "You've been holding out on us!"

"Yeah, like, what the fuck?!" Asher chimes in. He presses his lips together and nods at me, impressed?

I feel like my heart just hitched a ride on a balloon and it's floating up to the sky. I feel proud.

But that feeling disappears when I look at Charlie. His arms are crossed and his eyebrows are so pinched now, they're practically touching.

"Who taught you that?"

"Ryan. Um, you know, Ryan Love," I say. I smile at him, hoping he'll return it. "I started taking lessons with her back in April."

His eyebrows shoot up now. "That long? And you didn't say anything?" He shakes his head. "Delilah, she's our competition."

"I don't think she thinks of us like that," I say with a laugh, but I can tell immediately from the way his eyes darken that that was not the right move.

"Why? What did she say?"

"Nothing bad. I promise. We're just . . . you know, friends. She's been really supportive, I guess." I put the guitar back on the stand and walk over to my backpack, pull out my notebook. "Um, I've been writing lyrics, too. For the whole thing, not just that one part."

Maybe if I stop talking about the guitar playing, which is firmly Charlie's zone, and focus on something else, he'll stop looking at me like a traitor.

"Yeah, let's hear 'em," Beau says, and Asher nods in agreement. Charlie says nothing.

So I read some of my favorite lines from my notebook, most of them written after everything that happened in May. About being in the spotlight, but in a way I didn't choose. About others taking something I'm proud of and twisting it, tainting it for their own needs.

I can hear the shakiness in my voice, and I know the words don't sound as good as they would if I was singing them on stage, when I have that electric feeling coursing through my whole body. But still, I'm so proud that I'm even doing this thing that would have been the premise of an anxiety nightmare just last week.

When I'm done, I inhale, exhale, and then risk looking up at them.

"Sounds like you're reading from your journal," Asher says

with a smirk, and Beau smacks him on the back.

"Don't be a dick, bro."

Beau smiles at me, and it's not fake or placating, which would be the worst. "I really liked it, Delilah. There's some real potential here that we—"

"Hey, the journal thing wasn't a diss!" Asher cuts in. "I liked it too! Fucking Kurt Cobain took his lyrics from his journal, I'm pretty sure. Not that you're Kurt Cobain, Delilah." Beau smacks his back again. "Not that you're *not* Kurt Cobain, either!"

"Thanks, Asher." I smile at him.

"No prob."

We all turn to Charlie in unison, because even if we'd never admit it out loud, his opinion holds more weight. He started this band, and Asher and Beau always take his lead.

Charlie shrugs, and my heart breaks before he even says a word.

"It's cute, but, like . . . it's not what we do. I think you know that."

"Well, maybe not yet," I rush to say. "But it could be. Or maybe we could work on it together to get it closer to—"

"No, it's not right," he says, shutting me down. But then the coldness disappears and he grins at me, batting his long lashes. It's the same way he's always looked at me, the way that used to make me feel like a plant leaning toward the sun. "I'm not saying you won't get there, but . . . yeah, leave the music-writing to us, kid. You get to be out there in the front, looking beautiful."

He reaches out to put his hand around my shoulders, to pull me in close, but I step just out of his reach. My throat aches, like I've swallowed something sharp.

I stare at the floor as we all stand there in silence. I'm scared to look up, scared what my face might give away.

"Okay, I know what we need," Asher says finally. "Top three, uh, Kurt Cobain songs, g—"

"Dude, read the room," Beau says, shooting him a look. And that's nice and all, but where's the same energy for Charlie? I know he was their friend first, that this was their band . . . I just thought maybe I'd earned my place at this point too.

"I'm going to go," I say, grabbing my backpack.

"What about the fireworks?" Charlie asks. As if nothing of importance just happened.

I shrug. "I'm good." And then I head out of the garage, throwing a wave behind me. No one follows me.

As I sit at the stop, waiting for the holiday schedule bus, I replay what happened, searching for what I did wrong. *Was I stupid for sharing with them? Was my music so cringey that reaction was warranted?*

But no. I'm not going to take that on. I was brave. I was the girl I want to be. So if they don't like that girl, then that's their problem, not mine.

But what does that mean for me and the band? What do I do next? I don't want to quit Fun Gi. I love performing too much, and how would I do it without them?

My phone buzzes in my pocket and a little seed of hope plants in my chest. Maybe it's Charlie. Maybe he's apologizing, telling me to come back.

It's not Charlie's name on my screen, though. It's Reggie's.

I know you said you were going to your dad's but you got
plans tonight? This is kinda a bs holiday that I'm not even sure
we should celebrate anymore. But also me and Yobani and
Greg are going to see the fireworks at Alamitos Beach 🙂

I feel my cheeks get tight as I smile at my phone.

Do I want to hang out with Reggie and his friends right now?
Yes. Of course! But also . . . I really want to go home and work on
this song some more. I want to make it better, closer to my vision,
so maybe I can perform it on my own someday, without the guys.
So no one—not even Charlie—can tell me it's not good.

I've got some stuff I need to do. I'm sorry!

Okay no worries

But tomorrow?

His response is immediate. I'm all yours.

LABOR DAY WEEKEND
REGGIE

I am going to try again with Delilah this weekend.

If you'd asked me back in June, I would've sworn I'd rather get into fistfight with a cloud giant rather than put myself out there with her after the swerve from hell. And if I get swerved again, damn . . . I'm done.

But I don't think that'll happen.

Maybe I'm completely delusional, but it's been months now of cracking jokes and long, deep conversations and sitting so, so close. And I don't think you do all that with someone you're gonna swerve. Unless you're, like, a sociopath about to have a podcast season, *60 Minutes* special, and Hulu show made about you, and Delilah isn't all that. She's perfect.

There have been moments where I've almost tried again this summer, when I was 99.7 percent sure that she wanted me to actually kiss her this time. Like that one day we were at her place watching *The Warriors*—which, yeah, is like the least romantic movie ever. Our thighs kept touching, though, and every time I reached for the popcorn, she did too, and I swear her fingers were shooting electricity right into mine, like she had Storm and Black Lightning's powers combined. But then Georgia came home and started hollering, "Warriors, come out and play!" because she heard it in some TikTok and the moment was gone. And then there was that time we were celebrating National Soft Serve Day—or something like that. The "holidays" have definitely become an excuse at this point. But we were at Shoreline Village, looking out at the water and licking our chocolate-dipped sprinkle cones, and the sun was setting, casting everything in this glowy, perfect light. There was no interruption, no reason to pull back this time . . . except that last 0.3 percent.

She could run away screaming. She could slap me and post my picture on one of those "Girls, beware!" Instagram accounts. She could *let* me kiss her once but be obviously not into it, and when I jump back immediately because I'm not a creep, I would be able to see that something was irreparably broken between us. And then our friendship, this friendship that means everything to me at this point, would be done.

Yeah . . . that last 0.3 percent is a real asshole.

But I feel like this weekend is the turning point, the now or never, the point of no return. She asked me to drive her up to a festival her band is playing in San Luis Obispo. She assumed I was going already because Ryan Love and the Valentines are playing, and I didn't correct her. I immediately informed Mom I'd have to skip the family barbecue and took the resulting guilt trip like a champ. I don't know why Delilah couldn't have hopped in her band's van . . . or tagged along with Ryan for that matter. But I didn't want to know. Four hours alone in a car with her, driving up the coast—that felt like a gift from the universe, an offering from whatever holiday mascot is in charge of Labor Day. A tree? No, that's Arbor Day . . . I don't know.

Anyway, I'm going to kiss Delilah this weekend.

I mean, I'm going to try. If she's clearly, obviously, 100 percent into it. If all the signs are there that I won't get swerved again and therefore crumble into a pile of dust on the ground forevermore. I'm going to do it then. For real this time.

DELILAH

I've decided I'm going to quit the band this weekend.

Even if it means I'll be bandless, even if I have to take a break from performing for a bit. At least I'll have stood up for myself. I'll have shown the guys—and myself—that I know my worth.

I thought I could make it work after Charlie's brutal rejection on the Fourth of July. He didn't say anything else about the song I played for him. In his eyes, the matter was resolved, so I could have easily just pretended like it never happened, too. Asher and Beau sure did. They may have been supportive at first, but once Charlie moved on, they followed his lead, which to me was just as devastating. And once I knew those feelings were there, once I knew where I really stood—it's like that was lurking under every interaction, every annoyance that I was able to brush off before.

There's how they handle all the band business without me—setting up more studio time with Neil at Brass Knuckle, committing to this festival in SLO that is admittedly a big deal but still really far away. No one asked for my input, just assumed I'd be down for whatever. There are also just the little things, like how I rarely even get passed the fucking aux cable in the car. As if I have nothing to contribute, no opinions about what we should listen to on the way to our shows.

And yet I'm front and center on all our social media. From the sheer number of solo shots on our Instagram, you'd think this was my band, my music. But it's all about the image, how I set them apart from different bands . . . because I'm Black. It's so clear to me now that Charlie wants the benefits of that without giving me any actual power. I went along with it for so long. Too long.

It's crazy how quickly things changed, how I started seeing him as irreversibly different, like the shifting portraits in the Haunted Mansion at Disneyland. What seemed so cool and confident before now reads as pretentious, try-hard . . . fake. I felt like I was faking it trying to fit in with him, with them—but what I was aspiring to wasn't even real in the first place.

I walk down the path from our apartment complex and spot Reggie's bright blue clunker of a car waiting for me at the curb. I didn't need a ride. I could have gone with the guys, toughed it out in Asher's mom's minivan one last time. But when I brought it up, Reggie agreed so readily, and I chose not to think too much about if he was really already driving four hours—five to six with traffic—to one of Ryan's shows.

I open the door and slide into Reggie's car. It smells like laundry detergent and cocoa butter, the scent I know so well now. Reggie beams at me and pumps his fist. "Road trip!"

I feel like a plug has been pulled up, and all the worry and tension is draining out of me, just the good stuff left behind.

I'm going to quit the band. After the show, after maybe my *last* show. But not yet. First I get to be right here with Reggie, enjoying this.

REGGIE

"Okay, first essential element of a successful road trip: music."

Delilah was biting her lip and her eyes looked stormy as she walked out the gate, but I swear as soon as she saw my car, her whole face lit up. I want to keep that smile there.

"The good news: Bessie here"—I tap the dash— "is so old that her cassette player is now vintage and cassettes are a thing musicians make again. The bad news: Bessie's cassette player ate my Anderson .Paak cassette tape last week, so now that's all she plays. And if I have to listen to that album one more time I'm gonna lose my mind."

"I thought you were supposed to end with the good news?"

"Yeah, you're probably right." I click my tongue, searching for one. "Okay, here's some more good news: This means you get to play radio DJ. All those stations, just waiting for you to discover them. Who knows what you'll find! It's . . . uh, very exciting."

"You're really selling that," she says, but I see that her smile gets even bigger, creating sunbursts on the sides of her eyes. She turns the dial on the stereo as I pull out onto the street, and soon "Lovely Day" is playing from Bessie's speakers.

"Bill Withers!" Delilah giggles, turning it up.

I snap and shake my finger at her. "Bill Withers."

"Okay, and what's the next essential element of a successful road trip?" she asks. "You got a number two?"

"I do, in fact," I say, right as we pull into the 7-Eleven parking lot. "Snacks!"

Ten minutes later, our arms are loaded up with Slurpees and chips and candy, even though it's only late morning and these are definitely not typical breakfast fare.

"So, Twizzlers? Really?" I say as I turn the key in the ignition. Except, instead of roaring to life, it starts making this very troubling clicking noise. I look at Delilah, and her eyes are wide and worried, probably a mirror image to mine.

C'mon, don't embarrass me, Bessie.

As if she can hear my pleas, Bessie does this weird gurgle thing, followed by a whine and then a deep rumble, like she's a pack-a-day smoker having a cough attack. But she's moving and that's all that matters.

"Bessie always comes through," I say to reassure Delilah, and she giggles and shakes her head.

"If you say so. Okay, now what were you saying about my Twizzlers, AKA the best road trip snack ever? I know you weren't trying to diss them."

"They taste like plastic," I say as we turn down Bellflower and toward the freeway.

"No, they don't." When I flash a side-eye at her though, she relents. "Okay, the regular ones totally do. But these are Twizzlers Pull-and-Peel. They're not the same. They're in an entirely different universe." She holds out the bag like it's some priceless artifact, and I laugh.

"The assessment still stands."

"Oh, that's just because you haven't been given the full Pull-and-Peel experience." She's keeping her face all serious but I can see the playful glint in her eyes. She gestures at my stash of chosen snacks in the back seat. "Plus they're better than Funyuns. They don't make your breath all funky."

My cheeks get hot as I realize what a stupid mistake I made buying those. Nothing makes a girl want to kiss you less than synthetic onion breath.

But that must not be on her mind, because she's back onto the Twizzlers. "They're not just a dessert. They're an experience."

"An experience?"

"Yes. Observe." Out of the corner of my eye, I see her pull off two of the strands, twist them together, and shape them around one of her fingers. "See—a ring."

"Is that what that is?"

"Ha! Shut up!" she says, hitting my shoulder. Gently, because I'm driving . . . or maybe just to linger there. "Georgia and I would always get these when we were stuck in the back seat for a long drive. We'd have competitions to see who could make the best creations. And then we'd eat them all."

"Who would win?"

"Me." She frames her face with her hands. "Give me a couple

minutes. I can make a very impressive flower."

"A flower? Nah, I want, like . . . a dinosaur or something. That would be a true test, especially if you're trying to win me over to your nasty candy."

"Hey, more for me!" She laughs and shrugs.

"So did you go on road trips a lot as a kid?"

"Yeah, I guess. My mom grew up going to Bass Lake, so she'd bring us there to see, you know, real seasons. And Georgia went to this fancy performing arts camp on the central coast. We took this drive, actually, to get there. The 405 to the 101. I always loved it, especially once we get further north and are driving alongside the ocean."

"Why didn't you go to the camp?"

"Because I'm not a performer," she says quickly. The carpool lane is moving slow, so I steal another look at her, and her eyebrows are pressed together tight. But then her face smooths out and her chin raises. "Well . . . I wasn't. But I am now."

"You are."

She nods once, with finality, like she really believes it. "Georgia and I are just so different, you know? Performing has always been her thing. She knew when she was so young, and I was always the quiet one. I think that's why my mom is so shocked by all this, the band thing. Sometimes I catch her watching the videos online and just, like . . . smiling. It's weird." The smile taking up Delilah's face now shows me that it's something much bigger than just weird to her. It's special. "Anyway, you probably know what it's like. You get stuck in those roles you've always played in your family. They don't expect you to ever change."

"Yeah, I completely get that."

"Is it the same way with your brother? Eric?"

"Mm-hmm. We're very different too. *Very* different."

And because of those differences, we've never really gotten along. Probably never will.

"I can't believe I still haven't met him. Or I guess, I have . . . but not really. Just that quick wave at the barbecue when we were heading out."

And if I keep playing it right—only inviting you over when everyone is gone, hanging out far away from my house otherwise—then you never will. Because you meeting Eric . . . that would be the absolute worst-case scenario.

But of course I don't actually *say* any of that. Instead I mumble, "Yeah, weird, right." I slap the steering wheel and point at the stereo, which is currently bumping "Respect" by Aretha Franklin. "Okay, now I know I said you were in control of the music. But if Bill Withers is what my mom played when she first started cleaning on Saturday mornings, this song is what she played when we didn't get our butts up fast enough to help her. I'm getting flashbacks to the floor shaking to the beat of R-E-S-P-E-C-T. That's, like, the only word I can spell without thinking about it. I'm getting triggered."

Her head falls back against the seat as she laughs, a cascade of shiny brown curls against the dull gray, and I want to freeze the scene in my brain so I never forget it. I get that feeling a lot, as we drive up the coast, sharing snacks and stories. I want to remember everything.

There's how the late-morning sun makes her skin golden,

especially her smooth right leg, up on the seat and leaning against the door. The way she sticks her tongue out the side of her mouth as she creates complicated shapes out of the Twizzlers Pull 'n' Peel, and then eats them with the biggest grin. How when we're driving through LA and the Valley, she talks shit to all the cars under her breath—for going too fast, too slow, not signaling. One time she even holds her hands up in exasperation at a big bro truck that was tailgating us and just laughs when the driver flips her off. And then there's her serious face as she's choosing music, like she's performing brain surgery or something.

Even as I'm living these moments, it's like my mind recognizes that they're special, fleeting, and I need to scoop them all up and tuck them somewhere safe, like a little kid whenever confetti falls from above.

We're past a long stretch of beaches and are driving through rolling hills, bleached yellow from a dry summer. Delilah turns the dial on the radio, cutting through static and country ballads until she lands on a song that makes her jump up in her seat and sing along. "I have nothing, nothing, nothing if I don't have yooooooou."

The song is an old-school belter, but Delilah's voice is quiet and restrained like it has been whenever she's sung a few snatches of lyrics throughout the drive, almost like it's sneaking out without her permission.

It's over just as soon as it started. "Oh, I love that one," she says, disappointed, as the synthesizer opening of another song starts. "Actually, that song reminds me of one of these drives. We—my mom, Georgia, and me. My dad would never make the drive. But yeah . . . when a really good song came on shuffle, one we all liked, we would roll the windows all the way down and sing at the top of our lungs. Whitney Houston was always one of Mom's favorites, and I think Georgia had seen the *Bodyguard* musical at the Pantages that year. We replayed it at least four times before a bug flew in the window and went up Georgia's nose. We were laughing so hard, Mom had to pull over."

Her whole face is sunshine. Her lips, pulled into that wide, wild smile are my favorite sight.

"Well, why aren't we doing that?" I reach up to turn the dial, but then pause. She's looking at me with a skeptical eyebrow arched, but then nods her permission. I keep turning until I land on a folksy pop song that I vaguely recognize. "Oh, this is my jam!" I shout, turning up the volume until I can feel it in my chest.

"I've never heard this song before in my life."

"You haven't? It was my favorite back in the day!" I try to sing along but I don't really know the lyrics except the "ho, hey" part that keeps repeating. I try to make up for that with enthusiasm, though. Her eyebrow goes up even higher.

"Favorite, huh?" she asks, with a smirk.

"Okay, maybe not my favorite. But I remember it. Well, the Kidz Bop version, at least. They used to play it all the time at the after-school program . . . You know how they change the words."

She laughs. "Sure, that's it."

I keep singing, right hand on the wheel while I crank Bessie's window down with my left. And the lyrics are pretty repetitive, so after the chorus a couple of times, I've pretty much got it down and I'm confidently warbling along: "I belong with you, you belong with me, you're my sweetheart!"

I shimmy my shoulders in her direction as I hit notes I definitely should not be trying to hit, and soon enough her window is down too and she's belting the song out with me.

I sound terrible, like injured-animal terrible, but it doesn't even matter. Because her curls are whipping around in the warm air, and I'm singing to her that she's my sweetheart, and she's singing it right back, beaming at me like she means it as much as I do.

DELILAH

I've sung in front of Reggie before. He's been to a whole bunch of shows at this point. But this . . . this feels different. Like when you're singing alone in your room and you can be totally free because there's no one there to judge you. I never feel like Reggie is judging me. If anything, he seems to see the best version of who I am.

We keep singing together with the windows down and the breeze sweeping our voices through the air. We sing along to Olivia Rodrigo and the O'Jays, Beyoncé and Blondie, turning the dial until we find something good, screaming the lyrics that we know and making up the ones that we don't. We sing until my throat feels sore, but my chest—so tight and tense before—has released and I'm breathing easier. It's like I just drank a big mug of chamomile tea, all cozied up in a blanket by the fire. That's the Reggie effect.

After a particularly enthusiastic rendition of a Britney Spears classic, I turn down the commercial that follows it. "I am impressed."

"Bet you didn't know I knew all the moves to that song," he says, doing another wobbly thing with his arm that Britney has definitely never endorsed. His car drifts a little bit on the winding road.

"I didn't and now it will be seared in my brain for all of eternity. So thanks for that," I say, giggling, and he laughs along with me. "We can totally listen to something else, too, if you need a break from these epic performances. My phone speakers are probably loud enough to play that podcast you like. *Role With It*? And, hey—"

"Nah, that would be so boring for you," he cuts in quickly. "Okay, now what is *that*? That can't be real." He points ahead of us to a giant billboard that reads: "Buellton: Home of the Split Pea Soup."

"Are those dudes just chilling in a big bowl of soup? I don't get it. And can a town really be famous for soup? They don't got anything else going on? That soup must be real dope."

The sign looks really familiar to me, and as we drive past it, something clicks. "Wait! I totally remember this place!"

"You've tried the soup then?" he asks. "Does it live up to the hype?"

I laugh. "Not the soup. I've never had split pea soup before, but I can say with absolute certainty that it's gross."

"Hey! What did split pea soup ever do to you?"

"That same exit, though! I remember stopping there on the way back from taking Georgia to camp. There's an ostrich zoo?"

He blinks at me. "An ostrich zoo?"

"Or, I don't know. Ostrich ranch? Ostrich farm? Ostrich . . . something. Whatever it's called, there's this place with, like, hundreds of ostriches. I would start crying immediately because I missed Georgia, and my mom would take me there to cheer me up. Or I guess to distract me, really."

"How much time does it say we have until San Luis Obispo?"

I check the maps app on my phone that we've been using to navigate. "A little over an hour."

Reggie nods and then he turns the wheel, swooping his car over to the right lane.

"What are you doing?"

"I'm taking you to see the ostriches!"

A little bit later, we've paid our admission to Ostrichland USA, and we're standing in front of a fence, as ostriches jut out their heads and snap their beaks to get to the food trays that we're both holding. A sign right below their long necks warns in green block letters, "YES, WE LIKE TO BITE!"

"This place used to cheer you up?" Reggie asks, his eyes wide.

"Uh . . . that's what I remember."

"Because I kind of feel like we're those stupid people in *Jurassic World*, trying to chill with dinosaurs on vacation."

"They do kind of look like raptors, don't they?"

Reggie shudders. "They do. I don't like it."

"Well, we paid extra for the food," I say, taking a tentative step toward the fence. "We don't want to waste it."

"I would be okay wasting it. If it means I don't lose an arm."

"C'mon . . . I used to do this as a kid. It'll be fine." As if on cue, a little girl in overalls and pink flip-flops walks over and lifts up her tray. The ostriches start eating frantically as the girl giggles and her mom films the whole thing. When they're finished, she skips away, and the ostriches turn back to us in an, admittedly, menacing manner.

"We have to do this. We're taunting them."

Reggie lets out a big exhale and then starts bobbing his head like he's pumping himself up. He takes two long strides forward, so he's standing closer to the fence than me, and then slowly lifts up his food tray. The ostriches' heads jerk toward him, mouths wide. Reggie shrieks in terror, food goes flying, and next thing I know, he's sprinting toward the car. That tray belongs to the ostriches now.

I'm still falling over in laughter when I finally catch up to him, cheeks and sides aching.

"No. Nah. That's not how I'm about to go out!" Reggie says, shaking his head. "Did you see the way that tall one was staring me down? He's already had a taste of human flesh! You could see it in his eyes!"

"Your—scream!" I gasp out in between laughs. "That pitch! And—oh my god. I didn't know you could run that fast!!"

"I mean, when it's life or death!" he yells, but now there's a smile on his face. "I have a responsibility here! I gotta get you to your show!"

"Oh yeah? 'Cause I don't think you turned around once to see if I was taken by the ostriches." I smirk at him and cross my arms.

"Yeah—um, 'cause, well . . . I knew you'd be all right," he

says. "You'd already conquered them as a child. You're the experienced ostrich fighter here."

That sets us off into a whole 'nother fit of laughter, the kind that makes tears pop out and it hard to catch your breath. And I find myself wishing that we didn't have to go to the show. That we could take our time and make this a proper road trip, stopping at all the cool and bizarre places like this along the way. I wish it could stay just us.

So it kind of feels like a joke, or maybe a fairy godmother's wish-granting gone rogue, when Reggie's car doesn't start.

REGGIE

"Oh shit," I mumble as I turn the key in the ignition for the fourth, maybe fifth, time. I've lost count. But like every time before, there's no roaring, not even a troubling gurgle. Bessie just keeps clicking. And no matter what stories I try to tell myself, I feel it in my gut: she's not starting up anytime soon.

My mind starts spinning, trying to figure out how I'm going to save this trip and get Delilah to her show. Of course, my AAA membership just lapsed like two weeks ago. Mom kept telling me she was going to take me off theirs, that it was my responsibility to pay for it now, and I kept saying, "Yeah, yeah, yeah. I'll handle it." But I didn't handle it. And I can't go calling my mom, asking her to do me a solid and sign me back up, because well . . . she may think I'm sleeping over at Yobani's tonight. She may think that because I told her that. And if I call asking for help now, she'll find a way to kill me from a hundred-something miles away, and my ghost will be no help to Delilah.

But—"I can call you a Lyft," I say, turning to her. Her eyebrows shoot up, and I realize I've been totally silent in disaster control mode. She might not even know fully what's going on. "Bessie isn't starting, and I don't think she's going to make some miraculous recovery in the next hour." I pull out my phone and check the time. "You still have a while before your show, so there's plenty of time to take a Lyft."

She's already shaking her head. "Reggie, it's over seventy miles away. That's going to cost a million dollars."

"It's fine. I have money saved from Cultured and from my birthday. I really don't mind—"

"No. That would be such a waste. Plus, I can't leave you here alone to deal with this."

"It could take forever. You could miss your show."

"I'm not gonna miss the show," she says with confidence, which I don't think is, like, really backed up by the facts of the situation here. "We'll find someone to help us. I'm sure it's a quick fix. Bessie here is a tough broad." She pats the dash. "Now do you have Triple A?"

Something on my face must give away the answer to that because she quickly continues. "Okay, no Triple A. Well, we can just call a nearby mechanic? Maybe they can send a tow."

A few minutes later, though, we've called all the car shops in the vicinity and have gotten either busy signals or no answer. And, I mean, I get that it's a Sunday on a holiday weekend or whatever, but damn. The universe is not on our side.

"Okay, new plan," Delilah says, holding up her phone so I can see a map. "This shop isn't far, just right in town. We can walk there and see if anyone can help us."

So we set off on the side of the road, leaving Bessie behind to fend for herself with the terrifying raptor birds. The two-lane road is lined with tall trees, but the late-summer sun is still burning down. It's so hot I can literally feel the exact moment my antiperspirant says, "You're on your own, bro," and peaces out on me. And even though I'm keeping up a perfectly normal conversation with Delilah, all I'm thinking about is my dripping pits and whether I can get away with a smell check. And how even if I'm slick enough so Delilah doesn't see me, some dude with a phone in one of these cars speeding past us will, and then I'll be captured on camera and made into a meme that will follow me around for the rest of my life.

"Oh, I remember this place!" Delilah shouts, oblivious to my BO-sniffing dilemma. We're standing in front of a blue-and-white sign that reads "Welcome to Solvang" in old-timey lettering. "Just wait. We're almost there!"

Almost there means another half mile and approximately five-billion quarts of stinky sweat. But at least I can see what got her so excited. We've basically stepped into a dream world—or at least the set of one of those creepy, claymation movies that are always on perpetual rerun at Christmastime. There's a sea of white buildings with sloped roofs and dark wooden beams, cobblestone streets, and at least three windmills that I can count peeking up into the bright blue sky.

"Whoa," I say to Delilah as a man struts past us in lederhosen like it's no big deal.

"Right?" Delilah sighs back, her eyes bright with excitement. This place looks like where Santa goes on vacation.

But Karl, the owner of the auto shop, doesn't look anything like Santa, with his stringy gray hair and frame so thin it's possible he'd snap right in half if he was hit with a strong gust of wind. And he's not jolly at all when, after his tow truck driver hauls in Bessie, he tells me that I need a new alternator to make her go again, and that he can't make that happen until tomorrow, maybe. If he gets around to it.

"It's a holiday weekend. You're not the only one trying to make a long drive in a car that can't take it."

"She—I mean, *my car* has always been just fine. I take it in for checkups twice a year."

"Sorry," he adds with a shrug that looks very not-sorry. "You can check back later if you want. But I wouldn't count on it. Tomorrow morning is the best I can do."

I leave my phone number and we walk outside of the shop. It's aggressively cheery, the polar opposite of Karl's vibe, with bright red paint, intricately carved white trim, and yellow flowers bursting out of an oversized wooden clog.

"So what now?" I ask.

"Ebelskivers," Delilah answers, nodding her head with certainty, and I blink at her. Is she having a sudden, panic-induced loss of language?

"Ebelskivers," she repeats again. "They're these . . . pancake ball things, I guess? But way more delicious than that sounds. They're soft and fluffy and filled with jam. I remember getting them when I would drive through with my mom. After the ostriches." She points to a windmill that has café tables set out front. "I bet they have ebelskivers."

I blink at her some more, confused, so she laughs and adds, "I promise ebelskivers are a lot less scary than the ostriches."

"You joke, but if those fences weren't there, those suckers would take us down with no regrets." I shake my head. "But no, I meant, like, your show? How are we going to get you to your show?"

I check the time on my phone. "We have two hours until you go on, and it's about an hour away. So you can still make it, but it will be cutting it close, you know, with traffic. We could always call Ryan and see if they're all still driving, or I bet she would come and pick you up. And I know you say a Lyft is too much, but I really don't mind—"

"Reggie," Delilah cuts me off. "I'm not going to the show."

"What do you mean? We don't have to give up yet."

"I'm not going. I—I don't think it's worth it."

I study her face: stormy eyes and a tight jaw.

"Is it 'cause you're nervous? You don't have to be nervous. I mean, I know this festival is a big deal or whatever, but you're going to kill it. You always do."

"I'm not nervous," she says, looking me straight in the eye so I know it's true.

"Then what's going on, Delilah? You can talk to me."

"I know." She inhales deeply, her shoulders almost reaching her ears, and then lets out a long breath. "But first ebelskivers?"

I nod. "First ebelskivers."

DELILAH

"That asshole." His face is hardened in fury, but it's also speckled with powdered sugar from the ebelskivers. So I kind of want to just pinch his cheeks, it's so cute.

"I can't believe that. Charlie thinks he's like, what? The arbiter of good music? And to act like your only job is to stand there and look pretty? I mean, you *are* pretty. You're the prettiest person I've ever seen, but that doesn't mean you can't also write music just as good as his. Better than his! That's probably what he's scared of."

I wish I had a rewind button, because did he just say what I thought he said? The prettiest person he's ever seen?

But he continues on with his rant. "And why didn't Asher and Beau stand up for you? Like, what's their problem? They should be just as loyal to you as they are to him." He takes another bite of ebelskiver and chews it like the pastry insulted his mother. "Man, of course you don't want to go to the show. They're disrespecting you, and still using *you* to get the band more attention at the same time? Fuck . . . they don't deserve you, Delilah."

I sigh and shake my head. "Yeah, I can't help but wonder if I would even be in the band . . . if I wasn't a girl. And Black. Do you . . . do you know what I mean? Is that stupid to even think about?"

"It's not stupid. And I'm not gonna lie to you and say they—*Charlie*—didn't think of it that way. Because I don't know. We've established that he's an asshole." He reaches across the table and brushes his fingertips against mine, and it's electric. "But like I've told you, you are the one who brought attention to this band after they were floating on for so long. And it's not just because of your race or your gender—even if they were trying to make it out that way, like you were some sort of token. That's *their* baggage, not yours. Because you've got the talent. You've got the passion. You've got something special that everyone sees when you're on stage. You can't let those dicks take that—that *knowing* away from you." He puts his hand up to his chest, where his heart is. "You can't let their opinions of you affect what you know about yourself. And I haven't heard your song yet, but I know you. And you're extraordinary, Delilah. So if you're putting your heart into something, it's extraordinary too. You deserve to make music with people that recognize how lucky they are to . . . to be with you."

I search his face for some clue, some tell, that I'm missing. Because how can someone be this perfect? To be so confident in who he is, but in who I am, too. To see the best in me even when I can't see it in myself. All while not asking for anything in return, or seeing me just for what I can do for him.

How is this boy real? How did I get so lucky?

"Thank you." It's all I say. Even though I want to thread my fingers through his. Even though I want to jump up and throw myself onto his lap and kiss him like I've known I want to do for weeks. Even though I want to finally confess everything I'm sure I'm feeling now.

"You don't have to thank me," he says with a shrug. "I should be thanking you for introducing me to this life-changing dessert."

"You're right. You should." I smile. "Also, there's powdered sugar all over your face."

His eyes go wide in embarrassment, and he reaches up to wipe his cheeks, but that just makes it even worse.

"Did I get it?"

"No—right there," I say in between giggles.

"Here?"

"No, there," I say, miming it on my own face, but this isn't working. "Here—let me." I reach across the table to wipe the last bit of sugar lingering on the side of his mouth, and when my pinkie finger brushes his lips, just barely, he nearly jumps out of his seat.

"You okay?"

"I'm good. I'm straight," he says, clearing his throat and looking everywhere but me. "So, um, yeah. You better text them. The band, I mean. Tell them you're not coming. Even though they don't even deserve that from you."

"You're right. I'll do it now."

The responses come in immediately.

I can almost feel the heat from the flames surely shooting out of Charlie's ears.

Are you fucking kidding me??

What the fuck Delilah

We can't go on without you

How could you do this to us??

Where are you??????

Asher's text is less angry, but equally infuriating: Look I know Charlie was a douche to you but you don't have to take it out on me and Beau

Beau just sends: Are you okay?

That's the only text I respond to. Yes I'm fine. I'm sorry. I'll talk to you guys tomorrow.

"You good?" Reggie asks, concern written all over his face.

"I'm good." I nod a couple times, as if I can convince myself. "It's just that—"

Am I doing this because it's the right thing for me? Or is it because I want to stick it to Charlie, hit him where it hurts. I can't deny that I feel some sort of satisfaction that he'll really have to reckon with the fact that they need me. That I'm not just an eye-catching bow on the top of their already assembled gift, pretty but not necessary. No, I'm something essential, vital. But does it make me a bad person that I want to send that message? Am I being selfish?

I don't even say any of this out loud to Reggie, but it's like he can read my mind.

"You're not doing anything wrong, Delilah," he says, a gentle smile on his lips. "There's no shame in putting yourself first. Even if other people are, like, inconvenienced or uncomfortable . . . that doesn't mean you're wrong."

His words feel like medicine spreading through my body. They give me permission to feel okay, to relax. And I know I need to work on giving myself that permission, too, without any outside forces. But still, it feels good to have someone else there, sturdy and sure, helping me along.

REGGIE

Okay, so that's handled. And Delilah 100 percent did the right thing, no gray area there. If those dicks aren't going to appreciate all that she is, then fuck them and their stupid-named band. They don't deserve her. And I'm not trying to pull an I-told-you-so here, but I *knew* that stubbly bro was bad news from the moment he popped up and kissed her cheek on New Year's Eve, like he was laying down some type of claim.

But the thing is, if we're skipping her show and Bessie isn't going to be ready until tomorrow, then . . . what are we doing tonight?

This question has been whispering in my head ever since Karl first gave us the prognosis, but at that moment, the worry was only for myself. Now the question is being screamed into a bullhorn, because it's not just me, it's Delilah too. Where are we going to sleep? *How* are we going to sleep? It's just the two of us, over a hundred miles away from home . . . what does this mean??

I can't, like, actually *say* any of this out loud, though, without coming off as a total creeper. So I put it out of my mind when we explore the different shops, flipping through children's books inside of a converted windmill and taking selfies in Santa hats in one of many Christmas-themed stores. I keep quiet when we split a big platter of schnitzel in another windmill for dinner. But then it starts to get dark, and when we check on Karl one more time, he very grumpily declares, "Tomorrow morning. If you don't bug me again." And it can't be put off any longer.

"So . . ." I start.

"So . . ." she repeats.

"For tonight . . ."

"I guess we need somewhere to stay?"

"Yeah, it looks like we do."

"So, we, uh . . ."

"Should we get, like . . . a hotel?"

DELILAH

I've known the night was going to end like this ever since I decided not to go to the show. It's the only thing we can do if we're not going to call our parents and fess up to our mess. And that isn't an option. I already got permission from Mom to sleep over at Ryan's after the show, because I knew she would be bothered if she knew how late we would actually be driving back, and *that* was a stretch. I would be grounded forever if she knew where I was right now.

Still, when Reggie actually speaks those words aloud, and turns the thing we're both thinking into an actual plan, my heart starts beating double time. And I'm suddenly hyperaware of my breath, the position of my body, as if there's a spotlight shining and putting all of me on display.

"Yeah . . . yeah, I guess we should."

I keep stealing looks at him as we walk down the street in silence, trying to interpret his every move. Like, is he wringing his hands together like that because he's nervous, or because he's trying to come up with a delicate way to let me down? And I couldn't even blame him after what happened in June and how unclear I've been this summer as I tried to figure myself out. It's possible he doesn't feel the same way about me now, that he doesn't still want to kiss me.

But I think he does. Want to kiss me.

I want to kiss him, too.

Staying in a hotel together, in this town that looks like something out of a Hallmark Christmas movie, seems like an obvious push from the universe, from our holiday fairy godmothers, to finally take the step toward something more. But it's also a lot of pressure.

"Does this look okay?" he asks, nodding toward a white building decorated with royal-blue beams. There's a red, lit-up sign that reads "Vacancy" hanging in the window.

"Yeah. Let's check it out."

Reggie opens the door for me, and we both walk inside the lobby. The AC is cranked up so high that goose bumps appear on my arms instantly, and there are crackling flames going in the massive stone fireplace in the corner, bookended on each side by cushy leather sofas. I don't know who this energy-wasting display is for, though, because the lobby is empty except for a blond guy standing behind the front desk wearing a jacket that looks like it belongs to Kristoff from *Frozen*, and a name tag that reads "Todd." A tinkly bell over the door jingled when we came in, so he must know we're here, but he stays hunched over his cell phone, an intense look on his face.

"Excuse me," Reggie says, waving his hand.

"Are you eighteen?" Todd asks. His eyes don't leave his phone.

"Um, no?" I didn't even think about that. I'm sixteen, seventeen later this month. And even though Reggie is a senior now, he's a young senior. He just turned seventeen this summer. I don't think we even *can* rent a hotel room for the night.

"Then I can't help you," Todd says, confirming my fears.

So now what? We call our parents, tell them what's going on? I'll still be hearing about it when I'm fifty if my mom has to drive hours away on a Sunday night and pick me up from a hotel *with a boy*.

I look at Reggie to see if he's panicking too, but he's already walking toward the desk. Todd is staring at his phone with his eyebrows pinched together tight, rubbing his right hand over his cheek repeatedly.

Reggie leans toward the phone and squints. "Hearthstone?"

That makes Todd look up. But he just rolls his eyes, and mumbles, "Mm-hmm." His eyes are back on his screen a second later.

Reggie squints at the screen again, though. "Play Puzzle Box of Yogg-Saron."

Todd's head jerks up, and he looks at Reggie longer this time, narrowing his eyes in discernment. "But that's random. I could lose."

Reggie shrugs. "It's the best you got. And that timer is running out."

Todd exhales sharply, and I realize his whole body is moving like his leg is bouncing under the counter. He looks at the phone, looks at Reggie, and then looks at the phone again. Finally, he nods and taps something on the screen. A whirring, sparkly noise explodes from the phone, followed by a loud boom.

"Yeah! Let's go!" Todd shouts, jumping up. His stool clatters to the ground. "I had a hundred bucks on that game! My jerk cousin beats me every time, and he thinks he's the shit." He claps his hands and points at Reggie. "Good looking out, man!"

"Hey, no problem," Reggie says with a sly smile. "But now maybe . . . you could help *us* out?"

Todd laughs, shaking his head. He whips his head around, probably checking for his boss, and then grabs a plastic card from under the desk. "Deluxe king, second floor. The couple that was supposed to stay there just canceled like an hour ago, and it's too late for them to get their money back." He pushes the key card across the counter toward us. "But you *don't* get the continental breakfast. And if anyone asks if you talked to me, no, you didn't."

"But we—but we need, uh, two beds," Reggie stutters, but Todd's attention is already back to this Hearthstone game. "Take it or leave it, man. Now if you'll excuse me, I'm about to go double or nothing."

One bed. Reggie and I aren't just staying in the same hotel room. We're staying in the same hotel room *with one bed*. And I don't hate that idea . . . but I'm also completely freaking out.

"Did I really just save us with my nerd shit?" Reggie asks as we walk up the stairs. His eyes are focused on his feet, so I can't tell if he's freaking out too.

"You really did. That was impressive. Even if I don't totally get what happened."

Reggie lets out a low, hissy laugh. "It's this card game that you can play online. Kinda like Magic: The Gathering, but also kinda not? I used to be really into it before I, like . . . had friends?"

"Well, it came in handy, didn't it?"

"Yeah, take that, Mom and Dad!" he shouts with another laugh.

"Do your mom and dad give you a hard time about the . . . nerdy stuff?"

But Reggie doesn't answer, because we're standing in front of a door. The door to the hotel room with only one bed.

"Uh, here it is," he mumbles, sliding the key in the reader. It flashes green, and he pushes the door open, revealing a bed with a padded navy headboard, fluffy white comforter, and a sea of pillows.

My whole body gets tingly, and Reggie starts talking fast.

"I—uh, yeah, I'm totally going to sleep on the floor. Like, you don't even have to worry. I'm not going to, like, you know—yeah. I can even sleep in the hallway if that makes you more comfortable. And, like, guard the door! I'll totally guard the door!"

"Reggie . . ." I say, giggling. "You don't have to guard the door."

"Well, I will. I will guard the door." He's nodding so much, I worry his head is going to bob right off, and I can feel the waves of anxiety rolling off him.

"Let's just, um, watch a movie?" I suggest, pointing at the flatscreen in the corner. "And then we can discuss . . . sleeping arrangements."

"Yeah. Uh, yes, let's." He lets out a long breath, clearly relieved. "I got the snacks," he adds, digging in his backpack and pulling out some candy he bought at the chocolate shop earlier.

Except, the only movie we can find playing on TV is some cheesy romance with two thirty-somethings playing teens and not going more than five minutes without kissing or touching or doing . . . other things. And so even though I'm sitting up by the pillows and Reggie is sitting on the floor, his back against the bed, and even though we're sitting here munching on licorice and orange sticks and chocolate-covered marzipan, making jokes about the corniness with our mouths full and wearing the same sweaty clothes we've been in all day—basically the *least* romantic situation possible—all I can think about is kissing and touching and doing . . . other things with Reggie.

But does he want the same?

With most guys, this wouldn't even be a question. We're in a hotel room, miles away from any distractions or interruptions, and I think I'm giving out the vibes that I want this. That I want him. I don't want to think about Charlie, but Charlie would make a move right now—not because he cared about me, just because he could. I know Reggie cares about me, but I also know what message I gave him, loud and clear, when I rejected his kiss in June. How do I show him that it's different now, that I'm finally ready? How can I be sure this is still what he wants too?

"Well, uh, that was pretty good." He turns around as the movie credits roll, and I try to study his face for a sign. Except every sign—the way he's biting his lip, how much he's blinking—could be read one way . . . and also the complete opposite way.

"Yeah. It was good," I say.

"Good." Are we doomed to repeat this same adjective for the rest of the night?

"So, we better get to sleep. To drive back in the morning. I texted my mom that I was back at Ryan's, but she's going to start getting suspicious if I show up all late." He nods in agreement and stands up, and I do the same. My heartbeat is so thunderous, he must be able to hear it.

"Shit, we don't have toothbrushes or toothpaste . . . and oh no, your hair."

"My hair?" I ask, confused.

"Yeah, your hair. You probably don't have a bonnet. Or, like, a scarf? Whatever you use. My mom always forgets hers on trips and then sends my dad out to get her one at CVS. I can go to CVS if you want . . . or whatever the Solvang equivalent of a CVS is."

"No, no—that's okay." I'm actually really bad about consistently wearing my bonnet, and that's why my curls are permanently frizzy. But the fact that he's worrying about my curls? That's a sign.

"Wait, I have an idea." He holds up a finger and then walks over to the closet, pulling down some extra bedding. He holds out a pillowcase. "Maybe you can wrap this around it? I know it's not satin or anything, and actually, sorry, maybe this is a really stupid idea . . ."

"I'll try it," I say taking it from him. I wrap it around my head, tying it in the back and then I strike a pose. He looks at me funny, with his lips slightly parted and his eyelids heavy. His short, curly eyelashes sparkle in the low light of the room.

"What? I look ridiculous, don't I?" I start searching for a mirror, but he stops me, a finger lightly brushing my wrist. "No, you look beautiful. You always do."

Another sign. A *crystal-freaking-clear* sign.

This is it. He's going to kiss me. I want him to kiss me. My whole body is screaming for him to kiss me. He must feel it.

But a second later, he steps back, rubs the side of his head, and looks around the room. "Yeah . . . so yeah. Now that your hair is good, we're, uh, good."

There's that stupid word again. What in the world just happened?

"Anyway, so, I'm going to sleep on the floor," he says, taking another step back.

"You don't have to sleep on the floor, Reggie."

"Really, it's okay."

"No, actually it's not. Have you *seen* those black light videos of hotel rooms?" I smile big at him, wishing all the awkwardness away. Because this is all just so awkward. Why isn't he making a move? "If you sleep on the floor, you're going to catch some rare disease, like scarlet fever, and I can't have that on my conscience. Sleep on the bed. It's fine."

"Are you sure?" His voice is quiet, wobbly.

"I'm sure." I turn and get into the bed, so he can't protest anymore. Every time he does, it makes me doubt myself and my instincts even more.

"Okay, well, we can sleep head-to-toe," he says, taking the slowest steps ever to the other side. He puts a knee on the bed delicately, like he's testing the waters. "Except my feet are pretty funky. They're not, like, always this funky, but all the walking . . ."

I snort out a laugh. "It's fine," I repeat. "I'm comfortable. I promise."

That seems to be the last reassurance that he needs, because he finally, finally gets into the bed. There's still a significant space in between us, like there's an invisible line he's trying not to cross.

But I can still feel the warmth of his body and smell his scent—sweat, yes, but also the lingering smell of his cocoa butter lotion. I want to inch closer and lay my head on his chest. I want to press one perfect kiss to his lips. But it also feels too big, too bold, to make the first move. I wish I could know for sure it would end well.

"Should we turn out the light?" he asks. He takes his glasses off and puts them on the nightstand, and it's like seeing a secret side of him. I never noticed the thin rim of gray circling his dark brown eyes before, or the little indents his frames leave on the sides of his nose.

"Sure."

The room plunges into darkness, but it makes me even more aware. The rhythm of my breath matches his, and I feel like every single nerve ending on my body is on high alert. The bottom of my stomach aches, like it's reaching for him.

"Just so you know, I'd really like to hear your song one day." His voice is barely a whisper. "When you're ready, I mean."

"Thank you," I whisper back. "I really want to play it for you."

He exhales, and I swear his leg moves closer under the sheets. It feels like it's only a centimeter, a millimeter, away, like just a tiny nudge or a deep breath would close the distance.

But I don't move. I stay right where I am.

"Goodnight, Delilah."

"Goodnight, Reggie."

I listen to our mingled breaths until I finally fall asleep, still hoping for something that doesn't come.

REGGIE

I choked.

I completely fucking choked.

She was giving me the signs and everything. Her lips were plump and pursed, like she was offering them up, and her body was open and angled to me.

But every time I thought, *Yeah, this is it. I'm finally going to make a move*, my brain kept playing back the swerve. Except it had a background track that wasn't there the first time: Eric laughing at me with his friends, Tyrell and every asshole that's ever made fun of me. And it's like, why would Delilah want that guy, the weak, nerdy one that just sits there and takes it? I kept seeing her beautiful face transform into a pitying expression or, worse, a disgusted sneer, as soon as I tried to kiss her again, the total fool who didn't get the message the first time, and I just . . . couldn't do it. I couldn't risk Delilah looking at me that way, feeling that way about me. I don't know if I could come back from that.

So, as my eyes adjust to the darkness, I watch as she drifts off. It could be disappointment that settles all over her features, or it could be relief—I'm not going to find out tonight. Instead, I try to fix in my mind the little sighs she makes as she's asleep and the way that her eyelids flutter because I'm probably never going to see her again like this.

I don't know when I finally pass out, but it's late. Still, when I wake up at 6:12, according to the glowing red alarm clock, every inch of my skin is buzzing like I just drank three shots of espresso. And also my jeans, the jeans I slept in because I didn't want to freak her out by taking them off, are suddenly very tight.

I inch my body off the bed, careful not to wake her up, and tiptoe over to the bathroom. I take a piss, which takes care of one problem, and then I see what I got going on in the mirror. Smashed hair, crusty eye boogers, and oh no—I breathe into my palm—foul, *stanky* breath. If I had any tiny, infinitesimal hope left after screwing things up last night, well, that breath is going to murder it.

I gargle some water, scrub my teeth and my face with a washcloth. Not perfect, but better. When I walk back into the room, she's still sleeping, still making that sweet sighing noise, so I decide to go out and get us some food. Breakfast in bed has to offset the message I sent by freezing last night.

Twenty minutes later, I'm back with ebelskivers and orange juice from a bakery around the corner, and I'm feeling a whole lot better about my chances. Last night was one night. What me and Delilah have been building . . . it can't be messed up with one night.

Maybe I'll kiss her now. Yes, *now* is the right moment—when she won't feel pressured by a whole night ahead of us. Now there will be no awkwardness, no perceived expectations, just whatever she wants to do.

But when I open the door to our room, the bed is made and Delilah is standing there with her hair down and her shoes on.

"Should we call Karl?" she asks. Her jaw is set, her eyes determined. Maybe even angry. "I'm ready to go."

DELILAH

When I wake up Reggie is gone and my phone is full of passive-aggressive texts from Charlie. I'm so close to being where I want. *So close* that this in-between stage, my fingers grasping and just missing, is almost physically painful. I need to boldly go after what I want, without fear, or I'm going to be stuck in this purgatory forever.

So, I'm going to finally take action. Starting with quitting the band. Right now.

Well, not *right now* right now, because we still have to drive back to Long Beach. But as soon as possible.

"Should we call Karl? I'm ready to go," I say when Reggie walks into the room with a box of something that smells really good. He looks just as good, even in the same clothes from yesterday.

Something quickly passes across his face, something I can't read, but just as fast he's nodding and giving me a nose-wrinkling smile. "Yeah, of course! Fingers crossed Bessie is good to go."

And she is. After leaving our keys at the front desk with a confused woman named Patricia, we walk over to Karl's cherry-red car shop and Reggie's car is sitting right out front, blue hood sparkling in the early morning sun. Reggie pays Karl—I don't see how much, but it makes him wince when he sees it on the screen—and then we're back on the 101 again. We're not talking and singing, not like we were yesterday, but it's not awkward, thank god. It's the good kind of silence, the kind you can only exist in with someone you're 100 percent comfortable with. And I am with Reggie—all that happened last night, as disappointing as it was, only solidified that. There's no one else I'd rather do this drive with, to the soundtrack of the salty ocean air whipping in our open windows and Motown singers crooning on the radio. He makes my mind, my whole body, quiet down.

"Should I drop you off at home?" Reggie asks, when we drive past the blue-and-yellow beacon of IKEA off the side of the 405. It's a sign that we're almost back to Long Beach.

"No, actually . . . will you take me to Asher's?" I ask. "He lives over by El Dorado. I know it's kind of out of the way, but . . . yeah. I think I need to go there."

He takes his eyes of the road, a swift moment of consideration. "So you're doing this?"

"I'm doing this."

No *Are you sure*, no *Maybe you should wait until tomorrow*. With so few words, he gets me. He trusts me.

And I want to start trusting myself that much, too.

We pull up to Asher's midcentury modern house by the park about twenty minutes later. It's pretty small and has always looked kind of soulless to me, but I know it was designed by some fancy, important architect. Archer's mom made sure to tell me the first time I came over.

The minivan and Charlie's Volvo are out front, so I know they're back from SLO and that at least Charlie is still hanging around. I didn't really think this plan through, outside of just *right now*, so I'm glad they're together. It'll make this easier. They're probably all sitting around talking shit about me anyway.

"Do you want me to come with you?" Reggie asks as he cuts the car off.

"No. I've got this."

I walk down the familiar path to the garage, and even before I open the side door, I can hear their voices, playful and loud. But when I walk in, a hush falls over them. From the couch, Charlie crosses his arms over his chest and narrows his eyes. Beau's looking at me with concern, clearly holding back a lot of questions, but Asher looks everywhere else except at me.

"So, you're totally fine," Charlie says, looking me up and down exaggeratedly. "No broken bones, not even a scratch . . . I don't see any signs of an emergency."

He has a sarcastic smile on his face, so he can quickly claim he's just playing. But then he cocks his head to the side and shakes it, like he's called me in for an audience with him. Like he's sitting there in judgment of me.

And all of a sudden I'm mad. Ears roaring, chest burning mad.

Usually I would stamp it down, make it smaller, but I let it build. I let it fuel me, push me over the line so I can do what I want to do.

"I don't want to be in Fun Gi anymore."

"WHAT!" Asher yells, stumbling forward and knocking into his amp.

"Delilah, let's wait and—" Beau starts calmly, but Charlie cuts him off.

"C'mon, you don't mean that." He stands up with his hands out toward me, like he's trying not to spook something wild. "Don't do something you're going to regret just because you're emotional right now. We'll forgive you. We're just giving you a hard time. Be rational here, kid."

Kid. I used to bask in that nickname. It made me feel closer to them, to *him*, like I was a part of something special. Now it's like a match to the gasoline of my anger.

Charlie steps closer to put his arm around me, to placate me with his touch like I was so eager to accept before. But I step back, knocking his hand away from my shoulder.

"I am being rational. And I don't need your forgiveness," I say, each word a lick of flame.

"Well, I don't know about that," Charlie says, chuckling to himself. "You did, like, completely fuck us over by not showing up. It made us look really uncool in front of the festival people, and I'm not sure if you understand this, but it was already a big deal that we got that invite in the first place."

"Charlie, I'm sure she had a good reason," Beau says, clapping his shoulder.

"I mean, did she though?" Asher shakes his head. "If she's just bailing on us now."

"I know it's a big deal. And I know a big reason we got that invite is me."

Charlie throws his head back in a big laugh. "Are you joking?"

"It's true," I say, even though my body and my brain are throwing up alarm bells, alerting me that it's time to smooth this over, to run away. "You guys had been doing this for a while before me. And things only started changing, people only started paying attention, once I joined Fun Gi."

Asher snorts. "Um, hello, ego."

"And I know part of that is the novelty," I continue. "I know it's because there are no other bands on the scene with lead singers that look like me. And *I know*, I promise I do, that making music is teamwork. We're all working together to create what's getting people's attention now. It's not *just* me, it's all of us . . . collaborating."

"This is so—" Charlie starts, but I hold my hand up.

"Let me finish." He rolls his eyes, that infuriating smile still on his lips.

"Except, you couldn't even give me an equal part in this band. You had to diminish me and make me feel smaller than you, Charlie, even though I had just as much to bring to our music. And it wasn't only him." I turn to look at Asher and Beau. "You two didn't stand up for me either. I thought you were my friends."

Beau's mouth drops open like he's about to say something, but Charlie is already talking. "Is that what this is about? 'Cause

I didn't like your song?" His smile is morphing into a sneer. "You gotta get a thicker skin, Delilah. You gotta learn to pay your dues. We are the ones giving you an opportunity here."

Before I would have accepted that. I would have felt embarrassed, ashamed. Because isn't that what I thought before? Isn't that what I told Reggie that first night outside of The Mode?

But I don't believe that anymore.

"No," I say, clearly, firmly. "You weren't just giving me an opportunity. This was mutually beneficial. I gave this band as much as you gave me. And, you know, it seems to me like you gladly used me, used my Blackness, when it benefited the band and got you listeners that didn't care who you were before."

Charlie's mask of composure finally slips, and there's something mean, something ugly, there.

"Are you fucking serious?" he asks, his voice dripping venom. "Really, Delilah? Really? You're acting like I'm racist or something."

"I didn't say that."

"Well, good. Because that's so fucking stupid. You know it is, Delilah." He throws his hands up, like he's dealing with a petulant child. "You know my family has a—a *Black* Lives Matter sign on our lawn."

Behind him, Asher winces but doesn't say anything. Charlie continues, "With you . . . I—I don't even see color."

And there it is, all laid out. It's like by even bringing up the fact that I'm Black, even acknowledging that he sees me as Black too—it's suddenly become a challenge for him to prove he's not racist. Immediately his comfort, his needs, take precedent over everything else . . . I guess that's the way it's always been. I want to laugh, but I also want to scream. I see him so clearly now that I can't believe I ever saw him as any different before.

"I want you to see my color. It's part of who I am," I say, my words quieter now, calm. Because I've shown myself that I can be loud if I need to be. But also, I don't have to give anyone that much of me if I don't want to. I don't have to fight people who don't even deserve that. "And I know you do. That's okay. What's not okay is . . . *using* my color, using me, to benefit your music, and then turning around and keeping me out of everything else—making it clear that's all you thought I was good for."

Beau exhales loudly. "Damn. Delilah, I'm so sor—"

"Are you—nah. This is . . . you're just looking for excuses." Charlie sputters, shaking his head. He rubs his hand over his face, and all of a sudden the charming smile is back. "Listen," he says, voice warm and smooth again. "We both made mistakes here. We're both at fault. Can we just agree on that? Can we forgive each other?"

I know he wants me to take some of the blame—so he can tell himself the right story, so he doesn't have to accept that he did anything wrong. But I'm not going to do that for him.

I shrug. "Whatever you need to tell yourself, Charlie."

"Okay," he says, bobbing his head and waving his hand, like that's something minor we'll circle back to later. "But we don't need to make a decision now. Let's take a breather. We can talk more about it tomorrow."

"Yeah, Delilah. We need you," Beau says. His eyes are kind and his voice sounds genuine. It almost makes me reconsider. Because isn't that all I wanted? To be needed, appreciated in this band? But next to him, Asher's face is blank, and Charlie's lips are pressed so tight they're almost white. *They* are never going to tell me they need me.

"I know you do," I say, my eyes landing on all of them. "And I needed you too. But I don't anymore."

I turn and walk out the door. And as I make my way down the path, the roaring in my ears shifts to the roaring of waves, the sound of wind whipping through rolled-down windows. It's peace.

Reggie is leaning against his car, and the bright sun is making his brown skin look like it's lit from within. He shines. It's as if the universe is sending me a sign, brilliant and clear, un-ignorable. He raises his eyebrows, talking to me without any words, and I take long strides to close the space between us. Right before I reach him, though, I stop, and he tilts his head to the side, confused. I walk the rest of the way slowly, savoring the way he looks at me, the warmth radiating from his body as it reaches mine. We're toe to toe, and then nose to nose. I reach up to cradle his face in my hands and finally press my lips to his.

REGGIE

I'm standing there thinking about kissing Delilah, and all of a sudden I'm. Kissing. Delilah. And it feels like magic. Not just because it shifted from dream to *Oh shit, this is actually happening* faster than my brain can even process. But because her lips are so soft and her hair smells so good and her callused hands start on my cheeks but then move to my neck, my shoulders, pulling me closer. I wrap my arms around her waist and try to push down the feelings that I don't deserve this, that she's going to regret it as soon as it ends. Because this kiss is fast, feverish. It feels like months of feelings, of frustration, fighting to be known all at once.

When we finally pull away because I guess we have to breathe or whatever, I stare at her, starry-eyed and stunned.

"I've been wanting to do that, like, basically forever."

She rolls her eyes, a huge smile taking over her face. "Well, you didn't."

"I didn't. But also . . . I tried. And it didn't seem like it was what you wanted. It's hard to come back from that."

"I know. I'm sorry," she says. "I was just so worried about making sure it was right. I wanted to stand on my own first."

"And you do." I reach out and touch her hip, pulling her closer to me. "But let's be real. I think I'm the one in danger of losing myself here. I've already been gone."

She covers her face with her hands, but then smirks at me between her fingers. "Last night, though? I was sending all the signs. It got a little ridiculous."

"It did. I promise to just, like . . . ask you next time." I thread my fingers through the tiny curls at the back of her neck and brush our noses together before planting another kiss on her lips. She kisses me back, softer this time, and I can feel her smile blossom.

"I'll make this next part easy for you," she whispers. "You're my boyfriend now, Reggie Hubbard."

"Oh, am I?" I kiss both her cheeks, and then pull back to look at her and remind myself this is real.

"You are," she says. And even though her words are sure, something else flickers in her eyes. They ask a question.

"Well, I'm honored to call you my girlfriend, Delilah Cole," I say, hopefully erasing any doubt. I reach behind me and pull open Bessie's passenger door, holding her hand as she gets in. And then I practically sprint over to my side, all goofy, 'cause now that we've finally figured this out, I don't want to be away from her for even that long.

"Where to, sweetheart?" I ask. I want to suck the corny-ass word right back into my mouth as soon as I say it, because I'm not about to keep Delilah sounding like a grandpa. Or a virgin. Or a grandpa virgin. But thankfully her whole face lights up. She leans across the center console to brush a finger across my cheek.

"You get it, 'cause, like the song," I say, kissing her hand. "The one yesterday. In the car."

"I get it," she says, giggling. Her laugh, her vibe—everything about her is lighter. I don't know if it's what happened in there with the band, or if it's this, with us, but I'm grateful I get to witness it.

"I guess I probably need to go home." She sighs, twisting her lips to the side. "But first . . . can we just drive a little longer?"

"Of course." I say, one hand on the steering wheel, the other holding hers. "You pick the music."

WHO KNOWS?

DELILAH

"I was under the impression that this would be a fun, whimsical date! Not exercise!" Reggie shouts, as he pushes his legs forward double-time.

"It's fun! I'm having fun!"

I'm not having fun. Riding the swan pedal boats in the little man-made pond downtown sounded fun in theory, like one of those cute dates that couples do in movies. But it's at least ninety degrees out, because Southern California never gets the fall memo, and I can feel sweat pooling at the back of my neck and rolling down my spine. The only other people out on the boats are two pairs of tweens in dueling swans, cackling and hollering as they race back and forth on the water. We should have gone on the Ferris wheel instead.

"But seriously, are you trying to tell me something about my shrimpy legs?"

"Do shrimps have legs . . . or just claws?"

"Ah, she *conveniently* dodges the question!" He clutches his hands to his chest in mock offense. So I raise my eyebrows and shrug, like *You said it,* but then I smile and reach over to squeeze his left leg, showing him that I like them just fine.

He smiles back at me, that nose-wrinkling one that makes my whole body feel like a switch was flipped on. Then he leans in and kisses me deeply, his hands finding my hips.

Okay, so I guess the swan boats are a little bit fun.

And honestly, I would do anything with Reggie. Get my teeth cleaned, fold laundry, wait in the long Whole Foods line for my mom's specific brand of Greek yogurt. When I see him leaning against his car outside of my school—he drives across the city to be there every Monday, Wednesday, and Friday because of his senior early-out schedule—my heart beats at a faster tempo, and the butterflies in my chest start flapping their fluttery riffs, and there's the low, persistent pulse of my whole body on high alert. It's music. He makes everything, even the mundane, feel glossy and new, just a little more exciting.

I've already started trying to capture this feeling in a song. Something that might fit in Taylor Swift's *Lover* era . . . if she played electric guitar.

"Gross!"

"Get a room!"

The racing tweens are now only feet away, ogling us from their boats. One of them is holding up a brand-new iPhone, either filming us or himself, I can't tell.

"You think we can take 'em?" Reggie asks, a sly grin on his lips.

"Hell yeah."

"Hold on tight," he whispers to me, sneaking one last kiss.

"Last one to the dock is an ugly ogre!" he yells, pumping his not-at-all shrimpy legs as we leave the scrambling kids in our wake.

REGGIE

"Sometimes I think you're too good to be true."

It's Sunday morning, and we're sitting on steps, looking out at the boats docked in the marina. We already walked the farmers market, sampling peaches and figs and buttery pastries from the stands, and now we have a stack of pupusas and a giant pineapple agua fresca with two straws between us.

I almost cough up a big bite of beans and cheese when she says those words, but instead I study her face, pointing to my full mouth as an excuse. Has she found me out? Are these weeks of pure bliss about to come to their tragic, but not unexpected, end? I shouldn't be surprised . . . but I thought I would have more time.

But she isn't angry. Her lips and jaw get tight when that happens, and she's staring at me all heavy-lidded with her whole body facing my way. She doesn't *look* like someone who's realized that the whole personality I'm projecting to her is a fraud.

"Is that . . . good?" I ask tentatively.

"Yes, of course it's good," she says, beaming at me. "I just feel so lucky to be with you. You make me feel so special."

"You *are* special."

"And see, anyone can say that. But you show that. Even when you're so busy, with senior year and college applications and all this prep and negotiating for the podcast. You always make time for me."

My stomach dips, and it's not the good feeling I always get when she's this close to me, her bare shoulders offering themselves up as the perfect place to plant a kiss and her hand on my knee. No it's . . . guilt. And regret. Because no matter how good things get between us, there's always this, my initial lies, tainting everything, like how one red sock can ruin a whole load of laundry. We started this friendship with her thinking I'm someone—well, it's not *not* me, but just to the left of me. That's who she met, that's who kept her interested. And that was all fine and okay when we were just friends, seeing each other on random holidays once a month. But now that we're together, seeing each other as much as we can, it's required more lies, more half truths.

"I still don't fully get why it's taken months for you to start your run on the show. Is it really that big of a deal? Seems like they're making you jump through a lot of hoops."

Like that.

I shrug. "Yeah, most people don't know who Darren Lumb is, but for the people who do, he's like . . . nerd Beyoncé. So if I want to be on a season of the show, I gotta go through the motions, and, like, kiss the ring or whatever."

I can't even explain it away to make myself feel better. This is a complete lie. I mean, Darren Lumb *is* like Beyoncé to D&D superfans, but he's not making me fill out paperwork or negotiate anything. He invited me to come on *Role With It,* no conditions, easy as hell . . . and I turned him down. Even though talking to Darren and helping to shape a campaign on *Role With It* would be, like, the coolest thing ever, I just can't let go of all the reasons I told Delilah that day back in May when he first made the offer. I'm scared to be out there online, to let go of my anonymity. I'm scared what people will say when they know my name and my face—my internet trolls and the ones in my real life. But how do I say that to Delilah, when it goes against everything she understands about who I am?

God, I wish I could rewind to that first night and stop myself from fronting and trying to put on airs. Just be like, *Hey, I'm a huge nerd and very embarrassed by it, and that's why I admire you, someone putting yourself out there, because I am terrified to ever be my true, authentic self in front of anyone except the three friends I play a tabletop fantasy game with every Saturday instead of doing anything cool.*

But if I'd done that, we wouldn't be here right now.

She wouldn't be leaning in to kiss me, lips sweet with pineapple agua fresca.

"Sweetheart," I breathe in between each kiss, and she pulls back with a mischievous smile.

"Is that gonna be our thing?"

I hold my hands out and whip my head around like I'm lost. "What? Huh? Who are you? Where am I?"

"Because if it is. Well . . . I like it. A lot."

"Oh yeah?" I reach out and cup her face in my hand, stroking her cheek.

"Yeah. Even if that song is corny," she says with a smirk.

I throw my head back in a laugh. "Oh!"

"But yeah . . . I like being your sweetheart."

She leans her head on my shoulder, like it belongs there, and I know I'll do anything to keep us just as we are right now.

DELILAH

"What holiday is it today?" Reggie asks, his head resting on my pillow. My door is open and my mom is down the hallway, surely listening to every sound and ready to pounce at the first suspicious rustle. But even with those restrictions, Reggie here, on my bed, in my room—it feels intimate and right on the edge of something . . . more. Something I want. I wish we had figured out just how much we liked kissing each other when we were alone in that hotel room and didn't have to stop.

"Who knows? And do we still need the holidays? It seems to me the universe has done its job."

"I liked them," he says, scratching the side of his cheek. I reach my hand up to the scar on the right side of his lips, an open-ended parenthesis. It's become one of my favorite things about him because it's so faint that I only see it now that I can get so close, like it's a secret marking just for me.

He smiles and kisses my fingers. "But I guess I was using

them . . . sorta like an excuse?"

"What, an excuse to get me to hang out with you?" I say with a wink.

"No. I mean, well . . . that, too. Yes." He covers his face with his hands. "But I guess I was using them to, I don't know, like, hype myself up? When I would think you were out of my league—which you are, for the record—and, you know, get scared, I would use them as signs. That we were meant to be." He's peeking between his fingers, and I can see the insecurity in his eyes. I get flashes of this other side of him—vulnerable and unsure—every once in a while, and they feel like little gifts. Another part of Reggie that he doesn't share with anyone else because he's otherwise so confident and self-assured. It makes me want to show my secret sides to him too.

"Can I play you something?"

His eyes brighten and he starts nodding excitedly. "Yes. Yes, yes, yes."

So I walk over and grab Mabel from her case and sit down on Georgia's bed across from him. I feel my throat get tight with nerves because last time I risked this, it went nothing like I hoped. But I swallow that worry down. I take a deep breath and start to sing the new lyrics I've been working on, about how I feel right now. Like how I can be my whole self with Reggie because he's his whole self with me. My eyes study my fingers instead of him, as I pick out the notes and chords on Mabel as best as I can.

When I'm done, it takes me a second to look back up at his face, because I'm scared what I might find. I'm happy with what I'm creating. I'm proud of my work, and I'm not going to let anyone take that away from me. But this is different from just sharing it with Charlie, Asher, and Beau. If Reggie doesn't like my music . . . it'll be a lot more painful.

But every single one of his teeth is showing in the biggest grin, and he's staring at me all wide-eyed, like I'm something special.

"Delilah, that was—that was beautiful."

"Yeah?" Relief and joy bubbles up in my chest and comes out as a giggle.

"Um, yeah." He stands up from my bed and walks over to Georgia's, kneeling in front of me. "I mean it. I'm so fucking impressed. How did I get the coolest, most talented girlfriend ever?"

I can feel my cheeks burn. "Oh, stop."

"No, for real. Like, you need to record that right now because it's all I want to listen to . . . basically forever."

I roll my eyes, but his words fill me up with giddiness. "Well, nothing can really happen without a band," I say, trying to temper my feelings. "It needs something more, like a drumbeat that starts off slow, maybe a little . . . irregular? And then builds into something heavy—does that make sense? And then the bass, well, I don't really know, yet but—"

He kisses me, swift and sure.

"You'll figure it out," he says as he pulls away, our noses still touching. "I believe in you."

And when he says it, I believe in myself too.

HALLOWEEN

REGGIE

"Hey, yo, where's your costume, baby bro?" Eric says, grabbing my shoulder.

He's having friends over for Halloween—*not a party*, if my parents ask—so I was waiting until the very last second to leave my room and make a beeline for my car. I thought I would be done with all this hiding and sneaking around after Eric and his friends graduated in June. But they all stayed local for college and have continued to patrol our hallways like the Goombas in Super Mario Bros. And apparently I wasn't slick enough this time because I've somehow found myself in a crowd of Lakers, or at least guys dressed up like Lakers, standing at my front door.

"Yeah, isn't this your thing?" Tyrell asks. He has a dramatic unibrow drawn on and he's holding a fog machine. But I guess my lack of a costume is more important to him, because he sets it down and turns his attention to me with a douchey look in his eyes. "You could be wearing your like, unicorn horns, or whatever it is you fucking do, and no one would say *shit* to you tonight, bruh!"

"He's probably trying to play it cool 'cause of his girlfriend," Eric says, nudging Tyrell with his elbow. "That girl's about to be running if he pulls out the unicorn horn."

"I don't even own a unicorn horn," I mumble, but it's drowned out by Frankie hollering, "Reggie's got a girlfriend? This Reggie? No!"

"She white?" Tyrell asks, and they all explode into laughter. "This chick *has* to be white!"

"Hey, hey, now! You can't even be saying nothing to him, Tyrell." Eric slaps his shoulder. "Ain't like you got a girl here with you tonight . . . or any night!"

"Oh!" Frankie pumps a fist, and Tyrell covers his face and laughs.

Eric points at me and winks, and I don't get what he's trying to do. Is this supposed to mean something, him taking Tyrell down a notch? Is it supposed to make me feel better?

All I know is I don't want to spend any longer thinking about it. I weave my way around them and walk out the door to meet Delilah and my friends.

Everyone else is wearing costumes. And it's not like I can even claim I didn't get the memo, because Yobani sent out a significant number of memos. But the idea of being dressed up here at Pa's Pumpkin Patch, a very much public place, made my stomach feel sick. I don't want that kind of attention or eyes on me—I mean, look what I got with Eric and his friends when I was just trying to exist—and wearing a costume as an almost adult feels like an invitation for eyes on me.

Most of their costumes are pretty low-key, thank god. Leela and Ryan are two doctors from *Grey's Anatomy*, a show I didn't even realize was still on, and Yobani is Miles Morales, but he has a hoodie on with the mask pulled down around his neck because he kept bumping into little kids. Delilah is dressed like Poly Styrene from that band she likes, X-Ray Spex, with a bright red jacket and a captain's hat, which of course no one gets—she just looks really cool. Greg, though, went all out as Slarog, the cloud giant from our D&D campaigns. I'm talking grayish-white skin, a blue wig, some tall-ass boots that make him tower over us. He's even wearing this, like, metallic loincloth thing that he—for all of our sakes—put some gym shorts under. It's a lot.

"Mommy, is he Thanos?" a little boy in a Buzz Lightyear costume asks, squinting up at Greg.

"Thanos has purple skin," Greg explains. "Though it does appear blue at times in the movies due to the inconsistent lighting choices of the directors. But it's purple in comic book canon. Regardless, it is not gray."

Buzz's mom grabs his hand and pulls him away through the packed crowd.

"Good looking out, bro," Yobani laughs, patting Greg's heaving padded shoulder.

"I'm happy to help," Greg says with a shrug. "Hey, do you think they'll let us on the carousel? There's one horse with a missing right eye and a gold tooth that I used to ride on every year."

"Oh my god, yes!" Ryan shouts. "I need to see this horse immediately."

We decided on Pa's Pumpkin Patch for tonight because it's where we all used to come as kids. But after the initial wave of nostalgia passed, the rides look a lot smaller than I remember—and a lot rustier than their Disneyland counterparts, like they've seen some shit. Greg's horse friend definitely has a secret family and a pack-a-day smoking habit. And the actual field of pumpkins is overrun with parents carrying big-ass cameras and ring lights to photograph their drooling toddlers. All to what—post on their Instagrams? It's stupid. I don't know . . . maybe I'm just in a bad mood after what happened at home. I need a handful of fun-size candy bars, stat.

"So . . . I have to ask—" Delilah starts as we're standing in line for the carousel.

"How the show went last night?" Ryan asks.

Delilah's cheeks go pink as she nods hesitantly. Fun Gi played a show with the Valentines at The Mode last night, their first since Delilah left the band, and I know she's been wanting to ask Ryan about it ever since we arrived but is nervous about what she might hear. I squeeze her hand in encouragement.

"Oh, they fucking sucked!" Leela yells, and two dads in front of us dressed as Bert and Ernie turn around to give us dirty looks.

"They were . . . fine," Ryan says, pronouncing "fine" like the four-letter word it is. "Like they were fine before. But what the four of you had . . . man. It was different. Like, how your vocals danced around Charlie's riffs, that sharp and soft contrast, and how

Beau and Asher were always so in sync, like this sturdy backbone. It was just this perfect, like . . . *synergy*."

Delilah's face is a mixture of pride and melancholy. I know she misses it. Not being treated like a second-class member of the band, but being on stage, putting all of herself out there like that for an audience.

"You don't get that all the time. Some people never get it." Ryan pauses, maybe realizing how much she's killing the mood. She points at Delilah and smiles. "You, though? You were the spark. So you'll get it again, when the time is right."

"Plus, okay, I know I don't actually know anything about music, but I'm pretty sure Charlie massively screwed up that last song," Leela says, leaning in conspiratorially. "I mean, what even *was* that?"

"Tell me more!" Delilah laughs, leaning in too, and the three of them begin dissecting every second of the performance.

"Hey, you're one of those *Game of Thrones* dudes, aren't you?" Scooby-Doo, holding a baby Shaggy, has stopped in the middle of the one tiny walkway, blocking traffic to the pony rides. "The icy dudes that killed that other dude who could only say his name. Man, I loved him." He narrows his eyes, as if Greg might actually be guilty of killing Hodor.

"I believe you're referring to the White Walkers. I'm a cloud giant named Slarog, who actually looks nothing like the White Walkers."

Scooby-Doo's face brightens at that. "Oh yeah? Well, right on." He shuffles away, with baby Shaggy waving over his shoulder.

Greg turns back to me and Yobani, totally unaffected by the bizarre interaction that just took place. "Actually, they're doing some really innovative stuff with cloud giants in this newest season of *Role With It*. It's really making me see them in a whole new light."

"Oh my god, yeah, that twist with those cloud giant twins in the last episode." Yobani mimes a chef's kiss. "Brilliant."

"Reggie, what did you think about—" Greg starts, but then he taps his gray-painted forehead. "Ahh, sorry. I guess you're probably not listening to it."

Fuck.

Well, hopefully Delilah missed that, deep in her Fun Gi shit-talking sesh with Leela and Ryan.

"Why would he not be listening to it?" Delilah asks.

Fuuuuck.

I need to think fast.

"Because I don't want to be influenced, you know, when it's finally my turn to play a campaign on the show."

"But wait, I—" I shoot Yobani a pleading *Bro, just go with it* look and thankfully he gets it.

"Yeah, yeah that makes sense," he says. "Gotta keep a clear canvas."

Greg's thick eyebrows are furrowed, but Yobani jabs him with an elbow, and before he can say anything to blow up my spot, the tinkly music playing from the carousel's speakers starts blasting. It speeds up to three, four, times its normal tempo, and the ride's spins seem to match it. The kids on the horse scream in delight, throwing their hands up as their hair and candy baskets fly behind them.

"Is this supposed to be happening?"

"Uh . . . I don't think so.

"This! Is! Awesome!!" a tiny Oscar the Grouch screeches with each disturbingly faster cycle.

"Be careful! Hold on, Dashel!" a worried Ernie calls back.

We get out of there before we have to see just how many fun-size candy bars Oscar has already gobbled tonight.

I can feel Yobani's eyes burning a hole in the back of my head as we drive south down PCH, looking for a beach with an open fire pit. When we finally find a spot at Bolsa Chica, Greg asks Leela to take a picture of his costume with the sunset behind him, and Ryan and Delilah go along to hype him up.

"So are we going to talk about that?" Yobani asks as he unloads some firewood we picked up into the ring.

"Talk about what?"

He looks up at me and rolls his eyes, unimpressed with the play-dumb strategy.

"I just don't get it," he continues. "I thought that was all cleared up back in the spring. And, like, what a weird thing to lie about for so long. It really doesn't make sense to me, unless, I don't know, Delilah's some undercover *Role With It* superfan and we all didn't know about it."

"No, definitely not. That's why it's been so easy to like . . . dodge her questions about it."

Yobani blinks at me. "To lie, you mean."

"Yeah, okay," I sigh. "To lie. Or whatever."

"But why?" he asks. I can tell he's frustrated with me, but he's putting all those feelings into packing newspaper between the logs. "I know I was telling you to play all these games before, but Greg was right—"

"Oh man, I gotta get a recording of you saying that," I laugh, trying to lighten the mood. But Yobani doesn't bite.

"Greg was right," he repeats. "The games were stupid. And even if they weren't, like, this isn't even a good game. Lying about being on some niche podcast—though it definitely is the superior niche podcast—what does that even get you with Delilah?"

I glance around the beach and make sure they're still far away. I'm not about to be caught again.

"It's not just about the podcast. It's what being on the podcast represents, you know? It fits in with the guy she thinks I am."

"What does that even mean?"

"Delilah, she—she thinks I'm this totally cool, confident guy that doesn't care what anyone thinks. Like, the way I am with you guys . . . she thinks I'm that way in all parts of my life. With my family, online. That I'm always just living my truth or whatever, no matter who is around."

Yobani is quiet for a bit as he lights the newspaper and uses a stick to get the fire going. "Let me get this straight. Delilah knows you're a nerd, but she thinks you're a . . . cool nerd?"

"Exactly." I snort out a laugh. "See, it's really not that big of a deal. It's just, like, you know, little things."

Yobani sits down on the sand, the fire he built lighting up his face. "But the little things add up."

I shake my head and look away.

"Listen, I doubt she expects you to be perfect. And she seems to really like you, bro. I'm sure if you show her—"

"What, that I'm a scared, insecure wimp? That even my family thinks I'm a joke, but I don't have the balls to stand up to them—or anyone? You really think she's going to like all that?" The words make my throat burn as they fall out. Saying them out loud makes them feel even more true, which makes them hurt all the more.

"I think she'll surprise you. And I don't think you're being fair to yourself. Reg, you're—"

"I don't need some fake pep talk right now." I roll my eyes and kick at the sand with my feet.

"It's not fake. But okay, man." I hear him exhale loudly. "I just think . . . you're not even giving her a chance to prove you wrong. To, like, make her own choice here."

"You have no business giving me advice, Yo. It's senior year and you've never had a serious girlfriend."

The words aren't anything terribly new. We're always messing with each other, taking jabs, but . . . my tone. It's ugly and mean; it's meant to wound. And when I look up at Yobani, it seems like it did the trick.

His eyebrows are pressed together, and his lips are tight. Finally, he starts to slowly shake his head. "Okay, Reggie."

Everyone comes back soon after, and it's all light and fun again. Yobani cracks jokes about Greg's photoshoot and Greg excitedly shows off the "epic" shots and at some point Ryan starts singing some old Disney Channel song about monsters, and Delilah turns it into a duet. I keep trying to catch Yobani's eye and send him a silent apology, but eventually he pulls down his Miles Morales mask, shutting down that conversation for now.

I try to lose myself in this rare cold night—the weather always dips below seventy at Halloween and stays cool enough for sweaters until maybe MLK day, if we're lucky. I focus on how good it feels to be cuddled up under this blanket with Delilah, warm and cozy as our breath lingers in the chilly, salty air. I think about how this is everything I wanted, everything I dreamed about at the beginning of this year that's coming to an end.

But my mind keeps bouncing back to what Yobani said. He acted like it would be so easy, just a simple conversation, but I know it's not like that. Showing Delilah all of me, all of my vulnerabilities and anxieties and faults at this point—well, it would be like presenting her with Captain America and then whipping off a mask to show her she's really with that weirdo-looking CGI Steve Rogers. Except, I am wimpy CGI Steve Rogers at my best, so it would be like giving her, I don't know . . . wimpy CGI Steve Rogers's left pinkie finger or something.

Plus, for months, I've been encouraging her to take risks and put herself out there. How is she going to take it if she finds out I don't even do that myself? That I'm a fraud who walks, no, *runs* away from exposure, like a cockroach when a bright light flicks on. Would she still want me? I don't know. In her eyes, it could be a betrayal.

Delilah's hands creep under my shirt, sending sparks all up and down my spine, and she leans her head on my shoulder in the spot that I swear was created just for her.

I don't want to lose this.

But it's also not fair to her to be in this and not *be in this*.

Yobani is right. I know that. I need to allow her to make her own choice here. And if I never show her all of me and actually give her that choice, I'll always be questioning what we have.

But I want to make sure we're solid. That we have the best chance of weathering it through as one tough conversation and nothing more. I just need a little more time.

THANKSGIVING

DELILAH

It's the morning of Thanksgiving when I realize I'm in love with Reggie. Maybe. Probably.

Georgia was the first one to call it out, only a week ago.

"You really love that boy, don't you?" she said, just like that, without hesitation.

"What are you talking about?"

She smirked at me, put her hand on her hip. "Oh, you know exactly what I'm talking about, D. You used to be all . . ." She closed her eyes halfway and pressed her lips tight, with one little quirk on the right side. "But now you're all . . ." She stretched her face into a wide smile, like a deranged Cheshire Cat. "And I know it's because of him."

"God, I hope I don't look like that," I said, and she laughed.

"It's a good thing. I *like* seeing you like this."

"Even though I broke the 'pact'?" I asked, curling my fingers in air quotes.

She shrugged like it wasn't the huge deal I made it out to be in my mind. "I was worried, but instead of losing yourself in him, you're, like, even more yourself." She wiggled her whole body in my direction, making her voice low. "Because you looooooooove him."

I rolled my eyes. "You are so dramatic."

Her support has made me happy, because I had been so scared what she might think. But the rest of that . . . I tried to push the ridiculous idea out of my mind. It's too fast, too soon. I need to be rational about this.

But lying here with Reggie right now, our legs tangled together on my couch . . . it doesn't seem so far-fetched.

"We should probably go," he murmurs in my ear, kissing that spot right behind it that makes my lower stomach ache.

"Do we have to?" I whisper back, and he laughs. I can feel it on my neck, as his lips trail down from there to my collarbone.

Mom, Andre, and Georgia have already left for an earlier meal at Andre's parents' house, but Mom gave me permission to spend the day with Reggie and his family. And that's where we're headed, except he showed up an hour before we're due there, and we didn't want to waste the time.

"I wish we didn't, but if we show up late . . . my parents will know why we showed up late."

"Okay, you're right." I press one last kiss to his lips, and tuck my fingers into the very top of his waist band, so I can feel the soft skin there.

He groans. "You're killing me."

"I know." I stand up and smooth down the plaid T-shirt dress that I put on just for this occasion. As much as I want to stay here and get lost with Reggie, I also know how important today is. I've only had quick greetings and conversations with Reggie's family until now—it seems like we're always on the way to somewhere else. But today I'm going to spend the whole afternoon and evening with not just them, but his whole extended family at his grandma's place in Artesia. It feels like a test, and I don't want to mess it up. I want to show this boy that I maybe, probably love that I can fit right into his life.

He smiles up at me from the couch like I'm some kind of treasure. "You look great. They're gonna love you."

And I hope you do, too.

REGGIE

Inviting her to Thanksgiving dinner was sorta like a deadline for myself. I've been avoiding having her and my family in the same room for too long up until this point. I didn't want my parents to show how embarrassed they are of me with their head shakes and heavy sighs, or Eric to mock me mercilessly while I just stand there and take it, therefore revealing what an actual nerdy loser I am and losing her respect forever.

But there's no hiding at Thanksgiving. Not with the people that have been there for everything. *Everything* everything, like the time I was six and my cousin Jerry stepped on my Baneslayer Angel Magic card, making me cry so much that snot was bubbling up and dripping down my face.

They know me, the real me, and they're not about to let anything go.

So I knew I would have to come clean with Delilah about my insecurities and how I really navigate through the world: cautious

and quiet instead of the bold *Take me as I am* front I've been projecting to her.

But then I just . . . didn't.

The moment never felt right. There was always a reason not to.

And also, there's the fact that . . . I think I love her. Well, I *know*
I love her. And every time I thought about being completely honest
with her, my chest got tight and my stomach felt sick because it's
possible that she'll decide she doesn't want me anymore. That she'll
walk away.

But still, I know I need to let myself be vulnerable with her.
I need to show her all of me and give her a chance to accept that
person instead of this façade I've created.

First, though, I have to get through this dinner. And then I'll
tell her that I love her, and hopefully everything else I'll tell her
won't be such a big deal because she'll love me too.

DELILAH

My nerves make my insides feel all twisted as we walk up the path to the little orange, Spanish-style house, but they vanish as soon as Reggie's grandma Lenore flings the front door open.

"Is that my Reggie? Look at you, walking up here like a little adult. And now who is this beauty you've got here with you?" She doesn't wait for an answer before putting her arms out. "Both of you, come give Grandma a hug."

Grandma Lenore is wearing a velvet, floor-length green kaftan with golden curls piled high on her head, and her smooth brown skin is probably right there in the encyclopedia next to the term "Black don't crack." She is fabulous. Reggie had explained to me before that she's not his grandma by blood, just through marriage, but some of her spark has definitely transferred to him. They're both bold and secure in themselves in the same way; there's a family resemblance there.

She pulls us into a tight hug, and even though I just met her, it doesn't feel fake. There's real love there, as she smiles and winks my way when Reggie introduces me as his girlfriend.

And walking into her house is like getting another hug. It's full of people—warm and welcoming, lively and loud. There are kids in the corner, playing *Animal Crossing* on their Switches and arguing over an Uno game. Reggie's aunties and his cousin Jerry are finishing up the food in the kitchen, shouting instructions to each other over the beeping of timers, and the sound of hearty laughter and dominos slapping down sound like thunder coming from the garage, where his uncles and dad are congregated. The sound of the football game, playing on three separate TVs, is the constant soundtrack to it all.

"Oh, Delilah!" Reggie's mom greets me with a bright smile, the same as Reggie's. "I'm so happy you could spend the day with us."

"Thank you for inviting me, Mrs. Hubbard," I say, pushing down all the nerves that come with talking to my boyfriend's mom. This boyfriend that I probably love. "My mom wanted me to pass on her thanks for your hospitality."

"Oh, you don't have to thank me!" She leans in close and adds in a mock whisper, "Because I don't even do any of the work. One potato salad incident years ago, and now they don't even let me in the kitchen. Who's to say if it was on purpose or not?" She laughs and raises her eyebrows, and I join in, my nerves melting away.

"Now, I need to get your mom's number—"

"Yeah, I really don't think that is necessary," Reggie cuts in with a smirk.

She playfully pops his shoulder. "Yeah, me and Delilah's mom are 'bout to become real good friends, I think. We need to be comparing notes, spying on y'all, with the two of you getting so serious."

I look at Reggie to see how he reacts to that, and the steady look and slight nod he gives me back makes all the tension drain out of my body. If I told him I loved him . . . I think I know how he'd respond.

"Now let me introduce you to my brother, Ed. He's going to adore you!" Mrs. Hubbard puts her hand on my back and spends the next hour touring me around to all the relatives. And when we all stand in a big circle, holding hands to say grace before the meal, Reggie squeezes mine extra tight, meaningfully, and it really does feel like I belong right here.

There are so many people that everyone can't fit at one table, so we end up at an extra one in the living room with Reggie's brother and cousins: Eric, Jerry, Lenore (named after Grandma Lenore) and Wally—and their boyfriends, Alex and Kieran.

I try to follow their conversation as I work my way through my massive plate filled with turkey, ham, mac and cheese, greens, and candied yams. (The food feels like a hug too.) Their talk is like a dance, or maybe even a boxing match—but one between two old friends that ends in a handshake. They go from something innocuous, like the USC vs. UCLA game last week, to roasting Wally's "paddle feet" in seconds, and I feel like I'm gonna pull a muscle in my neck twisting it back and forth, trying to keep up. They all seem to take it and then dish it out right back, though, like when

Eric is teasing Lenore over her "bougie gap year" and saying she thinks she's better than them. Lenore grins slyly and says, "I got an A on that English 100 midterm paper that I know you totally bombed, so it seems like CSULB agrees I'm better than you, too." And Eric just laughs, taking a big bite of stuffing and nodding his head.

It's not until later, when Wally and Kieran have left to go see Kieran's family, that Reggie finally has an arrow launched his way and the playful vibe totally shifts.

"Okay, this"—Jerry says, pointing between the two of us—"I just gotta say it. *This* I don't get."

Eric throws both his hands up like we're in church. "Thank you! Delilah, you're real fucking cool." He whispers the "fucking," leaning in so the aunties don't hear. "So, like, what are you doing with my brother?"

I look to Reggie, thinking he'll jump in and throw it right back, like they've all been doing. Like I've seen *him* do with Yobani and Greg. But . . . something is wrong. Reggie's face is twisted into a grimace, and his shoulders are rolled forward, whole body tense. He doesn't look them or me in the eye.

I'm not sure what's going on, but I decide to take the lead here for him. "See, and I ask myself what he's doing with me," I say with a shrug. "I'm the lucky one here."

Alex and Lenore look at each other and murmur, "Awwww!" But Jerry and Eric explode into raucous laughter, slapping the table and throwing their heads back.

"How much—h-how much did he pay you—to say THAT!"

Eric gasps out in between laughs.

"She's a plant!" Jerry calls, clutching his sides.

I look to Reggie again, trying to figure out what I'm miss-ing here, but he's looking away and shaking his head. I know it's normal to take your families down a notch—Georgia and I do it all the time—but this feels off. Especially when Reggie isn't being the Reggie I know, the Reggie who doesn't care what other people think.

"Okay, I don't get what that's all about," I say, trying to keep a smile on my face. "But I mean it. Reggie is the coolest person I know, and just so—so . . . solid and sure of himself. I want to be more like him."

That sends them into another frenzy, and Lenore fixes them with a glare. "Y'all need to chill."

I turn to Reggie, my eyebrows raised in question, and when his eyes meet mine, finally, he just sighs and shakes his head again. "It's whatever. It's fine."

"If you out here talking 'bout *Reggie is the coolest person I know*, then you must be into that nerd shit like he is." Eric closes one eye and shakes a finger at me. "You got me, Delilah. You don't look like one of 'em!"

My chest burns, realizing finally that Eric is one of those people who think less of Reggie because he doesn't fit into some specified mold. He's talked about that before, but I don't think he's ever mentioned it with his brother . . . has he? No, I would have remembered that. And I'm so confused why Reggie's just sitting here silent when he's always told me he takes a stand—like he's pushed me to take a stand.

"Reggie is actually really well known for his 'nerd shit,'" I say, my voice tight. "He writes essays about Dungeons & Dragons that get thousands of views, and he was even invited onto this really famous podcast, *Role With It*, because they respect his knowledge of 'nerd shit' so much."

"Essays! This fool is out here writing essays for fun!" Eric laughs, and Jerry joins in.

But Alex clears his throat, cutting in. "That's so cool, Reggie. I love *Role With It*, listen to it every Friday when I'm braving the 405 to see this one." He smiles at Lenore. "What do you think of the new guy they added this season, Jason Henry? His views on racism and colonialism in the game are really interesting, and I like what he's bringing to this campaign. I think it was a perspective they, uh, desperately needed."

That seems to hit Reggie more than anything his brother and Jerry said. His eyes go wide and he sits back in his seat, away from me. But that doesn't make sense. None of this makes any sense. And wait, why is this other guy on the show doing the exact thing they wanted Reggie to do? Why would they bring on someone else, unless . . .

Oh.

REGGIE

The *should've*s are already starting in my head. I should've just sent an insult right back to Eric when he started this up to maybe, like, confuse him into cutting it out. I should've at least laughed along with him, like I was in on the joke, instead of sitting here all frozen and scared. I should've told him to shut up, should've taken Delilah's hand and walked away to get some sweet potato pie. I definitely, absolutely should've said something, anything, when Alex brought up the new guy on *Role With It*, the guy who apparently took up the spot that they were looking for me to fill.

But I didn't.

And now Delilah is looking at me with her brow furrowed, her lips twisted to the side, and it's like something clicks.

She stands up.

"I—I'm sorry. I just. Um. I need to go outside for a sec." She turns and walks out of the room, with purpose. And I guess that purpose is to get away from me.

That makes Eric and Jerry stop laughing, finally.

Jerry jerks a finger in Eric's direction. "Was it something he said?"

"You guys play too much," Lenore says, giving them an earth-shattering eye roll. "You should go check on her, Reggie. That seemed like . . . something more than just these assholes."

"Hey!" Eric shouts.

I stand up, trying to shoot everything I'm feeling toward him—anger, hurt, betrayal—in one look. "Why the fuck do you do this?"

Eric's head jerks back and his eyes go wide in surprise. I leave before he can give me some bullshit answer.

Delilah's already down at the corner when I step outside, so I jog to catch up with her.

She's standing super still, like I've noticed she always does when a migraine is coming, like her head might tip off her body if she makes one wrong move.

"Listen—"

"I already called a ride," she cuts me off, showing me the app on her phone. "It should be here in two minutes—oh, actually, one minute now."

"Delilah, let me drive you home. *Please.* Let's talk about this."

"So there's something to talk about, then? Something is going on?"

I consider smoothing this over, saying what I need to say to make this all smaller. The words flow through my head with ease, sit on the tip of my tongue. But I know I can't keep doing that. Not if I want this relationship with her to be all that I know it can be.

"Yes."

She looks at me, and it's like time slows down and I can see the moment that her heart breaks. "Okay."

"I promise it's not as bad as it looks, though. If we could just talk about it, then I know—"

"How will I even know if you're telling the truth? Because whatever that was in there—" She points toward the house. "One thing I'm pretty sure I gathered is that you haven't been honest with me."

"Delilah, I have been honest . . . about the important things at least."

"Oh, and who gets to decide what's important?" She exhales loudly and then holds her hand up. "You know what? We can talk, but not right now. I need to think."

And of course, right at that moment, a silver Honda Civic pulls up to the curb, and a woman with curly blond hair and a turkey hat rolls down the window. "Delilah?"

"Yes, that's me," she says, rushing to open the door. She turns back to me and I don't even recognize that expression she's giving me, probably because I haven't fucked up this much to deserve it before. "Can you tell your grandma I said thank you? And your parents too? Tell them I had a lovely night but something came up with my family."

"Delilah, please don't leave."

"I'll text you tomorrow."

Then she gets in the back seat and is driven away from me. From us.

BLACK FRIDAY
REGGIE

After ignoring my pleading texts all night, Delilah agrees to meet with me at the park a block from her complex. When she walks up, she's pulling her flannel around her like it's freezing. Her curls, usually bouncing everywhere like they're a sentient life force, are pulled back into a ponytail, and her eyes have deep bags under them. She looks like she got as little sleep as I did.

"Hey." I wave at her, and she nods back, giving me that tiny smile with the side of her lips just barely upturned. But she quickly removes even that little expression from her face.

"Should we . . ." I start, pointing to a bench. We're the only ones here—the rest of the world is probably shopping Black Friday deals from bed.

"Yeah. Sure."

Her hand is in between us as we sit down, and I try to take it, like I always do. But she pulls it back to her own lap, clasping her fingers together as if to protect them from me. My heart plummets to my stomach, like I'm on the worst roller coaster ever, and the little hope I was grasping on to starts to slowly slip away.

"So."

"So."

She takes a deep breath and then exhales slowly, steadying herself. "So. Yesterday was really good. Until it wasn't. Until it got just . . . very confusing. When we were with your cousins, that guy sitting next to me . . . it felt like I didn't know him. And, Reggie, I really hated feeling like I don't actually know you, my boyfriend."

She finally looks me in the eye then, her brown eyes big and questioning, and I know this is my moment to save everything. I start talking fast.

"You're right. You're so right. And see, I was thinking about it last night. You know how you're always talking about how you feel like a different person on stage? I think what I was doing . . . well, what I've *been* doing . . . I think it's sorta like that."

Something hot and angry flickers in her eyes, and I know immediately that I've said the wrong thing.

"That is not even close to the same thing," she says, her voice steely. "That was in the band. For show. I've always been real with you."

"Okay, yeah. I'm sorry. I only meant—"

She's already shaking her head, holding her hand up. "Stop. Just . . . actually, we need to back up. I need you to tell me exactly what I'm dealing with here, because I'm not even sure I fully understand." She sighs heavily. "Or, I think I do. But I was up all night, going back and forth between getting so . . . *pissed* at you, and then, like, gaslighting myself and telling myself that I'm overreacting.

That it's not a big deal. So I need to just hear it from you. All of it. What is happening, Reggie?"

Her voice cracks when she says my name, and it breaks something in me. I've told myself that all of this wasn't hurting anyone and that it was so minor, but seeing her like this—it's hard to keep that narrative going in my head. I owe her honesty. I owe her everything.

So, I tell her how I saw her on stage and fell in love immediately, except I don't say the L-word because I don't want this to be the first time she hears it from me. I tell her how I faked all that confidence sitting there on the curb outside of The Mode because I knew that a girl like her would never like an anxious, insecure guy like me, so I basically role-played cool. I couldn't hide my nerdy interests because of that stupid shirt, so I pretended to have no shame in what I like, even though I actually have, like, all of the shame. Even though my brother and his friends and assholes all my life have mocked me mercilessly for what I like. And it just . . . spiraled from there when I realized she liked that person and I might have a chance with her if I kept being him. New Reggie. New Reggie is secure in his dorkiness and his Blackness. New Reggie wouldn't be scared to put his name on his writing or show his face on an internationally famous podcast. And I told little lies that became big lies because I kept them going for so long. Because I was so scared to lose her.

When I'm done, when I've confessed everything, I study her face to see if there's any hope for us left.

DELILAH

As I listen to him speak, everything clicks into place. He always seemed too good to be true . . . because he was. I was falling for a character, an ideal, instead of a real person. But still, I'm trying to parse through all of it for the guy I know, the guy I connected with. Because what we had felt so real. How could it feel that way if so much of what he showed me was fake?

When he's finished, I can see him searching my face for absolution, and I want to give him that. I really do. I want to lean my head on his shoulder and wind our fingers together and have everything be okay again. But I know if I do that, the brokenness will always linger, a crack in the foundation that brings the whole building down eventually.

"The thing with your family," I finally say, my voice slow and tentative. "I can understand that . . . I guess. Almost. It's not your fault, that your brother makes fun of you. I just . . . I wish you would have told me it was like that."

"I should have. I know."

"And it's not a bad thing that you're not always this confident person, Reggie. It makes you human. I'm not always confident either. I *definitely* wasn't when we first met. You know I'm always doubting myself."

"I'm so glad you understand," he says, his eyes lighting up in relief.

I shake my head. "But what I can't get past was the lie. *A podcast?* What a stupid, small thing to lie about. And for so long—"

"I agree, it was just—"

"Let me finish." The words come out harsher than I intend, and I can see his eyes dim. "It makes me wonder what else you could be lying about."

"Nothing." His hands go out, big and dramatic, like he's signaling to a plane above. "Nothing. I promise I—"

"But I don't know that. I can't *trust* that. And also, there's the reason that you lied. To give me all this advice, push me to take risks." I let out a growl of frustration. "Here I was thinking you had it all figured out. I wanted to be more like you . . . and I didn't even really know you at all. Not the real you."

"It could be the real me, though!" His voice comes out strangled, and I see him swallow, trying to get it under control. He rubs at the sides of his eyes, and then whispers. "I—I think it's the me that I want to be, who I am deep down. Does that make sense? With you, it's like . . . I get to be my true self. I get to be free of all the bullshit."

It does make sense to me. And a part of me goes all gooey

inside, knowing that I am that person for him. But there's also the part of me that's flaming, burning mad over his deceit, and the part of me that's tense with worry that I'm letting myself get walked over again, like I've done so many times before. "I'm just so confused."

"I know I was stupid. I know I—I . . . I lied. I messed with your head. And I'm so, so sorry. I'll never stop saying that I'm sorry." He reaches for my hand, and I let him take it this time. "But what I know for sure, probably the *only* thing I know for sure, is that this year has been magic. And that's all because of you, Delilah. You are magic."

And I want to be that person for Reggie. I want to believe that I'm magic. But also, there's something about that label that feels stifling, restrictive. Magic sweeps away all the problems and makes everything better, everyone happy. Magic is the fairy godmother *poof*ing in to save the day, and who knows what happens to her after that? Who cares? That's exactly who I'm trying *not* to be anymore. And if that's what he thinks of me, then maybe this wasn't supposed to work out. I will only disappoint him in the long run . . . like he has disappointed me.

Maybe it's better to call it before either of us wastes any more time—like the years my parents wasted before they found the lives, and the people, that truly made them happy.

"I'm not magic. I'm not perfect." My throat feels raw as the realization of what's about to happen sets in. "I'm just . . . normal. And that's all I expected from you. For you to be your normal self."

"I know. And I will be, from now on. I'll never front or lie to you ever again."

"I don't know," I say, even though I do. Even now, when I know what I have to say, I'm trying to make it smaller, easier to digest. "It seems like maybe we both got caught up in something that—that wasn't really here."

"Don't say that. Please. You don't believe that, right?" He rubs at his eyes again, but a tear still escapes. It makes my chest feel tight and painful. "This is meant to be. That's why we kept meeting up like that, that's why . . . all the holidays. Sweetheart, please."

That name. I can't. I need to do this before I lose the will. I need to just do the hard thing and not worry about the reaction or hurting his feelings. He already hurt mine.

"It was all coincidences, Reggie," I say, taking my hand back. "And then we did it on purpose. Maybe to give this more meaning than it actually had."

I stand up and take that first painful step away from him.

REGGIE

She's done. I can see it in her face, instantly, almost like a switch was flipped.

So because nothing I say is going to make a difference, I might as well take the biggest risk and say the biggest thing.

"I love you."

"Don't say that." She starts shaking her head super fast, as if she's trying to shake the words out of her memory before I'm even done saying them.

I stand up and reach out toward her. "I do. I love you. And I—I wanted to be enough for you. That's why I made this—this huge mess."

"Reggie, you were enough for me."

"Was I? Because now that you're finding out who I really am— insecure and scared and, and nothing special—you're running for the door. You won't even acknowledge what I just said to you."

"You know that's not fair." There's no fight or feeling in her voice like before. She's already disengaging, and it's like I'm trying to grab ahold of something that might already be long gone. "It's that you weren't honest with me. It's that so much of us is built on . . . something that wasn't genuine."

I know it's true, but I can't let it be true. I can't let this be the end.

"Well, I'm being honest now. I will never lie to you again, Delilah."

"Now . . ." she starts, her eyes bright with tears she's holding in. She lets out a long sigh and then nods, like she's giving herself permission.

"Now it's too late. I can't do this anymore, Reggie."

WHO CARES?

DELILAH

"Are you gonna tell me what happened, or are you gonna just keep lying there cosplaying Taylor in the 'Teardrops on My Guitar' music video?"

Georgia's voice cuts through the silence of our dark room on Saturday afternoon. And I guess I am lying here with Mabel on my bed, so the comparison isn't totally off-base. But still. I've been crying off and on for hours, so my eyes are puffy and my pillow is damp and salty-smelling, and I don't actually know if I made the right decision or blew up something that could have been easily mended. But I do know that I currently feel like shit, and I can't foresee a future where I don't feel like shit, and I'm heartbroken and blindsided and confused. Long story short, I'm not in the mood.

"I mean, if you're gonna do this," she continues, oblivious or diabolical (either way, it's incredibly annoying), "you might as well go for it. Get you a gown, some eye gems. I can hook you up."

I let out a long, weary sigh, hoping that she'll get the message.

But of course she doesn't.

"Dreeeeeew loooooks . . . aaaaaaat meeeee. I fake a smile so he won't seeeeeeeeee!"

I press a pillow over my face to block out her singing, but that seems to make her just warble out the lyrics even louder.

"Georgia," I groan. "I just . . . can't. Not right now."

Her Taylor Swift impression, thankfully, stops, and it's quiet again. So I can track each footstep as she walks over to my bed. She reaches out and pats my leg, and I feel my body relax with her touch.

"Do you have a migraine? I'm sorry."

"No, I don't."

"Well . . . I'm here when you wanna talk, sissy. I love you."

"I love you too."

"And if you want me to sic the Von Trapp children on him, just let me know. They're still taking their roles from last season really seriously, even though we've moved on to *Matilda*, and will basically do anything I say."

My laugh is unexpected. It bubbles up my chest and out my nose, resulting in a large snort. Which makes Georgia start laughing too, loud and easy, until we're both have tears falling down our faces, but the good kind. And when she launches into another chorus of "Teardrops on My Guitar," I sing along this time.

REGGIE

My parents know something is wrong, but outside of some lack-luster *Tell us if you want to talk about it*s, they don't push it. That's just not their way.

But Eric isn't handled so easily—not because he cares, I don't think, but because he's nosy.

It starts with him storming into my room and pulling up the blinds. "Bro, open the windows in here or something. You looking like those people in those commercials before they start taking Zelemenica or Fromaxilexin or some other happy pill."

When that doesn't get his desired results, he tries standing at the door a couple days later, waving his hand in front of his nose. "I don't know what's going on with you man, but you gotta, like, shower. It is *rank* up in here!"

Finally, after almost a whole week has gone by, he strides in one evening after school, pulls my desk chair forward, and leans over the back with his hands under his chin, like a hip white teacher trying to connect to the youth by saying rap is poetry.

"Yo, just tell me what happened with your girl. Delilah. Did she dump you?"

I stare at the ceiling, saying the words I haven't said out loud to anyone yet, not even Yobani. "She's not talking to me, and I don't know if she ever will again."

I tried texting my apologies, and I even called a couple times—I'm that desperate. But she texted back Please stop, Reggie. And as much as I don't want to, I have to respect that.

"So y'all broke up then. What did you *do*?" Eric asks, eyes bugging.

I should tell him to leave my room again, but maybe it might feel good, like penance, to be mercilessly roasted for how I screwed things up with Delilah. Though, I already feel the lowest of the low, so I don't think there even *is* anything Eric can say to me now to make it worse.

I tell him everything that happened this year, starting with that first night and then detailing all my attempts after to be New Reggie till he totally blew up my spot on Thanksgiving by being such a dick. That's what I actually call him, a dick, and he doesn't even flinch or diss me back. I must look really pitiful if he showed restraint there.

"She's so mad. She doesn't even want to talk to me," I finish. "And she has a right to be mad. I was being so fake."

Eric scrunches his nose. "But I don't get it. You weren't being fake." He says it as if it's some inarguable fact. Like, the ocean is blue. Or version 3.5 is the best edition of Dungeons & Dragons.

I study him, trying to figure out how he's making fun of me. But his face looks weirdly sincere.

"I'm being legit right now. You weren't being fake. I mean, not gonna lie, referring to yourself as New Reggie *is* a little troubling, so I can see if she ditched you for that. You can't be doing that, man!" He laughs, but then stops when I don't join in. "Okay, not funny. I get it. But yeah . . . seems like she knew a lot about you. The important stuff, at least. You were being real about that."

I stare at him some more, searching for the joke, but it doesn't seem to be there. So, either Eric started taking an acting class at CSULB this semester, or he's . . . being kind?

I decide to just go with it and accept whatever consequences come from it later.

"Is that a cop-out though?" I ask, pushing down all the instincts inside of me that are screaming *Danger! Turn back now!* "I tried to tell her that, or something like that, when I was pleading my case. And she didn't want to hear it."

"Well, you still did her wrong. You lied. And that's like rule number one with girls: don't lie." He leans forward on two chair legs. "Now, you apologized, right?"

I roll my eyes, irritated. "Of course."

"Good, then you just need to let her be in her feelings about it. It's up to her whether or not she wants to forgive you. And, yo, *don't* tell her to calm down. Trust me, I learned that the hard way."

"Uh, thanks," I say, standing up from my bed, trying to signal that this is the end of our brotherly bonding moment. It was decent, and even maybe a little insightful? But I know there's only so much restraint Eric can show. "Okay, well, I'm gonna—"

He cuts me off. "But I mean, yeah, you don't gotta keep being all Drake about it. You fucked up. It happens. It's 'cause you're still in, like, the identity versus confusion stage—I learned that in my Psych 100 class and, hey, I totally destroyed Lenore on *that* midterm. She left that part out!" He pumps his fist, but then realizes that might not be the most appropriate move right now and settles down. "Anyway, you'll get there to being real all the time." He clears his throat and looks at me almost . . . sheepish? Like he can actually hear how ridiculous that sounds, considering he makes fun of me more than anyone. "And it would probably be easier, huh? If you didn't have a brother criticizing every glimpse of that real you was trying to show?"

That makes me sit back down. Am I dreaming? Is he a hologram?

"But I mean . . . it was, like, our thing, right?" he asks with a smile.

I blink at him. "When did I agree for it to be our thing?"

"It's just, you know, how brothers are."

"Brothers? Or *brother*—singular? Because I never, like, questioned your entire identity. Or took shots at you in front of my friends."

His Adam's apple bobs as he swallows, looking everywhere but me in the room. I can tell he really took that in, and now we'll see if he slips into how it always is and laughs at me for being too sensitive . . . or does something else. Nothing about this conversation has been going the way I expect, so I really don't know which it will be.

"I—I didn't . . ." he finally starts, his voice quiet. "I didn't know you were so bothered by all that . . . well, until Thanksgiving."

I glare at him, raising an eyebrow, and he puts his hands up. "Okay, okay. You right, you right. Maybe I did. But I mean . . ." He lets out a long breath and rocks forward on the chair again, thinking. Finally he says, "I think I was just trying to help you in a way. Or I don't know, like . . . make things easier for you? I know that sounds real wild, but all that board game and fantasy stuff you like? *Someone's* going to have something to say, and isn't it better to hear it from me first? To, like, get ready for it. Because you already know I love you anyway. It's, uh . . . preemptive, or whatever."

I'm already shaking my head. "But by doing that, *you* are the one who's making it hard. And in front of your friends, other people—it's like you're giving them permission. Like Tyrell, he's an *asshole* to me, even when you're not around. You *know* that. I don't think he would pull that shit if you didn't do it first."

He purses his lips and rubs his chin, taking it all in. And then he starts nodding. "Yeah. I can see that. I can. And I'm sorry."

And with those words, it's like the deep wound between us has a thin scab over it, just like that.

"Why couldn't we have just sat down and had a conversation about all this sooner, instead of you hating me and roasting me for years?"

"Ha!" He throws his head back. "'Cause that would've been too easy!"

He claps his hands, grinning at me, but then his expression turns serious. "And for the record, I've never hated you, Reggie. You're my baby bro."

"Baby bro" usually sounds like an insult coming from him, but this time it feels like it used to when we were kids—paired with an invite to walk down to RiteAid for ice cream, or a PlayStation controller handed over to me on the couch.

"Well, I don't hate you, either." I smile at him, probably the first genuine smile I've sent his way in a while.

"Good," he says with a nod. "But, listen, I'm still never going to get this whole dragons thing."

I laugh. "That's fine, 'cause I don't think I'm ever going to get this whole sports thing either. Like, baseball! They stand there for, like, eighty percent of the game. How is that interesting?"

He shakes his head and starts laughing too. "Maybe we can teach each other."

There's a beat of silence as we both stare at each other, testing the waters, and then at the same time: "Nah!" "I'm good!"

"So what are you going to do to fix this with your girl?" he asks me later, like this is a totally normal thing we talk about, and maybe it will be now.

"I don't know yet. But it's gotta be big."

DELILAH

It's so much easier not going to the same school with Reggie or any of our mutual friends. Because there's no one to hide from, no one I have to give an explanation to. I've canceled hanging out with Ryan and Leela twice now, and if they knew why, they didn't say.

But I can't avoid Georgia. She gives me less than a week of moping before she throws herself on my bed and pulls the covers off me. "Do you have a migraine?"

"No."

"Then, okay, we're doing this now."

"I'd . . . rather not."

"Uh-uh. Nope! You missed school today and have listened to 'All Too Well' twenty-one times just since I've been home from rehearsal. I mean, yes, this is the best song in the world and you know I fully support the drama—but this is disturbing, even for me, D."

I roll my eyes at her to communicate just how annoyed I am

by her presence. But then I fill her in on all the messy details of the breakup anyway. I don't have a choice.

And by the end, even though I'm trying to hold it together, I totally fall apart.

"I felt so blindsided, like he had this whole other side of him," I cry. I can feel my eyes puffing up and the snot dripping down my face. It's ugly. "And it wasn't, like, earth-shattering, what he did, I know. I could have just forgiven him, but, but I don't want to be that chill girl anymore that lets everything go. I'm not her anymore. I'm not chill!"

"So not chill," Georgia echoes, rubbing my back in small, soothing circles.

"And if I did just shrug and smooth it over, wouldn't he always see me that way? As passive? I don't want to be passive anymore in my own life!"

"You don't have to be—"

"I don't want to be like Mom!" I wail.

"Okay, I was following you, but you lost me there, sis. Back up—what does Mom have to do with this?"

"I mean—I mean—I want to be like Mom, but not the part where she wasted all this time on the wrong person. She's so much happier now! And I don't want to make the same mistake and be with someone who doesn't see me as I am." I wipe my dripping nose on my comforter and Georgia is kind enough not to call me on it. "He thought I was perfect, that's why *he* was trying to be perfect. I feel like—like he's been putting me on this . . . pedestal, not even seeing the real me. And I can never be that perfect person, not without losing myself. So it feels like it's better to end it now before I get even more attached to him, and this—this just hurts even more."

My body shakes in another sob, and it feels good, like I'm cleaning out my insides, purging all the hurt I've been feeling this week, and maybe also a lot longer. Georgia sits next to me, hugging me close, until the crying slows into intermittent blubberings and then just little sniffles.

"Can I tell you what I think now?" Georgia asks. "I can also sit here with my lips zipped, too. I won't be offended."

"Give it to me," I say, leaning against her.

"It seems . . . well, to me at least, that you were both putting each other on pedestals," she started, tentatively. "The way you always talked about him, like *he* was perfect. It was like he was your guru, or something. Very Jean Valjean and Cosette—or no, *My Fair Lady*! Yes, definitely some Eliza vibes there." My eyes flare and she gets back on track. "Anyway, it's okay and all, to admire him. And I like Reggie—I like you two together. I liked how you kept being your best self around him and taking risks, instead of losing who you are. But you don't need some guy's permission to do all that. You can be that for yourself."

My mind reels trying to take in what she's saying. Did I put Reggie on a pedestal? I definitely thought he was perfect, which I now know is not true. Would I have liked—loved—him the same if he'd been straight with me from the beginning? If I wasn't so focused on learning from him, being more like him?

"So you're saying we shouldn't be together?" I ask, and I wince, scared to hear her answer.

"No!" She bats at the air, like that idea is a pesky fly. "You know I love me a pact, but it really shouldn't be up to me, not really. It should be up to you!" Her playful grin turns a little more serious. "But I do think maybe you two need to readjust your expectations of each other . . . and just, like, let the other person be human instead of perfect."

I chew on that for a bit. What would me and Reggie be like if we saw each other for just who we are? Flawed, with a lot to learn, but also authentic and capable of change . . . together.

"But what if he's the wrong person? Again? Like—"

"Charlie? Oh, D, he's not as bad as Charlie. *No one* is as bad as Charlie. I don't know what you were thinking there." I give her my best big sister glare, and she wrinkles her nose and smiles.

"Back to your question, though. You just, won't know now. You can't. Like Mom didn't know until she went through it, and I know it was hard for her, for all of us, but still—she got us in the deal. I think she would say it was worth it."

And I know Georgia is right. Mom's happier because of what she went through. She knew it was right with Andre because it was so wrong before. So maybe you can't protect yourself from the wrong. All you can do is be yourself—fully, authentically—until the right person sees and loves that.

"How did you get so smart?"

"Musicals." She shrugs. "So, in conclusion, there's no way to see the future. So, stop trying!" She swats my shoulder, and I fall back, pretending to be hurt. "But what you need to decide is, does he make you happy now?"

I'm definitely not happy now. I'm the lowest I've been in a long time, since Mom and Dad were in the worst of their fighting. But I *was* happy, really happy. Performing at The Echo and knowing he was in the audience, talking about my deepest insecurities at the Juneteenth barbecue and being completely validated, laughing so hard I almost peed myself at Ostrichland . . . playing him my song.

"I don't know," I say to Georgia. And I really don't know how to put this all into words, so someone else can understand.

"I mean, you know what you should do then."

"Cry and watch Netflix Christmas movies?" I try.

"Yes, that. Definitely that." She smiles, hugging me tight. "But after that . . . well, WWTD?"

"T?"

She rolls her eyes at me, and points at my speakers, which are still playing "All Too Well" on a loop.

"Oh! T!"

I don't pick up my guitar for a few more days. I'm scared that nothing will come out, that I won't have anything to say.

But once I give myself permission to try, to just play for fun, the notes come and the right words arrive soon after.

And it has Taylor Swift's vulnerability and Poly Styrene's power. It has the technical skills that I learned from Ryan, and the unapologetic boldness I learned from my mom. It has Georgia's dramatic flair. But it doesn't sound like them.

It sounds like me.

REGGIE

It takes me another week to figure out what I want to do, and then *another* week to get the nerve to call Yobani. We've been . . . *fine* ever since Halloween, but fine isn't enough to ask someone to help me do something wild to win back the girl I love. And fine definitely isn't what Yobani deserves from me after all our years of friendship.

I FaceTime him and he answers on the first ring.

"I'm sorry."

His face quickly settles from shock into a smirk. "Go on."

"I was acting like I was better than you, like I knew so much more than you, and I don't really know shit."

"Okay, I'm glad we're on the same page here."

"And you were just trying to help and, like, hold me accountable, and I threw it back at you. Even though I should have listened."

"It's true. I was dropping knowledge and you shoulda been taking notes."

"I should have. You were being a good friend, and I was being a total dick."

"And an *ugly* one too, with, like, a crooked tip and some sort of STD—one of those rare ones we had to take that test on in health class."

I raise my lip in disgust, and he shrugs. "All right, I forgive you."

"You do?"

"Yeah, as long as you agree that you were an ugly, warty dick."

"I was an ugly, warty dick," I repeat.

He nods, satisfied. "Cool. Now what's the plan to get Delilah to forgive you?"

"Are you sure you want to help me? Because you totally don't have to help me."

"Of course I want to, Reg." He grins. "If only to save our D&D game. It's been getting *reeeeeal* melodramatic lately, and Trickery does not thrive in those conditions."

I lay out my plan, and he cheers and then cracks up, making me promise that he can be the one to tell Greg and Leela.

After I get off the phone with him, the panic starts to creep in over this big risk I'm taking, and I'm terrified that it all might be for nothing anyway. But I know that if I don't start right this second, those feelings will take over and I'll lose my nerve. So, I open up my transcribing app and start drafting an email I should have sent a long time ago.

Okay so . . . I know it's in the name, but how tight are tights
actually supposed to be?

There's no crying in theater, Reggie!

I don't care how many times you ask, bro. There is no way
that Trickery is going to be involved in this

Booooooo!!!!!!!

CHRISTMAS EVE

REGGIE

I decide to put the plan into action on Christmas Eve because it's a nod to our weird, wonderful beginning, how we were pulled together on these days with so much meaning, almost as if there was a string tying us together all along. But whether or not those were coincidences or divine intervention from Santa or a groundhog or whatever—this is me taking control and declaring who I am, what I want. Taking a ridiculous but hopefully romantic risk, and then living with the consequences.

"Siiiiiiilent niiiiiight! Hooooooooly niiiiiiight!"

"You better sing it, Mae!"

But first I have to get past my family.

Mom and Dad are currently dancing around the living room, belting along to the Temptations' version of "Silent Night." Mom is doing her best to hit that high falsetto, and Dad is bellowing out the bass in between big gulps of eggnog.

I'm hoping this Christmas Eve tradition of theirs will be

distraction enough so I have a chance to slip past them unnoticed, but—

"Reggie, where do you think you're going?"

"And *what* have you got on?"

There's the problem of my costume.

I'm currently wearing pointy elf ears, a purple flowing cape, and green tights tucked into tall boots, with an intricate design of sparkling gems across my forehead—courtesy of Georgia and her theater department connections. It's all part of the plan.

I rack my brain for a way to explain this getup without getting into too much detail or talking specifically about D&D. Because no matter what, I'm gonna do this—no delicate suggestions from my mom or disapproving looks from my dad are going to stop me. But I also don't want their judgment to cast a cloud over this whole special moment.

Before I can even get a word out, Eric sprints into the room, jumping between me and Mom and Dad. "This is who Reggie is! And you—you . . . you need to accept him!"

Dad's raises one thick eyebrow, and Mom puts her hands on her hips, head cocked to the side in confusion.

Finally, Dad says, slowly, "Reggie is . . . an elf?"

Eric starts nodding, furiously. "Yep. He is, and I'm going to support him in that. Well, he's not an elf all the time, or at least I don't think so. But. Um. Well. You want to explain, baby bro?"

They all turn and stare at me expectantly. And looking between them, I know it's not the most appropriate response, but I can't help it. I laugh. Like the kind of laughing that makes you fall forward, sides hurting and eyes streaming. I laugh until I'm gasping for air.

"An elf! Am I trying to be an elf?!"

This just makes my parents look even more confused, and it's starting to shift toward concern. But Eric has wide eyes and an excited grin, like how he looks when he's watching a particularly good *Super Smash Bros.* match.

I take a deep breath, trying to get myself together. "I'm not, like, coming out as an elf." This sounds so ridiculous that another laugh escapes.

"Then . . ." Dad starts, and his eyebrow gets dangerously close to hitting his hairline.

"Then why are you dressed like one, baby?" Mom asks.

"Tell them, Reggie," Eric says. "I've got your back!" He crosses his arms all tough, and I think he's taking this a little too far, but I appreciate the effort.

"I'm dressed like an elf because . . . well, because I'm trying to win Delilah back."

Dad lets out a snort. "Dressed like an elf?"

"I know you miss her and I think . . . it's . . . *good* that you want to mend things between the two of you," Mom says, clearly trying to select the exact right words. "But are you sure . . . this would be, um, attractive to her?"

"Of course it won't, Mae." Dad shakes his head. "Reggie, you need to go upstairs and change before you do anything."

"I'm not going to change," I say, my voice steady and strong.

Dad's jaw tightens at my tone. "I'm just trying to help you here, and I'm not sure where this attitude is coming from."

My chest gets tight, and I consider ending the conversation right here. Because no matter how I try to explain myself, I'm just going to get the same confused, disappointed look Dad always gives me when I talk about the things I like. How could he possibly understand that Delilah—if she still wants me at all—will want me like this, confidently myself. I mean, not that I'm *an elf*, but, like . . . it'll all come together soon.

"It's cool, Reggie," Eric says, nodding at me. "Just, like, speak your truth."

And I still think he's overcorrecting and being way too extra, but . . . I guess it's kinda nice, or whatever.

I take a deep breath and decide just to try. This whole night is going to be completely out of my comfort zone, so I might as well take a chance with my parents, too. "Delilah likes . . . or I guess, *liked* me the way I am," I say. "She knew how much I loved D&D and that I spent, like, a huge chunk of my life playing D&D and thinking about D&D and writing about D&D—yeah, I haven't told you about that. I do that, too. But yeah, she knew all about that, and it wasn't a negative in her mind. The only thing that was a negative was that I didn't let myself be vulnerable with her, not really. I put on a front and was dishonest. And a big part of that was because I felt like there was something wrong with me and that she'd never stick around if she saw all of me."

"Oh, Reggie! There's nothing wrong with you," Mom coos, stepping forward to pat my cape-covered shoulder.

"Yeah, well, that's not always the message I get around this house," I say, stealing a glance at Dad. His eyebrows are furrowed.

"Yeah, I've kind of been a dick to him," Eric cuts in.

"Language." Mom gives him a warning look.

"Sorry! I mean, I've been . . . making fun of him and stuff. And it's made Reggie scared to be himself, you know what I mean? He thinks we all look down on him because he likes these dragon games and all the other nerd sh—stuff."

"You think we *all* look down on you?" Mom asks, blinking fast.

"It feels like you do." This time, I look straight at Dad when I speak, and he stares back.

"Are you talking to me, son?" he asks.

"Not just to you, no," I say quickly, but I stop myself. I can't let myself backtrack here. I take a deep breath. "But I definitely feel it from you. A lot. You're always trying to push me toward sports, and it feels like that's because you're ashamed of how I prefer to spend my time instead. Like . . . like . . . you're ashamed of me."

Dad winces, like my words physically hurt him. "I'm not ashamed—I could never be ashamed of you, my boy."

My voice is smaller than I want it to be, but I get the words out. "Well, that's not the message I get from you."

He lets out a long exhale and rubs his hands over the top of his head, like he's searching for the right words. I steel myself for something that's going to hurt, but when he finally meets my gaze again, his eyes are watery and wide. "I'm really sorry for that. I love you, Reggie. Even if I don't always understand you, I love you. Fully. I guess I just want there to be more we can connect over."

Our eyes are locked, and it's like he can read my mind.

"But I can try and understand what you like, too, to make that connection happen. Instead of trying to make you like sports like me . . . to try and change you. Maybe we can meet in the middle more."

"We all can," Mom says, squeezing my shoulder. "Because you're our baby, and we love you just the way you are. We're gonna learn to love your dragon games, too. I'm sorry there was even a question in your mind about that, Reggie."

"I—I appreciate you both saying that. And I love you too."

"Come here," Dad says, pulling me and Mom into an embrace. Eric crashes in too, wrapping his arms around us. "Group hug!"

And it's not perfect. It's not like every hurt is erased. But that's okay. I said what I was feeling—boldly, clearly—and I was heard. I was accepted. It feels like hope.

From the speakers, Marvin Gaye starts singing about purple snowflakes, and Dad steps back, looking my outfit up and down again.

"You gotta have real confidence to pull off green tights," he says, letting out a hissy laugh. "I'm impressed."

"But now where did those things even come from?" Mom asks. "I know I didn't buy them for you!"

"Delilah's sister hooked me up." I smile and pose for them.

"Back to the game plan, though, bro," Eric says, rubbing his hands together. "Aren't you running behind?"

"No, I'm good." I hold up my phone. "It doesn't start until I send this, um, text. And I'm not going to do that until I drive over to her house."

"In your car?" Dad laughs, shaking his head. "Nah, nah! I can't let my boy show up in a hoopty! We'll drive you. Where are my keys?"

So that's how I end up outside of Delilah's apartment building in the back seat of my dad's car with my entire family, finger hovering over a button that's going to determine what happens with the greatest girl I've ever known.

There are lights hung on every balcony and staircase, casting the night in a warm, festive glow that makes anything seem possible—even Delilah forgiving me and giving me another chance.

I take a deep breath, in and out, and tell myself that I'll be fine either way. But I can't lie to myself. I know I won't. I push send on the text anyway.

Can I send you something?

DELILAH

It's funny, because I've been wanting to text Reggie the exact same words for over a week now, but I kept talking myself out of it. He might think it's strange, when there's so much we would need to talk about first. And even though I think I know that I want to be with him now . . . he might not feel the same anymore. When I finished recording my new song, though—just a rough version on the voice memo app on my phone—he was the first person I wanted to share it with.

"What does it say?" Georgia asks. She's paused the weird Netflix Christmas movie we were watching with one actress playing six characters.

"Hey, that was getting good!" Andre says, waving at the screen.

Mom shakes her head. "Baby, how do they all look the same? It just doesn't make any sense."

"It doesn't have to," Andre replies. "Suspension of disbelief! It's the holiday magic!"

"Well?" Georgia leans in, trying to look at my screen, but the smug grin on her face makes me think she may already know more than she's letting on.

Yes, I text back, and seconds later, he sends me a link to an episode of *Role With It*.

I press play.

ROLE WITH IT PODCAST, SEASON 12, EPISODE 7: TRANSCRIPT

Darren Lumb: Welcome, welcome, to a special episode of *Role With It*, and listeners, buckle up! Because this episode is going to be a wild ride. We're taking a break from our regular campaign to give a devoted listener a chance to bare his heart and make a grand gesture—even grander than when Berkum Hollowbraid sacrificed his immortality for his love, Gwawen, in season ten.

Yobani: That season was epic!

Darren Lumb: [chuckles] Thanks. Now, you'll probably recognize this listener. He's made quite the name for himself writing necessary critiques of Dungeons & Dragons. I know I've found his writing incredibly helpful. Please welcome to *Role With It* for the first time, Keepin' It d100.

Reggie: Actually, I'm gonna go by my real name. Reggie. Um, Reggie Hubbard.

Darren Lumb: All right, sweet. Okay, well, *Reggie*, I'm a big fan, so I'm so glad to have you here. And from what I understand, you're going to tell us a story.

Reggie: Yep. [takes an audible breath] I am.

Darren Lumb: And you've got some friends here with you to help you out.

Yobani: Yes, me! Yobani Alvarez. But you can also call me Trickery.

[faint grumbling in background]

Darren Lumb: [laughs] Okay, and you are?

Greg: Greg Hesse. I'm so honored to meet you, Darren, sir—

Yobani: For the record, Greg is here as more of an assistant host to my main hosting job, and I [rustling] . . . I am going to stop now. So, Darren, if it's okay with you, we're just going to get into it.

Darren Lumb: Take it away!

Yobani: Okay, today we are going to tell you the story of—

Greg: Gather round, adventurers, and we shall tell you the tale of the great Regeldan Hubbendra. An elven wizard, revered throughout the realm for both his noble heart and his extraordinary spell-casting abilities, the only of their kind—

Yobani: Yeah, I still can't get down with that name.

Greg: It is in line with elven naming conventions.

Reggie: You guys!

Yobani: Right, so this . . . *Regeldan*—he was a good dude, people liked him, but he always felt like a piece was missing, and he thought the one way to fix that was to find love.

Greg: And he set his sights on the beautiful Delia Lonesong—

Yobani: See, that's a better name.

Greg: Delia was a bard, admired and celebrated by all for the magical songs she played on her enchanted lyre.

Yobani: And Regeldan, he just knew that if he could make this Delia love him, everything would be all right. All his problems would be gone.

Greg: So he ventured deep into the Fungaloid Cave to retrieve a fabled greatsword.

Yobani: With that, he battled the crooked, warty dwarf, Dickilus, in order to cross the great underground city of Khindarul.

Greg: From there he traveled to Delia's kingdom, dodging cloud giants and diatrymas, and when he arrived, he could hear the notes of her beguiling ballads trickling down from her tall tower. And well, why don't you tell us what happened next, Regeldan?

Reggie: Standing there at Delia's tower, Regeldan—or I guess . . . I started feeling really unsure about this whole quest. What would this beautiful and brilliant bard want with a lowly elf like me? So at the last minute, I cast a spell—

Greg: The shapechange spell.

Reggie: Yeah, the shapechange spell, which cloaked my true form from Delia, making me look bigger and stronger and more impressive than I actually was.

Yobani: Homeboy was looking like a buffed-up dragonborn!

Reggie: But as soon as I presented myself to Delia and told her the tale of how I came to be here in front of her, offering my undying love, she wasn't fooled by my spell. You see, she had truesight—a rare ability that allowed her to see through all illusions. And once she realized my deception, she rightfully sent me away.

Yobani: Regeldan had to work on himself, because no girl is about to like an elf pulling all this smoke-and-mirrors BS!

Greg: And so our hero returned to his kingdom, his quest unfulfilled.

Reggie: I thought I needed to be perfect, the ideal. I thought I would never be enough for Delia as I am, but in trying to deceive her, I robbed her of the chance to make her own decision. I treated her as a prize instead of as her own individual. And I was wrong, so wrong. I know that now. I'm ready to be authentic. I'm ready to give Delia all that she deserves.

Darren Lumb: So Regeldan, er, Reggie . . . it sounds like you really love this girl, don't you?

[long pause]

Reggie: I do. I really do. And, well, if she's listening. I want to say—I know I might not deserve it, but I hope you'll let me prove that to you. I'm so sorry, and I'm willing to do whatever it takes. And if there's even a small chance that you might feel the same . . . well, you can step outside.

DELILAH

I look at Georgia, silently asking her, *Does that mean what I think it means?*

She smiles brightly, clapping her hands and nodding fast. Mom and Andre are now staring at me with the same, if not more, interest than they gave that weird Netflix movie.

"Lilah-girl . . . uh, what was that?" Mom asks.

Andre points to the door. "Are you gonna go outside? 'Cause I'm about to go outside."

I slowly stand up, but then I'm speeding to the door. I have a fleeting thought that maybe I should change out of the matching Black Santa pajamas that we're all wearing, but it's too late. I'm already out the door, down the first set of steps to the landing overlooking the courtyard.

And that's when I see Reggie. Or at least I think it's Reggie. It's hard to tell at first, because it's dark, but also because the figure standing below looks like . . . an elf?

But then the elf smiles that nose-wrinkling smile that makes my insides flip and flutter.

"I did that!" Georgia calls from behind me. "Well, me and Harold in the costume department."

"I don't get it. Why is this boy dressed like that?"

"Just go with it, Annie!"

Before I even make the conscious decision to do so, I'm running down the rest of the steps until I'm standing in front of Reggie. Or Regeldan.

"Hi."

"Hi."

"That was really . . . something."

"A good something?"

"A very good something." I reach for his hand. It's decked out in a plethora of gold rings that feel cool against my skin as I clasp our fingers together. "Okay, so, I know I told you to be yourself and I still very much believe that, but . . . is that really available for anyone to listen to?"

He lets out a low hissy laugh, and my whole body warms up, despite the cold.

"It is. But really, it's just for you. It always was for you."

"But you got to do it for you, too," I say, arching an eyebrow at him.

He nods. "I know. And I will. I'm not scared anymore."

"I don't expect you to be fearless. I don't expect you to be perfect. I guess I realized that . . . I did that as much as you did, creating this idealized version of you in my head. And it didn't give you the space to be authentic." I can feel my tears welling up, and I let them spill out. I let him see all of me. "I want you, Reggie, just as you are."

He reaches up to wipe my cheeks, and then he lets his hand rest there. "And I promise that's who I'll be from now on. Because I love you, Delilah."

The words hit me in the chest, stopping my breath.

"I thought I loved you right when I met you, but I hadn't earned it yet, that feeling. Because I didn't know you yet. But now I do. I know your talent and how bright you shine. I know your worries and your fears, which you've shared with me, so bravely, even when I didn't deserve it. And I know you're not perfect—I don't expect you to be perfect either. But, sweetheart, you're a treasure to me all the same."

I look into his eyes I know so well, and I'm sure this is right. This is what I want. And I may not know what comes next—I don't know if this is a detour or the finish line. But I know it's worth the risk.

REGGIE

And, there. I've said it. And I don't regret it, because it's true. That's what I want to lead with from now on: what's true. No matter who's watching, no matter what they might think—that's going to be the one rule in my *Player's Handbook* of life from now on.

Still, my heart stops beating as I wait for what comes next. It could be good, it could be bad—but I know I've given it my all.

Delilah's answer rises on her face like the sun: first her lips curve into a smile, a real one, then her freckly nose widens, and finally a starburst of lines appear at the corners of her eyes, just like when she sings.

"I love you too, Reggie."

Our families clap and holler, and it feels like a dream. But as I lean in to kiss her, I know it's better. It's real.

NEW YEAR'S EVE (AGAIN)

REGGIE

I really love New Year's Eve.

It's a fresh start. A chance to ask questions about yourself before you spend the year answering them. It's a time for change even bigger than you may be able to imagine.

But I especially love New Year's Eve because it'll always be when Delilah and I met.

"This lady any good?"

I'm spending the night at The Mode again, but instead of coming here reluctantly, trying to escape my brother and his friends, I'm standing behind the merch table, selling shirts for my girlfriend. She doesn't have much—just a few shirts that Greg helped her make—but they're already almost gone.

"She's the best," I say to the guy standing in front of me, considering one of those final T-shirts. He wearing a denim jacket covered in patches and has his lime-green hair fashioned into spikes. "You can see for yourself in a minute, actually. She's about to go on."

The guy narrows his eyes at me and then starts pointing. "Wait a minute. Aren't you Keepin' It d100? Yeah, you are! Man, I fucking love your essays!"

I study his face, looking for a sign that he's messing with me, a plant sent in by Yobani. But no . . . his expression looks genuinely excited, and it makes me excited, too.

"Yeah, that's me." I smile. "You play D&D?"

He doesn't *look* like someone who does plays D&D, but I guess I should know by now there's no one kind of D&D player.

"Play? Uh, I consider it more of a lifestyle," he says, crossing his arms. "But hey, that one you put up last week. My favorite, no lie. I listened to your *Role With It* episode, too . . . didn't really get it, kinda weird. But *that essay*, man—finally posting your face and name, and just, like, saying *suck it* to anyone who has a problem with that . . . Dude, that was legit!"

"Well, I don't know if I said *suck it* exact—"

"Hey, you're right! She is starting!" he shouts when the first strums of guitar sound from the stage. "Nice to meet you, man!" And with that, my first fan disappears into the crowd.

A lot really *can* happen in one year. And I can't wait to find out what this next one brings now that I'm meeting each day, each moment, as myself.

DELILAH

"You ready?" Ryan asks, strapping on her bass guitar.

I knew it was a long shot when I asked Jimmy for just a few minutes of stage time. New Year's Eve is a big night, one of the biggest at The Mode, and I'm basically starting over from scratch. But I was surprised, ecstatic, when he said yes. It probably helped that Ryan offered to give up some of the Valentines' set time—and put together a bass line that brought my song to the next level.

"Oh, she's got this," Beau says, sitting down at his throne behind the drums. "No stage fright or bubble guts for this one."

He texted me an apology after Christmas, said that I had been right and he was still kicking himself over staying silent that day with Charlie. And when he asked how he could make it up to me, I sent him the rough version of my song. He sent me back a shuffly beat that brought it all together and then offered to back us up tonight. I don't know if Charlie knows. I don't care.

I remember being so scared last year. I remember feeling like

I hadn't earned my place, that I didn't belong. But now I know I belong wherever I want to be. The only person who can count me out is myself.

I search the crowd—which I realize, with a rush, is filled with faces I recognize from other audiences—and spot Reggie. His beaming smile is the last boost I need to push down the nerves and step up to the mic. This is just the first show of many with him right there in the front row, the guy who sees me and loves me exactly as I am.

I keep my eyes wide open as I sing to him.

ACKNOWLEDGMENTS

First, thank you to Sherry at Lice Removal by Magic Hands for delousing my children and talking me down the week my revision was due. Without your help, it's very possible I might have just thrown my laptop into the ocean, and no one would be holding this book in their hands right now.

Alessandra Balzer, I could go on for hours about how much I love working with you (and I do, whenever I have the chance!). You showed me so much grace and understanding as I worked on this book, and your trust that I could do this kept me going so many days when I was absolutely certain I could not. I'm so proud of this world I'm creating—and it only exists because you gave me the permission at the beginning to build it and helped me develop the skills I needed to do it well.

I probably have the worst personality type to be working in this industry because I cry often and spend a lot of time thinking about how everyone secretly hates me. So who knows where I would be without the kind, brilliant, and fierce Taylor Haggerty by my side!

Taylor, thank you for always reminding me of my worth and helping me to believe all that is possible for my career. Your positive energy and encouragement have carried me through the most difficult moments. And I'm so grateful to everyone at Root Literary for their unending support, especially Jasmine Brown and Melanie Figueroa.

Thank you, Heather Baror-Shapiro and Debbie Deuble Hill, for helping me to bring my stories to more people than I ever imagined.

I've been lucky to work with such an incredible group of people at Balzer + Bray / HarperCollins over the years. I hope I finally get to meet you all in person one day and give you big hugs! Thank you to Caitlin Johnson, Aubrey Churchward, Abby Dommert, Shannon Cox, Donna Bray, Suzanne Murphy, Andrea Pappenheimer, Kerry Moynagh, Kathy Faber, Jen Wygand, Nellie Kurtzman, Audrey Diestelkamp, Patty Rosati, Mimi Rankin, Sonia Sells, Raven Andrus, Megan Carr, Emily Logan, Savannah Daniels, Jessie Gang, Catherine Lee, Alexandra Rakaczki, Alison Kerr Miller, Jaime Herbeck, and everyone else who works so hard and makes my dreams come true.

Michelle D'Urbano, you continue to work magic with your beautiful illustrations. You've helped create the kinds of covers I searched for as a kid, and you make so many readers who pick up my books feel seen and valued now. Thank you for always getting it so right.

Christina Hammonds Reed and Brandy Colbert, I'm so grateful that books have brought you both into my life because our friendship has been so healing for me. Thank you for your perspective and wisdom and for being my safe space.

Thank you to all the wonderful authors who have encouraged me over this past year, given me advice, and helped this job to feel less lonely: Danielle Parker, Susan Lee, Leah Johnson, Tracy Deonn, Karen Strong, Julian Winters, Jordan Ifueko, Jamie Pacton, Julie Murphy, Aminah Mae Safi, Nicola Yoon, Becky Albertalli, Ronni Davis, Sarah Enni, Sarah Henning, Marissa Meyer, Ashley Woodfolk, Debbi Michiko Florence, Ibi Zoboi, Rita Williams-Garcia, Isabel Ibañez, Kristin Dwyer, Kelly McWilliams, Farrah Penn, Jason June, Emily Henry, Rose Brock, Sarah Mlynowski, and Kwame Mbalia.

To my readers: I haven't been able to meet many of you yet, but the few events I could do this year showed me you're the coolest, kindest, best-dressed bunch around. Thank you for spending your time with parts of my heart, sharing your stories with me, and being my touchstone as I wrote this book. Lots of love especially to: Jackie, Katherine, Jypsy, Tobi, Megan, Jesse, Emani, Martha, Doria, Zoe, Jordan, Lyssa, Lynessa, Emily, and Victoria.

Tabor Allen, I never could have imagined I'd be writing your name here. But I'm glad we don't hate each other anymore, and I'm so grateful for all your help making this book feel authentic. Thank you also to Danny Miller, Neal Marquez, and Chris Schlarb for being a part of so many good memories.

I get asked a lot how I balance writing and motherhood, and the secret is: I don't! I'm a mess! It's only because of all the wonderful people in our community that it seems like I have it together. Shavonne James, Dr. Mireya Hernandez, and Shannon Kennedy: thank you for helping me feel well. Bridget Jones, Mari-Ann Migliazzo, Kyle Becker, and Alexa King: thank you for loving my kids and treating them with such compassion and care. And Sonia Ramirez: thank you for keeping this ship from sinking. We love you and would be lost without you!

Mom, whether it was stacks of fantasy novels and a binder full of Pokémon cards, or cut-up vintage dresses and truly awful emo bangs—you've always let me like whatever I like and be exactly who I am. Thank you for continuing to mother me through every stage and providing a shining example of a life well lived. And Dad, thank you for being my one-man hype team, checking the stock at every Target and Barnes & Noble in a fifty-mile radius, and sharing my books with your accountant, barber, and golf buddies. So much of what I do is to make you proud because you've been such a role model to me.

Rachal, there's a reason all my books' little sisters are geniuses who have to help their clueless big sisters get it together. You are the best person I know and I'm so thankful I get to learn from you. Eddie, thank you for making my sister so happy and for your exceptional contributions to the sibling group chat. And Bryan, thank you for teaching me how to be funny. I'm still not as funny as you, but I tried really hard in this book.

Joe, thank you for listening to every single idea and reading every single page. Thank you for teaching me how to play D&D, even though I didn't follow the rules and got on your nerves. Thank you for being solid and steady and for making me feel safe to take big risks and dream the biggest dreams. I love you more and more every day.

My girls, you are my brightest joys and greatest loves. Coretta, thank you for inspiring me with your endless creativity, and Tallulah, thank you for constantly motivating me with your belief in what's possible. I love you more than anything in the whole wide world.

And Taylor Swift, thank you for writing all my favorite songs.